ABOUT TANIA JOYCE

Tania Joyce is an author of contemporary, rockstar and new adult romance novels. Her stories thread romance, drama and passion into beautiful locations ranging from the dazzling lights and glitter of New York to the luscious vineyards in the Hunter Valley.

She's widely traveled, has a diverse background in the corporate world and has a love for sparkles, shoes and shiraz.

Tania draws on her real-life experiences and combines them with her very vivid imagination to form the foundation of her novels. She likes to write about strong-minded, career-oriented heroes and heroines that go through drama-filled hell, have steamy encounters and risk everything as they endeavor to find their happily-ever-after.

Tania calls Brisbane, Australia, home. She shuffles the hours in her day between family life and writing. One day she hopes to find balance!

She loves to hear from her readers.

Visit: www.taniajoyce.com
or email her at: tania@taniajoyce.com

I0593631

BROKEN BRIDGES

The Flintlocks Rockstar Romance Series – Book 2
by
Tania Joyce

BROKEN BRIDGES by Tania Joyce
Published by Gatwick Enterprises 2023
Brisbane, Australia.

BROKEN BRIDGES
The Flintlocks Rockstar Romance Series – Book 2
EPUB format: ISBN: 978-0-6455547-0-0
Paperback: ISBN: 978-0-6455547-3-1
ASIN: B0B8XWT552

Cover Photography by: Wander Aguiar Photography
Model: Chris Lynch
Edited by: Creating Ink

For more information on the author please visit: www.taniajoyce.com

Keywords and Subjects
New adult romance, young adult romance, contemporary romance, rockstar romance, rock star romance, forced proximity, gay to bisexual romance (pansexual, sexual fluidity), LGBTQI+ romance, celebrity romance, Hollywood romance, movie star romance, rocker, band, musician, bassist, music romance.

Love is love.

Chapter 1

LEWIS

Four months. Six days. Ten hours. That was how much time had passed since I'd gotten down on one knee, proposed to the love of my life, *and* had been hit with a heartbreaking, soul-crushing . . . 'no!'. After drowning my sorrows, I'd arrived home . . . and he was gone. That had been the last battering my heart could take.

In the past six months, I'd lost my band, my grandfather, and my lover. New York, the city I'd adored, had taken everything I'd cherished away from me. It had broken my spirit, crushed my soul, and left me shattered. I had sixty days to clear out of my place, Pop's condo in Brooklyn. I had to sell it to pay off his mountain of debt. With no other family nearby and my friends pursuing new dreams, there was nothing left for me on the East Coast. I'd had enough failures, losses, and delusions to last a lifetime. I needed to escape. Get a new life. Start afresh . . . again.

But as I stepped off the plane in Los Angeles, six days before Christmas, I questioned my sanity. This was maybe even too far-fetched for me.

Auditioning for The Flintlocks, a rock band who were

more popular and more successful than my former group, The Saylors, had ever been, was ludicrous. I doubted I had the level of talent they were looking for. But the chance to write songs, record another album, and hear the tracks on the airwaves again had been a dream of mine for more than ten years. I'd given twelve years of my life to The Saylors. We'd amounted to less than nothing. We'd been a one-hit wonder. Our albums had never taken off. Our continual fights and arguments, different creative ideas, diverse interests, and total dysfunction had destroyed us. Yet another family of mine had fallen apart.

At thirty years old, I'd learned too many valuable life lessons. I refused to be taken advantage of anymore, I wouldn't let my ideas go unheard, I wouldn't be complacent . . . and I'd never be blinded by love again.

I wouldn't repeat the same mistakes, so something had to change.

Was a new band and city the answer? Who fucking knew? But I had nothing left to lose.

I grabbed my duffel bag off the luggage carousel and collected my bass guitar from the bulky items counter. Weaving through the busy crowd, I made my way outside and jumped in a taxi. As the driver headed toward Ashlem Studios in West Hollywood, my head spun, and doubts pummeled my mind. *This is madness.* But then my thoughts reset with new resolve. My ex, Emilio, was wrong. I was hungry for success but our views on what that was differed. He wanted fame and fortune—I wanted happiness, a family, and to live off my music. I'd always known who I was and what I wanted. Following my heart had often led me astray. But now that was dead. So nothing would hold me back. Not anymore.

I can do this. I need this.

As I stepped out of the taxi, winter sunshine and a faint cool breeze hit me. I tightened my grip on my guitar case and stared up at the small chrome Ashlem Studios sign above the entrance to the two-story brick building. I pulled off my beanie, ruffled my fingers through my chin-length, shaggy blond hair, and closed my eyes.

Pop, wish me luck.

Taking a deep breath, I strode through the heavy glass doors. I walked across the glossy tiled foyer, checked off my name at the reception desk, then climbed the stairs to the second floor. Butterflies stirred low in my gut like a restless orchestra ready to play as I headed along the corridor lined with platinum album awards and photos of artists. One day, I'd grace the walls of a record company. *One day.*

The door to the audition room swung open. A petite chick who looked about twenty, dressed in black tights and a red tartan skirt, and carrying a bass guitar, walked out of the studio.

"Good luck." She grunted and threw me a daunting smile as she passed me. "You're gonna need it."

That didn't help my nerves. "Um . . . thanks."

"Lewis?" Hayden, my former bandmate, and closest friend, stood in the doorway. He hadn't changed—he had the same short brown hair and cut physique as always. He greeted me with open arms. "Holy shit, man. It's been too long."

"It certainly has." A year seemed like a lifetime. I dropped my bag on the ground and gave him a big, tight hug, slapping him on the back. My God, it was good to see him. I missed him like crazy. Nothing like traveling to the other side of the country for an audition and the rare opportunity to see my best buddy who lived across the river from me in Manhattan. "How've you been? How was tour?"

"Fantastic." He stepped back and ruffled my hair. "Look at you with long hair."

"Fuck off." Chuckling, I slapped his hand away. "I just haven't gotten my ass to a barber in months. It's grown out."

"Dude, don't cut it. It's awesome."

"O-kay." I gave him a sideways glance to make sure he wasn't joking. "Thanks. I think."

"I mean it. It suits you." He play-punched my arm, then took a long, slow, deep breath. His eyes lit up as he flicked his finger at nothing in particular in the hallway. "So, what do you think of this place?"

My chest swelled. "I can't believe you guys work with Ashlem *and* you own a recording studio back home."

Since he'd left The Saylors five years ago to join Everhide, the world's largest rock band, he'd found his rightful home as their drummer. He'd been close friends with Kyle, Gemma, and Hunter for years, and belonged with them more than anyone else. Now they owned their own label—EH4 Records—and would produce the album for The Flintlocks. Ashlem, one of the largest independent artist entertainment management groups on the planet, would handle distribution, promotion, and the tour.

"It's still surreal." Hayden rubbed the back of his head. "Every day, I pinch myself to make sure I'm not dreaming."

"I would too. I'm so happy for you." I really was. He deserved every success. I missed him and hated that we didn't see each other often anymore. He had a new life, a wife, and a kid. But no matter where in the world we were, we'd always be friends.

Hayden thumbed toward the studio behind him. "You ready for this?"

My pulse jumped. Nausea swirled in my gut. A cold sweat had broken out on the back of my neck. Why was I so nervous? I'd played for years at bars, music venues, and festivals, and had performed at some big shows when we'd had our hit. This was ridiculous. Pushing my fluster aside, I nodded. "I'm as ready as I'll ever be. I can't thank you enough for thinking of me. How have the auditions been going?"

"Not good." Hayden grimaced and scratched the side of his cheek. "Flint and the guys just haven't been impressed by anyone. They auditioned twelve people yesterday and have seen nine bassists today. You're the last one."

"Shit. Are their expectations unrealistic?" They had a right to be high. Finding someone to replace Phil, Flint's brother, who'd been killed in a car accident, would be tough. I could only do my best.

"I don't think so." Hayden shrugged. "They're just looking for an edge in someone. When they hear it, see it, feel it, they'll know. When it's right, it's right."

"Here's hoping. I've flown my ass to LA, so I'm gonna give it my best shot."

"Damn right you will."

I glanced over his shoulder but couldn't see anyone inside the studio. "Do they know we know each other?"

"Yes. They recognized our old band on your application." He shot up his palms. "But I promise, I've said nothing to influence their decision. You have the talent and skill, so knock 'em dead with some of that magic you used to churn out when we jammed."

"Magic, huh?" It would be nice to experience that again.

"You got this." Hayden placed his hand on my shoulder and gave me an encouraging nudge. "Go break a leg. We'll head out for a beer afterwards."

"I look forward to it." It would be nice spending two days here in LA with him at Kyle and Gemma's house before he headed to London for gigs. We needed a good catch up.

Hayden opened the door wider for me. I picked up my gear and stepped inside.

This was just another audition.

Just a couple of songs.

No.

Grit set in my gut.

My life was a mess. I needed a fresh start.

I needed a new band and music to breathe.

I wanted this.

This had to happen.

It's showtime!

Chapter 2

LEWIS

I sucked in a deep breath and walked into the studio's huge rehearsal space. I spun around slowly, taking in the drums, guitars, keyboards, mics, amps, and speakers. *Holy crap!* This place was incredible, all light and bright and clean. Beat the hell out of the dingy basement I used to practice in.

"Good luck." Hayden slapped me on the back then joined the guys at the far end of the room. Flint, Cole, and Slip, a.k.a. Sebastian—the members of The Flintlocks, Blake— their manager, and Kyle—Everhide's bassist, stood huddled around a desk, talking.

"Give us one sec," Flint called out. "Can you patch in there by the drums, please?"

"Sure." I took a long second to eye him up and down. Dressed in tight black jeans and a white T-shirt, and with jet-black hair and icy blue eyes, Flint was hot as fuck. But he had a girlfriend, Sutton. I'd done my research . . . on all of them.

"You need anything?" Kyle hollered.

I shrugged off my denim jacket and tossed it onto a nearby chair. Just being in the same room as Kyle raised my body temperature. It had always done that since I'd met him twelve years ago via Hayden. The guy had a charisma and manner that did it for me. Pity he was straight. "No. Thanks, Kyle. I'm good." *If my nerves could disappear, I'd be fucking great.*

Whatever the men were talking about had them hurtling fiery whispers at each other. Were they frustrated over the auditions and unable to agree on a bassist? One or more of them liked the previous girl but the others didn't? Were they just over the long day and tired?

Maybe all the above.

Their low voices didn't ease the knots in my stomach. But playing would.

I grabbed my bass out of its case and plugged it in.

Taking a seat on a stool, I thumbed the strings, played a few chords and scales. No feedback or delay came through the amp. *All good. I'm set.*

But fuck.

Was I wasting my time?

What edge could I inject into a cookie-cutter audition? Playing two of The Flintlocks' songs—a pop-rock upbeat number, "Move Me", and the bass-heavy track "Drunk On You" was easy. Not even a challenge. How could I stand out from the other contenders?

I flicked my hair off my face and closed my eyes. My leg jiggled. Damn, I wanted this gig. Not just because it would be a phenomenal job and an incredible opportunity, but because I loved the band's music. Their energy captivated me. I'd watched their live performances online. The connection they'd had with each other on stage had hit me hard. I hadn't had that kind of bond with my band in years.

I craved it again.

Clearing my head, I filled my lungs to capacity, then let my breath out slowly. The deep thrum and reverberations from my bass coursed from my fingertips up my arms and settled in my chest. I morphed from playing the low and slow bassline of "Riders On The Storm" by The Doors, to the faster-paced "Mr. Brightside" by The Killers, to then tapping out "Hysteria" by Muse.

I chuckled. I didn't know where that combination of songs had come from. But I'd loved it.

"Lewis? . . . Lewis? . . . LEWIS?" Flint called across the room, breaking me out of my zone.

I palmed my strings to kill the sound. "Oh, shit. Sorry. I was warming up."

Flint's eyes brightened as he quirked half a grin. Slip gaped. Cole raised a questioning eyebrow. Blake and Kyle bobbed their heads. Hayden's face lit with a enormous smile.

"Dude." Flint jutted his chin at me. "That was some move, ripping out Muse."

He knew the song? Awesome. "It wasn't a move. It's a great track that kicks ass on the bass."

Kyle widened his stance and folded his arms. "But it's one of the hardest bass-heavy songs to play."

I bet Kyle, with his wicked talent, could've played it in his sleep. "Maybe. But it rocks."

"Absolutely true." Flint led the group of men over to join me and we went through introductions. After I shook their hands, Flint headed to the electric guitars. He picked up the Fender and hooked the strap over his head. "Let's see what you've got."

Wait. What? "Don't you want me to play the songs for the audition?" I flicked my cable out of the way and moved aside so Flint could stand beside me.

"Yes. With us." A touch of cockiness sliced through Flint's tone as he strummed the electric's strings. The twang reverberated through the speaker, filling the room with a new buzz. "Clearly you know your way around a bass, so let's see how you nail timing."

"You wanna play with me?" *Shit. Okay.* I'd never done that for an audition before. And I'd been to plenty over the past few months. I'd tried out for some small start-up bands, a couple of no-name groups hitting the festival circuit, and several back-street Broadway shows. But nothing had come off. Nothing had gelled.

"Yep." Flint nodded.

"Alrighty, then." I rose to my feet and moved the stool aside.

Slip swiped another electric off its stand and stepped in next to Flint. Blake, Hayden, and Kyle returned to the desk and gave me the thumbs up. Having an audience turned up the dial on the butterflies in my gut.

Cole grabbed his drumsticks out of his bag and took a seat behind the drum kit. "Let's start with 'Move Me,' and go straight into 'Drunk On You.' Ready?"

I shook the jitters from my fingers and set them over my strings. I stretched my head from side to side, then nodded. "Yep." *I can do this.*

Cole tapped his drumsticks together. "One. And-a two. And-a three."

The second Cole hit the drums, my heartrate doubled. The moment Flint and Slip struck their electrics, my breath quickened. *Get it together, idiot.* I joined in at the end of the intro and shivers ran up my spine. Oh, yeah . . . these guys could play.

And Flint could sing, all seductive with a touch of raspy badass rocker.

By the time we hit the verse, the music had taken over me and my nerves had subsided. The hum in the air was more electric than the voltage coursing through the power cables.

My adrenaline kicked in as we transitioned into the second song. I couldn't contain my grin when they sped up the tempo then slowed it down. Was this a test to see if I was on-point with listening to the rhythm? Letting the drummer set the pace? This wasn't my first time playing. I never missed a beat.

Flint sang the last note of the song, then muted his strings with his palm. He panted and nodded. "Fuck. That was good. *Really* good."

"Thanks." I puffed my hair off my face, still high on the rush from playing.

"So what's your story, Lewis?" Slip continued to play a soft tune on his guitar. "What happened to The Saylors?"

Cole leaped from his stool behind the drums and joined us, taking a seat on an amp beside Slip.

I took three steps back and sank onto the stool. Resting my bass across my lap, I sifted through a million memories—the gigs, the travels, the struggles. How could I sum up twelve years of highs and lows?

I glanced at Hayden. He'd been lucky to avoid most of the disaster.

"Once Hayden left, it was never the same. The move we'd made a few years ago to play in Boston didn't go to plan. Life pulled us in different directions. Our regular gig at a bar became less regular. We fought all the time. Reg, our lead guitarist, knocked up his girlfriend and had to get a day job to pay the bills. Kilt, our lead singer, released another solo single but it flopped. Basil, Kilt's brother who'd replaced Hayden, spent more time in rehab than playing drums. And me?" An ache shuddered through my chest. "I lived between the two cities. I spent more time back in New York, seeing and making music with my ex who DJ'd. As a band, we lost unity and focus, and fell apart. So after twelve years, we called it quits."

"I'm sorry to hear that." Flint tilted his head toward his bandmates. "We've been together since we were nine. That's sixteen years." Profound love, gratitude, and respect flooded his eyes as he glanced at Slip and Cole. I used to get nothing but glares of contempt from Kilt. "We've certainly had our ups and downs, but we've always remained best of friends."

"That's cool." *Was he rubbing salt into my wounds?*

Slip stopped strumming; his dark brown eyes drilled into me with curiosity and concern. "We listened to some of your demos. They're good. Do you prefer the DJ scene to playing in a band?"

"Fuck no." I shook my head. Hadn't they read my application? Bass was life. Not working with DJs or at random times as a session musician at a local indie studio, nor bartending. "It's been a hobby that's helped pay the bills. I've licensed a track to a telecom company for an ad campaign, and done some loops and mixes for other DJs, but it's not where my heart lies. Performing is. Playing bass every day is."

"What about writing songs?" Cole swiveled a drumstick around in his hands.

"Yeah. I've written quite a few tracks over the years. Unfortunately, everything I've created since I wrote the hit for The Saylors hasn't been good enough for Kilt. He is a narcissistic prick who controls everything." Kilt had squashed so many of my ideas, I'd given up on putting them forward. To keep the peace, I'd just played his music and gone along with his direction. I'd focused on having fun . . . and prayed for our next break to come. It never had. What a fool I'd been. I'd wasted too much of my life, and I'd been muzzled for way too long.

"You're not wrong about Kilt," Hayden mumbled. "I don't miss him at all."

"No. Not one bit." I wouldn't go down that path again. The embers stirred in my gut as I turned to Flint. "So that's something I want to be upfront and honest about. If that's the way you operate, with it's-my-way-or-the-highway bullshit, I'm not interested in taking this further." Was I killing my chances?

Probably. But I refused to end up in another soul-crushing environment.

"No way." Cole shook his head. His electric green eyes shimmered as he circled his finger through the air, taking in Slip, Flint, and himself. "We're a team. Flint used to write all the lyrics with Phil, but for this album, we've all pitched in to create the songs and music. We still have some refining to do before we hit the studio next month."

Nothing like a tight deadline. "I like that. I just wanted you to know I'm more than a bassist. I'd love the opportunity to work with you and add some magic to your tracks."

"Add magic, huh?" Flint folded his arms. A challenge glinted in his eyes. "Alright then. What do you think of 'Move Me?' Any suggestions for improvement?"

The song I'd just played for the audition? Shit. Me and my big mouth, thinking I could make their songs better than what they'd written. This could make or break the deal. "It's not recorded yet, right?"

"Nope." Slip took the hairband off his wrist and tied back his sun-bleached dark blond hair. "It's a potential track for the new album."

"Honestly?" Should I tell him the truth? *Yes.* That was why I was here. "The lyrics are great, the overall music composition is good, but the bridge and chorus could do with some work."

"How so?" Flint narrowed his eyes.

I swallowed hard. He'd written this song. Could he handle constructive criticism?

Was this what Hayden had meant when he'd said I should show them some magic? I had an ear for music. I could hear what a song needed—that little sound or bit of pizzazz to make it unique. Hayden nodded.

Flames flickered to life in my belly and mingled with my wayward nerves. It was now or never. "I'm more of a hands-on guy. Let me show you." I wriggled on the stool, repositioned my bass against by belly, then strummed the strings. As I played the bridge, the tune morphed inside my mind. New notes and progressions formed. "Rather than quicken the tempo when you transition into the chorus, I'd take advantage of Flint's vocal range and slow it down, go all swoon-worthy and high, then segue into a vivacious belt. Hammer on the bass, pause, then slap the melody. Like this." I flew my fingers over the strings, plucked and strummed hard, then muted the sound. "There. Something like that."

"Holy shit." Slip's eyes widened. "That was insane."

"Um . . . thanks." A small smile tugged the corner of my lips.

"Did you just come up with that?" Cole's brows pinched together.

"Kinda." I scratched the tip of my chin. "When I was practicing the song for the audition, I just *felt* like the track could use a twist. It would give it much more of an emotional punch."

"Fuck." Flint swung his guitar back behind his shoulder. "You just ripped the crap out of our song."

"Yeah, I did. But you asked." *Shit.* Should I have kept my mouth shut? Was it a good ripping, or was I out the door?

"Told you he was good," Hayden hollered from the desk. Sitting beside him, Kyle and Blake gave I'm-impressed nods.

Flint flicked his finger toward my strings. "Your technique is brilliant. But what you just did was exactly what we wanted to see." A low, reserved level of excitement hovered in his voice. "We've auditioned more than twenty people and you're the first one who's offered some improvements. Everyone else has just said they loved the track as it is. We know it's crap and needs work. It needs flair. I'm impressed with what you just played."

Holy shit! I placed my hand on my chest. My heart raced way too fast. "Wow. Thank you." No one had praised my suggestions in a long time. It felt good, but I didn't want to get ahead of myself. "If you want to see what else I can do, I'll play any song you throw me at."

"I can vouch for that," Hayden piped up again.

I shot him a *dude, shhh* glare, but my grin grew wider and wider.

Cole leaned forward on the amp. As he rested his elbows on his knees, he rolled his drumsticks between his hands. "So, why us, Lewis? Why do you want to join The Flintlocks?"

I'm nearly homeless. I miss performing. I want to record a fucking album. Stability would be nice, too. But they weren't my only motivations. I shuffled on my seat and draped my arm across the top of my bass. "I don't just want a job. I want to be involved in the creative process. Grow and be a part of your future. I want to become one of you, feel like I truly belong, add value, and form an integral part of your family. That takes time, trust, and mutual respect. I'm prepared to work my ass off to ensure that happens. I've listened to all your music, and watched dozens of your performances. This is the genre I love. I dig the gritty, unique edge in your music . . . and you're all a lot better-looking than my previous band. No offence, Hayds." I winked at him.

"None taken." He laughed, swinging on his chair.

"Do you understand what's on offer?" Flint rested his hand on his mic and crossed his ankles.

Holy shit! We were talking business. This was getting serious. Could they hear my heart pounding against my ribs? "I read the email. Something about milestones."

"Yes." Flint's voice dropped. As he glanced at the floor, his hair fell forward, curtaining his eyes.

This must have been tough on him, on all of them, moving on from the loss of Phil. I could relate to what they were going through.

Drawing his shoulders back, Flint took a deep breath and fiddled with the strap on his guitar. "We only want to go through this process of looking for a bassist once. It's our soul intention to find someone who wants to join us for life. But we want to ensure we find the right fit, so we've set a few milestones." He held out his hand and counted on his fingers. "The first one is to record our album in New York. Anything you write or create with us will be written into our royalty agreements and our employment contract. You'll be compensated for your time and effort in a more favorable manner than a session musician because we want to get the best out of you. The second milestone, if recording goes well, is the promotion of our first single across the US. Milestone three is the album launch and promo of two more singles. The final milestone is the world tour that kicks off in November. Each step has a bonus payment, kinda like a slice of our advance." A subtle smile quivered across his lips as he tucked his fingers into the front pocket of his jeans. "These stages could tie you to us for the next eighteen months. If you survive them, I'd say you'll be stuck with us for a very long time. You down with that?"

My pulse thudded with an unsteady beat. I understood the reason for the milestones. They'd want the ability to get rid of me or vice versa if we didn't work well together. If I passed milestone one, it'd be a huge call to pack up my life and move here to LA knowing it might not last more than a couple of months. But it was a risk I was willing to take. "I wouldn't be here if I wasn't. I'm ready to give you my blood, sweat, and tears and put as much distance between me and the East Coast as possible."

"Why?" Slip quirked a grin. "Who was she?"

"He, actually." I strummed my bass, low and slow. Music was the only thing that eased the pain. "Emilio and I were together for five years, but it didn't work out. I've moved on." *Well . . . I was trying.*

"Sorry, man. That sucks." Cole shook his head. "Five years? Fuck. I don't keep any chick around for more than five minutes."

"You guys got issues with me being gay?" They wouldn't be the first, if they did.

Slip jerked his chin back. "No. None. But you're not alone in the failed relationships department. We've all been there, done that. Haven't we, bud?" Slip clutched Flint's shoulder and gave it a friendly squeeze. "The only thing that has come out of them are some killer hangovers and some wicked lyrics."

"True." Flint grinned. "But there'll be no more breakups for me. I've found my girl."

"Yeah." Slip nodded. "Sutton's awesome."

Flint turned to me. The vibe radiating off him morphed from chill to electric intrigue. "But maybe fate played its hand. It's put you on a path that led you here. I've never seen anyone other than Kyle play bass like that. Not even Phil was that good."

Shit. If these guys kept it up, I'd start feeling good about myself. I didn't want to get my hopes up. I didn't need any more delusions. "I breathe bass."

A smile charged across Flint's face. He slid his hand down the neck of his guitar, struck the strings, and played, "When You Were Young" by The Killers. I joined in, matching his beat and rhythm and pace. A hum vibrated through my veins and lingered in the center of my chest. God, I loved that feeling.

Slip joined in. Cole returned to the drums. Kyle leaped from his chair at the desk and took to the keys. Hayden, a single snare. For twenty minutes, we churned out hits by The Killers. We let the music take over. This . . . was what I missed. This . . . was magic.

At the end of the fourth song, Flint called, "Okay. Enough." Combing his fingers through his sweaty hair, he swept the long strands off his eyes. "That was cool."

Damn. He was hard to read.

"What do you think?" He glanced at the guys, then turned to Blake. "You feeling it?"

Blake nodded.

I held my breath.

Flint swung around to face me. "Are you able to come here for a session tomorrow? We'd like to run through a couple tracks with you and see where this goes."

Shit yeah. "That would be awesome. Are there any other callbacks?"

"No." Flint shook his head. "Just you."

"Sweeeet." I kept my tone calm and casual, but on the inside, I was pumping my fist and screaming *fuck yes.* "I'll be here."

The following day, I played for five hours with The Flintlocks. With each minute that passed, it grew harder and harder to sit on my simmering excitement. We gelled. We jammed. We jived. I hadn't been around people who inspired, encouraged, and respected me in years.

But with nothing more than a handshake and a thank you, they sent me home after the session, saying they'd call me later that evening.

The wait almost killed me.

My cell phone rang just after nine. I answered it and held my breath.

"Lewis?" Flint's sultry voice came through my cell phone speaker. "From the moment you played The Killers, one of my favorite bands, you intrigued me. You, ripping my song apart stung, but it's what I wanted to see. Slip loved some of the suggestions you made and how quickly you picked up the tracks. Cole can't deny you're talented but is concerned with you being five years older than us. He's worried you won't keep up with his partying." Flint's tone remained consistent and professional; it was hard to gauge his emotion and direction.

Was I in? Fuck. "Is that another challenge?"

"Maybe. Your nerves were shocking, and deep down, it's hard for us to replace Phil." Then his voice softened. "But they're things we're willing to work through and will get better with time. We all agree you've got something we want. The edge we've been looking for. We'd love you to join us in recording the album, and hopefully beyond. You in?"

Holy shit! "Yes." My heart somersaulted and backflipped. I punched the air and hollered. "Oh my God, yes. That'd be awesome."

"Is there any chance of delaying your flight back to New York for a few more days? We'd love to run through the rest of the songs for the album with you."

Holy freaking wow. I had no sessional work until mid-January, and I didn't care if I lost my crappy bar job. I'd easily find another. "Yes . . . yes. I can do that." I bit down on my knuckles to stop myself from shrieking and shouting. *They want me. YES!*

"Well then . . . welcome to The Flintlocks."

Those words were music to my ears. "Thank you. I promise, I won't let you down."

This was the chance of a lifetime. The break I needed. I wanted this so much. It felt right.

I was a Flintlock.

I wasn't going to fuck this up.

Chapter 3

TIA

I reached for the doorbell. My hand quaked as I pressed the buzzer. Unease rolled through my guts. I hadn't seen my brother, Cole, for ten months. Not since Phil's funeral.

Losing Phil had left a huge hole in my heart. So had every excruciating month since then. Phil's death hadn't been the only thing that had kept me away from the people I cared about. My secrets and heartache had played their part. I'd tried to move on. Forget. But I'd failed. Thanks to another horrid blow, I'd had to say goodbye to the life and career I'd built in Chicago and return to LA, the city I'd been desperate to escape.

Staying with Cole would help me settle into living on the West Coast again and adjust to the crappy hand I'd been dealt before I found my own place.

The huge frosted-glass door opened.

Cole's six-foot-two, zero body fat, ripped frame filled the doorway. Years of drumming had given him a physique most guys would die for. I used to be able to outrun him, tackle him to the ground, and never let him win a play-fight. But those days were long gone. His handsome face lit with a radiant grin.

Dressed in designer jeans and a button-down, he was ready to head out. He didn't have to wait for me. We could've caught up tomorrow.

"Tia." He shot forward and wrapped his arms around me. Crushing me against his hard chest, he squeezed me tight. "Oh. It's so good to see you, baby sis."

"Hey, Cole." Before I suffocated in his strong hold or was knocked unconscious by his overpowering spicy cologne, I pulled out of his embrace. "Sorry I'm late. The plane was delayed, and traffic was shit."

"But you made it." Opening the front door wider, he waved me inside. "Come in. Come in."

My smile faltered. Grabbing my suitcase handle, I took a deep breath. "Sure."

Here I go.

I limped inside, wheeling my suitcase behind me. Three days out from Christmas and not one decoration was on display in the foyer. No fairy lights. No tree. No tinsel. He'd probably been waiting for me to put them up.

Cole's brow furrowed as his gaze fell to my leg. I left my luggage by the door and hobbled toward the living room. The pain in my ankle was on the brink of being unbearable.

He closed the door, then pointed to my foot. "Why are you limping? Did you slip on the stairs?"

I wished that was all I'd done. "No, I didn't slip. It's a bit more serious than that."

I dumped my purse onto the sofa. As I shrugged off my coat and tossed it beside my bag, my stomach lurched. I had to come clean. That was why I was here. I sank onto the seat, smoothed my hands over my dress pants, and rubbed at the ache in my knee. "Can we talk for a moment?"

"Sure." He headed over to the bar. "You want a bourbon?"

"Yes. That'd be great." I hadn't drunk alcohol in months,

but something to take the edge off would be nice. I stuffed a cushion behind my back to make myself comfortable.

Cole's luxurious modern home, high up in Laurel Canyon, was ridiculously big for someone who lived alone. His six-bedrooms house had a towering atrium over the extensive living and kitchen area, a spectacular, wall-length gas fireplace, a home theater, custom music studio, games room and tech galore. It was a true bachelor pad.

Nothing had changed since I was last here. No new music awards or photos had been added to the glass shelves by the massive TV. All the perfectly placed cushions, throws, and floor rugs in coordinated shades of dark green were set against oatmeal-colored furniture, making the place look like it was staged to sell. But he never would. With spectacular views across the secluded canyon toward the endless expanse of the city, it felt like he lived on top of the world, not in the center of Los Angeles.

I rested my arm on the back of the sofa. "Where's the rest of my welcome party?" Flint and Slip, the other two members of his band—my crazy friends too—were never far away.

"The guys and Sutton headed to the club about half an hour ago. Blake and April have us out every other night at some swanky bar or event, generating hype for our new album. It's a tough job, but someone has to do it."

His band's manager and their PA/publicist were ruthless when it came to promotional opportunities and kept the boys in line. They worked hard for their money. I knew. I'd caused them enough grief when I'd lived here too.

Cole handed me a bourbon and took a seat adjacent to me. "So? What happened to your leg?"

My heart cinched like a harness pulled too tight. I was glad the others weren't here so I could talk to Cole first. I'd kept secrets from him for way too long. But I'd needed time to accept that I'd never be the same. "A lot has happened over the past few months. I haven't told you everything that's been going on." Tears burned at the back of my eyes. "Nor have I been honest about why I had to give up the show I loved and move back to LA."

"Gotta say, I was shocked." He took a sip of his neat vodka. "You loved Chicago. You loved your show."

"I did. But I couldn't do it anymore." The cracks in my chest that had taken months to stitch together threatened to open. I took a deep breath and tried to hold onto my composure. I had to get through this.

Confusion dug divots into his brow. "Why?"

Nausea rocked my guts. "Physically . . . I can't do stunts anymore." I put down my glass on the coffee table. My hands trembled as I rolled up the right leg on my flared dress pants. "Because of this."

"Holy shit." Cole choked on a mouthful of his drink and shot forward. His gaze raked over my mangled leg. "What the fuck?"

A tangle of seven finger-width, six-inch long, red scars snaked over the side of my calf like angry tentacles. Several large dark marks dotted my knee and sliced across my ankle. Every time I looked at them, it reminded me of everything I'd lost—my career, the fun I used to have, and my boyfriend. Since I was ten, I'd wanted to be an action star, and perform my own stunts in movies and on television. So I'd trained. I'd done every course possible—acting, fighting, wirework, driving skills, and firearms. I fell in love with stunt work more than acting, and wasn't afraid to have a go at anything. At the end of my first year at college, I landed the Chicago-based role on *Through The Smoke*. My dream job had come to fruition. Now, it'd been incinerated.

Not being able to do stunt work ever again was like losing a limb.

I almost had.

"What happened?" Tears welled on the rims of his eyes.

"I was injured on set." Working on a fire and rescue show, some of the stunts we'd done were insane. We'd meticulously prepared for them. We'd rehearsed them. Every safety measure had been in place. But sometimes things went wrong. "Rhett and I were doing a scene on top of an old building. We had to run from the fire and jump across a gap to the next rooftop. But when the explosion went off, the blast was too big. It threw us off our mark. Rhett's safety wire saved him. Mine failed. I hit a metal stair landing. My right leg took all the impact, shattering my ankle, snapping my tibia, and breaking my knee. But the platform was rusted. My leg fell through. My calf was ripped to shreds against the shards of steel."

So much for safety boots and clothing. They hadn't protected me enough.

"Fuck." The color drained from his face. "Why didn't you tell me you'd been hurt?"

I shook my head, fighting back my stinging tears. "Everything got so fucked up." Mainly my head. "I went into complete denial. I didn't want to admit that my leg was ruined. After the accident, I spent a couple weeks in the hospital and had multiple surgeries to pin the bones back together. I was adamant I'd get better . . . so determined . . . but I didn't. And then Rhett left me." My co-star, my boyfriend, gone. He'd trampled on my heart and tossed me aside without a second thought.

"Rhett?" Cole scratched his brow as if trying to make sense of everything. "After all the shit you two went through, he dumped you?"

"Yeah." My chest hurt just thinking about my ex. "He went back to Michaela, his ex-wife." I'd been a fool to think we'd survive the distance.

"He what? What did you do?"

Me? My heart constricted. Why did Cole always assume it was my fault? I loved a good time, but I never messed with people's hearts. Not ever. I wished the men I'd been involved with had felt the same way. I was so done with love.

Cole half-grinned, injecting tease into his tone. "Did you wear him out? Couldn't he keep up with you?"

"That was never a problem." I threw Cole a wicked smirk, but reality was quick to return. I stared at my scars. "Rhett was the ringleader half the time."

We'd been inseparable from the moment we'd met on set. We'd partied hard and played hard. He'd made me forget why I'd left LA. We'd caused a scandal when we'd started dating three years ago. I'd just turned twenty. Rhett had been thirty-seven. He'd left his Bel-Air billionaire wife and kid to be with me. But I was labeled the homewrecker, the slutty skank, the young floozy who had lured him away from the LA elite. *He'd pursued me!* That truth had never been printed online. The slandering and bullying comments had been impossible to ignore.

"The night before my accident, I'd brought up the idea of moving in together. We'd discussed getting married and having kids within a year or two. He wanted time to think it over. A few days after the accident, when I was in hospital, he called it quits. He said I was too young. He didn't want more children and he still loved Michaela. Always had."

"Asshole."

I couldn't argue with that. Not anymore.

We'd both been unable to let go of our pasts.

Cole reached over and clutched my hand. "I'm sorry. I never liked the guy so I'm not upset it ended."

"Didn't think you would be." I rolled down my dress pants. Cole had warned me not to date him, but like always, I hadn't listened. "Rhett will never slow down. He's a big kid just out to have fun. I'll never be able to do all the things we loved doing again. There's no more mountain biking, rafting, or skiing for me. He doesn't want me anymore because I'm injured." *Nobody would.*

Gone were my days of wearing shorts—not that I'd done that very often. From the schoolyard to red-carpet events, I'd been trolled and teased for my solid build and my masculine dress-sense. I liked jeans, suits, and tailored dress pants rather than sparkly dresses and miniskirts. I didn't need more hurtful gossip and cruel comments about my hideous injuries and scars.

"Tia, I know you." Cole's assuring tone never faltered. "A fucked leg won't keep you down. You're a wild spirit that can't be tamed."

I sank deeper into the sofa. I'd been trying for months to be okay, but I'd failed. "Was."

"I won't buy that bullshit for a second."

Why wasn't he listening? I wasn't the same person anymore. My spirit had been severed. The acting and stunt career I loved was over. The job I'd lived for every day had been annihilated. Nothing would ever give me that rush of adrenaline ever again.

Cole came to sit beside me and drew me into a hug. "I'm so sorry you got hurt. I always worried about you. You could've told me about the accident. About Rhett. We tell each other everything." I didn't miss the hurt in his tone.

But arching an eyebrow, I gave him a cynical sideways glance. He hadn't told me everything either. I wasn't the only one with secrets.

"I would've been by your side in a heartbeat." He rubbed my arm. "You didn't need to go through this alone."

Yes, I did. I was stubborn, pigheaded and had thought otherwise. "There was nothing you could've done. You had your own problems to deal with. Flint wasn't in a good place. He needed you more than I did. I didn't want to burden anyone.

I was determined not to let my injuries set me back. But they have. No matter how much physical therapy I do, my leg never gets better."

"When did this happen?"

"Early June." I picked at the rim of my glass.

"Six months ago?" Shock rattled his voice. "Fuck. So this is why you've left the show?"

"Yeah. Production resumed a few weeks after the investigations into the accident had finished. It was found to be a freak incident. I went back to work after three months off, but it wasn't the same. How could I stay when I couldn't do the stunt work? They re-wrote my character to accommodate my injury, but everyone just looked at me in pity. I didn't want to be on set, watching everyone do the things I loved and not being a part of the action. It was too soul-crushing. So I talked to the studio, took the insurance payout, and made the decision to leave."

"But you've landed a new role." Cole's voice jumped up a notch. "That's good, right?"

Was it? Doubts fired in my head like rounds from a machine gun. The blaze in my heart was for stunt work, not acting. Playing an unlucky-in-love lawyer was so far removed from anything I'd ever wanted to do. I wasn't sure it was me. "I took the first role that came my way. I was afraid no one would employ me if they knew I was injured, so I lied. If they find out that my injury is more than a limp, I could lose the part. I'm a liability. An insurance risk."

"Nah." Cole swatted the air with his hand. "They're lucky to have you. You're freaking Tia Tanner. An A-list TV star. You're an asset to any show."

If I could just get excited about my new role, everything would be fine. "Here's hoping."

"You'll love it, I'm sure." He gave me another hug. "I'm so

glad you're home. Christmas wouldn't be the same without you. It's gonna be fun having you live here with me."

"Yeah." I rested my head against his shoulder. "I'm not gonna lie to you, Cole. I'm still struggling to accept I'll never be the same again. I'll get there. I'm down but not out." Somehow, I had to bury the old me and come to grips with the new one. The one who was crippled, scarred and afraid of being hurt. I was always up for a challenge, but a complete lifestyle and personality overhaul had never been on my list.

I had to find something I could do and would excite me every day. I had no idea what that was. I'd better find something quick, or I'd go stir crazy.

Cole kissed my temple. "I'll do anything I can to help."

"Thanks." I summoned a weak smile. "It will be nice to spend some time together before you release another album and tour."

"Absolutely." He chinked his vodka against my bourbon. "Tanner trouble together again."

"Cheers." I'd lost track of the good times we'd had and the chaos we'd caused when we were younger. Most of it had included drinking, drugs, music and wild parties. I wasn't sure I fit into my brother's world anymore.

"I can't wait for you to hear the new tracks. We're still finessing them to record and getting our new bassist up to speed."

Pain stabbed the center of my chest. "You found someone?" Seeing the band play without Phil would be hard. But we all had to move on. Even me.

"Yeah." Reservation and excitement lurked through Cole's voice. "Lewis is way more talented than Phil ever was."

"Shit. That's a huge call."

"Yeah, it is." Cole took a mouthful of his drink and swallowed hard. "We've only known the guy for three days. He seems alright. He's already helped us tweak one of our songs for the better, he's a bit reserved, and could turn out to be a dick. But if he's going to be a Flintlock, he'd better know how to party." Cole slapped my thigh. "So get your dancing shoes on; it's time to head out. Or is your leg too sore?"

Every cell in my body screamed at me to stay at home. I was afraid of being knocked, falling, or tripping. "It aches like a bitch. I can't stand for too long. But I won't let it stop me from living." Pity my heart didn't believe the crap that dribbled from my mouth. "I want to see the guys. It's been too long. I'll freshen up first." And take a strong painkiller or two.

"Awesome." Cole stood and dragged me to my feet. "You get ready. I'll rack up a round of shots to have before we head out."

Half an hour later, we entered a trendy nightclub in West Hollywood. As we weaved through the sea of people, I kept my head down to avoid being stopped by fans.

In the VIP section, Slip, Flint, and Sutton—I recognized her from our show's casting briefs and online pictures—sat around tables drinking and chatting, ignoring the ogles and photos being taken by onlookers. The moment they saw us, they jumped to their feet and hugged me hello.

Flint squeezed me extra tight. "Tee, so good to see you." Cole's best friend was the biggest sweetheart. We'd known each other since I was seven. He and Slip were family, through and through.

Flint drew his girlfriend to her feet. "Tia, I'd like you to meet Sutton."

"Argh!" Sutton screamed and flung her arms around me. "It's so nice to meet you. I can't wait to work together. I'm so excited about our new show."

"Same." I laughed, lied, and soaked in her contagious energy. I needed a good dose of positive vibes . . . and my drinks and my painkillers to kick in. I'd just arrived at the club and my ankle already throbbed.

Sutton held my shoulders at arm's length. "My God, you're the spitting image of your brother."

Yep. Same dark brown hair—his short, mine long. Same green eyes. Same nose. But we were two years apart and I was five inches shorter. I eyed her up and down. Her legs were as long as the 101 Interstate highway, and her sweet face was as round as a peach. Her gorgeous dark blue eyes drank me in, and not a hair was out of place in her perfectly styled blonde bob. "And you're stunning. I see why you captured Flint's eye." *Oh, yeah. She is so Flint's type.*

"I'm not sure who fell for who first." She slipped her arm around his waist and kissed his cheek. "But we're madly in love and happy."

"That's awesome." I play-punched Flint in the arm. "Good for you."

"Missed you." He half-hugged me again, then thumbed toward the bottle of vodka. "Hope you still know how to party?"

"It's like riding a bicycle, isn't it?" But fuck . . . I couldn't do *that* anymore.

"Good. Then get this into you." He poured shots of vodka and handed them to everyone. Raising his glass, he hollered, "To Tia. May she never leave us again."

"Never." I downed my shot. As long as LA didn't fuck with me again, I'd be fine.

I swallowed hard and licked my lips. The cold vodka hit the center of my chest. *Mmm, yum!* But bourbon was better. So was the buzz coursing through my veins.

My painkillers had kicked in. *Finally!*

Wobbling, I thrust out my glass for a refill. "Hit me again."

After a few more shots, I couldn't feel my leg. Or my lips . . . or my arms . . . or my feet. *Perfect.* Before the pain returned, I needed to dance . . . well, sway and boogie on the spot. I grabbed Cole's hand and hobbled onto the dance floor. We laughed and jigged around. Flint and Sutton joined us. She was adorable. Definitely a match for Flint. So much nicer than Lena, his last girlfriend.

But as the crowd jostled around us, a heavy blanket of warm air washed over me. I glanced toward the side of the dance floor. Through my hazy vision, I homed in on a hot guy with tousled shoulder-length, blond hair, dancing with another man. He moved his toned physique in perfect sync with the music, swaying his hips and rocking his shoulders. He was impeccably dressed in a black designer button-down, bootleg jeans and studded belt. His chiseled jawline highlighted his gorgeous lips and refined chin. The hairs on my arms stood on end. *Wow!* I hadn't been captivated by a man in years. Not since Rhett in Chicago. This guy was next level. Hot. Sexy. Made my panties wet just looking at him.

He moved closer to his friend and whispered in his ear. A cute smile curled across his lips.

Cole nudged my arm, then followed my line of sight. "Who are you checking out?"

"The blond."

Cole hooked his arm around my shoulders and burst out laughing. "That, my dear baby sister . . . is our new bassist. Lewis."

My heartbeat quickened. "Your bassist?"

"Yes."

Hmmm. Heat rushed to my core, pooled between my legs. Maybe LA wouldn't be so bad after all.

Then Lewis erased the gap between him and his partner. He cupped the guy's face, drew their lips together, and kissed him. Hard. Long. All tongue.

Oh wow. I couldn't look away.

Lewis's hands circled the man's head and clutched his hair.

His partner groped and grabbed Lewis's ass. The fire blazing between them ignited the room, blasting me where I stood.

But my heart catapulted backward. My stomach hit the ground with a thud.

Crap. That would be right.

Just my fucking luck.

The first guy I was attracted to in months . . . was gay.

Chapter 4

LEWIS

I dragged my drunk ass over to the bar for another drink. Benson, the guy I'd been dancing with, kissing, and getting hot under the collar for, had to leave. Go home to his boyfriend. *Prick.*

I could pick 'em, couldn't I? *Not.*

The first step I'd taken to move on from Emilio and the guy had turned out to be a dick. He'd been a great kisser and a sexy dancer, but a dirty rotten cheater. *Good riddance.* Maybe I should swear off men. My fun night celebrating with The Flintlocks had taken a dent, but it was nothing another drink wouldn't fix. Time to put Benson out of my mind. Reset. Party on.

Slip wove through the crowd, who were herding toward the bar like thirsty sheep. He eased in beside me and slapped my shoulder. "No luck with that dude?"

"Nah. He turned out to be a jerk." The taste of the Benson's Grasshopper Martini lingered on my tongue, and the scent of his musky cologne still filled my senses. I hated the smell of musk. So no loss.

Slip jutted his chin toward the group of guys standing at a

nearby high table. I'd noticed their I'm-interested gazes when I'd left the dance floor. Maybe not all was lost when it came to finding a moving-on hookup.

Overloaded with a ton of vodka, Slip swayed on his feet. "Wait a few minutes. I'm sure one of those guys will ask you to dance after the way you burned up the dance floor. Damn, you've got some moves."

"Uh . . . thanks." I nudged Slip's ribs with my elbow. "You want some lessons?"

I'd only known Slip for three days, but we seemed to have the same sense of humor and loved music more than anything.

"None needed." He leaned in closer and pointed to a blonde standing at the far end of the bar with her friend. As she sipped her cocktail, she threw come-fuck-me eyes in his direction. Slip's killer smile curled across his lips as he winked at her. "I have some moves of my own." With his bronzed skin and surfer-dude looks, no wonder he pulled in the women. He slapped me on the back. "I'm out of here. Catch you soon."

"Later." I flicked my hand in a drunken wave. He took off, meandering through the mass of people toward the girls. I leaned against the bar counter and waited for service.

"Lewis." Cole's voice hollered from somewhere behind me.

I whipped around. Cole and a stunning . . . no, gorgeous . . . brunette headed toward me. *Well, I'll be damned.* I might like men, but I could appreciate a good-looking chick when I saw one.

Oh, wait . . . She looked familiar. *Oh . . . shit.*

"Lewis?" Cole hooked his arm around the young lady's shoulders. "I'd like you to meet my sister, Tia."

Sister? My mouth ran dry. I swallowed hard. When I'd researched the band online, I hadn't delved into their families. Was it wrong to have a fan moment? I wiped my clammy palms on the back of my jeans, then held out my shaky hand. "Hi."

Tia slipped her fingers around mine and shook my hand, firm and strong . . . and a strange ripple snaked across my skin.

Her electric-green eyes shimmered with a glassy haze, and she swayed back and forth on her feet. "Nice to meet you. Soooo, you're the new bassist."

Yep, she'd had a few too many drinks and was possibly high, but that didn't stop my heart rate doubling. "Yeah. And you're on the show *Through The Smoke*, right?"

"*Was* . . . past tense." Her thick fake lashes couldn't mask the sorrow that flashed in her eyes. She scooped her long dark hair over her shoulder, straightened, and pasted on a flimsy smile. "I had to leave because of an injury. Messed up my leg."

"Shit. I'm sorry to hear that." But she looked fine from what I could see. Her heavy makeup, black skinny jeans that looked like they'd been painted onto her skin, and sequined T-shirt gave off a hardcore party animal vibe. *Just like her brother.* Scanning the even curves of her body from the ground up, I stopped at her well-toned, almost muscular arms. *Hmm.* I had a thing for arms. Nothing too bulky—I just liked them sexy and strong. I'd love those arms wrapped around my shoulders when we fu—

Wait. What?

I'd clearly had way too much to drink. Maybe I was still turned on from making out with Benson. Maybe I was a little starstruck. Maybe both. *Yep.* That was it. "I love your show. It won't be the same without you. Are you alright?"

"No." She shrugged like it was no big deal. "But I will be."

The current of anguish threading through her tone struck a chord inside my chest. I knew all too well how life-changing events could rip your heart out. Break you. Set you on a path you never saw coming. And time didn't always heal the wounds.

"Tia, you'll be fine." Cole ruffled Tia's hair, as if he were oblivious to the waver in her eyes. "Lewis, don't be fooled by Tee. She's a hell-raiser and troublemaker. She can talk smack, smut, and shit better than the rest of us. And she'll out-drink and out-party everyone."

I doubted she could in her current state.

"Is that a challenge?" I raised an eyebrow and threw her an I'm-game-if-you-are stare.

"God, no." She closed her eyes and shook her head. "I used to outdo the guys, but they'll run circles around me now."

"Never." Cole kissed her on the cheek, then hugged her tight. "I'm so glad you're here."

"Yeah. Me too." She patted his cheek and cuddled him.

I had a huge family but didn't get along with the majority of them like Tia and Cole seemed to. That had been my family's fault, not mine. I was better off without them.

I straightened my shoulders and thumbed toward the bar behind me. "Can I get you two a drink?"

"Nah, I'm good." With a mischievous grin, Cole pointed in Slip's direction. "Looks like Slip might need some help with those two ladies. I better go offer my assistance. Lewis, are you okay to keep Tee company?"

"Sure."

"I warn you." Cole waggled his finger at me. "Don't let her lead you astray."

I smirked. I'd like to see her try. "I'm sure we'll be fine. Have fun."

"Cool. Catch up soon." Cole took off toward the far end of the bar.

Chuckling, I turned to Tia. "Those guys are awesome."

"Yeah. I love them to bits." Her gaze, full of sisterly love, followed Cole. "And they like their women."

"They can have them. Not my scene." I threw her a saucy grin, then flicked my finger toward the wall of spirits and liquors lining the shelves behind the counter. "So . . . what's your poison?"

She arched one finely sculpted eyebrow. A playful smile curled across her lips. "Are we talking about drinks or *my* sexual preference?"

That made me laugh. I loved a no-boundaries sense of humor. "Drinks. Definitely drinks."

"Bourbon. Jim Beam, thanks . . . And, FYI, men."

"Me too." I tried not to smile, but my lips twitched and quivered.

She leaned toward me. That was better so we didn't have to shout over the loud music. As she rested her hand on my arm, the scent of her jasmine-infused perfume filled my head. *Hmm. Nice. Much better than musk.* Her eyes narrowed into seductive slits and glinted in the flashing club lights. "And I like black."

Okay. Cole was right. She certainly had some sass. Was it wrong to like her quirky banter, full of sexual innuendo? *Probably.* But some harmless fun never hurt anyone, right? "Are we talking about aged bourbon or preference in men?"

She caught her lower lip between her teeth and ran her fingers down the line of buttons on my shirt. "The whiskey. But I like both to have a bit of age."

"Age has never bothered me. It's what's on the inside that counts."

"True."

With our gazes locked, warm air stirred around us. The buzz from the booze made my head spin. Ignoring the partygoers, the music, and the jostle, I inched forward a fraction and lowered my voice. "And how do you like it?"

Looking up at me from beneath her thick eyelashes, she toyed with my collar. "Sex or my drink?"

I chuckled and shook my head. For some unknown reason, her touch sent weird, wicked electric pulses to every one of my nerve endings. My heart thudded to a strange beat. But my wits were intact. I caught her hands and lowered them to her side. I didn't want her to get the wrong idea. "Your drink."

Her eyes flashed with a sexiness that sent a jolt to my dick. No woman had ever been able to do that before.

She lifted her chin. "I like *it* many ways. But for my drink, straight will do. On ice."

I drew my shoulders back and pinched my brows together. "And just so *we're* straight, you know I'm not."

"Yeah, I do." She wrinkled her nose. "But you're hot. And I was just messing around with you."

My sanity warped as my gaze slid down toward her chest and back up again. She had a decent set of tits. There was nothing wrong with looking, right? But reality snapped back into place. *Definitely not for me.* "Do you always flirt with strangers?"

The color drained from her face. "Oh, shit. Did I go too far? It's no excuse, but after a few drinks, I have no filter. Growing up with Cole and the guys, and hanging out with men all day, I'm used to wisecracks and dirty talk. I'm sorry if I offended you. It wouldn't be the first time my mouth has gotten me into trouble."

I glanced at her soft pink lips. *Oh yeah. I can see why.* Those lips could render a man useless. I swallowed hard and flicked the thought aside. *What is wrong with me?* I needed more alcohol. And quick.

Finally catching the bartender's attention, I ordered and paid for our drinks. *Double shots.*

Thirsty partygoers aiming for the bar bumped into us. The dickhead behind Tia shoved her against my chest. I caught her arm to steady her on her feet. My fingers twitched, begging to feel her toned muscles. With all my strength, I tried to resist but failed. I swiped my thumb over her soft, silky flesh. *Hmm. So firm. Smooth . . . shit. Stop.* "Are you okay?"

"Yeah." She winced and hobbled. "Are you?"

"Yes. I'm fine." But my head certainly wasn't. Blood had

rushed to places in my body that shouldn't be affected by her. We needed to get out of this mosh pit of a bar queue. "Is your leg hurting?"

"Uh-huh."

The bartender placed our drinks on the counter. I picked them up, turned to Tia, and pointed toward our table. "Let's go sit down."

But before she moved, she eased between my arms. She slid her hands up my chest and rested them on my shoulders. "We could've gotten table service."

"I know, but I like mingling with common folk." I was one. I wasn't accustomed to privilege and the celebrity life The Flintlocks and other famous people led. Guess I had to get used to it. "You could've said something if you didn't want to stay."

Humor touched her smile. "Our conversation was too entertaining, and I liked being crushed against your body."

"I can't argue with that." My dick still didn't know what had happened. "Let's go."

As she walked toward our table, she limped. My stomach lurched. I'd been hurt before. The scars on my body hadn't caused any permanent damage, but the ones on my heart and soul ran deep. I prayed Tia's injuries weren't as serious.

At our table, Flint and Sutton were smooching and cuddling. The heat radiating off them was hot enough to melt a polar ice cap.

"Hey, you two? Enough." Giggling, Tia slapped her hand on the table to break them apart. "We don't need to see that."

Our presence didn't stop them from kissing. Flint circled his hand over Sutton's back and flipped us the bird.

Seeing people in love was hard after I'd had my heart sliced in two. But I refused to let the damage rule me. Having fun, moving on, and laughing were the best forms of medicine. I needed to overdose on all three.

I slid onto the chair beside Tia and handed her a coaster. "What's wrong with them making out? Don't you like to watch?"

"Oh, I like to watch." She grabbed the coaster in my hand, but I didn't let it go. She smiled, leaned in closer, and whispered in my ear, "I liked the show of you kissing that guy on the dance floor before."

Why did I like that notion?

She sat back, tugged the coaster out of my hand, and took a decent sip of her drink.

"What did you like about it?" I lifted my drink toward my mouth and glanced at her over the rim of my glass. "Did you want to join in?"

Shit! What if she said yes? If she'd edged between us on dance floor, I wasn't sure I would've asked her to leave. *Fuck.* I downed a mouthful of my drink and swallowed hard, praying the alcohol would knock some sense into me.

"No." She shook her head. Cute wrinkles formed on the bridge of her nose. "I like a lot of things, but not threesomes. I've had a couple. Not my thing."

Thank goodness, she'd said no. "Not mine either. They're overrated." Too many hands, arms, and legs, and not enough cock to go around.

"What happened to the dance floor guy?"

"He turned out to be an asshole."

She shrugged. "A lot of men are." Sting hovered in her tone.

"We're not all bad." I took another sip of my bourbon, savoring the burn as it slid down my throat.

"No, but the good ones are either taken or gay." She circled her palm at me.

"Sorry about that."

"Don't be." She slapped then rubbed my thigh. "You're cool. Don't ever change. You'll fit in well with the guys."

Heat pooled beneath her touch. My leg tingled. *Damn.* I

caught her hand just above my knee. But I didn't remove it . . . or let go. I scanned her face, intrigued by her. "I hope so."

"You've got some big shoes to fill." She glanced at my crotch then met my eyes. "But from what I can tell, you'll measure up."

I laughed and removed her hand from my leg. "You like causing trouble?"

Her shoulders slumped. "I used to. Sorry, I'm a bit of a mess tonight. Alcohol and painkillers aren't a good mix."

That explained the glassy eyes.

I'd honestly never met anyone like her. She had a tough exterior, was a flirtatious barrel of laughs, but her eyes gave away to being damaged on the inside. Maybe that was why I was captivated. No one was perfect. And maybe we had too much in common.

She rested her elbow on the table and cupped her chin in her hand. "So what were you doing before you joined the guys?"

"I'm from Brooklyn. I was in a band called The Saylors, but we broke up six months ago."

"The Saylors?" She pinched her eyebrows together. Her eyes darkened as if she were sifting through her brain. "Never heard of them. Sorry."

"Don't be. We were shit. Not for lack of talent but lack of unified direction. My best friend, Hayden, left The Saylors a few years ago and joined Everhide. It went downhill after that."

"I've met Hayden a few times. He's really nice. Was he your boyfriend before he married Lexi?"

"Um . . . no. Never." I chuckled and stared into my glass. "We're just best friends. I had a serious boyfriend. Past tense. But not looking for a new one."

"Me either." She glided her hand up my arm and over my shoulder, then draped it across the back of my chair. Her lips hovered dangerously close to my ear as she pointed across the VIP area. "But a hookup could be fun. There are four guys over at that table eye-fucking you."

Dragging my gaze away from her, I glanced across the floor toward the same men Slip had pointed out earlier.

I nudged her side gently. "They could be checking out you." She was the superstar. Hell, I'd even checked her out and I wasn't into women.

"Nope." Her laugh sent a current rippling across my skin. *Shit.* I liked that when I shouldn't. She jabbed her finger against my bicep. "Definitely you. You should ask one of them to dance."

"Is that a dare?" *But I was at a table. In a VIP section. Having a drink with Tia Fucking Tanner! I didn't want to leave.*

"Yes."

Our eyes met. Every time I looked at her, the wires in my brain scrambled to make sense of the something-but-nothing hovering in the air. Confusion was all that remained.

I wanted to spend the night talking to her, laughing, and making dirty jokes.

I wanted to touch her soft skin. Drink in her intoxicating perfume. Stay right where I was.

Why? What is with that?

I'd been through a lot of shit in my life, numerous ups and downs, but this was unchartered territory. I didn't understand it and didn't want to.

I'd never been into women.

Not ever.

I wasn't about to change.

With the opportunity to play with The Flintlocks on the line, I wasn't going to fuck up my chances. I needed to focus on music, not Tia. I'd had too much to drink. It had been too long since I'd had sex. I needed space to clear my head.

I forced myself to look away from Tia and glanced toward the men. They were an excuse to escape. I'd go over, have a drink and a chat. *Yep.* That was a plan. Tia had Sutton and Flint to talk to once they came up for air.

I gave Tia an okay-I'm-game nod. "They're all even on the looks scale. Who do you think I should ask to dance?"

She rubbed my back. "The one in the red shirt. He's got a Ryan Gosling vibe."

Shame it isn't the real Ryan. I'd do him in a nanosecond. "Okay." I downed the last mouthful of my bourbon then placed the glass on the table. As I stood, I combed my fingers through my hair, then straightened my collar. "Wish me luck."

She swatted the air. "You won't need it."

I took a step toward the guys but stopped. I looked back over my shoulder at Tia and pasted on a devilish grin. "Are you going to watch?"

"Oh, yeah. You fucking bet."

Shit. What hell had I landed in?

Chapter 5

TIA

Three cups of coffee by nine in the morning hadn't erased the dull hangover from last night. It'd been the first time I'd been out partying since my accident. Now I was paying the price. Too much dancing had exacerbated the pain in my ankle. I should've known not to overdo it. Shouldn't have gone out. But being with Cole and the guys again, and drinking alcohol combined with painkillers, had made me temporarily forget about my injuries. So had meeting Lewis.

I hadn't had that much fun bantering and making jokes in months. Each teasing nudge of his arm or leg against mine, each touch of his hand and sexy glance my way, had been hot enough to melt my panties. My body temperature still hadn't returned to normal. But to think there was something more between us would be foolish. Downright stupid. I'd wasted enough years of my life being with men who'd claimed to adore me only to be tossed aside for *something* or *someone* they'd loved more than me. I wasn't about to waste another second with a guy who wasn't even into women to begin with.

With no plans for the day, I tagged along with Cole to Flint's house to listen to the tracks for their album. I couldn't wait to hear the demos they'd been working on.

Carrying a takeout tray of steaming coffees, I shuffled along behind Cole and Slip toward Flint's music studio. Slip opened the door, and we stepped inside. The stench of masculine sweat, deodorant, and aftershave hit me like a karate kick. The sight of Phil's bass mounted on the far wall nearly dropped me to the floor. *God, I missed him.* It felt like a lifetime had passed since I'd been there at the beginning of the year. The huge room, decked out with band equipment at one end, and two sofas and a matching chair at the other, could be mistaken for a live recording studio, not just a rehearsal space.

Flint sat on one of the sofas, strumming his electric guitar. Lewis sat opposite him, plucking his bass. Notebooks, Flint's laptop, and two energy drinks littered the coffee table between them. Lewis pivoted his head toward me. A small smile curled at the corner of his mouth, then he winked. My knees weakened, and my heart skipped a beat. *Stupid heart. But damn!* He'd looked sexy as hell last night at the club, but in faded ripped jeans and an old sweatshirt, he had me hotter and more bothered than I should be. I shouldn't be reacting like this to someone who was off-limits. *Fuck. I'm a screw-up.*

"You're late." Flint half-grinned and glared at Cole and Slip. "We agreed on ten o'clock, not eleven."

"Flint, it's my fault." I hobbled over to him and handed him a coffee. "I needed to strap my ankle." Even after sleeping with an icepack on, it had swollen to the size of a baseball.

Over more shots of vodka and bourbon at the club last night, I'd told the guys about my injury. Like Cole, they'd been adamant that nothing, not even a messed-up leg, would keep me down. I wished I could believe them.

Flint stood his guitar against the sofa and took a sip of his cappuccino. "And if I remember correctly, Tee, you're not a morning person."

"Nope." I ruffled his soft black hair. "Neither are you." I wasn't looking forward to early starts again when my new show kicked off in January. There wasn't enough caffeine in the world to make the mornings easier.

"No, I'm not." He wriggled his eyebrows "But Sutton is. She made sure I was up before she went shopping." A shit-eating grin slid across his face. "Sex was worth it."

My shoulders slumped. I hadn't had sex in months. No guy would want someone with a limp and ugly scars. Thank God for vibrators. I went through batteries by the truckload.

I shuffled around the coffee table and handed Lewis a coffee. Ignoring the flutter in my tummy, I sank onto the seat beside him. "Cappuccino. Hope you like it?"

He took the cup. "Thank you. You're a lifesaver." Redness rimmed his stunning silver eyes. A pale tinge of gray hued his skin. *Oh yeah.* He wasn't running at one hundred percent, hungover from too much bourbon and God only knew what else he'd downed before I'd arrived with Cole. "If it's got caffeine in it, I'm good."

"Guys?" Flint licked and wiped foam from his upper lip. "Lewis and I have been running through two more songs. Some of the progressions he's come up with are good and might work for 'So Long.'"

"Are you trying to impress the boss?" Chuckling, Cole walked behind Lewis and playfully clipped him on the back of his head. Cole took a seat next to Flint, nearly missing the edge of the sofa, but was quick to clamber onto the cushion. He could possibly still be drunk. Thank goodness Slip had picked us up and driven us here, although . . . he didn't look much better.

"No." Lewis shook his head. "I'm only offering some suggestions. You don't have to use them. It's just nice to be heard for a change."

Hmmm. I took a mouthful of my coffee. I could listen to Lewis's kinky-edged voice all day long.

Flint slapped Cole on the leg, hard. "Don't spin shit to Lewis. I'm not the boss. Everyone's equal."

"Yes, boss." Slip slid onto the single chair at the other end of the sofas. He tossed his cell phone and keys onto the coffee table then buried his face in his hands.

"You're such a dick." Flint flicked his long hair off his eyes and laughed.

"Can't you handle big nights, Slip?" Lewis raised a questioning eyebrow.

Slip pressed his fingers against his temples and rubbed them in circles. "Ergh! Not when I mix drinks."

Placing my hand against my stomach, I could relate to Slip's current state of health. The cocktail of bourbon and vodka I'd drunk last night wasn't stilling well in my gut. The coffees may come back if I'd belched. But as I shuffled on the sofa, an inch closer to Lewis, the temperature between us jumped. The skin on my arm tingled.

Lewis's gaze dropped to my wrist. His brows pinched together. *Did he feel that?*

Ergh!

I was too hungover to deal with this shit. I was sure it was just a side effect from the alcohol seeping from every one of my pores, creating a toxic vapor in the air.

I eased a few inches away from him and rested my head back. I should've stayed in bed.

Lewis turned to Slip. "So, Cole hooked up with a Bella Hadid lookalike. Did you have any luck last night?"

"Nope." Slip continued to rub his temples.

I giggled. I loved that the guys didn't always get lucky. It kept them grounded, real, and their cocky arrogance at a tolerable level. I hoped they never changed as they grew more popular. "These guys aren't as irresistible as they think they are." Stretching out my leg, I massaged my aching knee. "What about you, Lewis? Any luck with Mr. Gosling?"

When I'd left with Cole and his hookup to head home, Lewis had been outside, leaning against a car, talking to the same guy.

"No." He nudged my good leg with his knee. "The conversations you and I had were much more entertaining than the ones I'd had with him and his friends. They were stockbrokers."

"Hmm." I summoned a low, seductive tone. "Doesn't talking about fondling your finances, hot stocks, and sexy trades get you off?"

Laughing, he lowered his chin. His gorgeous hair fell forward, brushing against his cheeks. "Well, it didn't with them, but if you keep talking like that I might change my mind."

Yeah . . . I highly doubt that.

Grinning, Cole leaned forward and rested his elbows on his knees. "God, I've missed your smart mouth, Tee. I warned you, Lewis; there's never a dull moment when she's around."

Lewis bobbed his head. "So I've gathered."

But my stomach nosedived and hit the floor. Cole was wrong. The past few months had been nothing but dull. My life had consisted of watching shows on every TV streaming service available, reading, or having my psychologist or physical therapist visit my apartment. My days of causing havoc were over. I didn't go out anywhere. Last night had been a special occasion to see the guys and meet Sutton. Until work on my new show started in late January, I'd be doing the same thing I'd done in Chicago for the past few months. *Nothing.* But at least here in LA, my *nothing* enabled me to come to Flint's and listen to the guys play. That would take my mind off my aches, pains, and worries.

Cole flicked his finger back and forth between Lewis and

me. "What was with you two last night? Every time I saw you talking, I didn't know whether you wanted to kill each other or fuck."

Lewis tensed, clutching his bass against his belly. "Uh . . . no. Neither. We were just spinning shit and had some good laughs. I don't play on both sides of the fence."

Shame. I'd let him dig in my dirt any day.

Lewis placed his hand on my knee, giving it a gentle shake and tap. "We had a great time getting to know one another."

Oh my . . . his touch. Fire coiled beneath my leggings. It shot up my thigh and pooled in my core. My pulse quickened, pounding in my head. This was not happening. *Stop. Stop now.* But my gaze fell to his hand. Thick silver signet rings decorated his three center fingers. Tattoos peeked out from beneath the cuff of his sweatshirt. *What are they of?* I followed the line of his arm and met his breathtaking eyes. He stared back at me and smiled.

My breath hitched. My leg tensed. *Shit.*

He quickly withdrew his hand and fidgeted with his rings.

Time to draw on my acting skills. Time to ensure that the guys didn't suspect that I was mental. "True, but I also learned I shouldn't take oxycodone and alcohol together."

A deep laugh burst from Cole. "You were high?"

"A little hazy." Despite being buzzed, it had been the first time I'd had fun in months. But I couldn't drink and drug myself up to the eyeballs every day. That would be a sure way to get fired from my new role.

"That explains everything." Cole tilted his head toward me. "Just like the old days, right?"

"I wish." My heart shriveled to the size of a pebble. My wild days were long gone. My future involved sedate activities like adult coloring books and Sudoku. That was the level of excitement in store for me. Yay! *NOT!*

"Well, you two were entertaining." Cole jutted his chin toward Lewis. "But you are gay, right? Or do I have to warn you not to fuck around with my sister? She's off-limits."

I sneered at Cole. I loved that he cared about me, but I could take care of myself.

Humor shimmered in Lewis's eyes. "You have nothing to worry about."

"Good." Cole straightened and clapped his hands. "Now let's get rid of these hangovers and play some music."

Finally. It had been three years since their last album. I loved hearing the songs before they hit the studio, before they morphed, and were mixed and mastered into final versions.

Flint grabbed his guitar and placed it across his lap. "First, Lewis and I will play you some of the changes we've come up with for 'So Long.' Let us know what you think. That okay?"

"Absolutely." Cole grabbed the top open notebook off the coffee table. He flicked through the pages covered in Flint's handwriting, music notes, scribbles, and lyrics. "Tia's gonna hang around. She can help record a clean demo for the studio."

"That'd be awesome." Slip rubbed his tired eyes. "Can't have you just lazing about doing nothing, Tee."

Lewis's eyebrows shot skyward. "You have hidden talents?"

"Many." I threw him a saucy smile. "Want me to show you them sometime?"

"If it involves music, I'm in."

Figures. He was just like the rest of the band. Music was all that mattered.

I drained the last mouthful of my coffee and placed the cup on the table. "Growing up around these guys who played every day for hours, I learned how to use their sound and lighting equipment. I took a few classes at college, and I even ran a couple of shows for them when they started out. I've helped at random gigs when I've come home. I know my way around a mixer with my eyes closed."

"Did you ever want to play with them?" Lewis asked.

"God no." I tugged the cuffs of my sweater over my hands. "My parents forced me to learn piano. I hated it. Plus, the boys never wanted a girl in their band."

"True." Cole swiped up his coffee and took a big sip. "But you loved pressing our buttons."

"I sure did." And flicking switches. Like the one that had turned on being in the same room as Lewis. Just sitting next to him caused heat to rise in my cheeks and had my fingers twitching with the urge to touch him. Now I had to work out how to turn it off. But as I was a sucker for punishment, I leaned against Lewis's arm and pointed to each of the guys. "See? Cole thinks he controls the band with his drums. Flint believes he's the leader because he sings. Slip claims to be the life of the show on his electric. Phil thought he was in charge with his basslines. But in reality, it was me, or whoever sat at the control panel, who held them by the balls. I could kill their voices or their instruments with the turn of a dial."

"You like that?" Narrowing his eyes, Lewis lifted his chin a fraction. "You like being in control? Dominating the guys? Having them at your mercy?"

"Always." I threw him a mischievous smile.

"No games, Tia." Flint smacked his coffee cup down onto the table. "You can help as long as you don't fuck around. We've got to get Lewis up to speed before we hit the studio. Got it?"

"Yes, boss." I pouted.

Flint groaned then smiled a big, gorgeous smile.

As we lazed on the sofas, Flint and Lewis did a few run-throughs of the song they'd been working on. They discussed the alternative intros and listened to a variety of beats Lewis strummed. None stuck as much as the one he and Flint had first played. Lewis's suggestions, tied with Flint's incredible voice, added a new layer of seduction to the lyrics. After the final okay from everyone, Flint and Lewis played the track. Flint sang, soft and low.

It's been so long since my heart beat,
It's been so long since I felt anything.
Thought my days would fall apart,
Thought my nights would be endlessly dark.
I walked alone for way too long,
I cried too many tears at home alone.
The fire inside me had gone out,
All I wanted to do was scream and shout.
But I wouldn't let losing you crush my soul,
The pain inside me had to go.

I couldn't take my eyes off Lewis. His hand caressed the neck of his bass, and his fingers glided across the strings like they floated on air. Would his touch on my skin be that gentle or would his calloused fingertips scratch?

Shit! What the fuck was I doing? I needed to get him out of my head. Would spending time with him kill this weirdness or make it worse? Was my life set on repeat? What the hell was it about bassists?

"Can we record the whole song?" Slip edged forward on his seat and rubbed his hands together, no doubt eager to get on his strings. "It's wicked."

Flint slipped his fingers down the neck of his guitar; the sound sliced the air. "Tee, you up for that?"

"Sure am." I got up from the sofa, wincing as I put weight onto my ankle. As I lumbered over to the desk and mixer, I glanced over my shoulder. Lewis tracked my every move. He wasn't making it easy to kill the strange, undeniable, totally fucked-up attraction I felt toward him.

Cole brought Flint's laptop over to the desk and plugged it into the monitors. "This is the latest version of the audio software. It hasn't changed much since you probably last used it."

"Thanks." I sank onto the office chair and scanned the equipment. The recording software filled the screens. Lights on the control panel flashed green. I glided my fingers over the channel levers. My fingertips tingled. Dials and buttons begged to be turned and pressed. *Oh yeah.* This could be fun. "Just give me a few minutes and I'll be back up to speed."

"Good." He kissed the top of my head. "Now behave." He pointed at me as he walked toward his drums.

"Always."

I put on the headphones and clicked through the software. The audio program had a new interface, but the functions were the same.

The guys' took to their instruments and practiced the song. Their hangovers disappeared within a couple of run-thoughs. With every booming beat, the old me simmered to life. I had to cause a little bit of havoc. I slid the dial down on Slip's channel, delaying his electric through the amp. I killed Flint's mic and loaded Lewis's bass with too much reverb.

The guys laughed and shook their heads.

Cole shot up from his stool and pegged a drumstick at me. He missed. The stick smacked against the wall behind me and fell at my feet. A huge grin beamed across his face. "I have not missed you messing around."

I wrinkled my nose and reset the channels. "Yes, you have."

He lowered his butt onto the stool. "Okay. Maybe a little. Now throw me my stick so we can get this change recorded."

I picked up Cole's drumstick and tossed it to him. It hit the cymbal with a clang.

Lewis chuckled and plucked his bass. "Never a dull moment, right?"

"Never." Cole grumbled but his eyes shimmered with love.

He twirled his stick around his fingers, then pumped his bass pedal. "We all set?"

"Yes." I flicked the switch and set the software to record. "Go."

They ran through the track twice. Every time they reached the end of the song, I drew in a deep breath. I missed this— hanging out with the guys, and their music. But the hole in my heart crushed my ribs. I missed Phil.

Would Lewis be able to fill his shoes? If he added a touch of magic to each song like he'd just done to that track, Cole would be right. Lewis could be more talented than Phil. He played with more pizazz. Phil had possessed character. Lewis had a charisma that sucked me in. The energy radiating off him when he played, the sparkle in his eyes and the way he moved and danced, all held me captive.

With every passing beat, butterflies fluttered in my belly, and my body temperature soared.

He smiled. I smiled back.

His grin grew bigger.

What the fuck?

This wasn't healthy. I didn't need to add more problems to my long list. My therapy bills had been huge enough. What would a new therapist say about my attraction to an unattainable man? *Shit.* I didn't want to find out. They'd have me committed.

Lewis was only in LA for two more days. Since every second I spent with him made me feel things I shouldn't be feeling, it would be best to avoid coming to Flint's. I didn't have to be around the band.

If Lewis moved here after recording the album, I'd only see him at random events and get-togethers.

I could handle that, right?

LA was a big city.

Surely, I could avoid him.

Chapter 6

TIA

At the end of recording the demo, I took off my headphones and tossed them onto the desk. The electric groove from the sultry, sexy beat still coursed through my veins. *Damn.* They were good. I couldn't wait to hear the rest of the songs.

"Let's have a break." Flint placed his guitar on the stand next to his mic. "I need food, and my phone has been vibrating against my ass for five minutes." He grabbed it out of the back pocket of his jeans and scanned the screen. "Fuck. It's Sutton. I better return her call. She's Christmas shopping and has probably bought half of The Grove."

Slip stowed his guitar. "You guys want burgers from In-N-Out?" He headed over to the coffee table and swiped his keys and cell phone off the surface. "I'll go pick 'em up. Delivery takes forever."

"Sure." Flint rubbed the back of his neck, not taking his eyes off his cell phone as he headed toward the far window to make his call. "I'll have a Double-Double."

"We don't have In-N-Out back home." Lewis unhooked his bass and placed it on the stand. "I've never had it. But if they have something like a regular burger and fries, I'm in."

"Sure do." Cole headed toward the door. "I'll go with Slip. You two want to come for a drive?"

"Um . . ." Lewis turned a shade of pale green and swiped his hand down one cheek, then the other. "I'll pass. I'm still a bit queasy. I'll hang here if that's okay?"

"Cool." Slip shoved Cole toward the door. "Tia will keep you company. Won't you, Tee?"

"Um . . . yeah . . . sure." But what if *I* wanted to go for a drive? I didn't. But that was beside the point.

We left Flint in the music room, talking to Sutton about gifts for his parents, and we headed down the hallway. Slip and Cole took off. The loud rumble of Slip's Camaro reverberated throughout the house as he sped out of the driveway. As I followed Lewis into the kitchen, I pulled my sweater over my hands, and tucked my fingers underneath my armpits to keep them warm. "Your changes to the song were awesome."

"Thanks." He grabbed a coffee cup out of the cupboard near the rangehood. He'd been staying here at Flint's for the past couple of days and seemed to know his way around the place. "You want one?"

"No, I'm good." I leaned against the sink to take the weight off my leg. "Have you written a lot of music?"

He placed the cup underneath the coffee machine and pressed the button. It whirred to life, grinding the coffee beans, then seconds later, thick black liquid trickled out of the spouts into the cup. "Yeah, I have. I've created a ton of songs, riffs and cool beats. The majority have been just for fun."

"I like what I heard today. Have the guys listened to any of your songs?"

"No." He rested his hip against the counter, waiting for his coffee to finish brewing. "Only my instrumental demos I posted online for the audition, and I've played them a few riffs and loops over the past few days as we've works on their tracks."

"Make sure they hear some of them."

"I will . . . one day. I know my place for this album. I have milestones to reach. I don't want to push the boundaries. I'm happy to just be involved."

"There is no harm in asking them to listen to a few tracks. They'd be cool with it. Whether they take anything onboard is up to them."

"I'm beyond stoked they're listening to my ideas. That's a big step up from my last band." I didn't miss the snark in his tone. Clearly, The Saylors hadn't ended on good terms. He gave me a sideways glance. "I'm impressed you know your way around the channel mixer and audio software."

"I'm not just a pretty face." I grabbed a glass of water and took a mouthful.

"No . . . no, you're more than that." His gaze raked over me, sending shivers down my spine. "You are intriguing and full of surprises. I like that."

Heat flooded my cheeks. "Good. I like you too. I mean . . . your playing. Your music. In the band." *Shit. Stop mumbling.*

"Got it." He chuckled, grabbing the milk out of the fridge.

I wiped my palms on my leggings. I wasn't sure being in the same space as Lewis was a good thing. "Do you have plans for Christmas? Do you spend it with family?"

"Um." He poured milk into the frother and turned it on. "No. They're in Ohio." His tone took on a cold, lifeless edge. "I haven't spent Christmas, nor many other occasions with them, since I was sixteen."

"Why's that?" *Shit. Had I been too abrupt again? Yep.*

He puffed air through his nose. "I'm the black sheep of the family. My parents never approved of my *lifestyle*."

"For being gay or a musician?"

Gray clouds drifted across his eyes, but he was quick to

blink them away. "Both."

I hugged my glass against my chest and softened my tone. "That must be hard." I could relate on the job front. My parents had wanted Cole and me to have corporate careers, not pursue the arts. They were workaholics and traveled a lot. We hadn't spent any of the holidays with them since I was fourteen. It was for the best—it prevented World War III.

Lewis tipped the milk into his coffee and stirred it in. "It was at first, but living in Brooklyn with my pop was awesome. He was this crazy old man who ran a bowling alley and the local community bridge club. Everyone loved him. But he died three months ago."

"I'm sorry to hear that. Losing someone sucks. Phil was like a brother to me." No . . . he was so much more than that. He was my *everything. Fuck!* "We were the same age. We always tried to outdo each other at everything and always caused mischief. We raised havoc across Pasadena."

"That doesn't surprise me." He opened the pantry door and stepped inside the long skinny aisle that ran down the center of the packed shelves. I'd never seen that much food in Flint's pantry ever. Must be Sutton's influence.

Lewis's hand moved in time with his gaze as he scanned up and down the shelves. A groove pinched between his brows. "Were you two an item?"

The hole in my chest that had remained since losing Phil lurched. Nausea flooded my gut. Were some secrets best left buried? Literally? "Have the guys told you about the dibs rule?"

Intrigue flashed in his eyes. "Dibs rule? What's that?"

What was the dibs rule? The cause of too many fucked up problems and even more dangerous secrets.

But whatever Lewis was looking for in the pantry still hadn't been located.

I interrupted our line of conversation. "Do you need help

finding something?"

"Sugar!" Lewis pointed his tensed hand at the eye-height shelf. "It was here yesterday. In a little blue container."

"It has to be there." I stepped into the pantry and skimmed the shelves, unable to see the container. Lewis tensed and shuffled farther along, turned, and resumed looking on the other side. He opened one container that contained pasta, closed it, and placed it back on the shelf. "So what's the dibs rule?"

"It's The Flintlocks' bro code." I peered inside a tin containing rice, shut it, then placed it back where I'd taken it from. "After Flint and Phil got into a fight over this girl, Shelby, in high school, they made up this rule that they couldn't hit on each other's girlfriends, their friends, any exes, or hot interests. It was to avoid causing problems in the band. I fell under the dibs rule as Cole's sister."

Lewis rested his hand on the shelf beside his head and turned to me. His silver eyes drilled into mine. He stepped toward me, stopping less than a foot away. The air around us grew heavy. My mouth ran dry. I swallowed hard.

Lowering his voice, he said, "So if Slip's brothers are hot, I can't hit on them?"

With his gaze locked onto mine, he reached past me. His arm brushed my hair as he grabbed a jar. I lost the ability to breathe. My knees weakened. Visions of slamming him against the shelves, ripping off his clothes, kissing him like a crazed animal, and fucking him like the rock star he was flashed before my eyes. *Crap.*

I staggered back a step. He was too close. Too hot. Too much. "Sorry, Slip's brothers are straight. But even if they weren't, you couldn't touch them. Not if you want to stay in the band and keep your balls intact."

"Noted. But I've never been one to follow the rules,

especially ones made in high school. Nobody, nor some silly dibs rule, will dictate who I can be with." He waved the jar of sugar in front of my face. "Found it. Different container." A small smile slid across his lips.

Heat radiated across my skin. Did he know the effect he had on me? Or was I having a mental breakdown?

We made our way out of the pantry.

Thankful for the cool air and space, I hobbled around the kitchen counter and took a seat on one of the stools. "I'm with you on the dibs rule. It's stupid and has caused more problems than they realize." And no doubt would cause more. Every member of the band had broken it. I knew that for a fact. Me included.

Lewis chuckled, low and soft, as he scooped one spoon of sugar into his coffee. "So, which of the guys did you fuck?"

Damn. Was it that obvious? I slumped and slid my arms onto the counter. "Phil." My voice came out in a pained whisper. "We were best friends. We went to different schools and were together in junior and senior year. Part of the thrill was sneaking around. But he ended it just after the guys got signed. Music was more important. He loved the band and wanted to honor the dibs rule." *He loved them more than me.*

I drew myself upright and pushed the memories into the recesses of my mind. "Unfortunately, as they guys grew more popular, Phil got swept up in the lifestyle, the drugs, the alcohol, and God only knows what else. I hated seeing him with other women. So I left town and got a new life."

"Now I've done that several times." Lewis sipped on his coffee. "Nothing wrong with a fresh start."

"No. It was what I needed to do. Meeting someone new helped. But that didn't last either." Chicago had turned into a shit show as well. "But the guys don't know Phil and I were together. If you don't mind, I'd like it to stay that way. Losing him has been hard enough without unpacking more painful memories." *A bit too late for that.*

He raised his cup toward me. "We all have past relationships we'd like to bury."

"Mine literally is." I quirked my lips into a small smile.

"Shit." He winced. "Sorry."

"Don't be." I straightened. "Despite their crazy rules, these guys are awesome. They're my family. We love each other more than anything, and we'd do anything for each other."

"I like that. You seem to get along well." He came around the counter and sat on the stool beside me. "My family and I aren't close. I only keep in touch with three out of my six siblings. I don't talk to my parents. My pop and my band were my family, but now they're gone."

I clutched his forearm and gave it a quick squeeze but removed my hand just as fast. "Well, hopefully you've found a new one."

"I hope so too." He picked up his cup and blew into it. "I know Phil meant the world to you and these guys. That will never be forgotten, but I hope to be part of their future and build a new legacy."

"Yeah. Are you ready for that ride?"

"Yes."

"Good. You'd better be certain about that if you become a Flintlock. The guys have a wild reputation. Once promo starts, the media will dig up dirt on you. So you'd better be honest with them and April, their personal assistant and publicist, so they can be prepared."

He stared toward the far kitchen wall, took a steady breath, then lowered his chin. "I don't have anything to hide."

Oh, he had secrets. We all did. "No mystery children? No criminal background? No scandalous love affairs?" I could give him some pointers on the last one.

"No children. No criminal record but I was caught having sex in public once. I was let off with a warning. Think the cop liked me." He chuckled then sipped his coffee. Sadness swallowed his eyes. "My fucked-up family is about it."

"You'll fit right here into LA then. Everyone's a mess in this town."

"Can't be worse than New York. Let's hope I survive recording and make the move at the end of February."

"If you're lucky, I might show you 'round when you do." Providing this uncanny draw I had toward him had died by then.

"Yeah . . . I'd like that."

As Flint came out of the music room, the boys arrived home with In-N-Out. The scent of fried food made my tummy grumble. We took seats at Flint's huge wooden dining table and dug into our burgers and fries. The conversation revolved around which song to work on during the afternoon.

But Cole kept swiping and reading something on his cell phone. Every message made him wince and groan. "Fuck! You wouldn't believe it."

"What?" Slip said with his mouth full of fries.

"There's been another huge dump of snow up at Big Bear. It's the best season ever. We should go snowboarding. We won't have a vacation for months once we start recording and rehearsing, and promo kicks in."

"You mean, go up there for Christmas?" Flint picked up his cup of cola and sucked on the straw.

"Yeah." Cole chewed and swallowed a bit of his burger. "You can spend the morning with your folks, then we can head up after lunch. Slip's spending Christmas Eve with his family. Tia and I have no plans. We don't have to be in New York until the thirtieth."

My calf muscle seized just thinking about snowboarding.

Another activity I'd loved that was no longer in my future. "I can't board anymore."

"So?" Cole grimaced. "Come and hang out."

"Tee, Sutton will come." Flint wiped his fingers on a napkin. "She's not a big skier. You two can go shopping or to the spa, and stay toasty warm while us guys hit the slopes."

I slumped my shoulders. "Flint, you know I'm not one for being pampered at a spa." I hated long fingernails and facials, but I loved a good deep-tissue massage.

"You scrub up okay when you have to." Flint threw me a sly smile. "I've seen you on the red carpet."

"That's work."

"I don't know, Tee." Slip dipped his head to one side. "I'm sensing change in you. There might be a princess inside of you yet."

I pegged a fry at him. "No chance." I had to change my life, but it wouldn't involve becoming a princess. "I'm a dragon slayer, not a princess who needs rescuing."

"What about you, Lewis?" Flint asked. "Do you have plans for Christmas?"

"Nothing that is set in concrete. On Christmas Day, I usually go to lunch with a bunch of friends. But other than that, with Pop gone, no boyfriend, and Hayden in London with the rest of Everhide, I guess I'll be home alone for most of the holidays." He shot a breath of air through his nose. "That sounds kinda sad, doesn't it?"

"Yes. We can't have that." Cole rubbed his hands together, like he always did when he came up with a wicked idea. "Would you like to come with us? My parents own a cabin up at Big Bear, so accommodation is covered. We can board all day, then run through the songs or hit a tavern or two at night."

"Um . . . I don't have gear for the mountains." Bewilderment swept across Lewis's face. "I came to LA for two days, and I've been here for four. Clothing is an issue."

"We're the same size." Slip waved a few fries at Lewis. "I've got a ski jacket and pants you can borrow, and a hoodie or two. We've got spare boards. If you can grab a few other things to last another few days, are you in? It would be a great opportunity to get to know you better."

Lewis took a bite of his burger. As he chewed, he looked at me across the table. Doubt and concern flickered through his eyes.

Why was he looking at me like that? I had nothing to do with this invitation.

But, *oh yeah*. The invisible threads of tension between us grew tighter and tighter. Heat crept up my neck and settled in my cheeks. I didn't like it one little bit.

He swallowed hard and dragged his gaze away from me and turned to the guys. His worry morphed into cool excitement. "I'd love to. I'm in."

Shit. My blood pressure pounded against my temples. Why did the universe keep putting Lewis in my path? *Stuck in the mountains. In a cabin. With him. Crap. Crap. Crap.* Maybe I needed saving. My sanity needed rescuing if nothing else.

"Awesome." Cole tossed a small fry into his mouth. "Let's hit the slopes."

But Lewis glanced at me. Fire and ice flickered through the silver shards in his eyes. I wasn't imagining things. There was something between us. But Lewis didn't look happy about it.

He wasn't the only one.

Chapter 7

LEWIS

Two days later, just after a late lunch on Christmas Day, we headed toward the mountains. I'd lost my bar job back home to be here. This trip to Big Bear had better be worth it.

I planned on being around for a long time, so this strange pull I had toward Tia had to end so we could be friends. Was that even possible? Concern dug and drove into my brain, inching deeper and deeper. The way she looked at me sent unwarranted warmth coiling through my veins. She was attractive. Smart. Funny. But that was it. I didn't *feel* anything for Tia. No, I didn't. *I didn't. I didn't. I didn't.*

Upon nightfall, Slip pulled up beside Cole's Lamborghini SUV in front of a luxurious lodge covered in snow. *Holy shit!* I peered out the windshield. The two-story monstrosity with its panoramic windows, massive deck, and views across the valley looked like a freaking hotel. "When Cole said '*cabin,*' I was expecting something tiny with shared rooms and bunk beds."

"Uh . . . nope." Slip jumped out of the car and slammed the door shut. Following him, I hopped out and headed toward the trunk. With each step, my breath misted, and thick, fresh snow crunched underneath my boots. The sickly stench of smoke from all the lodgings fireplaces filled the air.

Slip opened the back and yanked out his bag and guitar. "This joint is top-notch. Six rooms. Seven bathrooms. A hot tub. You can snowboard straight down to the chairlift over there." He waved half-heartedly into the dark.

I grabbed my duffel bag, bass, and a portable amp, and followed him inside the cabin. The short vacation would do me a world of good too. I hadn't had a break in years. "I'm glad I stayed."

"It'll do for a few days." Slip dumped his belongings at the base of the wide wooden staircase.

Wow! I spun around, taking in the huge windows, stone fireplace, enormous blue U-shaped sofa in the sunken living area, and gourmet kitchen at the back of the lodge where the others were unpacking food and making drinks.

Before my bag had hit the ground, Cole shoved a neat bourbon in my hand. "Welcome to Tanner Manor. Glad you could stay."

I took the glass. "You might not say that when I whip your ass on the slopes tomorrow."

"Bring it."

I could get used to this extravagant, spontaneous lifestyle very easily. I just needed to pass some milestones.

We joined the others in the kitchen for drinks. It was juvenile, but I kept my distance from Tia, standing as far away from her as possible. After pizza and more drinks around the fireplace, we had an early night.

The next morning, I hit the slopes with the guys. We boarded every trail. In fits of laughter, we tried to outperform each other, showing off with tricks on the rails, half-pipe, and jumps. But by mid-afternoon, my borrowed boots had rubbed my feet like a bitch.

Sitting on the snow at the top of the chairlift, I clipped into my board for another run down the slope, but one of my heels burned and screamed in agony. I'd persevered with the pain for long enough. "Fuck, guys. I'm gonna have to go via the cabin and get some Band-Aids. I have a blister or two. My foot's killing me."

"Pussy." Slip chuckled, stood, and dusted the snow from his gloves.

"Never." I jumped to my feet and shuffled toward the downhill run.

"Don't worry about coming back out." Cole slid beside me and pointed toward the far mountain. "Looks like a snowstorm is coming. We'll only get another run or two in anyway."

"And visibility is shit." Flint glided past me, putting on his mirrored goggles. "We'll meet you back at the cabin."

"Sweet. I'll have hot chocolates waiting."

"Spike them and you're on." Slip took off. "See you soon."

We sped down the slope, darting in and out of the trees, jumping over mounds of snow and zigzagging around each other. Halfway down the hill, I hollered goodbye and headed toward our cabin. The guys took off in the other direction toward the chairlifts.

After packing my board and boots away in the dry room, I peeled off my wooly socks and examined the damage. One heel was fine. But the other? Raw, red skin and watery ooze leaked from the wound the size of two dimes. *Fuck.* Shower first, then I'd deal with my blister.

Ten minutes later, I dragged myself out of the shower and dressed in jeans and a black hoodie.

Halfway down the stairs, I balked. My breath hitched. *Crap.* Tia sat on the sofa, flicking through social media feeds on her cell phone.

"Hey?" I called out softly.

She spun her head around. "Oh. Hi. I didn't think anyone was here."

"The guys are still boarding. I got a blister." I grabbed the first-aid kit off the top of the fridge and sat on the opposite end of the sofa. "Where's Sutton?"

"She wanted a mani-pedi, so she'll be at least another hour. I hate sitting still for that long. It drives me crazy." She wriggled her socked toes on her outstretched legs.

"You really don't like being pampered?"

She dropped her cell phone beside her hip. "Not really. I tolerate the salon when I have to go to events. That's it."

"What do you do to relax?" I opened the first-aid box. Ointments and dressings and tweezers sat neatly in position like none of the items had been used before.

"I'm not much of a relaxer. Not even since being injured." She fidgeted with the cuffs on her sweater.

That was obvious. "You need to learn to chill."

"I try to." She stared out at the snow-covered hills. Sadness clouded her eyes. "But I'd much rather be out on the slopes."

My stomach sank. Her injury had affected her more than she liked to let on. But she didn't have to put on a tough front for me. I'd been through some rough shit in my life. Music had been the only thing that had helped me through. I wouldn't know what I'd do if I couldn't play anymore. I could only try to understand what she was going through after having to give up the job she loved.

I threw her a mischievous smile. "It was great out there. Great powder."

"Okay. You can shut up now." She picked up a cushion and threw it at my head.

"Ow!" Laughing, I grabbed the cushion and tossed it back to her. Maybe I could help a fraction by showing her things she could do. Having fun was the best medicine. "You may not be able to ski or board, but you can ride, right? Tomorrow, we'll take that snowmobile out back for a spin and cruise around the trails."

She slumped deeper into the sofa. As she watched the fire flicker, worry etched her brow. "Nah. I'm good. I don't want to break my other leg. I don't want to get hurt again."

Was that her main concern? I could understand that.

"We can go steady. I promise." It'd require restraint not to gun the snowmobile over the mountain, but I could behave when necessary.

"No thanks. I'm fine."

She wasn't. I'd have to think of something else she could do. Something that involved everyone so I wasn't alone in the same room as her. Like I was then. Just the scent of her perfume made my head spin.

But my blister stung, pulling me to a halt.

I hooked my ankle up onto my other knee and re-examined my sore. The red raw flesh and flap of broken skin looked worse than before. I grabbed the antiseptic cream and dabbed it on. *Oh shiiiit!* Clenching my teeth, I flopped back against the sofa. I closed my eyes and rode out the burn and sting.

Tia puffed air through her nose. "Wuss. It's a tiny blister."

"It fucking hurts." I grimaced, relieved when the pain subsided.

Sitting forward, I sifted through the box of various sized Band-Aids and dressings, looking for something big enough and suitable to cover the tear on my skin.

"You want some help?" Tia asked.

"You know what I should use to cover blisters?"

"Absolutely." She shuffled to sit beside me.

Hmm. I scanned her shapely legs and arms. She made sweatpants and a matching Tommy Hilfiger hoodie look like couture. I should've put more than two inches between us, but

I didn't. Couldn't. *Crap.*

Grabbing the box, she sorted through the packets of gauze, bandages, and dressings. "Fixing wounds was sometimes a daily requirement at my last job. We were always ripping our hands on ropes, touching cables that were hot, cutting ourselves on props."

"Occupational hazards?"

"Yeah." The light in her eyes disappeared.

"You miss your show, don't you?"

"Every fucking day."

"But you love acting, right?"

"I loved stunt work more than acting. I keep telling myself this new role is the right move to accommodate my injury, but I'm not ecstatic about the part." She grabbed some non-stick dressing and ripped the packet open. "The problem is, I don't know who I am or what I want to do anymore."

With gentle touches, soft dabs and swipes, she cleaned and covered my ghastly blister. Her warm hand curled around my foot as she inspected her work.

"You shouldn't be so hard on yourself," I said. "Give yourself time to work shit out. You had a serious accident. Allow yourself to be sad, angry, fucked off at the world. This show may not be what you want. But it's a step toward finding out what is. Life isn't a straight and easy road. Believe me, I know."

"I've always been more of a 'jump first, ask questions later' kind of girl."

I glanced at my foot. Her hand had slipped underneath my jeans and rubbed the back of my ankle. My pulse quickened. Shivers ran up my leg and jolted toward my groin. *Fuck.* I pulled my foot away. "Um. Thanks. My blister feels better."

She shuffled to the other end of the sofa. "Sure. Any time."

"How about a drink?" I jumped up. Yes, something to kill all traces of her touch. "Would you like a bourbon?" I needed something stronger than hot chocolate, spiked or not.

"Yeah." She fidgeted with the ties on her hoodie. "That would be great."

Half an hour later, the guys and Sutton still hadn't returned. Tia and I were onto our second whiskey, talking about the band as we sat on the sofa in front of the fireplace. But Tia kept rolling her ankle and wincing as if in pain.

I couldn't have that.

I put my drink down and waved at her to give me her foot. "Here. I give a hell foot rub."

"Really?" Her eyes hooded as if it was desperately what she wanted, but she also was a touch hesitant.

So was I when it came to touching her. Yet I'd offered. I wasn't one to back down.

"Yep." I shuffled to face her and took her ankle in my hand. But as I ripped her sock off, she shrieked.

"Wait. Don't." She pulled her foot out of my hold. The color drained from her face.

Shit! What had I done? I held up my hands. Her sock dangled from my fingertips. "Don't what?"

"I didn't need my sock off." She winced. "I . . . I have scars."

I placed my fingertips on her foot and traced the long red marks that zigzagged across her dainty ankle. Just touching her bare skin sent a flurry of shocks rippling beneath my skin. "They're fine."

She shook her head and drew her leg away. Tears welled in her eyes. "They're not. They're ugly. The ones up my leg and knee are horrid. I hate them. They're so gross."

"I have a huge one on my back. When I was seven, my brother Lyndon pushed me into a wrought-iron fence—one with pointy poles. The tip cut underneath my shoulder blade. I have a five-inch scar. See?" I turned and lifted my hoodie to show her the mark.

"Shit." Her cool fingertips traced the couple inches of keloid tissue on my back.

"We all have scars." I lowered my top and turned around. I waved her sock at her. "But if it would make you feel better, would you like to put your sock back on?"

"Yes. I'm sorry."

"Don't be. I didn't mean to make you uncomfortable."

"Thank you." She swiped a tear off her cheek. "I used to have nice legs."

"They still are." Once she put on her wooly sock, I took her foot again. "Now. Where were we?"

I worked my fingers into the base of her foot, taking it easy at first, then deepening my strokes. As I drove my thumbs into the ball of her foot, rubbed her toes, and massaged the arch, she slowly relaxed. I eased into working the sides of her ankle where her scars were.

"Oh my God." A little moan fell from her mouth and her eyes fluttered closed. "That's so good."

She bit her lip.

Fuck. She shouldn't do that.

"Harder" fell from her lips.

Blood surged through my body. My dick jolted. I laughed it off. The buzz from the alcohol must have kicked in. Straightening my leg along the outside of hers, I tucked my foot in beside her hip. "Is that okay? I need to stretch."

"You want a massage too?" She smiled over the rim of her glass. "I'm not sure my hands are as magic as yours?"

I drove my thumb into her arch, and she moaned again. "Years of bass playing. I have strong fingers."

Her fine eyebrow shot upward. "So you're good at fingering things?"

I let out a low chuckle as I rubbed her toes and worked her instep. "Yeah. I can do this all day . . . and all night."

"You want to prove that?"

"Uh . . . no."

Giggling, she sank lower on the sofa. Her cell phone pinged. She grabbed it from beside her and scanned the screen. The glint in her eyes vanished.

"What's up?" I eased off my rubbing.

"Um . . . It's my ex, Rhett." She spun her phone around and showed me a picture of him and some woman at a red-carpet event. "I still follow him on Instagram."

"Rhett Newton was your ex? Lucky you. He's hot." He was one of the reasons why I loved her show. Something about buffed, sweaty firemen did it for me.

"Yep. He chased me and left his wife for me, then the second I got injured, he dumped me and went back to her."

Damn. She'd done it again. Her tone was tough and flippant like nothing bothered her, but it held a bassline backloaded with heartache.

I circled my hand around her foot in a soothing rub. "Why are you still following him?"

"Self-sabotage. My daily dose of torture."

I chuckled. *Yep. I get that.* "I'm with you. I followed my ex on Insta for ages too." But I hadn't looked at any of his posts for months. I'd moved on. Well . . . I was trying to.

She slapped my shin next to her. "Oh. What's his name? I wanna see a picture."

I took a deep breath to make sure my heart was in check. *Nope. It wasn't. Fuck.* "Emilio Rivas."

She typed on her screen, then her eyes lit up. "Oh my God. He's gorgeous."

The breath in my lungs ached. "Yes, he is." He had thick black hair, golden skin, and hazel eyes, and a Brazilian body that just begged to be touched.

"How long ago did it end?"

I took a swig of bourbon and swallowed it, letting it burn the back of my throat. "Four months ago. We were together for five years."

She dialed down her voice to just above a whisper. "Can I ask what happened?"

I stared into the fireplace, wishing it would incinerate my memories. "Um . . . I proposed. He turned me down."

"YOU PROPOSED?" Her voice rebounded off the rafters. The whites of her eyes blazed bright. Her mouth hung open. "Holy shit."

"Yeah. I'd thought everything between us was great. We were happy and in love. I'd bought a ring. I'd prepared a whole speech. I got down on one knee at our favorite Italian restaurant and he said no." When he'd said he didn't love me anymore, it had crushed my heart. When he'd said he'd tired of my volatile career, it had stabbed my stomach. When he'd moved to Miami without me, it had scarred my soul. I'd helped build his career, then he'd left. "Turns out, he loved himself and his DJing more than me. He moved to Florida the day after I proposed, and I haven't heard from him since."

"Fuck." She placed her cell phone on the coffee table. "That breakup tops mine."

"I don't know about that." We'd both failed in the love department. "Mine was hard to comprehend when there was no prior warning."

"Yep. Mine was out of the blue too . . . kinda. We both had issues letting go of our exes."

"Every breakup hurts. The depth just varies and the time to heal differs."

"Yeah." She half-giggled as she pointed to her knee. "You saw my leg, right?"

"Yes. I did." I ran my hand up the back of her calf, over the top of her sweatpants. "And there is nothing wrong with your scars. They tell a story. They're you. They show that you are strong and a survivor."

"Thank you." Her small smile hinted at gratitude. She slid her other foot up the inside of my thigh and wriggled her socked toes. "Can you give this foot a rub too? It's feeling left out."

"Can't have that now, can we?" I placed her sore foot on the sofa between my spread thighs and set to work on her other foot.

Her little moans returned as I massaged the ball of her foot. Each one struck something strange inside my system. What was it about Tia that shook the wiring in my brain? She was beautiful. Broken. Intriguing. And I liked her wicked sense of humor. Was that wrong? No. So why was I unnerved? I didn't need this shit storm to brew any further.

I rested her heel on my thigh and reached over to grab my drink off the coffee table. But as I leaned sideways, her foot slipped into my groin. *Shit.* My dick twitched and throbbed. If she wiggled her toes, she'd know the effect she was having on me. And that wasn't good. I didn't want her to get the wrong idea. Should I just pretend that my cock wasn't hardening? *Sure.*

Straightening, I wriggled back onto the seat and sipped my drink.

But as our gazes locked, electricity charged the air. Her expression was as blank as an unpainted canvas, but the intensity in her eyes scalded me. She slowly licked her lips.

Flexing her toes, she brushed the side of my dick.

Shit!

I froze. My heart pounded against my rib cage. I liked her touching me when I shouldn't. I liked her looking at me when I shouldn't. This was wrong. So, so wrong. I grabbed her foot and moved it onto the sofa. "Tia. No."

I couldn't mess around with Cole's sister. I might not have believed in the dibs rule, but I didn't need to play with fire. I couldn't jeopardize my chances with the band. And I wasn't into her.

The door swung open and in strode the guys, shaking the snow from their coats and beanies. They stamped the snow from their shoes and left them by the door.

I leaped to my feet and charged into the kitchen to hide the strain in my jeans.

My skin prickled as Cole glanced from me to Tia as he hung up his coat. "What have you two been up to?"

The baffled look on Tia's face reflected the same chaos pummeling inside my head. But with a flick of her hair back over her shoulder and a sigh, she sank deeper into the sofa. No trace of our spark remained. "Lewis just gave me a foot massage to ease my sore ankle. We've had a couple of bourbons while we've waited for you to come home."

"That all?" He questioned Tia, his eyes narrowed.

Shit. Had Cole sensed the unexplainable vibe between us when he'd walked in? *Fuck.*

"Yes," Tia chided. "That's it. I can't do much else."

"I'm just teasing you." His gruff laugh filled the air as he ruffled her hair. His carefree smile returned. "Sorry you missed the slopes. The snow was awesome."

"Fuck you," she groaned and smiled and slapped his hand away.

Crap. Had I imagined the buzz between Tia and me? Or was she a damn good actress, convincing her brother that nothing had happened? *Wait.* Nothing had happened. I'd given her a foot massage. We'd talked. Her foot had slipped and accidentally hit my dick. That was nothing, right?

"Well, rack up those hot drinks, Lewis." Slip yanked off his gloves and tossed them on the table. "We need to warm up."

"Sure." With aching balls, I grabbed mugs from the cupboard and begged my semi to disappear. I put a jug of milk in the microwave. While I waited for it to heat, I downed a shot of bourbon. So much for this vacation not screwing with my head.

"We missed you out there today, Tee." Flint hung up his ski jacket. "You would've loved the half-pipe."

"My skiing days are over."

"Nah." He pulled off his beanie then combed his fingers through his hair to mess it up. "You'll get better. Give it time."

But the dread set in stone on Tia's face said otherwise.

"Sutt texted a few minutes ago." Flint headed into the kitchen, his ski pants swooshing as he walked. "She'll be another thirty minutes. She's made us reservations at the tavern in the village."

Cole rested his butt on the back of the sofa. "That okay with you, Tee?"

"Nah. I've done enough today. You guys go. I'll be fine."

Why did she look at me when she said that?

"We'll catch the shuttle; you won't have to walk far." Cole clapped his hands and wrung them together. "Get your party boots on, girl. It's going to be a big night."

"I said no," Tia snapped.

"Fine. Be a party pooper." He came over to the kitchen and grabbed his spiked hot chocolate. He raised it toward Tia. "We're going. You'll miss out on a wicked night."

Cole downed the whole drink in a few gulps, then poured himself a shot of vodka. He downed that as well.

Damn, these guys knew how to drink. So did I. I may be older than them, but I was far from hanging up my party shoes.

But as the guys rushed upstairs to shower, and I made another round of hot chocolates, Tia watched my every move. Her face was impossible to read again. My stomach twisted and knotted. The pressure in my temples mounted. Clouds of confusion rolled in my head.

Why was I drawn to her? Why did my body react to her?

My chest shuddered and lurched.
Fuck. Fuck. Fuck.
I wasn't into guys *and girls*.
Was I?

Chapter 8

LEWIS

Just past midnight, I stumbled through the cabin door with the guys and Sutton, drunk off our asses. Laughing, we ripped off our boots and coats, dropped them on the floor and headed over to the sofa in front of the roaring fireplace. The trudge home from the shuttle stop in the freezing temperature had frozen my face. I needed to defrost. But finding Tia stretched out on the chaise in her black Batman flannel pajamas was enough to warm me from the inside out. No fire required.

Or maybe the obscene amount of bourbon I'd drunk had raised my body temperature. Either way, I was fucked up.

Tia shuffled straight and switched off the TV mounted on the far wall. "How was the tavern?"

"Oh, Tia." Sutton flopped onto the sofa and flung her arms around Tia's neck. "You missed out on an awesome night. We ate. We drank. We danced."

I chuckled as I stood near the fire. We'd also chatted to just about every person in the bar. The guys had taken it all in their stride, smiling and posing for photos, talking and having drinks with the guests. I hadn't had that kind of attention in years. My less-than-zero self-esteem hadn't minded the gentle stroke.

"I didn't miss out." Tia patted Sutton's arm but wrinkled her nose, no doubt at the stench of champagne I could smell on Sutton from where I stood. "I had a great night. I had a date with Vin Diesel. I'm up to *Fast & Furious 4* in my movie marathon."

"Vin?" I threw her a drunk grin. Swaying on my feet, I warmed my hands near the flames. "No Christmas holiday movies or New Year rom-coms?"

"Ew! No." She straightened a wooly blanket over her legs. "Not my thing. Action all the way. Michelle Rodriguez is my idol. She's so badass."

"And her ass is fucking hot in a pair of tight jeans." Cole smirked as he stumbled over to join me. He wriggled his butt toward the fire, then turned and staggered. If he wasn't careful, he'd fall face-first into the flames . . . or ignite. We both reeked of alcohol.

Slip sank onto the end of the sofa, placed his feet up on the coffee table, and ripped off his beanie. "The band tonight was good too. They weren't as good as us. But you should've been there, Tee."

"Yeah. Next time." Her nod lacked conviction.

I hadn't known Tia long, but her spark needed a good kick up the ass. Life was too short to mope around indoors all day. If I moved to LA in a couple months, I'd take her out . . . Wait. No. Cole should do it. He was her fucking brother.

Sutton grabbed a cushion and turned toward Flint. "Can you move over please, hun? I need to lie down." He shuffled along the sofa toward the corner so she could rest her head on his lap. "I'm spinning. I'll be okay in a second."

I raised a questioning eyebrow. *Or throw up.*

"You want me to take you to bed?" Flint leaned over and kissed her forehead.

"No. Play some music for me."

"Now that is a great idea." Flint eased himself out from beneath Sutton's head, leaped from the sofa, and headed over to the storage nook underneath the staircase. He grabbed his electric guitar from its case. "Guys, let's jam a few songs."

"Don't have to ask me twice." I stumbled over to the nook to grab my bass. After veering around the furniture, fumbling with cords, and plugging our guitars into the amps stowed by the wall, I sank onto the floor beside the fireplace. Bourbon sloshed in my belly. *Hmm. Any warmer and I'd be a hot toddy.*

Tia giggled. "Lewis, are you okay?"

She was kinda cute wrapped in her blanket and with her hair tied in a messy knot on top of her scalp. *Ergh!* I dropped my head back against the stones. This nonsense had to stop. "I'm just a little drunk." I set my bass across my lap and strummed the strings. *Better.*

Within minutes, Slip had his guitar, Cole had grabbed his small snare drum and sticks, and music flowed from our fingertips. Flint's swoony voice filled the room as we played covers of "Wonderwall" by Oasis, "Go Your Own Way" by Fleetwood Mac, and "I'm On Fire" by Bruce Springsteen. Sutton had passed out beside Flint before we'd made it to the end of the second song. I pursed my lips. Poor girl hadn't been able to keep up with us guys drinking. She'd tried. I'd give her ten points for effort.

Flint stroked her hair. "Our audience didn't last long."

"Hey?" Tia piped up. "I'm still here. Can you play some of your new stuff? That one about dreams?"

"'Shattered Dreams?'" Flint grimaced. "Yeah, I'm still not happy with that one. It needs a lot of work."

"And so does the intro on 'Fragile'. It's not right yet." Cole tapped his sticks against the rim of his drum. "Maybe while drunk we can come up with something better."

It wouldn't be the first time we'd played under the influence of alcohol.

We ran through "Shattered Dreams," then fell into playing "Fragile." I positioned my fingers over my strings, ready to join in after the electric guitar intro. But as I closed my eyes, the notes twisted and twirled through my head. *Yep.* Something about the beat was off. It was too reggae. Too boppy. Too . . . wrong. Then it hit me.

"Wait. I might have something that could work." I placed my bass down, shot to my feet, and swiped my laptop off the sideboard. Returning to sit on the end of the sofa by Tia's outstretched feet, I turned my computer on and scrolled through my folders of files. The riff I wanted them to hear blared inside my head. "Hold on a sec. It's here somewhere."

"Are you ripping another one of our songs apart?" Humor glinted in Flint's eyes as he continued to strum the tune softly on his guitar. But was that bite I'd detected in his tone?

"No, man." *Crap.* Should I keep my mouth shut until we know each other better? I didn't want them kicking my ass to the curb for being too cocky. "It was just an idea for the start. I can find it later."

"Lewis." Slip slid his fingers down the neck of his guitar. The sound sliced the air. "You need to own your shit. You're good. We don't mind listening to your ideas. That's why you're here. Flint's just messing with you."

Flint grinned. His head wobbled with a drunken nod. "I am. Totally."

"Okay. Good." *Thank fuck.* I was still getting used to the guys' digs and jokes and wicked senses of humor. I'd only known them for a week, but we seemed to share the same warped level of shit-stirring and sarcastic banter. I had to trust them more, trust my gut, and be bold enough to have my say. Not everyone was an asshole like Kilt from my previous band.

"You need to chill, bud," Cole slurred. "We're a team. We

work together. But if you ram nothing but your shit down our throats, I'll kick your ass out the door." Cole smiled but was serious.

"Trust me—that's not my style. I honestly love the songs you've written for this album. Like you said, some still need finessing. I wanna help you do that."

Over the past week, these guys hadn't taken all my suggestions onboard. Many of my ideas had been tossed aside. But they'd listened to each one, worked with what they liked, and refined my input. That was freaking awesome. I hadn't realized how much of a battering my confidence had taken over the years thanks to Kilt's obsessive control over our band and Emilio's over me. Thank God both relationships had ended. Each day I spent with these guys, my faith in my talent grew. Being surrounded by like-minded people helped. Attitude was key. Slip was right. I was fucking good.

Yeah, but don't push it.

Dick!

Cole waved his finger at my laptop. "Now. Play whatever it is you want us to hear."

"Will do." Blinking away the alcoholic haze from my vision, I searched my files again and found the folder I was looking for. I scrolled down the list.

Tia curled in beside me and edged closer to the screen.

I breathed her sweet scent in. I swayed toward her. *Hmm.* She smelled of honey. I'd done some interesting things with honey during my time. Picturing doing those things to Tia . . . not good. Shaking the thoughts from my head, I skimmed my fingertips over the touchpad.

"Are they songs you've written or just sound files?" she asked.

"Both." I found the one I wanted and clicked play. "Here it is, guys. This intro. Would this work?"

My vibrant, bass-heavy tune came through the speakers. I fidgeted with my signet rings as I glanced at each of the guys to gauge their reaction. Slip closed his eyes; I wasn't sure if he'd passed out or was concentrating. Cole's brow furrowed as he tapped his sticks on his thigh in time with the rhythm. Flint edged forward on his seat; his ear turned toward the music.

After the twenty-second intro had played, just before the lyrics started, I hit stop.

"Wait?" Tia caught my arm. "I love that. Is that a whole song?"

"Yeah, it's nothing." I shrugged. "Just something I wrote last year." Lyrics and beats had often come to me during the long drives between Boston and Brooklyn.

"It's got a nice beat. Real nice." Flint bobbed his head as he stroked Sutton's hair. She was dead to the world. "Can you play the whole thing?"

I gaped, not sure if he was serious. "You want to listen to my song?"

"We surrrre do," he slurred and placed his guitar aside.

Encouragement sparkled in Tia's eyes. "Told you'd they'd listen. Show them what you've got."

"Um ... okay." My pulse quickened as I reset the track. "Don't cringe at my lyrics."

"Never." Cole belched, then waved me on. "Hit it."

Slip gave me the thumbs up. He hadn't passed out. Not like Sutton had.

Nausea and nerves rolled through my stomach. I pressed play. After the intro, my alto voice filled the speakers.

> *Another day breaks over the horizon,*
> *Another bed I wake up alone in.*
> *Another city I'm seeing,*
> *Different air to you I'm breathin'*
> *But now there'll be no more dreamin'*

I've been away for so damn long,
I've lost track of the hours and days.
But the difference about this morning,
I'm gonna pack my bags, be on my way.
Oh yeah, I'm coming home to you,
I'm coming home to you . . .

Slip shot forward and stared at the back of my laptop.

Cole stopped tapping his sticks.

Flint stared into the fire and rubbed the tip of his chin. At the end of the song, he said, "Play it again. Slow it down a fraction."

I replayed the track.

The air around me prickled. The guys looked at each other. Their facial expressions were neutral, but something new burned in the depths of their eyes. Tia clutched the blanket and stared at Flint.

What is happening? Fuck! Do they like the track? Hate it? Shit!

I raked my fingers through my hair. *Jeezus.* They were killing me.

At the end of the track, Flint shook his head, but the glint in his eyes blazed bright. "Damn, Lewis. I don't want the fucking intro . . . I want the whole freaking song."

The breath shot from my lungs. "What?"

He jutted his chin to Cole and Slip. "You think it will fit in with the rest of the tracks planned for the album?"

Holy shit! Flint wanted my music?

"Hold on." Cole's eyebrows pinched together and pointed at my laptop. "You want that on our album? But we didn't write it."

"No, we didn't." Flint shuffled forward a few inches. "But I know a good song when I hear it. You do too. You felt it. Heard it. I saw your reaction. I'm not saying it will make the final cut, but it's got potential. It's got to pass through a lot of hoops—our marketing team, Everhide, and Ashlem—not just us before it gets the final tick."

They wanted my song? *Holy shit!* The back of my eyes stung. "Is this just drunk talk? Please don't fuck with me." I threw Flint a stern glare.

"Nope." Flint ran his hand up and down his arm. "I got goose bumps, man. That doesn't happen very often."

My head spun. I placed my hand over my thundering heart to stop it leaping from my chest. "I'd be honored just to record it with you."

Cole dipped his chin at me but waved a drumstick at Flint. "Are you sure you want this asshole singing your song?"

"Hell yes. I'm thrilled to be here, but you wanting to record one of my songs is beyond anything I ever imagined."

Tia hooked her arm around my back and gave me a tight squeeze. "Isn't that exciting? Keep going like this and every track on the album will be yours."

"Hold on there, Tee." Slip chuckled. "We love what we've written for the album. There's no guarantee that the track will be part of the final selection. But it's good." He flicked a finger toward my laptop. "Have you got other songs we can listen to?"

"Yes. I have hundreds." *Which other songs should I play?* My mind rattled with options. "But that's one of my better ones."

"Awesome." Flint rubbed his thigh. "We'll listen to some of them later . . . when we're sober. I'm done for the night. I loved the track. It will be fun to record. You can teach it to us tomorrow. But right now, I'm gonna take my drunk ass and Sutton to bed."

"You want some help carrying her upstairs?" I placed my laptop on the coffee table, ready to assist if needed.

"Nah, man. I got it." Flint swayed as he stood. He scooped Sutton up in his arms and headed up the staircase. At the top there was a thud, a knock, and then . . .

"Ow!" Sutton wailed. "You hit my head. You trying to kill me?"

"Sorry, baby." Flint's low laugh was cut off by the slam of his bedroom door.

"Guess that's a wrap." Cole placed his snare on the coffee table. "You want help up the stairs, Tee?"

"Please." She held out her hands toward him.

Cole threw her a mischievous grin. As he hauled her to her feet, he bent at the waist. He hoisted her over his shoulder like a sack of potatoes and headed for the staircase.

"Cole? What the hell? Put me down. I'll walk." She laughed and slapped his butt as he carried her up to her room.

"You good, Lew?" Slip stood and stretched his arms above his head. "I'm gonna crash too."

"Yeah. I'll pack up and have some water." I needed bottles of it.

"Cool. Catch you sometime in the morning." Slip ambled upstairs and disappeared down the hallway.

Just before I closed my laptop, I stared at the screen, lit with the song I'd just played. My chest swelled. They'd loved "Coming Home." They wanted to record it.

Fuck yeah!

The fire in my belly burned.

I didn't want to get my hopes up. My dreams and ideas had been crushed before. But fuck, it was nice to ignite them again.

Bring on recording.

Bring on milestone one.

Chapter 9

TIA

During the last two days at Big Bear, the guys snowboarded during the daylight hours while Sutton and I watched movies and soaked in the huge hot tub on the back deck. My ankle thanked me for the therapeutic spa. At night, the guys had worked on their songs.

On our last evening, after dinner, I sat on the sofa, sipping my un-spiked hot chocolate, listening to the guys finesse another track. With every tweak they made, note they changed, or finalized version they ran through, warmth filled my chest. I loved every demo . . . except "Miss You." It was an incredible single, but it was about Phil. I hadn't been able to listen to it without shedding a tear. I didn't know how Flint managed to sing it. Every other song they'd written was full of raw rock and possessed their unique quirky edge. The excitement and buildup to hitting the studio after New Year's grew every day. Their energy was truly contagious.

I missed spending time with the band. Life and love had kept us apart for too long. But I'd need to move away again if Lewis's constant inquisitive glances, cute smiles, and smart, sexy one-liners kept stirring the butterflies in my belly.

They had to stop.

I wasn't stupid. I'd fallen for flirtatious crap like that before. I wouldn't do it again.

Lewis was gay. I fully respected that with all my heart and soul.

But shit. I tapped my fingernail against my mug. What if he was into women too?

Nope. Don't go there. He wasn't.

So why did my body keep messing with my mind?

As I watched him play and sing softly, heat coiled and swam through my core, rippled through my chest, and tingled the base of my scalp. Every time I looked at him, I wanted to do dirty things to him . . . in bed, in the hot tub, there on the sofa. *Fuck.* These thoughts had to end. If they didn't, it would only lead to heartache . . . *mine!*

Near midnight, the guys packed their gear away and headed toward bed. I wasn't tired, so I made another hot chocolate. After putting on my coat, beanie, and gloves, and slipping my cell phone into my pocket, I headed outside onto the front deck. Standing beside the gas heater, I leaned against the railing. I cradled my cup, letting the steam warm my face. In the dark of night, I peered down the valley toward the lake. Cabin lights twinkled through the trees. The soft, gentle breeze carried fresh snow onto the ground. The snow groomer engines hummed in the distance as they zoomed over the slopes. I closed my eyes, inhaled the mountain air, and savored the silence. You didn't get that often in LA.

The French door behind me creaked open.

"Hey?" Lewis said. "Are you okay?"

My heartbeat jumped a fraction. "Yeah. Fine. Just enjoying our last night here."

He tugged his beanie lower onto his head. The ends of his

blond hair fanned beneath the bottom edge. "It's freezing out here."

"I lived in Chicago." I sipped my drink. "This ain't cold."

"Yeah, I suppose Boston and Brooklyn were worse than this too." He stepped closer to catch the warmth from the heater. "So, I was just talking to Sutton. She got an email saying that your show's cast and crew meet-and-greet has been delayed until the fourteenth of January."

Shit. I placed my mug on the railing and grabbed my cell phone out of my pocket. I scanned my messages and read the one from the director. *Damn it.* He was right. "She's going to come to New York with us. You should too."

Tucking my cell phone away, I pursed my lips and slowly shook my head. *New York? Lewis? Nope.* "Not sure that's a good idea."

"Why?" His brow furrowed. "I'd love to show you around my hometown before I move."

I picked up my mug, blew into my hot chocolate, and arched an eyebrow. "Are you confident you'll be relocating to Cali?"

Not every time the guys had played together had gone smoothly. They'd argued, bantered, been pissed with each other. But when they finally nailed a track, it had been magical to listen to.

"Not exactly." He tucked his hands into the pockets of his parker. "So come so we can celebrate New Year's. See the sights. You can't stay stuck at home and do nothing."

I laughed, short and sharp, and shook my head. "Yes, I can. My leg won't handle the crowds and the walking around. After New Year's, you'll be spending eighteen hours a day in the studio. You won't have much free time."

He lowered his chin. "But if you don't come, and I don't make it past recording, then this is our last night together."

My ribs ached and shuddered. My head hurt with all the

chaos spinning through it. I had to stop spiraling. I dialed down my voice to just above a whisper. "Lewis, can you be honest with me?"

Worry flooded his silver eyes. "Yes."

I sucked in a deep breath. I had to know if I was concocting all this shit in my head. "Is there something between us? Or am I imagining things?"

He winced and closed his eyes. "What do you mean?"

"This." I stepped in close so our jackets touched. His eyes shot open and locked onto mine. "When I'm near you, your cheeks flush. You tense. A thousand questions and concerns darken your eyes. My heartbeat quickens. My skin tingles. A spark ignites in the air."

"Tia." Anguish turned his voice into a breathy whisper. He took a small step back. "I never believed in kindred spirits until I met you. I think that's what we are. Please don't twist this into something that it's not. I just want to be your friend."

My ears hurt hearing the truth, as did my chest, but it was the slap I needed to get my shit together. "Friends, right? Just friends."

"Yes."

"So why did you get turned on the other day when you gave me a foot massage?"

"Um . . ." His eyes shimmered with a playful glint. They always did that when he's been sexy. "You rubbed my dick with your foot. Hard not to."

"So why didn't you stop me?"

Two heartbeats passed before he swallowed hard. "I did." He swept my hair back over my shoulder, then rested his hand on my forearm and gave it a gentle squeeze. "Tia, I like you. I'm sorry if you want more, but that's not going to happen."

A sharp pain stabbed my heart. *Foolish heart.* Why was I hurting over being rejected by someone who wasn't mine?

Who'd never be mine? *Ergh!* At least I knew where I stood. It still didn't change the fact I'd rather be fucking him senseless than being his kindred spirit. "Okay. I can accept that. But if that is the case, can we tone down the sexy glances and flirty comments? They've made me question your intensions." Suggestive banter had been fun up until a certain point . . . but now it had become too much.

"Shit." He grimaced. "I'm so sorry. Can we just reset? Be friends?"

"Yeah. I'd like that." Somehow I'd get over this messed up mindfuck.

He play-punched my arm. "Can we do that in New York? Please? When the guys are at marketing meetings I'm not involved in, we can hang out."

I loved New York. I could drag Sutton along on any outings. That would surely help contain the flames between Lewis and me. But was staying at home a better option? *Yep.* "I'll think about it."

He shook his head. "Nope. Don't think. Just do. Tomorrow morning, I'll make sure the guys convince you to join us." Thumbing behind him, he backstepped toward the door. "But for now, I'm gonna get a couple hours sleep before we head off early. Catch you later. Night."

"Night."

He disappeared inside.

I sipped the last mouthful of my hot chocolate and licked the sweetness off my lips. Could Lewis and I be friends? I didn't have many. At school, I'd studied in the library or played sport to avoid the bullies. At home, I'd hung out with the guys. At college, people had used me to get to the band, then splashed our wild partying ways across social media. In Chicago, I'd socialized with the cast and crew at the beginning of the show, but Rhett had become my world. It was hard to find good friends these days. I needed ones I could trust and respect, and who didn't have ulterior motives. Ones who didn't care about my fame, who I knew, or my A-list status . . . and who didn't want to get in my pants.

That was Lewis.

Sutton was on that list too.

But did I want to go to New York and spend more time with Lewis? Was that a good thing?

Ergh! I'd sleep on it.

The next morning, Cole shoveled a forkful of pancakes into his mouth. "Come on, Tee. What if I fly you first class so you can stretch out your leg?"

Hmmm. My brother's attempt at bribery was tempting. My former studio had often flown me and my fellow castmates around the country to attend events in business or first-class. I'd often thought it was an unnecessary expense, but now the extra leg room was essential. "Flying isn't the only issue. I don't want to crash in a bedroom with you the whole time." I loved Cole, but sharing a bed in their three-bedroom rental apartment would push my limits . . . and I was sure he'd bring home random girls. I didn't want to sleep on the sofa.

Flint crunched on a piece of crispy bacon. "You won't have to. I'll call April. We'll upgrade so you can have your own room."

Okay, the trip was beginning to look more favorable. But I still wasn't convinced. "I don't know. My leg aches too much in the cold. It's freezing in New York."

"We have a thing called heating." Lewis placed a fresh cup of coffee in front of me.

I mouthed, '*Thank you.*'

Cole tossed a blueberry into the air and caught it in his mouth. "What about daily massages? I'll throw them in too."

Cole and the guys had always looked out for me. Maybe they'd missed me as much as I'd missed them. It would be fun to hang out and see them record. This was such a huge step for their career. They wouldn't have much free time. I'd hardly see Lewis. But having four different walls to stare at for two weeks wouldn't hurt. *I could do this.* "Fine. I'm in."

I guess I was going to New York.

After a long flight, we landed at JFK airport late in the evening. April had worked her magic and found us a new place to stay. The swanky four-bedroom apartment in the West Village was only a block away from Everhide's EH4 Records studio. The guys went straight into pre-production meetings and Lewis joined us for dinner before he returned to his pop's apartment in Brooklyn.

On New Year's Eve, I avoided the celebrations. I watched the ball drop and the fireworks from the comfort of the living room sofa on the massive flat-screen. *Perfect.*

Two days later, the guys hit the studio.

Sutton and I went along to watch a few sessions, but I'd spend most of my time at the apartment watching movies, reading, and enjoying the massages Cole had organized for me. Sutton shopped.

On the nights the guys finished early at the studio, we ventured to the bar across the road for dinner. The food was great, the live music, average. The heat between Lewis and me lingered. I was determined to get it under control—I just didn't know how. Until then, he provided me with a new form of entertainment.

When he'd ventured to the bar for another drink or socialized with the crowd, men gravitated toward him like he had some invisible force. Watching him in action, chatting, flirting, and occasionally stealing a kiss from a guy at the end of the night had become my new favorite pastime, my obsession. It did strange things to my heart. It was wrong. Oh, so wrong. But it turned me on. I got wet, wanting him to touch me. Kiss me. Drive me crazy. Ever since he'd given me a foot massage at the cabin, I'd wanted his hands on me again. I caught him staring at me sometimes. That gave me wicked images to play behind my closed eyelids when I went home to bed.

Being kindred spirits sucked.

I needed to get a new life.

I had other priorities to focus on: myself and my friendships.

That included establishing a normal, stable friendship with Lewis, not one that would have me returning to therapy for the rest of my days.

Staying true to his word, Lewis rocked up on my doorstep to show me some local sights when the other guys were at meetings. With Sutton out shopping, I buried my jitters, and we ventured over to Dumbo—Down Under the Manhattan Overpass—in Brooklyn. Because I couldn't walk far, and it was the middle of winter, our outing involved food. We'd spent the morning wandering through the market halls past quaint stalls, and eating delicious treats at fancy patisseries. The smells of freshly brewed coffee, sweet cakes, and Asian dishes made my mouth continually water. So did the scent of Lewis's cologne, but I tried not to focus on that.

After a hot chocolate at a café, we rugged up in our warm, wooly coats and strolled toward the river. We ended up at Jane's Carousal.

"You game?" Lewis tossed his empty cup into a trash can, then pointed toward the carousel.

"Go on that? A kids' ride?" I wrinkled my nose. "Why?"

He stepped in front of me. As he straightened my beanie and tightened my scarf, a humorous glint sparkled in his eyes. "Because it's fun."

"But my leg?"

"I'll lift you on. Come on." He took my gloved hand and dragged me toward the ticket office.

Ten minutes later, we joined twenty shrieking kids on the ride. I sat upon a feisty-looking gray pony, going up and down as the carousel rotated. Lewis rode the palomino beside me. Carnival music blared through the speakers.

Once we sailed past the attendant, Lewis spun around in the saddle, riding it backwards, waving his arm around in the air and hollering, "Whoa, there, pony." Twisting around to face forwards again, he rode it like a racehorse. He leaned over the horse's neck, covered his mount's eyes, and screamed, "Arrrrgh! We're gonna crash! We're going too fast. Stoooop."

A loud laugh burst from me, but the little girl next to him paled. She shrieked and cried, hurting my eardrums. Tears streamed down her rosy cheeks. It took two rotations of the carousel for Lewis to calm her down.

Poor kid. Poor Lewis. But it was too freaking funny.

Once the girl's tears had stopped, Lewis sighed with relief and turned to me. "I'm not that scary, am I?"

"She was afraid you and your horse would get hurt. You covered its eyes."

"Oh. Sorry, pony." He patted the plastic mane.

Giggling, I shook my head. "You're crazy."

He swung his leg over the horse and sat sidesaddle. A fresh, gorgeous smile lit his face. "Scaring a kid wasn't part of the plan. I just wanted you to have some fun and see you smile." His voice took on a somber tone. "You don't do that often enough."

I rested my head against my pony's shiny pole. "I haven't had much to smile about lately."

"Yes you have. You've moved home to LA, you're staying with your brother, you hang out with a pretty cool band every day, you've gone to Big Bear and now you're in New York. Focus on the good things in your life." He pointed toward my leg. "Don't let your injury stop you from living, no matter how hard some days might be. You may not be able to jump off buildings, run marathons, or snowboard anymore, but look at you?" Flicking his hand at me, he grinned. "You're riding a fucking carousel horse. That's wicked, right? Find the things you can do, and love doing, and work your way up from there."

My eyes stung, but my stomach fluttered. *Stupid stomach.* "This isn't the kind of riding I like to normally do. But you made it entertaining." I'd sooner mount him at any time of the day.

"Good." He flicked his scarf over his shoulder and sat straight. "Ride or die, Tia. Ride or die."

"Yeah. Thank you. I needed this." Simple things could be fun . . . and they didn't hurt my leg. I had to remember that.

At the end of the ride, Lewis placed his hands on my hips and lifted me off the horse. He held onto me until I was steady on my feet. But as I looked up to thank him, his warm breath hit my face. At only a couple of inches taller than me, his lips lingered too close to mine. Way. Too. Close. My heart rate doubled.

That zing still hovered between us.

That fire still burned.

Nope . . . kill it.

With all my might, I stepped away and hobbled toward the street.

Lewis kept a good foot of distance between us, our arms not touching like they'd done before. In silence, we caught a taxi over to Manhattan. He headed to the studio; I went back to the apartment and kept telling myself we were just friends.

We're friends. We're friends. JUST friends.

That had become my new mantra.

Chapter 10

TIA

With only two days left in New York before Sutton and I had to fly home for our show's pre-production meet-and-greet, the guys invited us to watch them play a few live tracks for Ashlem's marketing team. Ashlem wanted to see them in action rather than playing at the small recording studio, so Everhide had offered them their rehearsal studio in Brooklyn.

Sutton and I picked up a box of donuts, sweet pastries, and coffees for the band and headed across the river. I'd seen the guys play together, but them putting on a small show, even if it was for a tiny group, excited me. They were so good; I couldn't wait to see them pump out a few of their new songs.

"So, how do you think Lewis is going?" Sutton asked as we clambered out of the town car in front of the building. "Do you think he's a good fit for the band?"

I hooked my purse over my shoulder while balancing the tray of coffees in my other hand. "It's up to the guys—not me."

"Yeah. But you knew Phil. You know the guys better than anyone." Sutton clutched the goods from the bakery against her chest as she opened the heavy front door. We headed inside out of the chill and up the stairs. From the street, the place looked like a rundown old warehouse, but inside, the décor was urban chic. Black walls. Chrome lights. Polished timber floors . . . and soundproofing panels.

Before entering the rehearsal studio, Sutton stopped and turned toward me. "Do you think Lewis is the right choice?"

I took a deep breath. Taking out my feelings for Lewis, and the loss of Phil, did he blend into the band? Match their personality and style?

Yes. "He doesn't have an ego the size of the sun like Phil had. He's got this calm-yet-nervous edge, which I'm sure comes from being new. He's anxious about impressing the guys. He wants to show off his talent and skills to pass their milestones but not overstep their creative control on this album or come across as a dick. It's a fine line. But he lights up when he has a bass in his hand, and they connect when playing. That's cool. So, yes, I think he's great."

"Flint has his moments." Sutton sighed, slumping her shoulders. "More good than bad. He's intrigued by Lewis's talent, but it's been hard letting someone new into their circle. He misses Phil every day."

So do I. "But I'm glad they're moving on as a band. I'd hate them to not play anymore."

"Me too." Sutton heaved the door open, and we entered the music room.

"Whoa." I scanned the room. Everhide's rehearsal room was the size of two tennis courts, decked out with arrays of speakers, amps, mounted stage lights, and more equipment than a music shop. Five people dressed in a mix of expensive suits, leather jackets, and fancy button-downs stood with Blake and April by the far windows. They were no doubt Ashlem's marketing team. Everhide gathered near the mixers on the other side of the room, talking to Gena, The Flintlocks' sound and lighting engineer. Four security guards sat on equipment trunks in the far corner.

Our guys stood together, prepping their instruments and checking cables, but Lewis paced in front of the drums, mumbling under his breath. *Was he running through lyrics?* I headed toward them, eyeing the overhead trellises, rigging, and lighting. I stopped beside Cole. "Impressive setup for just running through a couple songs."

He grabbed a coffee off the tray and nodded. "It's insane, right? Falcon, our new promo and tour manager, and the team want to see us play to get more of a feel for our music."

"It's getting real." Excitement skipped through Slip's voice as he hooked his arm around my shoulders and shook me.

The tray of coffees wobbled in my hand. I grabbed it with my other one just in time to save the drinks from toppling onto the floor.

The energy bouncing between the guys rattled and rocked the room. It was just like before a big show. Their hype and vivacity always electrified the air and hit my soul.

Was there something in that? Being around the band again? There was something new brewing in the base of my belly that had nothing to do with Lewis. I just couldn't put my finger on what it was.

I interrupted Lewis's pacing and handed him a coffee. "Cappuccino. One sugar, right?"

"Perfect." His hand trembled as he wrapped his fingers around the cup. "Thank you."

Wait. "Are you nervous?" I hadn't expected that when he'd played in a band for years.

"Yeah." He nodded. "I've never played in front of this many execs before. Falcon's been to the studio, but the others haven't. I don't want to fuck up."

"You'll be fine." I play-punched his arm. "Remember the

first night we met? I said I liked to watch you in action. So you better give me a good show."

He chuckled and shook his head. "You're not helping."

"Yes, I am. Now you're worrying about me, not your playing."

"Trust me. I'll worry about both."

"Nah. You've got this." I spun on my heels and handed a coffee to Flint. "You good?"

"Sure am." Flint grabbed the cup, but before he took a drink, he kissed Sutton on the lips. "Ready to see us play, babe?"

"Always." She cupped his cheek. "Good luck."

"Tee? Come say hi to Gena quickly." Cole waved at me and walked toward the control panel. I hobbled after him as fast as I could.

"So good to see you. It's been too long." I gave Gena a huge hug and scanned the mixer and monitors in front of her. My fingers twitched, wanting to play with the buttons and dials. "Mind if I hang here while they perform?"

"Sure. That'd be nice." She swayed on her feet and rubbed her tummy. "But I might not be very good company. I flew in last night and had curry from the corner store. It's not agreeing with my guts."

"Gena?" Worry lilted Cole's tone. "Are you going to be okay?"

"Yeah." She rubbed her perspiring brow. "Let's just get through this set so I can go back to the hotel and sleep it off."

"Deal." Cole clapped his hands. "We're ready."

Five minutes later, after I'd said quick hellos to Everhide and Kara and Lexi, Blake whistled. Everyone fell silent and most took a seat on one of the chairs lined in a row in the middle of the room. Blake poised his fingers in the shape of a gun and pointed at the band. "Okay, fellas. Show Falcon and the team what you've got."

Nervous excitement skipped in the air.

Flint slipped on his guitar and stepped up to the mic. "Okay, ladies and gents. We've got Cole on drums." He waved behind him. "Slip on electric. Lewis on bass, and I'm Flint. Lewis has only been with us for three weeks. These are all new songs for the album and we're still working on them in the studio. If we fuck up, bear with us. But we'll do our best not to. Here we go."

With the thumbs-up from Blake, the guys hit their first song, "Fallen For You." Cole pummeled his drums. The loud beat reverberated across the floor. Slip and Flint ignited the amps with their electrics. Lewis's bass rocked the speakers. But no matter how much I tried, I couldn't draw my gaze away from Lewis. With every flick of his hair, strum of his fingers, and shimmer in his eyes, my pulse quickened. My core clenched. *Oh God. He was good.*

Flint took to the mic:

> *It was a moonlit night,*
> *Partying on the beach.*
> *Hanging out with friends.*
> *Dancing, drinking, singing,*
> *Not wanting the night to end.*
> *And then, I met you,*
> *On the edge of the shore.*
> *Eyes so blue,*
> *Most stunning I'd seen.*
> *Had you been heaven-sent?*
> *Oh yeah.*
> *I couldn't believe, couldn't believe me luck.*
>
> *You said you'd be mine,*
> *For all of time.*
> *But just as summer ended,*
> *You disappeared.*
> *You left me a note,*
> *Saying we were dead.*
> *Over. Done. Through. What the . . .*

I was broken and wounded.
Dizzy and blinded.
I didn't know what I was supposed to do.
But . . .
If somebody had warned me,
That love made you crazy,
I would never have fallen for you.
If somebody told me,
That love made your heart break,
I would never have fallen for you.

I smirked as Flint sang the lyrics. *Yep*. Love made you crazy. So did liking someone you could never have. For the first time in years, I couldn't wait to go back to LA and start my new job so I could put more distance between Lewis and me.

The guys played four more new songs, rounding out their set with a harder rock track, "Midnight."

As Cole's final strike to the cymbal reverberated through the air, everyone clapped and cheered and whistled. Jumping to his feet, Falcon, who wore a swanky leather jacket and skinny jeans better than Jon Bon Jovi did, led his team over to talk to the guys. Blake joined them as did a proud and excited-looking Everhide.

Gena nudged my arm. "Lewis is awesome, isn't he?"

"Yeah, totally." *Too awesome.*

"Hey?" She rubbed her tummy. "I'm really not feeling well. Can you excuse me? I desperately need the bathroom."

"Go for it."

The moment Gena left, I stepped in behind the mixer. The software controlling the lights and monitoring the channel inputs filled the two screens. Reaching for the buttons, my fingers tingled. My pulse jumped. And this time it wasn't from being in the same room as Lewis. It was the tech. The magic this equipment controlled. The show it could create.

Oh yeah.

Gena came back into the room a few minutes later, paler than before. She tapped Flint and Cole on the arm and drew them over to stand a few feet away from me. "Guys. I'm sorry. I'm not well. I need to go back to the hotel."

"Yeah, okay." Flint rubbed the back of his sweaty hair. "Don't worry about it. You need a doctor or something?"

"No. I'm sure this curry just needs to pass through me." She winced, clutching her belly.

Cole jerked his head toward me. "You want Tia to go with you?"

"No." Gena winced. "No one needs to be around what's coming out of my ass."

"Okay. Go." Cole grabbed her a bottle of water from his bag. "Get some rest. I'll have our driver take you to the hotel. He's just outside." He grabbed his cell phone from his jeans pocket, swiped the screen, and shot off a text. "I'll call you later to make sure you're okay."

"Thanks." Gena grabbed her purse from beside the desk. "You're an angel."

"I know." Cole threw her a smug, friendly grin. "Now get out of here."

Falcon called out to the guys. "Can we hear 'Fallen For You' again? Can you play the slower version you did in the studio the other day, and then the fast one you just played?"

"Yep." Cole turned to me; a challenge flashed in his eyes. "Would you like to manage the mixer for us? Or should I get Kyle to do it?"

My breath hitched. *Wow! Cole trusted me in front of Ashlem?* My gaze jumped from Cole, to the huge mixer, and back again. I could do this. I wanted to do this. "I'd love to." *I think.* "Maybe have Kyle on standby."

"I'll let him know. But I'm sure you'll be fine." Cole squeezed my arm, then walked backward toward Kyle and pointed at me. "Love you. Watch out for feedback if Slip jumps around too much."

"Will do." My heart raced as I ran my fingers over the channel faders, effects dials, and the equalization and gain knobs. I scanned the software on the monitor that manipulated the effects and angles of the stage lights. There was no preprogrammed show running; they were just set to 'auto' to flash with the beat. *Easy.*

The guys replayed the track—first, the slower version, then the fast, vibrant take. The second feedback came through Slip's amp, I turned down the gain, then I upped the volume on Flint's mic; he needed to be heard. Lewis's bass sounded better with a little more reverb.

At the end of the song, everyone at the back of the room clapped.

"Yes." Blake pumped his fist.

Excitement flared in Falcon's eyes as he stabbed his fingers at the guys. "That faster version is without a doubt your first single. You guys are gonna be bigger than Cold Play. And we're gonna make it happen."

The Ashlem team nodded with money-filled grins on their faces.

The band rushed together near Flint's mic and hugged.

"Fuck yeah. We're ready to do this," Slip hollered.

Lewis joined in the celebrations, but reservation flickered in his eyes. I guess he was still on the outer edge, not knowing if his future was with them or not.

"Um, Flint? Can I have a quick word?" Blake called out to him.

The smile slipped from Flint's face and was replaced by a worried frown. He dashed over to Blake and huddled by the far window. Cole and Slip were asked to join him after a few minutes.

As Everhide and the people from Ashlem congregated in small groups, talking about photoshoots and video clip meetings, promotional schedules and venue bookings, I gravitated toward Lewis and Sutton, who were talking to Hayden.

"What's going on?" I asked Lewis.

He shook his head. "I honestly don't know."

Blake and the guys broke apart and came over to join us.

Flint sucked in a deep breath and stuffed his hands in his front pockets. "Um, Lewis?" A distressed edge quivered through his voice. "You've done an amazing job for us in the studio so far. You've helped us finesse some tracks. You're a great bassist, but . . ."

Lewis's shoulders slumped. "But . . . I'm not what you're looking for?"

What? My heart lurched. *Oh, no. Were they dumping him? Here?*

"That's the thing . . ." Flint flicked back his hair. "We wanted someone who fit in well, who we connected with, and had the same vision as us—"

"But I thought I did."

My gut sank. I didn't miss the devastation in Lewis's tone. No one could.

"No, bud . . . you've fucking exceeded our expectations." Flint's tone jumped an octave. "We're only halfway through recording, but you've passed milestone one with flying colors. We're still finding our feet, and getting to know one another, and have to work on our live performances. But we want to record your song and finish the album with you. We don't want to risk someone else snapping you up. You're too fucking good. So pack your bags. Come to LA. We want you on promo with us."

"Holy shit." Tears welled in his eyes. He swiped his hand down his face and shook the shock from his expression. "I thought you were firing me."

"No, dude. We were just messing with you again." Slip chuckled, slapping Lewis on the back. "So, how about it? Are you ready to move across the country once we finish recording?"

"You fuckers." Lewis grinned, hooking his arm around Slip's neck. "You mean it?"

"Sure do." Cole nodded. "We still have milestones in place as a safety net. But don't screw up because we don't want to have to kick you to the curb."

"I won't." He hugged the guys. "Oh my God. This is brilliant. I want this so bad. I don't want to go back to my old job. So, thank you."

"Congratulations." I rubbed his arm, but fire blazed to life beneath my touch. *Shit.* I quickly withdrew my hand. "You earned it."

He hesitated for less than a second, then drew me into his embrace and rocked me from side to side. "Argh. I'm moving to LA."

"Awesome." I closed my eyes, inhaled his sweet, sweaty scent, and clenched my teeth to ride out the pain in my leg. Being crushed against his chest was worth it. "You'll love it."

He stepped back, energy radiated off his entire body. His gaze jumped from Flint, to Cole, to Slip. "I won't let you down. This is freaking incredible. Oh my gosh. You'll have to give me some ideas on where to live. I'll need to get an apartment near Flint's place since that's where we'll spend most of our time, right?" He spoke so fast I struggled to keep up.

Flint chuckled as he scratched his cheek. "We can do that. My mom's a rental property manager; she'll help you find something."

"Nah, that won't be necessary." Cole swatted the air. "You can stay with me for a while."

"What?" The color drained from my face.

Cole threw me a what-the-hell glare before turning to Lewis. "I have a huge house. Tia won't mind. You'll be so busy with promo and hopefully the tour. You can find a place after that."

Lewis rubbed the new stress lines that had formed on his brow. "Um . . . that's kind of you, but—"

"No buts," Cole cut him off. "The rental market is insane in LA. You'll be lucky to find a dog kennel to live in. We can't have that. Sutton has just moved in with Flint. You won't want to be around them while they're in their honeymoon phase. Slip's sleeping in his guest house while his home is under full renovation. My place is perfect. We can go for days living there and probably not even see each other. Right, Tee?"

"Um . . . yeah." *Shit.* A cold sweat broke out on the back of my neck.

Live with Lewis?

Fuckity fuck. Fuck. Fuck!

"That settles it then." Cole rubbed his hands together. "You're staying with me and Tia."

Lewis's gaze locked onto mine. My heart thundered against my ribs. *Oh, crap.* The buzz between us hadn't died. Cole had just added more fuel to the fire.

Lewis's Adam's apple lurched. "Looks like we'll be housemates."

Oh. This just got better and better. "Great. I can't wait."

Not!

Why did I have the feeling this inferno would destroy me?

Chapter 11

LEWIS

By mid-February, recording was done. After the long, tiring weeks in the studio, a booze-filled night with the guys to celebrate Slip's birthday . . . and remember Phil on the anniversary of his death . . . exhaustion ached every bone in my body. But wow . . . we'd recorded my song. And it would be released as a bonus track on the deluxe edition of the album. If I didn't live another day, I'd die a happy man. I was beyond stoked and overwhelmed, and most days, I felt like I'd landed in a parallel universe.

Working with The Flintlocks, Everhide, and the team at EH4 Records had blown my mind. Their attention to detail and production skills were phenomenal. The marketing group at Ashlem had been scheduling the promotion for The Flintlocks' singles, the album, and the tour dates from the moment the guys had signed with them back in early December. Now I'd passed milestone one and was going on the promo tour with the guys, I'd been brought into the mix of meetings and media preparation. They wanted to include me in interviews, photoshoots, and the filming of video clips. Our first single would drop in late March. The album's launch date had been locked in for May.

My head spun, trying to keep up.

Everyone treated me like I was truly part of the band. But it was hard to stop feeling like an impostor. The weight of replacing Phil pressed on my shoulders as April, our publicist and PA, prepped me for dealing with reporters and our media releases. Questions about who I was, where I'd come from, and whether I was worthy of taking Phil's place were addressed, and carefully worded responses were prepared. I'd never had media training before.

This shit was next level.

So much was happening and at an astonishing pace.

Life had changed.

I hoped I survived the ride.

Over the past few days, I'd had dinner with friends in Brooklyn and caught up with Reg, Basil, and even Kilt to tell them about my new ventures. All wished me good luck. But yesterday, on a snowy bleak day in Manhattan, saying goodbye to my best friend Hayden made me question if I'd made the right choice to move across the country. Every time I'd made big changes before, everything had turned to shit. Music. Relationships. Boston. Love. I couldn't afford to fuck this up. I had more milestones to pass. I had to keep my excitement and fears on a tight leash and pray that my track record wasn't set on repeat.

But I was done with New York.

I loved my new band.

I was ready to move to LA.

As I took one final look around Pop's empty condo, my chest shuddered. The dark timber floors, small picture windows and tiny kitchen with stained yellow countertops seemed to shed a tear from missing Pop too. So many memories had been created inside these walls—memories I'd treasure forever. Pop teaching me to play card games by the small gas heater. The stories he'd told me about Gran before she'd gotten sick with cancer. Living here with Emilio because we couldn't find or afford anywhere else. The Sunday morning laughs Pop and I had over bagels and coffee. Those last few weeks I'd spent with him, just the two of us, would be moments I'd always cherish. He'd passed away peacefully in his sleep, but his spirit was still here. I felt it.

I blinked away my welling tears, picked up my bass, and reached for the door handle. Looking back over my shoulder at the bare living room, I whispered, "Thank you, Pop. Thank you for loving me. Saving me. Being my friend. Hope you're winning Bridge in Heaven. I love you. And miss you every day. Oh . . . and don't haunt the new owners. They seem like nice people." But Pop would get a thrill out of that.

As the van drove me and the guys toward the airport in New Jersey, the Manhattan skyline disappeared behind us. New York had given me life, years of music and amazing friendships, but she'd broken me too. It was time to start again . . . for the fourth time.

But the idea of living with Cole and Tia made me nervous. Cole wasn't the issue—Tia was. The thought of seeing her again after a few weeks apart had my stomach tied in knots. I didn't understand the effect she had on me. Confusion slithered through my head like a snake in the grass—I didn't know if it was dangerous or not. But I was moving to LA for the music. The guys. Nothing else.

As I stepped onto Ashlem's private jet at Teterboro Airport, my heartbeat boomed like an amp set to max. I'd never been on a chartered flight or a plane this flashy before. Not ever. I'd been catapulted into a world I'd only ever dreamed about. I'd fallen into the life I'd always wanted. And I'd found the perfect band to do it with.

I slid onto the plush leather seat beside Flint.

"You ready?" He slapped my thigh.

"Yeah. I am." Overcome with exhilaration and fear, I rubbed at the tightness lingering in the depths of my chest. I was leaving my friends and hometown to embark on a new adventure. I had to keep it together. *Just breathe.*

"You're one of us now. Any time you want to jam, drink, or jump off a cliff, we're here for you."

"I hope I never want to jump off a cliff." Although I'd come close a few times.

"No. I mean if you are ever up, down, need help, or want to just hang, we'll be there. Promise."

"Same." I wasn't going to waste this opportunity. I had years of experience behind me. There'd be no foolish mistakes. I wouldn't let my heart lead me astray. Not again.

Flint rested his head against the back of the seat. "This is a new chapter for us too. We've never done anything this big before." He smoothed his hands over his jeans. Excitement rippled in his voice. "We did a ton of promo for our first two albums, but nothing on the scale that Everhide and Ashlem have planned for us. The promo alone for the three singles tops what we did for our entire second album. We've never toured internationally. That's gonna be wicked. Our fans will love you." He nudged me in the arm. "So enjoy the last few weeks of being anonymous. Get out and see LA while you can. At the end of next month, life will never be the same again."

"Good. It needed a shake-up." But not like the one Tia had injected into my system. That I could've done without. I was sure it was just a side effect from all the hype and tension I'd felt since my first audition, being selected and my eagerness to join the band.

Slip came down the aisle and thrust beers into our hands.

He slid into the seat opposite us. Cole flopped into the one beside him. Slip raised his bottle. "Here's to our album blowing up the charts. We're going to kick some ass."

"Cheers to that." I chinked my bottle against theirs. I hoped this was the last big move I ever made.

After the long flight, the late afternoon drive into the Hollywood Hills made my head spin. We passed multimillion-dollar mansions, fancy wrought-iron gates and manicured hedges and trees trimmed to perfection. But when we entered through the security gates and stopped outside Cole's two-story house, it was like I'd landed on a different planet. Flint's and Kyle's places had been flash, but Cole's was insane.

My pulse quickened as I stared at the frosted-glass front door. Would Tia be here? She should be at work. If the charge between us was still alive, I wouldn't be living here long. But surely, after weeks apart, it would've died. I had too many other issues around settling into a new city, meeting milestones and preparing for promo to worry about without throwing her into the mix.

Cole and I helped the driver unload our suitcases, and my guitars and gear from the van's trailer, and we stacked everything inside the foyer. My entire life fit into three large suitcases and two small equipment trunks. I may not have had many possessions, but from my clothing to my music gear, what I had was top-notch.

Sucking in a deep breath, I followed Cole into the huge living room with its towering atrium. Panoramic windows gave way to amazing views down a narrow canyon and across to LA in the distance. The city stretched as far as I could see to the southeast. I'd lived in tiny apartments or cramped houses all my life and had seen some fine homes, but Cole's exuded immaculate Hollywood luxury and style. I dropped my laptop bag on the modular sofa and stepped toward the windows.

"Nice joint."

Yep. I could handle living under this roof for the next year. I couldn't believe I was in LA.

"We've done okay for ourselves." Cole shrugged his shoulder as he stepped in beside me and tucked his hands into his baseball jacket pockets. I loved that the guys were down-to-earth and not over-the-top arrogant dickheads about their money and success. Cole opened the sliding door that led out onto the entertainment area, complete with a huge infinity lap pool and outdoor kitchen. "We were lucky to buy houses before the real estate boom. Want a quick tour?"

"Sure."

After showing me around outside, he led me back through the open dining area and waved half-heartedly at the games room and gym on the other side of the kitchen before he led me in the opposite direction, down a long hallway, past the home theater, music studio, office, and guest bedroom, and into the six-car garage. Only three cars filled the space.

Holy shit!

Cole pointed at the cars. "I mainly drive the Lambo SUV. But feel free to use the Corvette anytime. Wait." He slapped my arm with the back of his hand. "Can you drive?"

"Yes." I chuckled. "Just because it's not a common thing to do in New York doesn't mean I can't." I'd used Emilio's car back home. If I stayed in LA, I'd buy one eventually, but I wanted to be more secure in the band and settled before I made any big purchases.

"Oh . . . good."

"What about the Merc?" I scanned the slick red Mercedes SL Roadster, glistening beneath the bright lights.

"That's Tia's. She loved it so much she had it shipped from Chicago. She can't drive yet, so a town car picks her up every day to take her to the studio."

"She's not handling being hurt well, is she?"

"No." Heaviness weighed down his tone. "She's not herself. Now we're here for a while, I hope to change that. She used to be so outgoing . . . no . . . totally wild. I'm sure once her leg's better, she'll be fine." He slapped me on the shoulder as we ambled back through the house. "You two get along well."

"Yeah. We do." *Too well.*

After the tour upstairs, I settled into my new room. Cole had allocated me the one right next door to Tia's as it was the biggest and had its own bathroom. I didn't want to seem ungrateful, but shit . . . *right next to her*? I'd hear her. Feel her. Just catching the scent of her perfume when Cole had shown me the inside of her room had tortured my senses. What was wrong with me?

I liked Tia. We had fun. But was I *into* her? Surely not. No.

Having a shower didn't ease the mounting tension twisting between my shoulder blades. Neither did dinner and a few beers. As I grabbed two fresh Buds from the fridge, I glanced at my watch for the tenth time since arriving at the house, then toward the front door. I flopped back on the sofa next to Cole and handed him a bottle. "Tia works late."

"I have no idea what a normal day is for her." He cracked the top off his beer and took a sip. "Doubt it would be any more insane than what we do."

"True."

At nine o'clock, she fell through the door.

All my resolve and reassurance that the spark between us was nothing but a crazed notion went up in a puff of smoke. I could almost see the invisible threads drawing me too her. *Shit!*

"Hey." She dropped her purse by the staircase and hugged Cole . . . then me. "Welcome to your new home."

Her gorgeous arms lingered around me for two seconds too long. *Hmm. Lord, give me strength!* I wanted to bury my nose beneath her earlobe, let her long hair brush my face, breathe her in until I was drunk. *Crap. This has to stop. Stop now.* I needed to find the nearest gay bar and get my queer back. *Quick!* "Thanks, Tia. It's great to finally be here."

Tia hobbled into the kitchen and grabbed a bottle of water from the fridge. "I'm sorry I'm home late. It's been a really long day. My leg is killing me. I've eaten and need an early night. Can we catch up tomorrow?"

"Sure," Cole said.

"Look forward to it." I waved goodnight.

But we didn't see her in the morning. She left early for work. Cole and I rehearsed at Flint's until just after midnight.

Then someone hit the you-won't-have-time-to-shit button. Every day, I joined the three guys at intense marketing meetings, posed for wicked photoshoot after photoshoot, attended more harrowing media training, or practiced our promo set lists. I'd never worked this long and hard in my life. I loved every second of it. I'd learned more in the past two and a half months than I had in twelve years with The Saylors. No wonder we'd never made it. We had no clue on how to market ourselves or run a business.

My moments with Tia had been fleeting—quick hellos before she rushed out the door to work, quick goodnights when we got home from practice, quick catch-you-laters as Cole and I headed out most evenings. But no matter how often we asked, she never came with us to the clubs, bars, or parties we had to attend for publicity.

She needed to get out of the house for something other than work. But when we'd be able to take her out, I had no idea. Our schedule was hectic.

At the beginning of March, the band and I flew with our team to Mexico for four days to film the video for the first single. When we landed back in LA, we hit our prelaunch schedule hard—we had interviews with magazine editors, held private sessions for key industry representatives to hear the album, and rehearsed at every chance we got for the promotional tour.

But each time Cole and I walked through the door, one glance at Tia was all it took to unravel me.

Fuck this shit.

I had to put an end to this once and for all.

But how?

Yep. I had the answer.

I needed a wild night out.

I needed a hot hook up.

I needed one before the single launched next week.

Chapter 12

TIA

On the *Angels in LA* soundstage at Warner Bros. Studios, I leaned back in my director's chair, drove the balls of my hands into my eyes, and screamed inside my head. *Somebody shoot me, please? Or throw me off a building, chase me down the 101 in a high-speed car chase, or take me on in a fist fight.* Two months into working on my new show, I was bored out of my brains. I'd kill for some action.

Waiting to shoot my scene, with my hair twisted into a French knot and my makeup done, and dressed in a tailored Prada pantsuit, was slow torture. Going from action star to unlucky-in-love lawyer was mind-numbing. *Ergh!* Our pilot had passed screen testing; now I had three-and-a-half more months of season one to shoot. Did I want to keep doing this? Take up the option to re-sign for season two? What other acting options did I have? *None.*

So suck it up.

"Tia. You're on," Frank, our director, called me to join the other girls on set.

I slid off my chair and feigned a smile. *About time.*

Frank spoke like an abrupt asshole but was soft as a teddy bear once you got to know him. He loved everyone he worked with. He knew everybody's name—even the caterers and cleaners—had an eye for detail and hated wasting time. Somehow, with a click of his fingers and quick directions, he got the best out of everyone.

Digging my nails into my palm to distract me from the ache in my ankle, I walked toward Sutton, Mia, and Peyton, my fellow cast members. *Don't limp. You can do this. Fuck, my ankle hurts.* Thank God, I'd had my agent negotiate as part of my contract that my wardrobe only consisted of flat shoes and long pants or skirts to cover my scars. There was no way I could do this show in high heels.

"Hold up," Frank snapped. "Tia, what the hell have you done?"

Shit! My breath hitched. Had I limped? Had he seen? I didn't want anyone to know I was injured. I didn't want them to treat me differently.

He hollered over his shoulder, "Jill? Come fix Tia's face again. She's smudged the shit out of her eye shadow."

Oh . . . oops. No touching my face after being made up. Jill, our makeup artist, spent more time fixing my ruined makeup than prepping the other three girls for the day's shoot. This was another reason why I'd preferred action shows and stunt work. I'd hardly ever had to wear foundation, mascara, and lipstick.

After a quick fix, I joined the girls. We were about to film a friends-catching-up-for-dinner scene where Sutton's character, Sienna, a marketing executive at an advertising agency, would tell us she had the hots for her boss. I could relate to the drama of being attracted to someone you shouldn't be drawn too. Lewis still starred in too many of my hot dreams. Seeing him at home every night was a torturous hell, a sweet pleasure, and a pain because we got along so well. But next week, the guys would hit their promo tour and I'd have a month of reprieve. *Yay!*

"You okay?" Sutton asked. "How's the ankle?"

"Shh. It's fine." I smiled sweetly over my clenched teeth. As I took a seat beside her, the throbbing pain subsided. I picked up my glass of watered-down apple-juice, which passed for white wine, and was ready to roll.

The only things that helped me get through each day of filming were painkillers and these girls. The ladies were in their element, and we did have fun. Mia hardly had to act for her role as a quirky graphic designer at a fashion magazine. Peyton transformed from her meek bookworm self into this hard-ass professional *LA Times* editor. Sutton dazzled and thrived in her dream acting job.

We were halfway through filming the third take of the scene when there was a kerfuffle behind the camera crew. I spun around to see what had happened. My pulse hit the boom mic. Flint and Lewis stood by our camera assistant with huge grins smeared across their faces.

What the hell? Flint had been here a couple times over the past few weeks but not the other guys. Not Lewis. Visitors weren't banned, but security was strict. Sutton must have added him onto the approved list. *I'll kill her.* A heatwave washed over me. I tugged on the collar of my blouse. *Shit.* Had someone turned the air-conditioning off?

The second we finished the take, Sutton leaped from her seat and rushed over to Flint. She flung her arms around his neck and gave him a steamy kiss on the lips. A big grin lit his face. He seemed to relish the attention just as much as Sutton did.

I headed over to join them. Mia and Peyton followed.

As I neared Lewis, my pulse quickened. In designer jeans and a tight black T-shirt, and with his hair pulled back into a man bun, he made handsome devil look way too fucking hot. Some more time apart couldn't come soon enough.

Mia hungrily eyed him up and down. She'd just started dating Peyton in real-life. Whether she . . . or they . . . swung both ways or not, she was wasting her time with Lewis.

Mia dug her elbow into my arm. "Tia, are you going to introduce us, please?"

"Yeah. Sorry. Mia. Peyton. This is Lewis King, the bassist in Flint's band."

"Nice to meet you." He shook their hands. "Have fun filming today?"

"Yeah." Peyton shrugged, unflustered by the interruption. Not like I was. "Are you sticking around to watch our last take?"

"We sure are." Lewis's gaze drilled into me, making my insides quiver, then he winked. "Afterwards, we're kidnapping the girls to take them out for the evening."

"You are?" I raised an eyebrow. This was news to me.

"Yep." Flint nodded. "It's Duke's birthday."

Damn it. I hadn't seen him in more than a year. Duke and his band were mutual friends of The Flintlocks and mine. Chloe, his wife, was probably one of my best friends here in LA. But since moving back home, I hadn't called or caught up with anyone. I wasn't ready to do so. *So nope.* "You three can go. I'm not." My shoulders sagged. "I've had a long day. I want to go home."

"Tia. No." Flint waggled a finger at me. "You're coming. It's Friday night. Cole and Slip dropped us off here and insisted we manhandle you if necessary. So text your driver and tell him you've got other plans. You *are* coming, so don't argue."

I closed my eyes. My ankle ached. I didn't want to go out. *Fuck!*

"Tee?" Lewis softened his tone. "It's time to live a little."

I sneered at him. My stomach hurt. I hated that he was right.

"Okay, everyone." Frank joined us, hooking his arms around

Peyton's and Sutton's shoulders. "Flint, your hot ass keeps interrupting my crew. I have a show to film on a tight budget. Can I please have my ladies back and do one more take?"

"Absolutely." Flint held up his hands and grinned. "I'm not here. I'm invisible."

The gathering cluster of crew fluttering their eyelashes at Flint and Lewis said otherwise.

Frank jutted his chin at Lewis. "And who do you belong to?"

The sexiest of dimples formed near Lewis's mouth as he smiled. "I'm Lewis. Flint's bassist and Tia's housemate."

"Oh, great." Frank rolled his eyes. "More rock stars to deal with."

"Guess so." Lewis grinned.

"Fine." Frank pointed to our director's chairs. "Sit over there and don't make a sound while we finish this take."

"Will do." Lewis gave him a quick yes-sir salute. He stepped over to me and spoke in a low, sultry voice, close to my ear. "You've watched me perform many times. Now I get to watch you. Fair's fair, right? So you'd better put on a good show."

Heat crept into my cheeks. Shivers darted across my skin. This wasn't the kind of show my mind and body wanted to give him. "This won't be anywhere near as hot as me watching you make out with guys. You'll be bored in five minutes."

He laughed, soft and sexy. "I meant watching me play with the band, not my attempts to pick up men."

Crap! We were clearly on different wavelengths. Drawing my shoulders back, I threw him a saucy grin. "Good thing I've enjoyed both. But I'm sure you won't get the same level of satisfaction as I do from watching you."

"I'll be the judge of that."

"Okay." I spun on my good heel and made my way back on set. So much for toning things down. Our suggestive banter hadn't ceased. We still gave each other loads of crap, teased, and taunted each other. Flirting with him was like an addictive drug; I wasn't able to quit. I wanted him to watch me. But I'd preferred to have him do it when I wasn't on set or in character.

Thirty minutes later, we finished filming. Sutton and I changed into our regular clothes and said our goodbyes to the cast and crew. Then, the four of us jumped in Sutton's BMW and headed to Sun Valley.

Just after seven o'clock, we pulled to a halt on the curbside outside Duke's home, an old Spanish-styled place complete with white rendered walls and terracotta roof.

Sutton killed the engine, and we hopped out of the car.

Flint headed to the trunk. "It's a double celebration tonight. Duke's turning twenty-four, *and* he and his band have just signed with Everhide's EH4 Records to make their first album."

"An album?" My voice piqued. "That's brilliant." Now I was glad I came. Duke had been playing for as long as The Flintlocks had been but hadn't had anywhere near the same success. Duke and his boys deserved their break.

Flint opened the trunk and grabbed a gift bag covered in balloons. The bottles inside it chinked together. This night clearly had been preplanned. "Duke will be stoked you're here, Tee."

"Yeah. It will be good to catch up." I felt bad it had taken me this long to see the people I cared about.

Lewis offered to carry me up the steep steps, but I blatantly refused. Partly because I was pigheaded and could walk up a set of stairs, and partly because him touching me wasn't a good idea. I had enough issues controlling my body temperature around him without his hands actually on me.

The front door was wide open. We made our way through the foyer, the arched walkways, and terracotta-tiled hallway, and headed toward the music and chatter drifting inside from the patio.

Around a long wooden table covered in pizzas and drinks, our guys sat with Duke's boys and some of his stage crew, and a few faces I didn't recognize.

The moment Duke saw me, his hands shot into the air, and he shook his wavy brown curls. "Oh my fucking God. Tia!" He hollered loud enough for everyone miles away in Venice Beach to hear. He clambered off the bench seat, and rushed over to hug me. "How are you, girl?"

"I'm good, Duke." *Lie.* "Happy birthday."

"Best birthday surprise ever." He turned to Flint. "Always good to see you."

"Happy birthday." Flint shook Duke's hand and handed him the present.

Duke took it and peered inside the gift bag. His eyes widened as he nodded. "Sweet. Vodka. Looks like we'll be doing shots later."

"I never say no to vodka." Flint slid his arm around Sutton's waist. "You remember Sutton?"

"Sure do." Duke hugged her hello. "You can steal my stage anytime."

"No, never again." She giggled. "Happy birthday."

Flint grinned as he waved Lewis forward. "And this is Lewis. Our new bassist."

"Nice to meet you." Duke slapped his palm against Lewis's hand and drew him into a half-hug. "Grab a drink and come meet everyone." He waved toward the table. "Tia, Chloe will be bursting to see you."

I waved to his wife who was jiggling on her seat, and called out to her, "I'll just grab a drink."

"Hurry up, bitch," she yelled. "I've missed you."

Lewis jutted his chin toward Flint. "You and Sutton go sit. I'll help Tia with the drinks. Beer and champagne, right?"

"Yep, thanks." Flint took Sutton's hand, and they rushed

over to join the partygoers.

"What do you want to drink, Tee?" Digging into the cooler full of drinks on ice, Lewis pulled out two beers and the bottle of champagne for Sutton.

"Just water." I snapped a bottle out of a pack on the table. I still didn't drink anywhere near as much alcohol as I used to, and I needed to keep my wits around Lewis at a party.

He twisted the wire off the top of the champagne bottle and tossed it on the table. He threw me an inquisitive glance. "You and Duke seem *friendly.*"

Was he jealous? That was laughable. "We've known each other a long time. I met him and his band a few years ago at Hayley's Bar in Pasadena, where Cole and the guys used to play. I hung out with Chloe, his wife, who's his sound engineer."

"Oh. The dots connect." The corners of his mouth curled into a small smile as he tore the foil off the champagne bottle. "The guys took me to Hayley's for lunch two weeks ago. I met Molly, the owner. She adores Flint."

I grabbed a flute off the tray of glasses sitting on the far end of the table. "Yeah, Molly tells everyone she kickstarted their career. I don't think they've played there since Phil died—other than the few impromptu songs they did after Sutton coaxed Flint onto the stage last year."

"Cole and Slip told me about that." A tiny groove formed between his brows. "I didn't know he struggled so much after Phil's death and couldn't sing, write, or play. That must've been tough." He twisted and wriggled off the cork. *Pop.* No rocketing projectile was sent hurtling through the air.

"Losing him fucked us all up. But we're finally moving on with you." I held out the flute for him to fill in one hand and rubbed his forearm with the other. Without thinking, I ran my fingernails through the fine hairs on his arm, tracing the swirls of the tattoo on his skin.

Every muscle in his arm tensed. Panic darkened his eyes. He swallowed hard, lurching his Adam's apple. "Yes, and here's to not fucking that up." He took the flute out of my hand and poured the champagne, angling the glass so it wouldn't bubble over the top.

"I won't let you." I lowered my voice to barely above a whisper. "You're too good to lose." I meant that with every cell in my body. I'd never do anything to jeopardize the band. Their success came first—it always had and always would. And I needed to protect my sanity and my heart. It was best to keep a safe distance from Lewis. More than three feet at all times.

But the problem was, sometimes when he looked at me . . . leaned into me . . . brushed his hand against my skin. . . I was convinced he wanted to do away with being *just kindred spirits* as much as I did.

Delusions did my head in.

I cracked the lid off my water bottle and took a sip. "Let's go join the others. I'll introduce you to everyone."

He placed the champagne bottle back on ice. "I'd like that."

After we gave Sutton and Flint their drinks, I introduced Lewis to Duke's band—Evan, his bassist; Ezra, his lead guitarist; and Wolf, his drummer—Chloe, and a few other friends I knew. I took a seat next to Duke. Lewis sat opposite me, next to Chloe. I dug my elbow into Duke's arm. "Congratulations on the record deal. That's awesome."

"Thanks." Duke grabbed a slice of pepperoni pizza from the box in front of him. "We'll be forever in Sutton and Flint's debt. After she took over our show at Hayley's to sing to Flint, and the video went viral, everyone wanted to know who we were. Then Flint dropped our name to Everhide when they signed with them last year."

"That's so cool. When you release your album, I hope it goes to the top of the charts. After my guys', of course."

"I'd be down with that." He took a sip of his beer then wiped his lips. "I can't believe you're still hanging out with your brother."

"I actually live with him at the moment, and Lewis. But trust me, some days, I wish I could avoid them." I shot a sly smile at Lewis.

He grinned, sipped his beer, and nudged my good leg under the table. "Where's the fun in that?"

There was a fine line between fun and danger. Most of the time, I wasn't sure which way the scales would tip.

Chloe waved her beer at me. "If you ever need a change of scenery, want to come see Duke and the guys play, help, or hang out with me, you give me a call."

"I'd love that." That was one promise I'd keep.

Throughout the night, we mingled and shuffled about, and I talked to and met everyone at the party. I filled Chloe and Duke in on the details of my injury; they were horrified but gave me a big hug and offered to help me in any way possible. It was sweet, but there was nothing anyone could do.

The party grew louder. The music was turned up, and the alcohol and laughter flowed. Beer morphed into vodka, and more tales of the fun and mischief both bands had caused on and off the stage were shared. I didn't need to be reminded of the night Phil and I had let off a smoke machine in a hotel suite in San Diego, or the time I'd killed the lights at their gig in Reno, sending the entire venue into a blackout. It had been stupid fun at the time, but I wouldn't do those things again.

Near midnight, my guys, Sutton and I lazed about on the outdoor sofa in front of the gas firepit. Cole had been making moves on Violet, one of Chloe's friends, but he'd come over to join us. He kept giving her the sexy eye though. That was destined to end in a hookup. *Go, Cole.* Slip kept on texting someone on his cell phone. Flint and Sutton were snuggled together, kissing and whispering in each other's ears.

Nothing helped to kill my Lewis vibe, especially when he sat next to me. Close. Too close. His bare arm kept brushing against mine, sending sparks across my skin.

So much for distance.

Ergh! I was done with this shit.

I needed to get laid.

Was that my problem?

It had been nine months since I'd last had sex with Rhett. *Fuck, that was depressing.* Would hooking up with a random hot dude for some no-strings-attached sex cure my Lewis addiction?

I needed to try something. Anything.

Problem was . . . I hated one-night stands. I'd had my fair share in my first year at college during my get-over-Phil era. But all the guys I'd been with had bragged about it the next day on social media. I'd seen statuses like *'Scored with Tia,' 'Wild night with Tia,' 'Rocked all night with Tia,'* and *'Tia's as wild as her brother'. Ergh! Nope.* I didn't want any more of that shit.

Lewis's cell phone buzzed. He grabbed it out of his jacket pocket and read the screen. His eyes lit up. "Hey?" He spoke to no one in particular. "We don't have anything tomorrow night, do we? I have a friend in town. He's DJing at somewhere called Emerald Destruction. Anyone want to come?"

He flashed me the screen. I scanned the text:

> HEARD YOU WERE IN LA. WOULD LOVE TO CATCH UP.
> COME TO GIG SATURDAY NIGHT.
> AT CLUB: EMERALD DESTRUCTION. ON AT 11.
> YOUR NAME IS ON THE DOOR LIST.
> CALL ME IF YOU NEED ANYTHING.

"Wow." Cole rubbed the tip of his chin. "Emerald Destruction is one of the biggest nightclubs in LA. You have to be good to play there."

"Morgan is." Lewis shrugged. "He's just done a ton of gigs in Ibiza and Japan. Come on. It'll be fun."

"Sorry, bud." Flint clutched and gently shook Sutton's knee. "We're out. We're heading up to Bakersfield to have dinner with Sutt's brother for his birthday."

"I'm busy, too." A mischievous smile curled across Cole's lips. "The German twins, Nadia and Petra, are in town for LA Fashion Week. I'll be reacquainting myself with them . . . or I might still be giving it to Violet."

Giggling, I shook my head. My brother was so easygoing and had this steady, suave, yet sexy and smooth charisma that women fought over. They often ended up in his bed . . . or fucking him wherever, whenever. Sometimes that had led to trouble and even more secrets that I was convinced he didn't know I knew.

"What about you, Slip?" Lewis asked.

"No can do. With a night off, I'm catching up with . . . um . . . my brother, Theo."

"You are?" Cole's eyes widened. "You saw him at Christmas. You don't see him more often than that."

"We didn't get much time together. So sorry, Lewis." Slip shrugged. "I'm out."

"That's cool." Lewis tucked his cell phone away. "I'm happy to go by myself."

Cole drained the last mouthful of his beer and placed the bottle on the ground. "Tia needs a night out. She'll go with you."

My pulse jumped. Lewis tensed.

Us? Out together? Nope. I tucked my hair behind my ear. "Uh . . . no. That's not my scene anymore."

"Tia?" Cole pleaded. "Go. You love dance music."

I'd used to. I'd loved raves and discos and nightclubbing. They were fun. But my ankle wouldn't accommodate the dancing and crowds anymore. "No." Firmness set in my tone.

"I'll need security at a place like that. I'm not a nobody. The crowd will be too much. I can't dance or stand around all night, so what's the point?"

"It's fine." Lewis let out a relieved breath. "I don't mind going solo."

"Bullshit." Cole glared at me. "Tia, please. Go. Get out of the fucking house."

Lewis picked at the label on his bottle, *pick, pick, pick,* then he gave me a sideways glance. "Do you wanna come? I'll call Morgan and get him to reserve us a VIP table. We can just sit and listen."

"No."

He dialed up the sexiness in his voice and leaned a fraction closer. "There will be hot guys everywhere. We can check them out. Maybe hook up. Who knows where the night will lead us?"

That sounded bearable, even entertaining. But he didn't have to do this for my brother's sake or mine. *Crap.* I'd just told myself I needed some action. Maybe I should consider going.

No. The crowds would be insane. My ankle already throbbed. "I'll attract too much attention."

"Nah," Flint said. "If you're worried, hire security for the night."

Lewis's eyes glinted as he scanned the length of my arm. "You certainly turn heads, but there's a strict 'no phones' policy at his gigs. He's protective of his shows. There'll just be good music and some fun. So what do you say? You want to come with me?"

My pulse strummed too fast. *Out with Lewis?* We were *just* kindred spirits, right? "Do you ever take no for an answer?"

"Yes. But for this? No."

He should. "You're impossible, you know that?" I half snarled, half smiled. I needed a good kick up the ass. We were *friends.* I had to accept that, move on, and get over my I-wanna-fuck-you attraction. Avoiding him hadn't lessened my pull toward him, so maybe spending time with him would. It was worth a shot. If that didn't work, moving out of Cole's place would be my only option. "Fine. I'll organize security. But we'll have dinner first. There's an awesome Spanish restaurant near that club. I might have to use my celebrity status to get a table, but it will be worth it."

He laughed. "Are you trying to impress me?"

"Nope." I shook my head. "You're in training for what's yet to come."

"I need all the help I can get."

So did I.

I'd just agreed to go out with Lewis.

And I had to be on my best behavior.

Chapter 13

LEWIS

As I waited on the sofa for Tia to come downstairs, sweat broke out on the back of my neck. I kneaded the knots tightening in my shoulders. Why had I insisted she come out with me tonight? Me and my big mouth after one too many drinks. My head ached from the constant frazzle and the twisting of wires in my brain when I was around her.

I didn't understand my attraction toward Tia. More importantly, I didn't want to. My focus was on the band, not her. But for one night, I needed to put aside the chaos hurtling through my mind and take her out. She needed this. She'd been cooped up in this house for months. Other than to work, Flint's place, and Duke's, she hadn't been anywhere. A night of loud music, a rocking DJ set, and a room full of hot LA men would do us both a world of good.

When I heard her bedroom door open, I looked up. Tia hobbled downstairs in a pair of black wide-legged dress pants, and a sleeveless midriff top. She carried a clutch and a metallic silver trench coat. Dark smoky makeup and bright red lipstick highlighted her gorgeous green eyes and accentuated her fine lips. But they weren't the only things about her that stole my breath. Her beautiful long hair had been hidden beneath a silver bobbed wig. Total disco vibe.

I stood and wiped my hands on the back pockets of my jeans. "Tia, you look amazing." *Stunning.*

"Thank you. So do you. Nice threads." She picked a piece of lint off my black blazer. "LA fashion is finally rubbing off on you."

"That's Kara's doing. All my gear is from her styling us now." I had more clothes selected and fitted to wear for promo than I'd owned in my entire life. They felt good. I looked good. I'd own that.

Cute wrinkles formed across the bridge of her nose. "You'd make dirty rags look hot."

Warmth crept up my neck. "Thank you." I reached out and toyed with the silver ends of her wig. "What's this for?"

"Disguise." She shrugged on her coat, then hooked her clutch over her shoulder. "It doesn't always work, but with my leg, I don't want to be swamped by overzealous fans and get hurt."

"You won't. I'll keep you safe."

But doubt darkened her eyes. I wouldn't let anyone hurt her, not ever.

Fidgeting, she tugged and straightened the hemline of her short top. "Lewis, we don't have to do this."

"Wh-why not?" My voice snagged in my throat. *She* had nothing to worry about. We had security and a VIP table. But me? I'd be in agony all night. Just looking at her made my dick ache. And that ache shouldn't exist. Not for her.

"I'm happy to stay at home."

"I know, but you're not." I grabbed my cell phone, wallet, and keys off the coffee table, and tucked them into my blazer. "Like riding a carousel horse. You can do this. I'll carry you if I have to. We'll have dinner, and a few drinks, listen to Morgan's set, and check out guys. We'll have fun. I promise." If the rampant butterflies swarming through my gut subsided, everything would be fine.

"I'll hold you to that." She tied the sash on her coat.

"Good. Let's go."

I took her hand, led her out the door, and helped her into our waiting town car.

Time to ride or die.

At ten-thirty, just after dinner, we entered the huge club on Sunset Boulevard. We checked in our coats and cell phones at the cloakroom, then Pedro, Tia's security guard for the evening, plowed us a path through the crowd in the direction of the VIP section on the opposite side of the venue. Music reverberated and boomed through the huge speakers mounted on the ceiling. A fog machine on the stage billowed smoke into the air. Green, blue, and red lasers flashed and flickered across the gyrating partygoers.

"Holy fuck." I yelled at Tia as we followed Pedro. "This place is massive."

"Welcome to LA." She clutched onto the back of my T-shirt. "Please don't lose me. I'll never find you."

Maybe we'd had too much wine at dinner, but I liked the desperate plea in her voice. "I won't. We have to meet Morgan by the stage first. Let's go." I tapped Pedro on the shoulder and pointed toward the stage. He nodded and changed course. I entwined my fingers with Tia's and wove through the crowd. Holding her hand seemed so natural; the warmth meandering up my arm, strange. I threw her a little smile. I'd kept telling myself to stop touching her and flirting with her, but I couldn't. We'd demolished a bottle of wine at dinner. More alcohol wouldn't help this situation, but I needed another drink . . . or ten.

"Lewis." Morgan hugged me hello, then turned to Tia. His eyes brightened. "Well, holy shit. You're on *Through The Smoke*. Tia, right? I love your show. Nice wig. Poor disguise, girlfriend. Lewis, why didn't you tell me you were hanging out with star power?"

I chuckled. "I'm moving up in the world."

"About fucking time." He squeezed my arm. There were no tiny shockwaves rippling through the air or beneath my shirtsleeve like I'd gotten from Tia's touch. And Morgan, with his dark skin and golden eyes, was totally doable.

I placed my hand on the small of Tia's back. My fingertips found a sliver of bare skin beneath the bottom of her shirt. *Hmm. So soft.*

No, focus. "Tia, Morgan is super talented. We met in New York about four years ago through Emilio. He's one of the best DJs in the country."

Morgan swiped his hand through the air. "Oh, keep talking me up, baby. I love it." His ego was still as big as Mount Everest. He flicked me on the bicep with the back of his hand. "But what the hell are you doing in LA? I've seen some posts on social."

"I've moved here to play in a new band. You'll find out all the details on Tuesday when our first single is released."

"Oh, I'm intrigued. I can't wait." Morgan tilted his chin toward the dance floor. "You two ready to dance?"

"Tia's got a sore ankle, so we're here to watch. But you never know what might happen after a few drinks." I needed to hit the dance floor with some hot guy and work up a sweat. Hopefully Tia would meet someone too.

Morgan stepped in close to me and whisper-yelled into my ear so I could hear him over the music. "Lew, if my memory serves me correctly, you love a little something to get you in the mood to party." He dipped his hand into his jacket, then took my hand. He pressed two round tablets into my palm and closed my fingers over them. "Enjoy the show on me. We'll talk after my set."

Grinning, I tucked the pills into my jeans. I'd save them for another day. Tia raised one inquisitive eyebrow. Taking party drugs around her wouldn't be a smart idea. I didn't need to get more fucked up than I already was.

We headed to the VIP section. Tia opted for a bar table at the back of the area to avoid recognition, and we ordered a bottle of bourbon. Pedro lingered off to the side, hanging out with a few other security guards. I didn't see any other celebrities— just dozens of rich LA socialites with more money than sense.

I slid onto a stool adjacent to Tia so we could talk and watch Morgan's set. Moments later, a waiter placed a bottle of Jim Beam Black and two shot glasses in front of us along with bottles of water. I reached for my wallet in my back pocket, but Tia caught my arm.

"I've got this. I have nothing else to spend my hard-earned money on these days, so let me buy the drinks. You paid for dinner." She grabbed her Platinum AMEX out of her clutch and swiped it across the waiter's POS terminal. With a sweet smile, she sent him on his way.

"Thank you. But I don't mind paying." Even though we were just friends, it felt like the gentlemanly thing to do. I wasn't rolling in cash, but I wasn't destitute either. I poured the shots and chinked my glass against hers. "Here's to the night ahead."

"Cheers."

We downed the shots. The cold bourbon burned my throat and sent fire coursing through my veins. *God.* I'd needed that. After the wine at dinner, we were already tipsy, so this would definitely put us in the party mood.

With a flicker of lights and a booming bass beat, Morgan's set took over the club. People on the dance floor screamed and hollered, jumped, and waved their hands in the air. The music rattled my eardrums and pummeled the center of my chest. The reverberations hummed through the floor and zipped up my legs. *Yep.* That was good.

Tia nudged her knee against my leg. "So, are we just gonna sit here and check out hot guys? Are you aiming to hook up?"

Grinning, I racked up another round of shots. I should hook up. Other than making out with a few random guys on nights out, I hadn't slept with anyone since Emilio. "Maybe. We'll see how the night pans out."

"I don't mind if you do." She wriggled and straightened her wig, the colored disco lights catching the silver strands like a rainbow. "Just let me know if you take off with someone so I can make my own way home."

I handed her a shot. "Get this into you, and we'll see what happens."

She downed it without hesitation. She hadn't drunk at Duke's last night, but she wasn't holding back tonight. I'd be carrying her out of here if she wasn't careful. But maybe we both needed to let loose and stop worrying about everything bombarding our lives—work, LA, each other. Was that even possible?

She licked her lips like they were the best thing to taste on the planet. *Oh fuck, that was sexy.* That . . . didn't ease my worry. Grabbing the bottle of bourbon, she twisted off the lid, then poured more shots. "What do you look for in a guy?"

I knocked down the bourbon and scanned the crowd on the dance floor and the guys laughing in the corner of the VIP section. She leaned against my arm, so we didn't have to yell over the music. The moment our bare skin touched, heat meandered through my veins.

I trailed my gaze across her fine fingers, along her delicate wrist, over her elbow and toned biceps, then up to her bare shoulder. I met her eyes. Her stunning green irises shimmered like emeralds in the club lights. "Um . . . toned arms, not too buffed, always attract me. Nice body. A smile that makes you want to drop to your knees the moment they look at you."

Tia tilted her head to the side. Her silver hair fell forward, brushing the edge of her cheek. She narrowed her eyes into sexy slits, pouted and pursed her lips, then smiled a devilish smile.

I swallowed hard, willed the blood away from my dick, then chuckled. "Yeah . . . a smile like that."

Damn actress. But I couldn't look away. Neither did Tia. *Shit.* She shouldn't look at me like that. Like she wanted me. It did strange things to my heartbeat every single time. Breaking my trance, I let out a long, slow breath and lifted my chin. "Does anyone here catch your eye?"

"Yes." She tapped my arm. "But he's not available."

I winced. Did she mean me? *Fuck.* I downed another shot, licked my lips, and let out an awkward laugh. More wires in my head frayed. Too much alcohol buzzed through my body. I'd better not drink anymore. "You up for dancing or is your leg too sore?"

"I'll be able to shuffle and sway for a bit." She knocked back another shot like it was water. She slid to her feet, easing in close to me. "But I'll need some help."

"With what?" I edged off my stool and caught her arm.

She erased the gap between us, leaving barely any room for air. Our lips hovered three inches apart. My stomach flipped, and my pulse quickened. Her jasmine perfume held me captive. She caught her bottom lip between her teeth as she slid her hand down my chest, over my stomach, then dipped it into the front pocket of my jeans. I flinched but didn't pull away. *God.* Her fingers were half an inch away from my dick. It twitched, liking the attention.

Crap.

With a sexy smile, she withdrew her hand and held her curled fingers against her chest. "This will help. We can't let these pills go to waste."

I brushed her hair off her face. "What would your brother say if I got you high?"

"He'd want an E too. You've read about my brother's band, right?"

"Yes. That's why we get on so well." *Most days, anyway.*

She popped the pill into her mouth and washed it down with a mouthful of bourbon, straight from the bottle. "Let's get fucked up and dance."

Smiling, I shook my head. "You're not what I expected."

"Trust me. Neither are you." She licked her index finger, placed the second pill on it, and hovered it half an inch from my lips. "Are you game?"

According to many, mainly most of my family, I was going to hell for my sins anyway. I may as well add this to the list. "Always."

With my gaze locked onto Tia's, I sucked her finger into my mouth and licked the pill off the tip. Then, I drew her whole finger into my mouth and swirled and flicked my tongue around it. Her breath hitched. A shockwave jolted my dick. My heart beat way too fast. *Damn. What brought that move on? Fuck!*

I should leave. Walk away. But something about her lured me deeper. And deeper. And deeper.

Drugs. Alcohol. Her. This was a dangerous combination. What had I gotten myself into?

I poured another round of shots. So much for not drinking. "Let's dance."

We drank the bourbon and slammed the glasses onto the table.

She held out her hand. "Show me the way."

I led her onto the dance floor, heading for the center. We

squeezed past a group of guys that reeked of pot, several couples making out, and girls who were so drunk they only managed to stay upright thanks to the mass of people around them. Morgan stood at his turntable on stage with headphones on, spinning out the tunes. Lights flashed around us. Bodies gyrated, jumped up and down, and spun around to the music.

I drew Tia to a halt. "This okay?" It was so packed, we only had about a square foot of space each to move.

"We'll see how it goes."

Facing each other, we stepped to the beat, swaying and dancing on the spot. But within two songs, her eyes had narrowed, and they shimmered in the flashing lights. She half smiled. *Yep.* The drugs had kicked in. Mine had too. Every part of my body hummed and buzzed. Laughing, I let the loud disco thrum take over me. I jumped around Tia. We bumped hips, shuffled from side to side, and hollered out the songs. She'd finally let loose. I loved it. I loved that despite her struggles and injuries, she'd come out tonight. She was smiling and hopefully having fun.

As Tia swayed to the rhythm, she raised her arms in the air, giving me an eyeful of her midriff. Every time she looked at me, my heartbeat thudded a touch faster, and the temperature of my blood rose a couple of degrees.

Don't think anything of it. It's just the drugs and alcohol. I hated that I had to keep telling myself that.

Needing a distraction, I grabbed her sideways around the waist. I picked her up, holding her hip against mine, and spun in a circle, twice.

But dizziness swam through my head. "Sorry. That seemed like a good idea at the time." I placed her on her feet, took her hand and twirled her 'round like a ballerina.

"I'm fine." Giggling, she stopped spinning and her back crashed into my chest. Holding her hips, I froze.

Her laughter ceased. She clutched my arms. With each deep breath she took, the rise and fall of her rib cage hit mine with a hypnotic rhythm.

Shit. I closed my eyes and rested my cheek against the side of her head. Her sweet perfume filled my senses. Her body was so aligned with mine no light could pass between us.

Dancing was supposed to take my mind off Tia, not make things worse.

"Lewis?" She slid her fingers down my forearms, then covered my hands with hers. "Dance with me."

A fevered rush shot through my veins. My dick strained in my jeans.

I'm not into her. Just fucking keep it together.

"Please?"

It was just a dance. No harm, right?

But the minute I moved, my body took on a mind of its own. Snaking my hands across her stomach, I drew her closer into my chest. When I glanced down, the arches of her perfect hand-sized boobs peeked out the front of her low-cut shirt. They taunted me, begged me to touch them. *No.* I snapped my eyes shut. *Don't go there.*

Problem was, I already had.

FUCK!

I wanted to scream, shout, push her away, run, touch every inch of her, taste her, hold her so close until I was even more delirious than I was now. Confusion thundered and clattered around inside my head, ripping it in two. *Why?* The scent of her skin was a gazillion times more potent than the bourbon and drugs I'd swallowed. Why did girls have to smell so good? *No.* Why did Tia smell so good?

She swayed slowly from side to side.

I resisted, fought with all my might, clenched my teeth, then ... followed her lead.

As the partygoers around us jumped and bounced to the beat, we danced in slow motion. Locked in a tiny trippy bubble, I ignored the world around us.

In perfect sync, we stepped in time to the music. Sweeping and roaming my hands across the soft smooth skin of her stomach, I tickled her. Her tummy muscles flinched and quivered.

She rolled her hips against mine, brushing and pressing her butt into my crotch. Tilting my hips, I drove my strained hard-on against her ass. There was no denying the effect she had on me. *Crap. This wasn't good.*

"Hmm." The moan that fell from her lips only made me harder.

She slid her hand down my thigh then squeezed it, digging her short nails into my flesh. "I like the way you dance."

Were we moving? I didn't know what was happening anymore.

She spun to face me. Her breath was too sharp and short. Our gazes met. Fire and doubt blazed in the depths of her eyes, just like it burned in the back of my brain. As I circled my thumbs across the bare flesh of her hips, heat blazed beneath my fingertips. She placed her hands on my chest, then ran them over my shoulders.

This ... wasn't nothing. This wasn't normal.

She shouldn't be this close. Shouldn't be holding me. Touching me. Devouring me with her gaze.

I wanted this to stop, but my body and words failed me ... because I couldn't.

Everything about her hypnotized me. Cradling the back of my neck, she combed her fingernails through my loose hair. I was trapped in a bubble, unable to burst free. Every muscle in my body screamed and burned and craved more of her. Wanted her. I shouldn't be feeling like this. Not for her. Not ever.

Why? Why her?

Anguish crushed my heart as I pressed my forehead against hers and whispered, "Tia?"

"Just dance with me." Her voice was a breathy whisper laced with too much heat. The tension in her body was wound as tight as mine.

The problem was, I didn't want to just dance. My gaze fell to her lips. So perfect and pink. I wanted to taste them. Put an end to this insanity.

Her hand ran down my back, leaving shivers in its wake. She clutched my ass and drew our groins closer together. She moved and rocked and gyrated against me. *Fuck!* Every cell in my body had come alive. *She* made me feel alive. Something I hadn't felt in months. Something I'd never experienced with a woman.

I'd never thought that this would be possible. It scared the living shit out of me.

She lifted her chin. Her lips hovered an inch from mine. The flames in our entwined breaths were enough to ignite the building. "Lewis? . . . Please . . . kiss me."

The want in her voice struck the center of my chest. The music thrummed like loud gongs inside my head. My heart pounded so hard against my ribs they were close to cracking.

I dug my fingers into her hips. My brain said no; my body said yes.

Fuuuuuck! I couldn't take this anymore.

All my restraint. My resolve. My control. Everything about who I was . . . snapped.

"You'll be the death of me." I cupped the back of her head and drew her lips to mine.

She moaned against my mouth, weakening my knees. My world tipped on its axis. *Fuck.* The sweet taste of bourbon on her lips was my undoing. I kissed her, unable to stop. The moment my tongue flicked, touched, and dueled with hers, jolts of electricity shocked every nerve ending in my body. Her soft licks and playful teases turned into a hot, fiery hunger. No one had ever tasted so divine.

In a haze, I got lost in her kisses. I devoured and savored each mind-blowing one. So soft. Sweet. Sexy. And such a fucking turn-on. A new ache grew hotter inside me, one of lust and desire.

Her hands knotted into my hair and tugged me forward. "I have wanted to kiss you from the moment we met."

Something hammered deep inside my head, something like *stop*, but the fog blocked all reasoning and sense. "Hope I didn't disappoint you."

"Definitely not." As she slid her sore knee up the outside of my thigh, she rocked her hips against mine, pressing and rubbing her crotch into my zipper.

Sweet motherfuck—but crap. Was her foot hurting? I ran my hand around her thigh and caught beneath her leg. "You okay?" I whispered against her lips. Had she had enough dancing? We should stop. Yes, we should stop.

In a fucking hot minute.

"Oh yeah. I'm good." She crushed her lips to mine, stealing my breath. Our kisses were the hottest I'd ever had. Full of fire and way too much sizzle. Easing my hand toward her ass, my fingertips blazed against the silky fabric of her dress pants. I smiled against her lips. "I like the feel of your pants."

"I like what's in yours." She drove her hips against me, gyrating and rubbing harder. *Shit.* My hard-on ached, threatening to burst from its confines. I hadn't been this turned on in months. Heightened by the ecstasy intoxicating my system, I was caught in this mad rush.

I wanted more.

Ignoring the mass of dancers around us, I trailed kisses

down the side of her neck. Her head fell to the side giving me a clear path to her soft skin. As I licked and nipped her flesh, I made my way toward her ear. "You taste so good."

"Shh. Just kiss me," she murmured. Curling her hands through my hair, she pulled my lips back to hers.

My God, I was on fire, burning from the inside out. I ran my hands up her back, down her arms, then clutched her butt, pressing her tidy body against mine. *So good.* I slipped my hands onto her waist, then ran them slowly up and down her sides. She arched toward me as if wanting to get closer and closer. I'd never wanted to touch every inch of someone so badly. I slid my hand toward her breast and teased my thumb across the lower arch. She didn't stop me. So, I didn't. Easing my palm upward, I skimmed my fingertips over her hardened nipple. Her breath hitched. Her lips parted. As I took the weight of her breast in my hand, I squeezed it gently. *Oh, wow.* So firm, yet squishy, yet so fucking hot.

A wicked smile curled across her sexy lips. "You can touch me anywhere. I won't say no."

My mind was blown enough for one night. "You shouldn't get high."

She covered my hand with hers and held it against her boob. "You shouldn't stop."

I was a lost cause. I couldn't get my brain to tell my body to quit this even if I tried.

Her lips found mine again. I drowned in our kisses. The drugs held me by the balls. This night hadn't gone to plan. The consequences flickered through my mind. *Fuck . . . this is Cole's sister.* Confusion twisted every fiber of my body and hurtled through my skull. *She's a girl.* But the swipe of Tia's tongue against mine swept the turmoil aside. Sweating and grinding against each other, we moved as one. Dancing. Touching. Kissing. As my hand slid down her back and onto her bare flesh,

I swear I heard a sizzle.

The partygoers crowded around us. Some danced. Some made out. Some seemed too drunk to care. Tia and I were in our own little world that was getting hotter by the second.

She cupped my cheek, hooked my messy, damp hair behind my ear. "You make me feel *everything. Everywhere.* I've been dead for too long."

The undercurrent of pain in her tone hit me in the chest. I'd been the same. Numb. Lost. But she'd awoken something in me that I didn't understand. "This wasn't what I had in mind tonight."

"Me either." She kissed me hard as she swayed on her feet.

I glided my hands over her toned arms. Heat swirled beneath my fingertips. I could touch her arms, caress them, feel them all day long. But kissing her lips was something completely different—a whole new level of heaven. They molded to mine, and each nip, bite, taste, lick, and soul-consuming touch was hot enough to melt the Arctic.

"Lewis?" she murmured against my lips. "I want you."

Her hand disappeared from my back and slid between us. She ran it along the length of my zipper and cupped my rock-hard cock through my jeans.

My muscles tensed. Oh, dragging her to the restrooms and having those sweet lips wrapped around my cock . . .

NO!

What the fuck?

Panic gripped every inch of my body. My head spun faster and faster.

I squeezed my eyes shut to block Tia. The music. The fire in my veins.

She reached for my zipper, but I grabbed her wrist. Fear seized my heart.

I yanked my lips away from hers. The back of my eyes

burned. "Shit. Shit. *Shit.* I'm sorry. I can't do this."

Her mouth gaped. Disappointment and confusion and hurt welled in her eyes.

Snapping out of my daze, I charged past her and headed back to our table.

"Lewis. Wait. What's wrong?" She limped and staggered after me.

"Tia. Please." I raked my fingers through my hair. "We shouldn't have done that."

"We did nothing wrong."

"Everything about this is wrong. Can we just go home?"

She caught my arm. "Talk to me."

"Fuck, Tia. Enough." My heart constricted. My head throbbed. My balls wanted to explode. Every part of me ached. *I fucking kissed a girl.* Not in some party dare. But a girl who'd left me questioning everything about myself. "I need to get out of here. Are you coming or not?"

"Fine." She grabbed her clutch off her table and waved at Pedro for him to follow. "This isn't over."

"Oh, yes, it is." I stormed over to the cloakroom, collected our belongings, and led her out of the club.

Before I lost my sanity, this was over.

So over.

Fuck!

Chapter 14

LEWIS

"ARRRRRRGH!" I screamed at the blazing morning sun as I sped toward Flint's house in Cole's black Corvette. Winding through the hills, I struggled to draw breath. I hadn't slept a wink. Last night, my kiss with Tia at the club had gotten out of control. It had gone beyond being high, drunk, and entranced by the music . . . It had been *her*. Her scent. Her laugh. Her touch. My head and heart were locked in an unrelenting battle.

Fuck.

How could I have kissed . . . no, not just kissed . . . made out with her? Tia had turned me on. My balls still ached, even after jerking off when I'd gotten home. I'd never questioned being gay. Nothing made sense anymore. I needed to set my head straight.

The only way to do that was with music.

With Flint away, I let myself into his house with the key and security code he'd given me and charged into the music room. I grabbed my bass and plugged it in. Frustration fed every strum, every pluck, every chord. I slapped the shit out of my strings. I couldn't strike them hard enough as I churned out heavy tracks by the Foo Fighters, Everhide, and the Red Hot Chili Peppers. The tangled wires in my head tightened. Grinding my teeth together, I played harder and harder. Louder and louder. *Strum. Strum. Strum.*

Every breath ripped my lungs. *What have I done? What is wrong with me?* Tia was Cole's sister, for fuck's sake. My lips still hurt from kissing her so hard. My scalp still tingled from where her fingers had knotted in my hair. My skin still burned from her touch.

Morphing into one of my own compositions, I hammered out the tune. No matter how much angry energy I poured into playing, my head thudded and thudded and thudded like a gazillion heavy metal drummers pounded on their snares all at once.

I've never been so frustrated,
Infatuated.
Confused and elated.
Is what I'm feeling just an illusion?
Am I lost in the delusion?
I want to scream and shout,
Then soar through the clouds.
I want to kiss your mouth,
Kick you out of my house.
Make love to you in bed,
Then wish this feeling would end.

Love has me in a world of confusion.
Is this all just an illusion?
Am I lost in a delusion?

"Hey? You okay?" Flint's groggy voice drifted across the room.

My breath stabbed my lungs as I spun around. *Shit!* My head ached as I tried to pack the turmoil tormenting my brain into the pit of my stomach, but thoughts of last night kept bombarding me. "Um . . . sorry. I didn't think anyone was here."

"It's okay. Our plans changed." In his pajama T-shirt and boxer shorts, Flint grabbed a stool and sat beside my amp. "Sutton's friend Maddy is in town for a quick visit. They're catching up today." Sutton constantly raved on about her best friend, Madison. She was an actress too and filmed her show in Vancouver. She came home every other weekend to see her mom, go to events, and catch up with friends.

I wiped my hand over my face, searching for some composure but failed. "I didn't mean to wake you."

"What's happened?"

Lowering my chin, I strummed out a low bassline. It matched the ache in my chest. "I'm still trying to figure that out."

"Wanna talk about it?"

Nausea flooded my gut. Days out from the launch of our single, this could blow up everything I'd worked hard for. The guys could kick me to the curb. But I wasn't going to lie. "Not really, but yeah." I put my bass on the stand and headed over to the sofas. Flint joined me.

Taking a seat opposite him, I leaned forward, resting my elbows on my knees. Where did I begin? "Last night at the club, Tia and I had a moment."

"A what?" Flint rubbed his eyes, his cheek, then his chin, as if still trying to wake up. "You and Tia? What kind of moment?"

"We had a lot to drink. The music was pumping. We slipped a molly and hit the dance floor. You know that moment when you're high and the beat takes over you and every sensation is heightened? It was so crowded. Tia and I were dancing. Close. *Too* close." Bile rose up my throat, adding to the sickening taste that was already in my mouth. "And . . . we kissed."

"You kissed Tia?" Disbelief rocked his tone. Then . . . he laughed. "Aren't you into dudes?"

The pounding in my head throbbed harder. That wasn't the reaction I'd expected. "Yes. I am. Absolutely."

"Well then, I wouldn't worry about it." He leaned back, straightening a cushion behind him. "We've all done crazy shit under the influence of drugs and booze."

How could he be so chill when I was losing my shit? "But you don't understand." My blood pressure still hovered in the danger zone. "Ever since I've met Tia, there's been this vibe between us. I can't shake it. It's not normal. It's not right. It's not me."

"Are you overthinking this? Or, oh shit . . ." Flint's eyes widened. "Did you fuck her?"

"No." But God, I'd come close to dragging her into the restrooms and having my way with her. I'd been turned on before, but with Tia, my whole body had ignited. I swallowed hard, willing my gut to settle. "I've never been into women. The only time I've kissed a girl was at college in a dare to win twenty bucks. I've only ever been into men." I'd known I was gay since I was twelve, if not before. I had my first kiss at fifteen. Dan had been in the band I'd played in at school. One afternoon, in my basement, our other friends had left to head home for the day. I'd been nervous as hell. So was he. We'd been touching and flirting with each other for weeks. But that fumbling, awkward kiss had been right. That kiss had set me alight. That kiss had led from one hot moment to another and in the heat of it all, we'd gone the whole way. I'd never looked back.

Flint's eyebrows shot upward. "You've never slept with a woman, just to experiment?"

"No. Never. I've never been attracted to women." I squeezed my eyes shut and shook my head. Visions of Tia danced behind my closed eyelids. No. No. *No!* "I ran away from home when I was sixteen because I was gay. I've always been gay."

"Wait . . .what?" Flint held up his palm. "You said you left home to live with your Pop, not run away."

My heart constricted and cracked. *Ran away. Left home. It's all the same to me.* "It's a time in my life I want to forget." But I'd never be able to erase the look of fear and hate in my mother's eyes when she'd busted me making out with Dan a few months later . . . nor the sting of my father's belt across my ass. "My parents are homophobic, conservative, religious, narrow-minded people. I ran away to avoid conversion therapy school. They wanted to send me to a reprogramming facility to change my sexual orientation."

"Holy fuck." The blood drained from Flint's face. "I didn't think conversion schools still existed."

"Yep, they do." That cold October night I'd left home, fourteen years ago, was still crystal clear in my mind, like it had happened yesterday. "The night before I was supposed to leave with the pastor, I grabbed my packed duffel bag, stole one hundred dollars out of my old man's wallet, and caught a bus to Brooklyn. I've never looked back. I had to leave. I didn't want to end up like my oldest brother, Lee. He's gay. The minute my parents caught him kissing a guy, they shipped him off to some horrid school."

"You dirty, sick boy!" The disgust in my father's tone when he'd beaten Lee still rattled in my ears.

As I glanced at Flint, my breath shuddered through my chest. "The school brainwashed Lee into thinking he was straight. They made him believe that being gay was deviant behavior. They'd fried his mind. He was never the same when he came home. My parents forced him to marry some chick they knew through a family at church. He's lived in an unhappy hell for fifteen years with a wife and had two kids because he's afraid to be his true self. He's still gay. I swear he is. I didn't want to face the same fate he did."

Lee was one of my three siblings I kept in touch with. The

other three held the same views as my parents, so we had nothing to do with each other.

Confusion rippled across Flint's brow. "What has this got to do with Tia?"

"WE KISSED!" Frustration elevated my tone. "For the first time in my life, I've questioned who I am. I'm into men, not women. My parents would be ecstatic if I ended up with a chick. I don't want them to be right. How fucked up is that?" *Fuck!* I'd had nothing to do with my folks for fourteen years. Not since Pop made me call them when I arrived in Brooklyn, to let them know I was safe. They'd told me to never step foot inside their house again. I'd been burned by their lack of love and rejection. Scarred from being disowned. Now, I felt nothing for them. *Fuck 'em.*

"Lewis." Flint's ice-blue eyes reflected the anguish that had lodged in my chest. "I don't think one kiss will alter who you are overnight. So stop stressing. But life changes. I can certainly vouch for that. So what if you're into men, and now into women as well. Maybe you're like David on *Schitt's Creek*—you're '*into the wine, not the label*.' Maybe you were just fucking high and had a bit of crazy fun. But at the end of the day, does it matter who you end up with? Love is love, right?"

"Yes. Of course, love is love." I slumped back in the sofa. But was I as narrow-minded as my parents if I couldn't accept the possibility that happiness could come in a different package? Was I now bisexual? *Shit.* I was too hungover for this crap. "I just never thought I'd end up in this position. I'm a grown man. I should be able to handle this crap instead of being freaked out."

Flint scratched his stubble. "I'd probably do the same thing if I'd made out with a man. But take a breath and chill. It's okay. In the last six months, you've lost loved ones, moved across the country, and started a new life. You've been going through some heavy shit. So has Tia. Maybe you've just connected over life changes. Don't read too much into it."

Flint's calmness and understanding eased a fraction of the pressure in my skull. I wouldn't have read anything into this issue with Tia if I honestly didn't *feel* something for her, but I did. And I didn't know how to process that. "She's just messed with my head."

"Tia will do that." Flint puffed air through his nose. "She probably tried to kiss you just to see if you would. She'd do anything to cause a stir. She's always been like that."

I hadn't gotten that impression, but I hadn't known her for long. "It wasn't some joke. But I messed up." As I stared out the big window into the garden, I rubbed the back of my neck. I had to prepare for any fallout this may have caused. "I'm sorry I broke the dibs rule. I don't want to cause problems in the band or be kicked out."

"Oh yeah, Cole will be pissed." Worry sifted through his eyes, but then he half-grinned and lifted his chin. "I should have a go at Tia for breaking the rules, not you. But listen . . ." He leaned forward and spoke with a soft tone that loosened some of the knots in my gut. "You're fine. We joke about the dibs rule, but we're not teenagers anymore. You can't help who you're attracted to or who you fall for. We'd never dictate who you could and could not date. The stupid dibs rule was an attempt to avoid hurting each other, but trust me, it hasn't worked." He rubbed his palms together, back and forth. Back and forth. "But Tia is like a sister to me. I'll always look out for her. So, is this what you're stressing about? Are you actually into her?"

Closing my eyes, I willed the fog in my brain to disappear. I couldn't deny that there was something between us, but it went beyond questioning my sexuality. Opening my heart to even the possibility of love had me breaking out in a cold sweat. I'd been burned badly. Falling hard for Emilio who hadn't felt the same way for me as I had for him had left a deep hole in my chest that would never heal. I'd promised myself to not let my heart lead me astray, and that was exactly what it was trying to do. Was I into Tia? *Yes ... no ... maybe ...* "No. I'm not." *Liar.*

Flint shrugged a shoulder. "Then we've got nothing to worry about, right?"

Cole stormed into the room and headed toward us. "Oh, we have a fuckload to worry about." Slip and Tia followed him.

As I stole a quick glance at Tia, my skin prickled. *I'm sorry* darkened her eyes.

But Cole drew closer.

I shuffled to the edge of the seat and tensed. I was no coward. If Cole wanted to deck me for kissing his sister, so be it. He couldn't make me feel any crappier than I already did.

But he stopped behind Flint and jammed his hands onto his hips. "Fuck."

Flint leaned back and looked over his shoulder at Cole. "This about last night?"

"You bet your ass it is," Cole seethed.

That wasn't good. Nor was the murderous fire in Cole's eyes.

Nausea pooled in the pit of my stomach. Was my time with The Flintlocks over?

Just because I'd kissed Tia?

Fuck.

I took a deep breath and prepared myself for the worst.

Chapter 15

LEWIS

"This is all over the Internet." Cole ripped his cell phone out of his shorts and shook it at me. "Someone had a phone in that club last night and posted photos of you two online. The media are going to throw this in our face when they research your past." He turned to Tia, who made her way toward the sofas with Slip. Worry etched into Cole's brow. "They'll drag your name through the mud, Tee. I don't want to see you hurt again."

Wait. What? I closed my eyes. My head throbbed. This wasn't about me? . . . Or the kiss? This was about protecting Tia?

"Will someone please tell me what the fuck is going on?" Slip flopped onto the sofa next to Flint. "Why was I called to an emergency meeting at this ridiculous hour?"

I wrung my hands together, jiggled my leg, and kept my eyes on Cole, who still looked hellbent on leaping over the sofa and pounding me with a gazillion punches. There was no point in lying to Slip. Flint would tell him anyway. "Tia and I got high . . . and kissed last night."

"No, we made out like wild, ravenous animals," Tia said saucily as she sank onto the seat beside Slip. She wasn't helping ease the situation.

"You *what?*" Slip's eyebrows shot skyward.

Cole growled, balled his hands, and paced behind them. "I had to leave Violet's for this. My cell phone wouldn't stop pinging with media alerts."

Sweat broke out on the back of my neck. I'd never hit the headlines for kissing someone before. This was another first. A first for all the wrong reasons.

Slip, however, laughed and hooked his arm around Tia's shoulders. "You cheeky little devil."

Tia raised one sexy shoulder. "It was some hot fun—"

That was an understatement. "But it shouldn't have happened." I slapped my hand across my chest. "Tia, I apologize. Things got out of hand. It won't happen again. As I just told Flint, I've never wanted to change or play on different teams— not since I ran away from home."

But as I caught her scent, I dropped my baseball bat, missed the ball and got struck out. I didn't know what team I was on anymore.

"It's okay." She tucked her shiny hair behind her ear. "We were high. Drunk. Shit happens."

How could she be so calm about this?

Or was she fucking acting?

She softened her voice. "I . . . I didn't know you ran away from home."

Cole stopped in his tracks. As he stared at me, his expression morphed from tensed turmoil to stressed concern. His shoulders slouched, and his tone dialed down a notch. "You ran away? Why?" He joined us on the sofas, taking a seat next to me. I told them everything—why I'd run away from home, about my family, and how I'd never meant to cause any issues. "Tia, I truly am sorry about last night."

"Think nothing of it." Leaning forward, and giving me an

eyeful of her cleavage in her low-cut T-shirt, she rubbed her ankle. We'd danced for a long time at the club; I hoped it wasn't too sore. Her tits jiggled as she massaged her heel. "You're not the first guy I've made out with."

Don't look at her boobs. Don't look. Don't look. Don't look.

She winked at me, and my pulse quickened. The air between us hummed and warped, as usual. *Shit.* I swallowed the dry lump in my throat. "But you're the first girl I've ever kissed like that."

"I'm honored. Flattered. But maybe next time we go out, we shouldn't get high." She glided her fingers over her ankle in slow, sensual strokes.

How did she make that look so freaking sexy? My fingers twitched, wanting to take over. I remembered how soft her bare skin felt, how warm she was to touch. *Wait . . . next time?* "No, no drugs" was all I could utter.

Slip pointed his palms toward heaven. "Yes. The old Tia is alive."

I didn't know the old Tia, but I couldn't deny last night had been fun for a few fevered minutes.

Cole shook his head. He sucked in a deep breath and glared at her. "Tee, this isn't good publicity for any of us."

"Lewis and I just kissed, not fucked." Fire flashed in Tia's eyes. "We're both single. We did nothing wrong. We'll handle whatever crap the media have said or will say about him being gay and me, a troublemaker. I've had much worse shit printed online about me and done much crazier things." Her voice came out strong, but an undercurrent of stress rippled beneath the surface. "If someone gets in my face about this, I'll just tell them to piss off, like I always do. It's none of their goddamn business. I don't want to cause problems, but you guys should know I can't go anywhere without it hitting the fucking headlines."

I slipped my cell phone out of my jeans' pocket and searched the Internet for images of us at the club. Grainy, dark pictures swamped several sites. There was no hiding or denying it was us. So much for her disguise. Bold headlines blazed beneath the newsfeeds: '*Tia Tanner Burned Up the Dance Floor with Mystery Man*,' '*Tia Tanner On Fire at Emerald Destruction*,' '*Another Tia Tanner Scandalous Affair*.' I didn't want us to be the cause of online ridicule or see her upset. Hopefully, this gossip would die quickly. "Tia, don't be sorry. You're right. We did nothing wrong. If asked, drunken fun was all it was."

A slinky smile inched across her lips as she thumbed over her shoulder toward the window. "Well then, you want to get wasted again, come down to the Chinese Theatre on Hollywood Boulevard, and make out some more? We could have some fun and create more hype for the album."

She didn't have to make jokes. She didn't have to lie and hide the fact the gossip had upset her. The press was the least of my worries. My sanity was a completely different matter.

"Tia, no." Cole rubbed his brow and shook his head. "Leave Lewis alone. The poor guy is traumatized enough."

That was one way of putting it. My brain was still spiraling.

"I'm just pissed this even happened." Cole's voice snagged in his throat. "I trusted you to have a night out with Tia, not hit the gossip pages. I understand this has shocked and upset you. That it's not who you are. But don't mess with my sister. You hear me?"

Panic slithered through my veins. I didn't want to thin my chances with the band any further. As I stared at Tia, I fidgeted with my signet rings and nodded . . . half-heartedly. "Yep. I can assure you, it won't happen again." I wanted to be certain, but I wasn't. I was unable to drag my eyes off her. My stomach flipped and fluttered. Kissing her had exacerbated our connection. It had made things more complicated. I was on a rocky road, unable to see where it ended or which way to turn. My growing feelings for her scared me. Was our bond so strong because we were going through so many life changes at the same time, as Flint had suggested, or was it something more? How the fuck could I find out without doing something we'd regret?

Tia lowered her chin. "Cole, it was some harmless fun. We're good." But I sensed she wasn't okay. *Shit. Neither am I.*

Flint waved his hand at me. "See? You were worried about nothing. Everyone's cool. Making out with Tia is pretty tame compared to some of the shit we've done."

Slip stretched his legs forward and crossed his ankles. "So true. You've got nothing on us, Lewis. Just about everything we've done gets splashed across the Internet. Some of the news has been good, some bad—the majority has been fabricated bullshit, but it's helped us sell millions of albums. You have to be prepared that someone, somewhere, is gonna drag you across hot coals, say shit about you, and make good fun look like a scandal."

"Yeah, but the gossip still makes you feel like shit and still hurts," Tia mumbled.

Slip rubbed her back. "Don't let it upset you, Tee. Remember, the way we handle it is to always be honest with each other. So don't stress." He dipped his chin at me, then returned his attention to Tia. "We've got your backs."

She rested her head against Slip's shoulder. "Thank you."

"I'm sure this will blow over if we keep our story straight." Some of my stresses dissipated, but the nausea and nerves didn't leave my gut. These guys truly were a rare find, but I didn't want to push the boundaries of their trust and faith in me. I was still new to the band and wasn't comfortable or secure in my position. I still had milestones to pass. They could kick me out at any time. Cole had me half out the door. The you-touch-my-sister-again-and-I'll-kill-you glares from him didn't ease my worries. "I've never had every move hit the headlines.

I'll be more careful in the future."

Flint bobbed his head. "Lewis, it's okay. But we're two days out from launch. Covering a drunken kiss will be easy, but are you okay if we tell Blake, April, and Falcon about your parents? We don't know what shit the press will have uncovered about your past or what crap they could spin in our direction during promo. We want to be prepared for anything."

Shit. I hadn't considered that my upbringing could cause a fallout. I'd never liked talking about my parents; they didn't deserve the time or breath. "Um . . . sure. I don't have anything to do with my folks anymore and vice versa. I want this launch and joining you guys to be about our music—not my personal life." My proposal to Emilio and our breakup had been discussed during our marketing meetings and media training. My past relationships and sometimes wild partying had been tame compared to these guys' reputations. "I honestly don't think I have any other skeletons in my closet."

"Alright then." Flint slapped his hands on his thighs and stood. "Since everyone is here, we may as well run through the set list again before Tuesday night. But first, I need to get out of my pajamas—that may involve a quickie with Sutton, who's still in bed—then I'll need a coffee."

"You do Sutton, I'll make coffee." Slip jumped to his feet and headed for the door. Cole and Tia followed.

"Um, Tia. You got a sec?" I rose and walked around behind the sofa.

She spun toward me. "Sure."

My pulse jumped a few bars. I had no idea what I wanted to say to her—I just wanted to make sure she was okay without the others around.

Halfway to the door, Cole stopped in his tracks. He turned to face me, and crossed his arms. He tilted his head to the side and an oh-yeah-I'm-listening smirk curled the corner of his mouth.

Flint shoved Cole on the shoulder, pushing him toward the exit. "Get out of here. Give them a minute to talk."

Cole stumbled. "But . . . but . . . I want to know what goes down."

"I know you do, but tough. Let's go."

Grinning, I puffed air through my nose. Tia was lucky to have a brother who looked out for her.

"What's up?" Pursing her lips, she shuffled toward me.

Damn. She was beautiful and rocked a pair of khaki cargo pants. I tucked my hands into the back pockets of my jeans to avoid touching her. "I want to apologize again for last night. A lot of crazy shit went down, and I should've handled the whole situation better. I just needed some time to process what happened. What shouldn't have happened."

"Lewis, you have nothing to apologize for. I'm sorry our kiss upset you so much. I don't want you to question who you are. We crossed boundaries that shouldn't have been crossed." Her shoulders slouched and too much sadness loomed in her eyes. "It was just nice to let loose for a night. For a few hours, I didn't have to pretend that I'm not in pain. I didn't have my brother breathing down my neck, being overprotective. I didn't have to watch every word I said, like I do around Sutton and the girls at work. I don't want them to know my heart isn't in our show. For a few moments, I had fun . . . with you."

An ache jolted through my chest. She hid so much from everyone, hid behind her jokes and laughs. I hated that she was hurting so much. The fact I'd helped her have a few hours away from her problems made me feel a touch better but not much. I half smiled. "It was a tortured fun."

She took a tiny step forward, leaving two feet of space between us. "I got to dance with the hottest guy in the club and had one of the hottest kisses I've ever had in my life. My panties are still wet."

My dick twitched. *Oh geez. Boner alert.* Images of dirty dancing with her last night flickered through my mind, our bodies gyrating, touching, moving as one. *Too hot.* I swallowed the huge lump in my throat. "We did burn up the dance floor."

"We did."

My gaze swept across her lips. I should step away. Should put more distance between us. But my feet remained glued to the spot. Lowering my voice, I whispered, "We just can't do that again." I wanted to believe the words that fell from my mouth. No . . . I had to believe them. I had to.

Her gaze drilled into me, hammering my head with hard blows. The fire that lingered between us sizzled. "Are you sure last night was nothing but drunken fun? That we should just put our kiss down to being nothing more than a crazy antic?"

"Yes." I lowered my chin and winced. Who was I kidding? "But the thing is . . . it wasn't, was it? You feel something for me, don't you?" *Like I do for you.*

"Lewis, I'm trying not to." The anguish in her voice reflected the same level of agony that had set into every muscle in my body. "You've made it clear where you stand. I respect that. I'll make every effort to stop teasing, touching and flirting with you."

Shit. I liked it when she did those things. But she was right. We were both at fault. Going forward, we had to be more careful and control ourselves. "Me too. Can we reset . . . again?"

"I'd like that."

"Cool. We'll be okay." I caught her arm and pulled her into my embrace, giving her a warm hug. *So much for no touching.* With my head resting against hers, I circled my hands over her back and held her close. *Mmm. So good.* "Let's just put last night behind us."

"Yeah."

But she didn't let go.

Neither did I.

Within a heartbeat, the silence in the room wrapped around us, chaining me to her.

Crap!

Her heartbeat strummed in time with mine.

Her hands pressed against my shoulder blades, sending warmth rippling across my skin beneath my T-shirt.

Closing my eyes, I nuzzled into her hair. The scent of her shampoo filled my senses, rushing in hot waves from my head down to my toes. The pounding in my brain resumed, crashing against my skull. I stilled, afraid to take a breath. "Tia?"

Drawing back, she placed her fingertips across my lips. "Shh. It's okay. You have the band to worry about—not me. Last night is forgotten."

I followed every move of her gorgeous lips. Lips I'd tasted and, for some fucked up reason, wanted to taste again. It took all my willpower to catch her hand and lower it to her side. "I'm not sure I'll forget in a hurry but yes."

She nodded, but longing still darkened her eyes. "Good, because this thing between us . . . is over. It's nothing."

Dizziness swam through my brain. My fingers twitched to hold her again.

She leaned in close; her lips hovered an inch from mine. Her hot breath sent goose bumps shooting across my skin and shivers down my arms. "What you're *feeling* . . . for *me* . . . is nothing."

My heart beat loud, like it had been plugged into an amp.

She took two steps back. For a split second, our eyes met. The electricity between us sparked and crackled. But then, she turned. As she limped toward the door, she swayed her sexy ass. *Damn.* Without looking back, she slipped out of the room.

Fuck!

I clutched a handful of my hair. My dick throbbed. My balls

ached.

This *nothing* was something.

She knew it. I knew it.

But what the fuck was I going to do about it?

Chapter 16

TIA

After having coffee at Flint's place, Sutton dropped me off at home. She'd invited me to join her and Maddy for lunch, but I had scenes to read.

I made it through one script before concentration eluded me. Stretching out on my bed, I grabbed my cell phone and surfed the Internet, searching for every story about last night. Acid churned in my gut as I read the online gossip articles. They all insinuated I was back to my old wild ways now I was single. *Nope* . . . That Tia was dead.

But every time a picture of Lewis and me filled the screen, a fevered rush shot through my system. The heat from his kiss still lingered on my lips. This morning, the embers between us hadn't gone out. I'd had complicated, messy relationships before, but this thing with Lewis was a whole new level of fucked up.

All logic and reason in my brain computed the facts. *He's gay. He isn't going to change. I don't want him to. Move the fuck on.*

That was what I planned to do. It was time to find a new

direction. Maybe a new career path. But who'd want to employ an injured twenty-three-year-old? The thing was, outside of acting and stunt work, I had no idea what interested me.

While the guys were away on promo for a month, I needed to do some serious soul-searching and Lewis-vibe-killing.

Near midnight, when he and Cole hadn't arrived home, I lay in bed, unable to sleep. A new ludicrous, hypothetical nonsense of being with Lewis tortured me, causing more havoc than a sixteen-car pileup. Would I be willing to take a chance on him if he was open to the idea of a relationship?

My head was quick to slap some don't-be-stupid sense into me.

There were too many reasons not to even contemplate the notion—like my brother, the band, my messed up self and past relationship failures. My heart was still too damaged thanks to Phil and Rhett. Lewis was fucking hot and fun to hang out with, but I had too many underlying reservations and doubts. I didn't want to be a temporary fix, a bit of fun, or a wild fling before he saw logic and realized he was still into men. That he loved them more than he could ever love me.

But what if he *was* into me?

Ergh! Stop. He isn't.

I needed sleep.

Maybe some warm milk would help.

After slipping on my robe, I clambered downstairs and headed toward the kitchen. But halfway across the glossy tiled floor, I stopped. Changing course, I shuffled down the hallway toward Cole's music room. I placed my palm on the door and let out a slow breath. Turning the handle, I pushed the door open, stepped inside, and switched on the downlights. Cole's huge Pearl drum kit filled the far corner, the golden cymbals glistening in the soft light. His desk was neat and tidy—not a pen or piece of paper was out of place. On the black two-seat sofa, the red cushions were set perfectly in line, and on the shelves, each cord, cable, and mic were stowed in an orderly pile. *Neat freak.*

I eased onto the sofa, drew a throw over my legs, and scanned the photos of Cole and the guys on the wall, then the framed one on the desk. I grabbed it, sat back down, and ran my fingertips over the glass.

Over Phil.

Heartache crushed my chest.

Why did I always fall for the wrong men? Complicated men. Men with too much fucking baggage. Men who weren't into women.

Phil. Rhett. Lewis.

I can pick 'em.

The door flew open. I jumped. My heart slammed against my ribs. "Holy shit, Cole. You scared the crap out of me." I hadn't heard the car enter the garage.

"Same." He sucked in a ragged breath. "What are you doing in here?"

I slumped into the sofa, questioning myself. "Trying to sort shit out."

He eased onto the seat beside me. "And you're doing that by holding a photo of us playing at The Forum?"

In the image, the guys pumped their fists in the air. Huge grins lit their faces. The last show of their second nationwide tour had been wild. Most of the after-party was still a blurry haze in my memory, thanks to too much alcohol. I hugged the photo against my chest. "I miss Phil."

"We all do." He smoothed his hand down the back of my hair. "Every fucking day."

"I'm glad you found someone to play with you."

"Lewis is certainly . . . different. Annoying. Talented. Cool fun . . . and messed up like the rest of us."

"Yeah, he is," I whispered, then waved toward the drums. "Are you gonna play now?" He often did that when he couldn't sleep.

"No. I'm done for the day." Cole rubbed the back of my head. "Lewis crashed. I was looking for you. Are you okay? After last night?"

Nope. But I would be. "Hopefully what happened will be old news by tomorrow."

"I doubt it. We've talked to Blake and April and have a meeting in the morning to work out a plan to deal with any fallout during the launch."

"I feel bad for Lewis. This throws him in the middle of a shit fest."

"He honestly didn't seem to care about the gossip. Kissing you worried him more than anything that has been printed online."

"Yeah." I picked at my thumbnail. "I'm sorry about that."

Cole placed his elbow on the back of the sofa then rested his head against his hand. "Was that all last night was? Some drugged-up, drunken fun?"

I'd witnessed the strain broken relationships had caused within the band; I didn't want to cause any more. And my issues with Lewis were mine to deal with, not Cole's. So I lied. "Yep. We had a good time and got carried away. That was all."

"Okay." He lowered his gaze and scratched at a stain on the sofa. "Because I don't want you to get messed up over someone who doesn't feel the same way as you do." The drop in his voice caught me off-guard. "I don't want that shit to happen to you."

My heart hurt. I hated how much his past had hurt him. "Are you talking about Aidan?" *Or Priah, his ex? Or someone else?* The list could be long.

Sadness clouded Cole's eyes. "Yeah."

"What happened wasn't your fault." In his senior year, Cole

had been into Aidan. Cole was adamant it never went beyond a couple of months of kissing and groping. I'd caught them making out a few times. But Cole was into women.

When he ended things with Aidan, Aidan had struggled with the breakup. Aidan had refused to believe it was over, was terrified of coming out, and afraid of his abusive parents. He'd OD'd and died a few years ago. Cole blamed himself for not staying in regular contact after high school. Losing a friend had cut up all the guys.

But fresh concerns pummeled my head.

"Is this what this is about? Are you into Lewis?" *Like I needed more fucking complications.*

"Ha. No," he chuckled. Relief flooded through me like a tsunami. "My experimental days are well and truly behind me. I was talking about you. I worry about you. I don't want to see you get hurt."

"I won't. It was nothing." Except when I closed my eyes, I could still feel Lewis's breath on my face. Feel his arms around me. Feel his lips against mine. I picked at a loose thread on the cuff of my silky robe. "After I left Flint's today, was he okay?"

"He seemed to be. He played hard, joked around, then had a fair few beers at dinner, hopefully to put what happened between you two behind him." Seriousness set into Cole's tone. "Tee, he's too fucking good. We don't want to lose him, so don't piss him off, or upset him, or fuck with his head like last night did. The milestones we've set are a two-way street. If he hates us or isn't happy, he could leave. We don't want that to happen."

Shit. I hadn't contemplated that.

"Don't mess around with him." He waggled a finger at me. "We don't need more problems in the band. We're finally in a good place. The shit is behind us."

I wasn't so sure about that. There was too much dirty laundry still laying around. I guess they all just wanted to bury their secrets, put the past behind them, and move forward. I should take that advise onboard. "Cole, you've nothing to worry about. Lewis and I are just friends."

"Good." Cole cradled the back of my head, drew me forward, and kissed the top of my scalp. "I'm sorry I got pissed at you. I don't want either of you to get hurt. But on the flip side, I was also stoked. You went out clubbing. You had fun. You danced. Just next time, don't stick your tongue down Lewis's throat."

"I won't." I play-punched him in the arm. But forgetting Lewis's kisses would be hard, if not impossible.

Cole jutted his chin at me. "You need to get out of the house more often."

"I will." *Time to focus on me, right?* "After this week, when you guys are away, I'm gonna make time to catch up with Chloe and Duke, have drinks with the girls after work, and go out to dinner with my agent."

"Awesome."

I slapped and rubbed his knee. "Are you ready for the launch, promo, and getting back on stage? Ready to deal with the shit that comes with touring?"

"Hell yeah." Fire ignited in Cole's eyes. "I can't wait to hit the road. It'll be strange without Phil. But I'm not complaining that Slip and I now get more girls to choose from. Having Lewis join us does have some advantages."

Giggling, I shoved him on the shoulder. "You're so bad."

He flicked his short hair off his forehead, and a mischievous smile curled across his lips. "Not always. Just sometimes. Just like you." He grabbed my hand and half-hugged me. "Now, are you ready to party with us at the launch on Tuesday tonight?"

"I'll be there." But I'll be laying as low as possible.

He squeezed me close. "It's going to be wicked."

I had no doubt it would be.

My guys knew how to rock!

Chapter 17

TIA

Backstage at Club Riot, the live music venue for the launch of the guy's new single, I grabbed a coffee from the catering kitchen and headed toward the foyer. Excitement skipped through the air as the club's staff and The Flintlocks' crew rushed around ensuring everything was ready for the press conference and mini show. Ashlem had gone to extremes to create hype for the release, and they'd delivered—teasers had been dropped on social media for weeks, billboards hinted at new music, and the guys had been to a multitude of music events, getting their faces in front of the cameras. Butterflies skipped through my stomach as I scanned the agenda on my cell phone again. The press conference in the venue's foyer would kick off at seven. The doors would open to ticket-holding fans at eight. The guys would take to the stage at nine, followed by a huge after-party. The single would hit the airwaves at midnight.

As I passed the open door to the dressing room, I stopped. I turned and took a few steps toward the guys to wish them luck one last time.

Everhide had flown in for the occasion. Kyle, Hunter, and

Gemma stood talking to Blake, April, and Falcon. All had cell phones in hand, no doubt going over last-minute checklists. Kara fussed over Flint's transmitter holder on the back of his belt. Penny, the guys' makeup artist, stood behind Slip's chair, straightening and styling his long hair. Cole lazed on the sofa, twirling his drumsticks, while Hayden tied his boots. *Cole, you lazy bastard.* Lexi darted around the room, taking photos. But Lewis, still not dressed for the show, paced the floor, fidgeting with his rings. He'd been nervous at sound check earlier; now, sheer terror skipped in his eyes. He mouthed *'hi'* but didn't break his stride.

Blake tucked his cell phone into his jacket pocket and dipped his chin at the guys. "Everything is ready." Circling his finger through the air, he pointed at Everhide and The Flintlocks' team. "We'll go out front and mingle with everyone. Falcon will get you when it's time for the press conference. Good luck. Have fun. We're gonna kick ass tonight."

"Hello." I waved. I wasn't sure whether anyone other than Lewis had noticed me enter the room. "I came to wish you luck too."

"Thanks, Tee." Cole jumped up to hug me, followed by Flint, Slip, and a stressed-out Lewis.

Slip glided over to the table and poured shots of vodka. "You here for one last drink, Tee?"

"No, thanks. I'm good."

As Blake, April and Falcon left the room, the guys and Everhide congregated around Slip for a drink. Before Lewis joined them, I caught his arm. "Are you okay? You look like you're gonna vomit."

Nodding, he winced and rubbed the center of his chest. "Highly possible. I haven't played a gig this big in a long time." His breaths were short and jagged. "I'm not sure I can do this. I'm worried I'll mess up. I'll forget the notes. Forget the lyrics.

Fall over."

Oh, crap. He wasn't just nervous; he had stage fright. Lewis needed to calm down or he'd pass out before he made it to the press junket. One thing I'd learned during my stunt training was how to visualize and focus. It helped execute every scene, see the outcomes, keep moving, and be prepared to adjust if things went wrong. *Hmph. I needed to apply that training to everyday life.* I took his hand and gave it a gentle squeeze. "You've got this. I've seen you play. You're incredible. You wouldn't be here otherwise."

He shook his head. "I'm not feeling it at the moment."

"You will. What's the one thing you want to achieve tonight?" *Instant fame? Sponsorship deals? Men throwing their boxer briefs at you?*

Furrows etched his brow. "Um . . . just to play well."

There was another reason why I liked him. He wasn't doing this for fame—just for his love of music. "And you will." I squeezed the side of his arm. "It won't matter if you miss a note. No one expects perfection. If you fuck up, close your eyes, take a breath, listen to the beat, and let the music guide you back to playing."

"It's not just that." He grabbed my hand and lowered it, but he didn't let go. The little tremble in his fingers matched the flutters in my stomach. "There'll be more people here tonight than I've played in front of in the past year."

Shit. Was he serious? But one thousand people was an excessive crowd for a launch. "Don't look at them." I caught his chin and our gazes locked. *Oh, yeah. He could look at me any time.* "Pick a spot on the far wall. Project any nerves toward it. If you get overwhelmed, shut your eyes and breathe." I waved at the band. "These guys have your back. Gena's got you covered on the mixer. And really, you could just stand on stage looking hot as you are, not play one single note, and everyone would fucking love you."

A small grin inched across his lips. "I'll try and remember that."

"And bear in mind . . ." I threw him a sexy smile. "I'll be watching you."

He pinched his brows together and lowered his chin. "Not helping, Tia."

"Shit. Sorry. No flirting, right?"

He grimaced and swallowed hard. Then he looked at me. A new apprehension shimmered through the silver shards in his eyes. "About that. We need to talk."

Hadn't we said everything we needed to say? If he still had concerns, I'd hear him out . . . later. I didn't want *us* to interfere with tonight. He had enough on his plate. I pulled my hand free of his and placed a finger over his lips. "Not now. This is your night. Focus. Enjoy it. Go break a leg. I'll see you after the show."

But as I headed toward the door, his gaze burned into my back.

I stole a quick glance over my shoulder and threw him a you've-got-this smile.

Flint ambled over to Lewis and handed him a shot. "What was that all about?"

Lewis raised his glass toward me. "Tips on settling the nerves. And wishing us luck."

"Here's to that." Slip joined them, slapping Lewis on the back. "But you'll be fine. Tonight, we're back in the game."

Cole stepped in beside them. They downed their shots and woohooed.

I sucked in a deep breath, filling my lungs to capacity. I was so happy for them. I'd loved and supported my brother and his band since they'd formed. They worked hard and deserved every success.

So did I.

New grit embedded into the pit of my gut. The guys had three days of promo here in LA, then they'd be gone for a month. I'd have time to work on me. I looked forward to exploring my options. But first, their launch. With almost one hundred media representatives coming tonight, I hoped the attention stayed on the band and not the commotion my kiss with Lewis had caused.

I left the dressing room and headed for the foyer. I hobbled past the rows of seating set up for the press conference and joined Sutton and her friend Maddy, who'd flown in for the night, at the bar. Hopefully, in the dim lighting and cordoned off area, surrounded by friends and family, I could avoid the reporters and cameras.

Right on time, security guards opened the venue's doors. The guests steamed in, checked off their names at the desk, grabbed their lanyards, a drink, and mingled in groups, waiting for the guys' press junket.

At seven sharp, April got the conference underway and everyone took a seat. When the guests had settled, she gave a quick summary of how the guys had met at the age of nine, lived on the same suburban street in Pasadena, and the successes they'd accomplished to date. Then her tone softened. "But last year, tragedy struck in February with the loss of the band's bassist, Phil Glover. After some time off, the boys were ready to rebuild. But who would fill Phil's shoes? . . . It took many auditions, but finally someone emerged from Brooklyn. With his music career at a crossroad, it was a destined find and perfect match. He brings a wealth of experience and unforeseen talent to the band. Please join me in giving a warm welcome to The Flintlocks—lead singer and guitarist, Flint Glover; drummer, Cole Tanner; lead guitarist, Sebastian 'Slip' Lipfield; and the newest member, bassist, Lewis King."

My heart raced as Flint led the guys into the room. The crowd cheered, whistled, and clapped as the boys posed in front of their logoed backdrop. Photographers jostled to snap shots of them; cameras flashed and flickered. Kara had outdone herself in dressing the guys. They wore coordinated but not matching outfits. Flint rocked a black leather jacket and button-down, Slip wore his token leather vest, Cole's toned arms bulged in his tight T-shirt, and Lewis stole my breath in black denim that looked like leather.

Hot damn!

Standing at the back of the crowd next to Sutton, I nudged her arm. "They look good."

"Oh, yeah." She wriggled and pouted. "I get all hot and flustered just looking at Flint."

I giggled. She had it bad for Flint.

The press jostled in their seats, waiting for question time. I didn't miss being in front of the cameras, or doing interviews, or getting dressed up. The stress levels were much lower when the focus wasn't on me. I liked that. But the night wasn't over yet. The place was crawling with media hounds.

The band settled onto chairs behind a long cloth-covered table. Lewis took a quick sip from his water and scanned the crowd. He smiled, but his shaky hands gave away his nerves.

April patted the air to quiet the guests and keep the agenda on track. "Guys, congratulations on the new single being released tonight. Flint, what can fans expect from the up-and-coming track and new album?"

"Awesome music." He flicked his long black hair off his face and smiled a sexy smile. His ice-blue eyes glinted in the bright lights. I pursed my lips to stop myself from laughing. He was such a show pony when he had to be for the band. "Having Lewis come onboard has given us a new edge. We're excited to release new music. Excited to have signed with Everhide's EH4 Records. And we're thrilled to be working with Ashlem

Entertainment."

Cole adjusted his mic. "We can't wait to hit the road over the next few weeks, visiting cities across the country. We'll be going to radio stations, appearing on TV talk shows, and performing at shopping malls and clubs. Our schedule is on our website and social accounts. Make sure y'all come see us play."

I folded my arms and leaned against a pillar at the back of the crowd. Maybe I should quit and go with them. I loved travel. Loved watching them play. *No . . . no, I can't do that.* I needed to sort out my life. Some decisions about my future had to be made sensibly and logically.

A reporter in a short-sleeve gray button-down shirt raised his hand. "So, Lewis? You're the big secret these guys have been keeping in the closet. How do you feel about making such a big jump from playing in a small Brooklyn-come-Boston bar band to a group as popular as The Flintlocks?"

Lewis leaned toward the mic and smiled his magical smile. "First of all, I came out of the closet a long time ago." Low laughter and chuckles rippled across the room. "And second? Yes, it's a big jump, but I'm ready. I was born to play with these guys."

A young male reporter with short brown hair and a tight polo shirt was quick to ask, "Are you touring the album?"

"We sure are." Slip nodded. "But more detail will be provided when the album is released in May."

Waving her fingers in the air, a Halle Berry lookalike didn't even wait for April's nod before she fired off her question. "Are you all single? I mean . . . the fans will want to know who's available and who's not?" She sat primed on the edge of her seat. Her gaze, unrelenting. My skin prickled. *Oh, yeah . . . tabloid reporter.* How did she get in here?

Flint laughed. "I'm well and truly off the market. Sutton is my girl."

Cole threw the audience a sexy, broad grin. "I'm always single."

Slip let out a nervous laugh. "Um . . . not looking at present."

My interest piqued. He'd spent way too much time texting someone recently. I'd place bets on the fact he was seeing someone, but clearly didn't want the guys to know who.

"And you, Lewis?" the reporter asked. "Some interesting photos of you and Tia Tanner surfaced on the weekend."

My breath hitched. A chill ran down my spine. Too many heads turned my way. *Shit!* I'd wanted to avoid this. But Lewis just grinned and replied with a level tone, "Tia is a good friend. We had a fun night and a little too much to drink. There's nothing more to it. I'm very single, and very gay, and for now, I'm just putting all my focus and energy into the band."

As I pasted on a sweet smile for the cameras, and the flashes flickered in my eyes, the hurt in my chest flared. I didn't need the reminder that the band came first. Or that he was into men. Or that my feelings for him had to be caged. I had a plan to do just that. Now if everyone stopped looking at me, I'd be fine. *Ergh.* I needed a stiff drink.

I abandoned Sutton and Maddy, headed for the bar, and downed two shots of bourbon.

As I grabbed a third, Gena rushed up to me. Tears streamed down her face. "Tia. I need your help. Come."

"Shit. Okay." I downed my shot and hobbled after her as quick as I could. "What's happened?"

We slipped inside the auditorium and veered toward the control booth. A few feet away, she spun to face me, wiping her tears and perspiration on her T-shirt sleeve. "Promise me you won't tell Cole and the guys."

"Tell them what?" *Crap.* Had some piece of expensive equipment been broken? Something wasn't working and couldn't be fixed in time?

"Just promise me." Her chin trembled.

"I'm not sure I can do that." I loved Gena—she'd been with the band for years, but Cole and the guys were my family. "I love my brother and if this fucks with him, sorry, no."

"Okay." Sniffling, she closed her eyes and nodded. "Just not tonight, alright?"

With an aching heart, I rubbed her arm. I hated dishing out tough love, but my guys came first. "They're on a high and about to play, then party the night away. It won't be an issue, will it?"

"I hope not." The color drained from her face as she rubbed her abdomen. "I'm pregnant."

"Oh, wow. Congratulations." *A baby?* I hadn't expected that. My ovaries twanged. Past plans to have a family with Rhett rattled my brain, but I was quick to flick them away. They were dead. *Stupid ovaries.*

"No." Her voice trembled. "It's not good. I'm sick. I can't stop throwing up."

Panicked, I glanced around the empty auditorium. The black walls, stage curtains, and floor offered no relief to the pressure rising in my chest. "Have you got someone to cover for you?" Surely Tristan, their lighting engineer, could manage. But this was a big show.

"I've called two backup crew but they're already at gigs. I don't have time to get anyone else here before the guys need to go on stage. Tristan has to monitor the lightning. Kent from the venue is tech support only; he won't run the show. Can . . . can you help, please? You've been to the rehearsals. You know the set. It's only if I need to rush to the bathroom."

"But . . ." My head spun as I scanned the huge channel mixer, the three monitors stationed throughout the booth, and the flashing audio switches. "Gena, I don't know the system well enough."

"Yes, you do." She clutched my hands. "I wouldn't ask unless

I was desperate."

I rubbed at the pressure mounting in my temples. What had happened to no stress? "Everhide is here. I'll get one of them to help."

"Tia? You can do this."

Could I? This was for Cole. I'd do anything for him. *Damn it.* "Fine. Give me a quick rundown." But I'd grab Kyle's cell number from Falcon as a backup.

"Thanks." Gena led me over to the monitors and rubbed her tummy. "I'm freaking out about being pregnant. This changes everything. I'm worried I won't be able to tour with the guys at the end of the year."

"You're having a baby, not dying."

"It feels like it." Her hand trembled as she wiped her brow.

"You'll be fine. I'm here if you need me."

"Thanks."

Thirty minutes later, ticketholders streamed into the venue and filled the auditorium. Five minutes out from showtime, Gena bolted for the restrooms.

Kyle hadn't come to help.

Shit.

I'd have to run the show.

Chapter 18

TIA

My heart thundered somewhere up near my throat. My stomach twisted and turned. Concertgoers filed past us into the auditorium and herded toward the stage. *Whoa. So many people.* I'd wanted to help Gena, not run the damn show. *Fuck.* I reread the set list. Reviewed the software settings. Ran my fingertips over the channel inputs. Everything was set.

Tristan swiveled on his chair beside me. "You got this, right?"

"Sure." Maybe . . . no . . . yes.

I shot Kyle a text. Called him. No answer. *Crap. Where is he?*

I slipped on the comms headset and adjusted the band to the correct size. Licking my dry lips, I lowered the mic into position in front of my mouth. I pressed the unmute button and checked in with Blake and Falcon backstage. "Hi. It's Tia. Is Kyle there with you?"

"Tia?" Blake hissed. "What the fuck?"

I wiped my clammy palms on my dress pants and stared at the stage. "It's okay. I got you. Gena's sick. But some help would be good."

"Kyle left with Gemma. Their daughter's ill."

Shit. "What about Hunter?"

"He's drunk with Hayden, schmoozing industry reps."

My stomach swayed. My fingers shook. But I closed my eyes and nodded. *I can do this.* "Okay. I'll run the show. I know the set. Are the guys ready?"

Radio silence.

Nothing.

Not a word.

"Blake?" I tapped the mouthpiece on my headset. "Are you there?"

Was he talking to the guys to see if they wanted to delay the concert's start time?

"Yes. Go." His terse voice came through my headset. I didn't miss the warning in his tone.

As I ran through final system checks, my ribs constricted. Why couldn't people take me seriously? I'd never mess with a show that was this big and important. I wasn't always out for a laugh. I'd changed. Life had changed. I could do this. I wanted to do this. "Alright then. On the count of three. One . . . two . . . three. Showtime."

With his eyes glued to his monitor, Tristan dimmed the lights, then pressed the button to retract the stage curtain. The packed auditorium erupted. The reverberations from their thunderous shouts, screams, and whistles vibrated across the floor, hummed through the air, and struck the center of my chest. *Oh yeah.* There it was . . . that rush, that hit of adrenaline I lived for. *Fuck.* I'd missed that.

"The guys are in position," Blake said through the headset. "Go."

I held my breath and pressed *enter* on the laptop. The projections rolled, lighting the screens at the back of the stage.

I flicked switches, turned dials, and pressed buttons.

The guys were live.

Cole's drumsticks slammed against the drums. Lights flooded the stage. Flint rushed to the front, grabbed his mic, and launched into singing their new single, "Fallen For You." Slip rocked to his left, but Lewis, on his right, stole my breath. Flicking his tousled hair, he looked straight at me.

Shit. Focus, Lewis. On something else. Not me.

I needed to concentrate too. There was no time to relax.

With music booming through the array of speakers and thudding through the amps, Flint held the crowd in the palm of his hand, zipping around the stage with his guitar or singing at his mic. Tweaking the sound mix, I lowered the reverb and modified the compression. The venue's acoustics were incredible, making my job a touch easier. But where the fuck was Gena?

By the time the guys struck the first note on the fourth song, Gena hadn't returned. I prayed she was okay. The guys had hit their hardest song to play live, the balancing of sound critical. Nerves quaked in my stomach; my fingers hovered over the mixer. With my ears tuned to every note, my eyes flitted to the guys, to the mics, to their instruments. Halfway through their complex track, Slip churned out a solo on his guitar. I amped up the volume on his audio feed, filling the room with the electric sound. Sliding the channel levers slowly, I transitioned the focus over to Cole thrashing on his drums, then I eased the balance over to Lewis strumming on his bass.

Oh yeah. He is good.

How had his last band not been a huge success with him playing bass and Hayden on drums? Two hidden talents, one brought into the spotlight thanks to Everhide . . . and now one thanks to The Flintlocks.

Flint stepped up to his mic to sing. I reset the panel and let out a deep breath. Tristan high-fived me. *Wow.* I'd nailed it.

After one more single off the album and two previously released hits, they brought the house down, blasting out the last note of the song. The standing ovation and the loud applause from the fans penetrated and pummeled my chest.

The noise. The crowd. The performance.

This ... is something. This ... is magic. It wasn't the same as pushing my body to the limit in fight scenes and action shots, but ... it was a high. A spike of adrenaline. Food for my soul.

Tristan jumped up and hugged me. "Argh. You did it. So cool."

"Yeah. Thanks." I held out my hands. "I'm still shaking."

Gena returned, green and pale even in the dim lights of the booth. "I'm so sorry. How did it go?"

I leaped from the chair and clapped my hands so quickly they were a blur. "It was amazing. Thank you."

"No. Thank you. I owe you one." She hugged me, then grabbed her purse and jacket. "I texted Blake and the guys. I'm gonna head home. I've promised I'll be at promo tomorrow."

"Okay. I'm just gonna help the crew pump out." I unplugged a cable and wound it up. I wanted to savor the high still intoxicated my veins for as long as possible. "Make sure you've got someone on standby. I can't fill in. I have to work." *Unfortunately.*

"Will do." She gave me another quick hug goodbye and headed out the door.

As I packed cords into an equipment trunk, my mind drifted to the guys' promo schedule. They'd be playing at new locations three or four times a day, plus doing interviews. Every day they'd be performing new shows, entertaining new crowds, and having new adventures. Jealousy lurked through my veins. I hated not being part of something exciting and fun on a daily basis.

An hour later, after helping Tristan and the road crew pack,

I ambled out into the foyer. The party, with more than two hundred friends, family, sponsors, influencers, VIP guests, and Ashlem executives, was in full swing. Music blared through the speakers. Alcohol flowed. Chatter filled the room. The minute I spied Cole through the mass of people, I rushed toward him and gave him a huge hug. "Ahhhh. You were amazing."

"That was so wicked." He squeezed me tight and rocked me from side to side. "I saw you at the mixer. Did you run the show?"

"Yeah. Gena wasn't well," I said as I congratulated Slip and Flint with big embraces.

"You're a lifesaver." Flint planted a sloppy kiss on my cheek. "Thank you."

Lewis rushed forward and flung his arms around me. He picked me up, spun me around, then placed me on my wonky feet. "That was insane, right? My God! It was so good to play up there. I'm still shaking."

"You nailed it. You were incredible."

"And you were perfect on audio. Thank you."

The crowd hovered around the guys, vying for their attention, but I clutched onto Lewis's arms for balance. "I was so nervous, but I did it."

"Look at you." Holding my hands, he stepped back. "That smile on your face is so good to see."

Warmth touched my cheeks. It felt good too. "You guys rocked. The single is going to be a huge hit. Congratulations." I leaned in to kiss his cheek, but he turned, and our lips connected. Fire shot through my veins and coiled up my spine. My heart pounded against my ribs. *No. Stop.* It took every ounce of my strength not to grab him and continue the kiss.

He drew back and pasted on a stunning smile as people jostled around us. But his darkening eyes told a different story. Heat and want simmered in their depths. *Oh . . . crap. That isn't good.*

He stepped in close and spoke into my ear. "I made it through thanks to your tips. I focused on a spot toward the back of the room. That just happened to be you."

I winced and pulled away. He was killing me. "Lewis, you're not making this easy."

"Neither are you." He waved toward the nearby bar where Cole and the guys were grabbing drinks. "Not sure if it will help, but would you like a bourbon?"

"Yes. Probably a whole bottle." But as I glanced over his shoulder, ice shot through my veins. My stomach cinched. "Oh shit." This was a surefire way to fuck up the night.

"What is it?" Lewis asked.

"Hopefully nothing. That reporter from the press conference has her eyes set on us." The Halle Berry lookalike stared in our direction as she sipped on her champagne.

Lewis arched an eyebrow. "And that's a bad thing?"

"Yes. We've caused enough headlines this week. It's best we're not seen alone together so we don't cause further speculation."

He lowered his chin and nodded. "I'm sorry, and I hate that you're right."

I play-punched his arm. "We can behave for one night."

"Speak for yourself." He winked.

Heat touched my cheeks as I lowered my hand. Oh, I so didn't want to behave. If he didn't stop teasing, we would be on the front page tomorrow. I didn't need drugs, alcohol, or a dance floor to cause a scene.

Cole broke through the crowd and handed us each a glass of bourbon. "Here you go. Get these into you."

"Thank you." I took the drink and had a sip.

"Let's go meet some more fans." A glint flickered in Cole's eyes as he tilted his head toward a table surrounded by a group of hot college-aged guys and girls drinking. *Oh yeah.* He was looking for a hookup. My bet was on the dark-haired Mediterranean-looking chick in the short green dress. Totally his tall, leggy model-type. "You coming, Tee?"

"Sure am." The quicker the better.

Following Cole and Lewis, I made all of two steps before someone caught my arm. I spun around, coming face to face with the reporter. *Damn it. So close to escaping.*

"Excuse me, Tia? Do you have a moment?" Her smile was warm and friendly, but I'd dealt with these types before. They buttered you up before they went in for the kill. "I'd like to ask you about the show."

You mean, Lewis.

Be nice. Be nice. Be nice.

I smeared on a honey-coated smile. "Sure."

Lewis and Cole had stopped as well and stepped in beside me.

"Everything okay?" Wariness hovered in Cole's tone as he eyed the reporter.

"Yes." I placed my hand on his arm and gave it a gentle tap. "I got this. You and Lewis go ahead. I'll catch up with you soon."

"You sure?" Cole rubbed my back.

"Yep."

Worry rippled through Lewis's eyes as he dipped his chin at me. "Holler if you need us."

I formed a half-megaphone with my hand. "HOLLER."

Chuckling, the guys shook their heads, turned, and disappeared into the crowd.

The petite woman thrust her hand out for me to shake. "I'm Gloria Pitman from *Entertainment On-show*. Nice to meet you."

A foul taste rose in my mouth. Of all the entertainment gossip sites, *Entertainment On-Show* was renowned for their clickbait headlines, scandalous and often untrue news articles.

I didn't want to give her a sliver of information that she'd twist and turn into tomorrow's top story.

I placed my hand in hers, but *ergh*, her fingers were wet and sticky, no doubt from spilling her champagne. . . at least, I hoped it was alcohol. "Evening."

I released my grip, flicked the droplets from my fingertips, then wiped my palm on the back of my dress pants. *Gross.*

Gloria raised her glass toward me. "It's good to see you back in LA."

"Thank you."

"I heard you're filming a new show."

Where from? Publicity for *Angels in LA* hadn't commenced yet. This city and its network of inside sources and gossipers did my head in. "Yes. That's correct."

"Why did you leave *Through The Smoke*?"

My stomach sank to the floor. I hated being reminded. "It was time for something new."

"Is it true you were injured on set?"

I drew my shoulders back. "Where did you hear that?"

"I interviewed Rhett Newton at the Emmys."

Asshole. He'd promised he wouldn't say anything. I didn't need that information to get back to my new job. I didn't want them to think I wasn't able. "Yes. But it was nothing serious." *Liar.*

She took a sip of her drink and waved her glass toward Cole and Lewis, who were talking to a group of partygoers. "The Flintlocks were awesome tonight. Lewis, the new bassist, is great. You two seem to be close."

My pulse quickened. *Oh, here comes the dig. Bring it.* "We're good friends."

"Wouldn't you say you're more than friends?"

"No." I took a dainty sip of my bourbon, when in reality, I wanted to knock back the whole damn drink and have another chaser or two.

"Those pictures online say otherwise." A slimy, suggestive smirk slithered across Gloria's lips as she raised a questioning eyebrow.

I shrugged, deflecting her attempt at getting a reaction out of me. I was an actress; I could control my emotions . . . *sometimes*. "You of all people should know not to believe everything you read online."

"Are you two dating?"

Her voice was causal and light, but it took all my effort not to punch her in the face. "My personal life is none of your business, but no, I'm not dating Lewis."

Her eyes narrowed. "I've seen bands fabricate stories to generate buzz for their music. Is that what the other night was about?"

That fucking boiled my blood. My grip on my glass tightened. No one accused my guys of such bullshit. "They don't need publicity stunts to attract attention."

"Is Lewis really gay?"

"Isn't it inappropriate these days to ask about someone's sexual identity or preference? And . . . if you're good at your job, you would've done your research."

"It's just you two seemed to be *very* into each other in those photos." She dug deeper and deeper without drawing a breath.

I was hanging onto all my media training and control by a thin thread. She'd pissed me off. I clicked my tongue. "Nope. We just friends and were having a good time."

Both her eyebrows shot skyward. "I don't make out with my friends like that."

I added bite to my tone. "Well maybe you need to find some new friends." I downed the rest of my bourbon and placed the empty glass on the nearby table.

As I straightened, I peered past Gloria's shoulder. Lewis

pointed at me and mouthed, *'Are you okay?'*

My heart fluttered and swelled. *Sweet, that he was worried about me.* I sucked in a deep breath and shook my head. I'd had enough of this reporter digging for dirt.

He downed his drink and licked his lips. *Hmmm. So sexy.*

'You want me?' He pointed to his chest.

Hmph! If only. Pursing my lips to hide my wayward smile, I lowered my chin.

"He's handsome."

Gloria had followed my line of sight. *Shit.*

"All the guys in the band are good-looking—not just Lewis."

"I don't see you ogling the others."

"Sorry to disappoint you, but I wasn't ogling." *I so was.* "Lewis is a friend. So stop with this line of questioning. You're wasting your time. Keep this up, I'll call security and have you removed."

"I'm just doing my job to find the truth."

Her blunt tone furled fire through my veins. "You want the truth?" My voice dialed up three notches. "Lewis told everyone in the press conference what happened. That was the truth. We got drunk. We kissed. We had a good laugh about it. We've moved on. So the fuck should you." *So much for keeping my cool. Not the first time I've lost my shit at a reporter.*

"Hey?" Lewis appeared by my side, his hand splaying across the small of my back. "Everything okay?"

"No." I glared at Gloria. "We're done."

"Lewis? Nice to meet you." Gloria shook his hand.

He greeted her politely but didn't stop touching me. "Thank you for coming to the show tonight. I hope you loved our new single, and enjoyed the music and a few drinks. But would you please excuse us? Tia, a couple of fans would love to meet you."

Gloria smirked. "Just friends, right?"

I wanted to wipe the smug smile off her face with my fist.

Lewis rubbed my back, calming me. "Yes. Goodnight."

Before I could thank him, Lewis drew me over to a group of guys. I was grateful for the distraction. The save. I could look after myself, but that had been nice. After a quick hello and a few photos, we joined the band. Then we mingled. We chatted to others.

Wherever we ventured around the room, I always found him. I always felt his gaze on me.

At midnight, the single dropped. The boys cheered and hugged, and more drinks flowed. Near two a.m., when the celebrations slowed, Lewis whispered in my ear, "You want to get out of here?"

A hot wave rushed over me.

I glanced at the gaggle of remaining guests, downing too many drinks. Cole was chatting up the girl in the green dress at the bar. Flint, Sutton, Maddy, and Slip were hanging out with Everhide. The exec team were onto an expensive bottle of American whiskey.

"But we have to stay." This was his big night.

"No, we don't." He shook his head. "This party is about to wrap. They won't miss us. You want to come with me?"

Like there is any other option. "Yes."

"Let's go." After a quick chat to the guys, he guided me through the crowd, down the corridor, and toward the rear exit. He opened the heavy back door.

We slipped into one of the band's waiting cars and disappeared into the night.

Chapter 19

TIA

The driver dropped us off at home, but rather than heading inside, Lewis took my hand, and we wandered up the street at a slow pace toward the dirt track that followed the ridge of the mountain. The stress of being around reporters, the high of the show, and the hype of meeting fans at the party had begun to fade from my mind, only to be replaced with a smoldering livewire from being alone with Lewis. Each smile, each touch of our hands, each stolen glance, blurred the lines of us just being friends.

We ambled along the track with the sea of LA lights sprawling endlessly to the south and a gentle breeze rustling through the dry grass. With each step, the simmering heat between us stirred. We couldn't go on like this. Either this had to evolve into something more before we went insane or one of us had to move out so our connection could be severed once and for all. With Lewis tied to my brother's band, I guess that would have to be me.

He fidgeted with my fingers. "That reporter, Gloria, was nice." Sarcasm rolled off his tongue.

I puffed air through my nose. *Nice deflection.* "Just another joyful day of dealing with the crappy press."

"Not all of them are bad."

"True. Just the tabloids and gossipmongers. Thanks for saving me."

"You're welcome. Cole was too occupied with that chick in green to come to your aid."

"He was in fine form, like always. Don't deny the guy some fun."

"Never."

Just short of a pathway lamppost, I tugged on Lewis's hand to stop. Leaning my butt against a wooden fence railing, I rolled and massaged my ankle. I'd walked far enough without resting for a few minutes. "Cole screws around to hide the fact he's just as messed up as the rest of us."

"I gathered that. Anyone who obsesses with running ten miles a day, rarely sleeps, and drums till all hours of the morning has issues. Slip's got shit going on too. We all do. The more I learn about each of the guys, about Phil, and how his death has affected everyone, I think Flint is the sanest out of everyone."

I stood straight and dusted the railing dirt off my hands. "Nobody's perfect."

"No. No one is." He edged in closer and tucked my hair behind my ear. He lowered his voice. "You don't have to be either. Not ever. Flaws and all, I still like you."

The breeze tousled the ends of his hair. My body quivered. I was mesmerized by the city light reflecting in his gorgeous eyes. "Is that all this is?" I whispered. "You just *like* me."

He lowered his chin. "I've being trying to convince myself every day that there is nothing more between us."

"And have you done that?"

"No." He turned to lean against the fence railing beside me. "I've come up here numerous times to think. The city seems so peaceful, yet the reality is it's full of mayhem and chaos as well as endless opportunity."

"It fills your head with dreams and hopes then rips them away."

"And brings changes you never saw coming."

I gave him a sideways glance. "Are you talking about the band?"

He half-smirked. "And you."

"What does that mean?" A tug-o-war pushed and pulled inside my head. "What are you saying? Do you want to be with me?"

He stared out over the cityscape. "I wish I could give you a straight yes-or-no answer."

I closed my eyes and took a steady breath. "But we've skirted around this for long enough. I like you. So much that it kinda hurts now. I don't understand why this attraction between us is so strong, intense, and just won't stop. It messes with my head every day. But we've reached a crossroad and have to choose what direction to take." My stomach swayed. Neither outcome would be easy. Any decision came with uncertain consequences. I pushed my past hurt down, deep inside my heart, and took a leap. "I'm open to the idea of seeing if this thing between us is real, if we can be more, but I'm also willing to leave, move out, or walk away to end it. I'm not going to waste another second of my life questioning what this is if you don't feel the same way."

Lewis took my hand and rested it against his thigh. "What you're asking isn't as simple as just dating someone new or opening up to the idea of falling for someone again. It's a complete change in who I am and all I've ever been."

I brushed my thumb over the back of his hand, tracing the veins and bones. "I don't want you to do something you'd regret or don't want to do. This isn't easy for me either. You're not just some guy I'm attracted to. You're a gay man. How can I be the person you want to be with when you've never been into women?"

"I've questioned myself a million times a day. Every time I see you or get a hint of your perfume, cables snap. At first, I didn't understand it, didn't want it, thought I was being foolish. But those feelings wouldn't go away. Some days, you're all I think about, and I struggle to comprehend why. Why you?" As he closed his eyes, deep grooves furrowed into his brow. "What would you do if you woke up tomorrow infatuated with a woman? If suddenly, your whole world was tipped upside down because of the way you felt?"

I tapped his leg. "I like cock, so it would be shocking and confusing."

He chuckled and shook his head. "Same. See my dilemma?"

"Yes." I entwined our fingers. "But if that woman felt as strongly about me as I did about her, it would be hard not to explore what that was."

"What if it turned out to be nothing?" Anguish wisped through his voice.

"We'd have taken a chance to find out."

"I've just told the world I'm gay. I can't suddenly be with a woman. The media would rip us apart for lying. The likes of Gloria would have a field day."

"I know. But . . . you're considering this?" My heartbeat quickened. "Us?"

"Tia."

The way my name fell from his lips tugged on my heart. I didn't want him to hurt any longer. "I don't want to fight this anymore. Just be honest with me, please?"

Concern flickered through his eyes. "I can't risk being kicked out of the band. Slip's cool, but your brother has issues with me. Some days, so does Flint."

"They're just protective. They don't want to see me, or

you get hurt. Letting you into their world after losing Phil is hard on them." On me too. There was no easy way forward. I stared out across the hillside. My head grappled for a solution. "Would . . . would it help to keep being together a secret until we are more certain about what we are?"

"This isn't a game. We're not kids."

"No. And I don't want to be somebody's behind-closed-doors girlfriend again, like I was with Phil. But maybe it's necessary for a while. For both of us. I used to take risks without question. I'd jump off buildings, run through fires, skydive from planes. But this attraction between us has raised more doubts than there are stars in the universe. I want to take every step with caution. Putting my heart on the line again is a huge gamble. But I'm willing to do that. I just want the chance to see where this goes."

He winced and nodded but then shook his head. "I've just got so much going on with the band. I've been burned and deluded by love before. I don't want to go down that road again. I'm not sure if I'm ready for another relationship."

"Neither was I. Yet here we are. If this turns out to be nothing, there are no issues. If it's something, how incredible would that be? But if this turns into a downright mess, I'll leave LA again. I'd never jeopardize your position in the band."

"Fuck, Tia. Cole's your brother. I would never ask you to leave. My plan was always to move out after the tour. I can do that earlier if needed."

"I don't want you to." I rubbed my thumb over the back of his hand. "We defy logic, but God, I want to find out what we can be. Are you open to the idea of exploring? Of just a maybe?"

"You're persistent, aren't you?" He sighed, stood, and turned to face me.

Had he had enough conversation and wanted to head home? *No.* "Lewis, I need an answer."

He glanced down at our entwined hands. "Can we try something first? Without being drunk, or high, or joking around . . . can I kiss you?"

Oh . . . okay. Hope filled my lungs to capacity. "Is this some kind of test? If you don't feel anything, that's it?"

"Something like that." A playful smile curled across his lips. "Okay."

He drew me to my feet. As he ran his hands up my arms, fire skipped across my skin. I slipped my arms around his waist, hooking my fingers into his studded belt. His heart beat so loud I could hear it. This was a big step for him. For us. I didn't miss the weight of the moment. "Are you sure about this?"

He cupped my face, inched closer. His breath brushed in soft wisps against my lips. "Yes."

He closed his eyes and pressed his lips to mine. My knees buckled, and I collapsed against his chest. *Oh. My. God.* My heart boomed louder and faster than his did. Dizziness spun through my head. With the softest of kisses, he swept his lips across mine. Touching. Teasing. Tasting. Delirium took over. Parting my lips, I deepened our kiss. With a flick of my tongue, I dove into his mouth. Smiling against my lips, he met my fevered rush. Our tongues entwined. Dueled. Danced. Gripping onto his belt tighter, I tugged him forward, crushing my breasts against his chest. He had to feel that!

A guttural groan rumbled deep in his throat.

Oh yeah! Hunger rolled through my belly. Heat coiled through my veins.

As he knotted his hands through my hair, he tilted his hips and drove his semi against my pants. "Shit." He raked his lips away from mine. Panting, he rested his forehead against my brow. His hot breath rushed across my face.

Smiling, I bit my lower lip, savoring the taste of his mouth. "Good shit or bad shit?"

Chuckling, he smoothed his hand over the back of my hair. "Good. Definitely good."

"So now what?" Did he want to rip my clothes off and fuck in front of the city? I'd be down for that.

"Timing sucks." He drew me against his chest, wrapping me in his warm embrace. "I leave in three days for a month. But when I get back from promo . . . maybe we could go on a few dates, see how that goes. We need to take this slow, okay?"

"I don't like slow but okay." I toyed with the buttons on his shirt. *Damn.* I'd love to rip them open. "If you feel a smidgen for me what I feel for you, you'll be counting down the days until you're home."

"Oh . . . I'm counting."

A beaming smile spread across my face. "So, we're doing this? You're willing to explore what this is between us?"

"Yes. After promo. So let's head back before you talk too much, and I change my mind."

I zipped my lips and took his hand.

Slowly, we ambled down the hill to Cole's house. I didn't want the night to end. The heat from our kiss lingered between us. He occasionally adjusted his balls. It wasn't my fault he'd gotten turned on . . . well . . . maybe. I'd be happy to relieve him.

At the top of the stairs, I let go of his hand and headed for my bedroom door. I wanted to kiss him again but I didn't want to push it. "Night"

He stood there. Agony blazed in his silver eyes. "Tia, are you sure about me? That this isn't just some passing infatuation?"

"I've known you long enough to be sure that it's not. It if it was, it would've died, not grown stronger. Why?"

"Because . . . fuck waiting until I get back. I want to explore . . . Now."

He closed the gap between us and crushed his lips against mine.

Chapter 20

LEWIS

With my lips connected to Tia's, we fell into her bedroom, and I kicked the door shut. The city lights threw a faint glow through the full-length windows, giving the room a dark blue tinge. Cupping her face, I guided her backward toward her bed. Everything about her—her touch, her smile, her sass, her soul—ignited my senses. I was there. There was no going back. Not ever. My heart had totally led me astray. This was without a doubt one of the craziest things I'd ever done. But I'd be foolish to not see if this fire brewing between us was destined to grow or burn us to a cinder.

"Is this okay?" I whispered against her lips. "Or do you want to wait?" My balls would object, but I wasn't an animal.

"I'm good." She tugged on my shirt. "I want you. In every possible way."

Kissing her was like taking cocaine and oxycodone together—a total fucking high. My fingers trembled as I caressed and stroked her sexy arms, circled her back, or buried them into her hair. Every touch was new. Different. Heightened.

She clawed at my buttons and undid my shirt. Clutching at

the edges, she peeled it from my shoulders and dropped it onto the floor.

My stomach dipped and dived. *Shit.* Taking a quick breath, I squeezed my eyes shut tight. I was more nervous than when I'd lost my virginity at fifteen. Everything was happening too fast. I couldn't keep up. "Tia?" I pressed my forehead against hers. "Can we slow down? I've . . . never done this before . . . with a woman."

Smiling, she ran her fingertips over my bare chest. Her cool, gentle touch blazed against my hot flesh. "I've never done it with a gay man."

She had a comeback for everything. I loved that about her. "First time for everything, right?"

"Yeah. You're just so gorgeous; I can't keep my hands off you."

"I'm not complaining." I traced the arch of her collarbone with the softest of strokes. "There's so much to take in. Your skin is so silky and smooth." I kissed her sweet lips. "You taste divine . . . and there's no stubble scratching my lips."

She giggled, wrinkling her nose. "Am I less hairy than you're used to?"

"Much less."

She raised her arms above her head. "Take my top off."

"Gladly." Running my fingertips down between her breasts, over the flat plane of her stomach, I caught the hemline. Clutching at the fabric, I yanked it over her head and tossed it on the floor. My heart rate doubled as I raked my gaze over her plain black bra and the teasing arch of her boobs bulging over the top of the smooth fabric. I wanted to take my time and explore every inch of her body, but . . . later. We didn't have many hours left until I had to leave for the promo. I didn't want to waste one second.

She stepped in close, melting against my chest. She trailed

steamy kisses up the side of my neck, along my jawline, then met my mouth. My eyes fluttered shut as our tongues entwined. Every touch and taste dialed up the heat coursing through my body.

"Do you wanna take my bra off?" Her breathy voice rushed across my lips.

I swallowed hard. I'd never been asked that before. "Uh-huh." I slid my hands up her back. Taking hold of the bra, my fingers trembled. Over our kisses, I twisted the clasp this way, then that. This way . . . then that. *Nope, no release.* I pushed and pulled the connection. *Nothing.* I tugged and tweaked at the elastic. *No give.* I jiggled the hooks, but the stupid thing still wouldn't budge.

I broke our kiss, stepped back, and splayed my hands. "How the fuck do you get that thing off?"

Tia pursed her lips to contain her laughter but failed. "Like this." She reached behind her back. Within a second, the straps fell loose on her shoulders.

Okay. I need to practice that.

Slowly, sexily she lowered the garment and eased it from her arms.

My balls jumped. Fuck this going slow shit. I caught Tia around the waist and crushed her against me. Her bare nipples pressing into my skin sent shudders and tingles across my body. As we kissed, the temperature between us grew hotter and hotter. With a gentle nudge, I lowered her onto the bed. We shuffled toward the pillows and kicked back the bed coverings. Nestling between her legs, I hovered over her and rocked my hips against hers. I needed more of her. All of her. "Tia? I'm dying here. I want you."

She moaned against my mouth. "Say that again?"

My heart drummed hard against my ribs, but there was no hesitation in my voice. "I want you." God, it felt good to admit that.

Her eyes glistened in the soft light as she tapped my ass. "Good. Now roll over."

Falling back onto the pillow, I hated losing contact with her for a second. She rolled onto her side and planted a mind-numbing kiss on my lips. Her fingernails scraped across my chest, down my stomach, and found the buckle on my belt. "Can I take off your jeans?"

A wave of reality slammed into me. Did I truly want this? Was I ready? One look into Tia's breathtaking green eyes and all my doubts disappeared. "Yeah."

I raised my hips and helped her ease my clothes off. My strained erection was happy to be released from the confines of my boxer briefs.

A sexy smile curled across her mouth. "I can work with this." She took hold of my cock and rubbed her thumb up the length and circled the tip.

The breath shot from my lungs. Tia . . . a woman . . . was touching me. Weird . . . But good. So fucking good. "It's all I got."

"It's more than enough." She sat upright and reached for the zipper on the side of her dress pants. But she stopped, then drew the sheet over her legs. Shame shimmered in her eyes. "You don't need to see my scars."

My chest ached. "Tia." I ran my hand up her spine. Threading my fingers beneath her hair, I caressed the back of her neck. "No scar is gonna scare me off. I saw some of them when we were at Big Bear." I crawled around in front of her and grabbed the top of her pants. "Trust me. It's okay."

"Lewis?" She winced, reaching out to stop me.

"You wanna fuck, these have to come off." I tugged on the waistband. "Yes? Or do you want to stop?" My body screamed *'no, don't stop,'* but I would if I had to.

She gnawed on her lip. Once. Twice. Three times. Then,

she nodded. "Off." She collapsed back against the pillow and covered her eyes with her arm.

I eased her pants and boyleg panties from her hips, then slid them down her thighs, over her knees, and off her ankles. In the soft light, I took her injured foot in my hand and traced her scars with my fingertips. The raised marks were like the one that sliced across the middle of my back. I threw her a saucy smile and dipped my head. Licking and kissing along the length of her calf, I followed each scar, making sure I didn't miss one. "Your leg feels and tastes alright to me?"

"Get up here." She flapped her hand at me.

Grinning, I meandered nips and kisses up her leg, across her hip bone, then over her stomach. The scent on her skin drove me wild. But I couldn't pass her boobs without exploring. I cupped one perfect breast, then the other. The weight? *Weird.* The flesh? *Firm yet soft.* The nipple? *So sexy.* Aching to taste her, I lowered my head and flicked my tongue over the hardened tip.

My cock twitched and throbbed. *Guess I like this.*

She flinched and arched toward me. "Mmm." *Guess she did too.*

I swirled my tongue around in a circle, blew softly, and sucked her nipple into my mouth. Goose bumps darted across her skin. I grinned as her bud hardened even more.

"Lewis." My name tumbled from her lips with urgency. Wriggling, she threaded her fingers through my hair. With a soft tug, she drew me back to her mouth.

The moment our lips connected, flames blazed through my body. I kissed her top lip, then her bottom lip. I wasn't sure if it was the lingering hint of bourbon on her tongue, or the magic in her touch, but I was hungry for more. I couldn't get enough. As I lowered my weight onto her, my dick pressed between our bellies. She draped her good leg over my butt and pulled me closer. Every swirl of her hand over my skin, scratch of her hard nails on my back, or dig of her long fingers into my flesh made me burn hotter. With a mind of their own, my hips rocked against hers. "Tia?" Did the agony in my voice tell her how much I wanted her?

"Let me grab a condom."

I hadn't had to use them in years. But fuck. I'd wear ten of them if she wanted me to.

She plucked one out of the box in her nightstand. I tore the packet open and rolled the sucker on. Tia watching me quickened my pulse. I didn't think I'd ever been this hard. Ever. And I'd had some fucking wild sex in my time.

I re-positioned myself over her, placed my hands either side of her head and gazed down into her stunning eyes. My heart thudded with a strange rhythm. Life was about to change . . . forever. Everything I was . . . was about to change. But I wanted this. I wanted her. No doubt in my mind.

She snaked her hands around my neck, then combed her fingers through my hair and scratched my scalp with her short fingernails. Tingles shot over my head and skipped down my spine. I liked fingernails. She cradled the side of my face, her breath hot and heavy. "You sure about this?"

"Yes. You?"

"Oh yeah." She wriggled, edging me closer to her opening. All the blood in my body rushed south. An inferno burned within my balls. If I didn't bury myself inside her soon, I was sure to blow my load. "Do you want me to touch you first?" I'd never felt up a girl. But if I recalled high school biology correctly, I knew where the essential spots were. *Hopefully.*

"I just want you inside me."

I brushed my lips against hers. "How can I stay in control when you say shit like that?"

"Stop overthinking this. You won't break me. Just do what

comes naturally."

"This isn't natural for me."

"I want it to be." She kissed the side of my neck. "Do what feels good. Do what feels right. If you want to stop, we can."

My heart pounded against hers. Our chests heaved in time. Resisting her was useless. "I don't want to stop."

She drew my lips onto hers. With a flick of her tongue, I was a lost man. Closing my eyes, I let her moves and touches guide me. Let the want in my body and hers take control. How hard could this be? Easing back a touch, I nudged my cock between her legs. Warmth engulfed the tip. *Oh geez. So good.* Then I nudged forward. Prodded. Nudged. Prodded. *Fuck. Nope. I sucked at this.*

Smiling against my lips, she slipped her hand between us. She took hold of me and guided me to the right spot. "There."

Whoa. This was it. My head spun. My heart thundered up somewhere near my throat. With our gazes locked, I pushed into her. Slowly. Carefully. *Oh. My. Fucking. God.* My breath shot from my lungs. Shudders spiraled up my spine in manic waves. Warmth . . . no, raw heat . . . and fire . . . and pleasure wrapped around my entire dick. "Holy fuck."

I closed my eyes. I didn't want to move. *No, wait.* Yes, I did.

Tia tilted her pelvis, clenched her insides around me, and drew me closer. "God, I've wanted to fuck you from the moment we met."

An animalistic moan fell from my lips. I nearly lost it. Being inside her was so freaking good. *Do what's natural, right?* Fucking was natural, and I could do that. I pulled back a fraction, then drove into her. I did it again, penetrating deeper and deeper each time. After a few more thrusts, I relaxed. *I've got this.*

Tia's eyelids fluttered closed, her lips parted, and her panting quickened. Her hands, roaming over my shoulders, squeezing my arms, and circling my back, electrified every hair on my body. She nuzzled and kissed the side of my neck. "Harder."

Without hesitating, I picked up the pace. Each thrust throbbed through my cock. My balls tightened. I wanted to kiss her, touch her, take my time, but being inside her stole my focus. This was too good. Sliding my hand down her side, I caught hold of her leg and raised it up near my hip. My breath hissed through my teeth. Maybe I shouldn't have done that because now the new angle pushed me closer to the edge. Too close. "Tia. Fuck. I'm gonna go."

"Me too. Go deeper."

"Like this?" I fought the rapture in my brain to pound into her. I drove inside her and stilled, giving her every inch I had to offer. Clutching and clawing at the bedsheet, I concentrated on not coming. Oh, but every move of her body and taste of her lips made it nearly impossible.

Her hips rocked and swayed and pulsed against mine. Her warmth surrounded and claimed me. Breathing her in, I closed my eyes. "You feel so fucking good."

"Yeah. You too." She rubbed and wriggled beneath me. Her fingers scraped across my shoulders and dug into my flesh.

Clenching my teeth, I couldn't take anymore. My body took over. I drove into her faster and faster. The strain in my cock, unbearable. "Argh. Fuck." I thrust into her hard. Once. Twice. Three times. My release exploded. Waves of hot pleasure shot through my veins, charged up my spine, and pooled at the base of my neck. As I convulsed and shuddered, the throbs in my dick were the most intense I'd ever experienced. I kept driving into her with slow, languid movements. *Shit.* If I kept this going, I'd come again. I didn't have an issue with that.

"Don't stop. Stay there." Her walls clenched around me like a vise. Her thighs squeezed around my hips, tighter and tighter.

She rocked and rubbed against me. *So. Damn. Good.* "Oh yeah. Hmm. That's it." The tension in her body snapped. Jerking and quaking beneath me, she giggled. The sexiest smile I'd ever seen curled across her lips. "Oh. Wow."

But as I closed my eyes, chaos erupted in my head. My pulse thudded in my temples. *Oh shit. What have I done? Shit. No...no...no. NO!* I sucked in several ragged deep breaths. Her scent filled every cell in my body like a calming vapor designed just for me. My dick pulsing and throbbing inside her erased any form of doubt. This was good . . . *really* good. I kissed her soft pink lips. "You okay?"

"Yeah. You?" She flattened her palm over my stampeding heart.

I stroked her hair, swiping the long strands off her brow. "My mind is officially blown."

"Not bad for your first time, right?"

I withdrew, wrapped the condom in some tissues from her nightstand, and tossed it on the floor. I'd deal with it later. After Tia cleaned herself up, I curled in beside her and drew her against my chest. Pulling the sheets over us, I kissed her temple. "I don't think once is enough to decide if this is a good thing or not." My heart rate still hadn't returned to normal.

"Definitely not. I'm happy to do that again anytime."

"Hmmm. I agree." I circled my fingertips across her back. Chaotic thoughts pummeled my brain. "Tia? Are you okay if we keep this between us for now? I meant what I said. I'd like to take you out . . . date. Make sure this is what we both want before we tell everyone. Is that okay?"

She glanced up at me. "Yes. We both need that. It will be nice to let this craziness we've fought over the past couple of months to settle. Sneaking around will be fun for a while." A glimmer of light flashed in her eyes. Why did I sense she was going to enjoy that element too much?

I stroked her hair, kissed her forehead. "It won't be for long—I promise. A few weeks, tops. You know how important the band is to me. I don't want to piss the guys off or blow my chances with them if they lose their shit at us being together." They'd been cool about a kiss, but dating Tia was a different ballgame. I wouldn't let the guys dictate who I could be with, but I had to make sure Tia was worth risking my career for. I had to be logical and sensible. Was that even possible when she was so damn tempting?

She eased onto the pillow beside me and brushed her soft lips across mine. "We didn't plan this well. It sucks you'll be away for four weeks."

I trailed my fingertips down the length of her arm. I wanted them wrapped around my shoulders, holding me close as I made her come. "I'll be counting down the days until I'm home."

"Same."

"How's the leg?"

"What leg?" She giggled as she played with the back of my hair. "But in the future, when we do this again and again and again"—she teased her lips against mine between each word—"we'll have to get creative because I can't bend my knee or put weight on my leg for too long."

I caught her hands. Pushing her back onto the pillow, I pinned our entwined fingers beside her head. "If we have to do missionary for the rest of our days, it's a sacrifice I'm willing to make."

She jerked her chin back. "What the fuck? I'm not." She caught my jaw in her hand and skidded her thumb across my lower lip. "I don't want to scare you off, but maybe before this goes any further, you should know I like to be . . . *adventurous*." She wriggled beneath me, and a mischievous glint sparkled in her eyes. "I like my toys, my games, and my cuffs. Pleasure, not pain. If you're not open to those things in the future, we should stop now. Or do you think you can handle me?"

My dick hardened. *Fuck. She was made for me.* I chuckled, low and soft. "You and I are going to get on very well."

She tugged her hands free and linked them behind my neck. "In that case, want to do some more exploring?"

"Hmm, we should."

She grabbed another condom. I rolled it on and buried myself inside her again. I had to leave in four hours. I had to sleep and pack. Cole could come home at any second. *Shit.* Until I passed the next milestone, and I secured my place in the band for tour, Tia and I had to stay under wraps.

I was walking on thin ice. Risking everything.

Was she worth it?

Fuck . . . I hoped so.

Chapter 21

LEWIS

After having less than three hours of sleep, I handed my suitcase and Cole's huge roller duffel to the concierge at the InterContinental Hotel in Downtown LA. With dark black Ray Bans covering my tired eyes, I entered the huge light-filled foyer, caught the elevator up to the seventieth floor, and walked along the Sky Lobby in search of my band. My stride had a touch of swagger and a new smile had been etched onto my face. Last night with Tia had been phenomenal, nerve-wracking, and life changing. Clearly, I'd survived. So much for dating and taking things slow. I had a history of going all-in fast. This had been no exception. But I was adamant about moving forward at a steady pace to make sure our infatuation wasn't a hot fuse that fizzled out quickly. Keeping what happened under wraps would be hard—especially with the guys. But thanks to our busy schedule over the coming weeks, our promotional tour would ensure I remained focused on the band, not Tia.

I headed toward the bar at the far end of the lobby. Flint and Slip lazed on a large gray sofa with April and Blake sitting opposite on comfy chairs.

"How are you holding up? Tia okay?" Flint asked over the rim of his coffee cup.

I'd told the guys last night before we'd left that she'd been tired, her leg had ached, and the reporter had upset her, and so I'd offered to take her home. Since it had been late, they'd thought nothing of it.

"I'm still on a high after our show. Tia's fine." Leaving her in bed had been hard, but music was why I was here.

"You tuck her into bed real good?" Slip's suggestive chuckle made me falter.

Did he suspect there was something between Tia and me? Or was this his sense of humor shining through. I played along, grinned and told a version of the truth. "There was no tucking." Only ripping off bedsheets and clothes, and a lot of fucking. But he didn't need to know that. I quickly changed the topic. "She doesn't like gossip reporters very much."

"Who does?" Flint lowered his sunglasses over his eyes. The sun blazed too brightly through the large windows that gave views across LA. We'd all had a big night. "Tia can get fired up, rather than remaining cool and calm during interviews."

"So I witnessed last night." I waved down a waiter and ordered a cappuccino, before continuing. "Gloria from *Entertainment On-Show* had a go at her about the pictures of us at Club Destruction and whether I was really gay, and whether we were just creating hype for the launch. That pissed her off. I interrupted, just in time."

"Geez, thank you." April covered her mouth with her fingertips as she quickly finished a bite of her blueberry muffin. "I haven't missed dealing with Tia's outbursts. But that news should die now you've launched the single. Initial posts online about the track and last night's show have been all positive."

"The single is already sitting at number ten on the charts. It's the best release we've ever had." Blake scrolled through his cell phone.

Flint pumped his fist. "Yes!"

Slip slapped his thigh. "Fuck yeah."

Me? The breath shot from my lungs. *We are on the charts!* "That's amazing."

Five minutes later, after the waiter delivered my cappuccino, Cole strode out of the elevator and ambled toward us, still dressed in the same clothes as he'd been wearing last night. The only new additions were the leather jacket, hooked on his finger and draped over his shoulder, and the dark shades covering his eyes. He screamed hot, smoldering rock star. Just about every guest in the lobby turned their head and raked their gaze over him . . . then us. *Cool!*

Cole never altered his pace.

"About time you turned up." Blake shook his head. "Hope she was worth it."

He flopped onto the sofa beside me and rested his head back on the seat. "She delivered. That's all that matters."

Go, Cole. "I brought your gear with me and checked it in." I sipped on my scorching-hot coffee. That was the only way to have it.

"Thanks, man." Cole didn't move. "You're a lifesaver."

"Now that we're all here . . ." April grabbed her tablet and opened the screen. "We can start. We have a huge day."

"First, here are your room keys." Blake dug into his jacket and handed us swipe cards. "Slip and Lewis are in one room. Cole and Flint, the other. You know the rules. In bed by two a.m. Ready for the day by seven. Not too much drinking. No drugs." He pointed to each one of us. "No going home to women's or men's houses; you fuck 'em in your room or the dressing room, or the restrooms . . . I don't care and don't want to know the finer details, but no leaving the designated venues and hotels. That's for your security and safety. Let's keep the shenanigans to a minimum. I don't want to spend half my fucking day herding you lot together. Got it?"

"Where's the fun in that?" Cole groaned. "You know we don't like rules."

"I know." Blake's shoulders slumped as if tired before promo had even started. "But I have to try to keep you in line."

"But you always fail." Cole chuckled, then turned to me. "You ready for this shit?"

"Yep." I nodded. I was more than ready.

By the time we hit our first promotional interview after lunch, our single had reached number six on the charts. *Freaking insane!* Based out of the hotel, we were ushered from radio stations to TV shows to venue appearances. The crowds we attracted were nothing like I'd ever witnessed before. At every stop, fans waved banners and photos, and screamed in excitement. I was treated like a celebrity even though I didn't *feel* like one. Joining The Flintlocks and being thrust into the spotlight had happened so fast. My brush with success in my early twenties and the years of experience I had under my belt gave me some foundation on how to handle this lifestyle, but I was often in over my head.

In my last few years of playing with The Saylors in pubs and small venues, no one had cared about us. People had come to listen to live music, not *us*, per se. I'd been invisible. No one had judged me. Now, the world's eyes watched my every move. On the outside, I could smile, wave, greet the fans, and answer any prying question in interviews, but deep down, unease lurked in the pit of my gut. I'd told the world I was gay but couldn't wait to be with Tia. Was that wrong? I didn't want to derail this ride I was on. Being careful of every step I made and every word I said took effort, but until I knew if Tia and I were something real, I had to be mindful. I couldn't change my game until I was sure I could give my heart and soul to her. Easy, right?

But Tia was on hold for now. I had four weeks to prove myself to the band to make the next milestone. Every time I took to the stage, Tia's focusing techniques helped me contain my nerves. My love of performing quickly took hold and had me playing up to the crowds. I'd gotten better at playing alongside the guys, learning their cues and silent stage talk. But as we waited in the green room to film *Miller's Late Show*, one of the biggest talk shows in LA, one that was watched by millions of people each night, my nerves returned. This was a huge deal. I didn't want to screw this up. Struggling to find focus, I texted Tia.

> HI. ABOUT TO FILM MILLER'S SHOW.

She replied:

> YOU NERVOUS?

Me:

> YEP. AFRAID OF MAKING A MISTAKE.

Her response was just as quick.

> FOCUS ON COMING HOME.
> PICKING UP WHERE WE LEFT OFF.

Chuckling, I replied:

> OKAY. THAT WORKS.

"Dude, are you okay?" Cole questioned me as he put his foot up on the coffee table and double-knotted his combat boots. "Two minutes ago, you looked like you wanted to throw up; now you've got a goofy smile on your face. Who are you texting?"

I tucked my cell phone into my jacket pocket. I didn't need him reading the texts from his sister. "Just a friend." That wasn't a lie. "It helps calm my nerves. I don't want to fuck up playing for one of the biggest late shows in LA."

"Stop stressing. We all get nervous. We've all screwed up on stage." Flint sat on the arm of the sofa and took a sip of his water. "One time in Salt Lake City, Cole's snare drum fell over. He kept playing until it was reset by our stagehand. Slip has jumped around so much he's ripped the cable out of his guitar. I've lost count of the number of times I've knocked over my mic. If something goes wrong, just keep playing. Fix the issue. Act like it wasn't a problem."

All those things or similar had happened to me and the guys in my former band when we'd started out. I just strived for perfection in performances and hated it when things went wrong.

Slip slapped his hand on my thigh. "Each show will get easier. So will the interviews and photoshoots and dealing with the fans. This is just the warmup for the next promo, and the one after that, and then the tour."

If I make it that far.

"Your life is now on show." Flint twisted the lid back onto his water bottle. "You'll get used to every tiny slip-up, trip, fart, scratch of your nose, and adjustment of your balls being posted online by someone."

"I'm getting there." Gossip didn't bother me. I knew most of it wasn't true and was clickbait, revenue raising fodder. *But shit.* How was I going to date Tia, an A-list TV star, without being caught? *Ergh!* We'd deal with that issue later.

Cole hooked his arm along the back of the sofa. "Just have fun. When I get nervous, I think about sex. You should try it. Every time you have a camera pointed at you, picture the person you last fucked. Stare down that lens like you want to give it to them again. The audience eats that shit up."

I lowered my chin and laughed. Oh, if he knew that person was Tia. "Okay. I'll try that."

"You'll be fine," Flint said. "Just watch your tempo on 'Changes.' You're coming in a beat too late in the chorus. Focus on that, not whoever you last banged."

Easier said than done.

Funny thing was . . . Cole's advice worked.

Images of Tia had flickered through my mind when we'd hit the set and TV cameras loomed in front of me. But even with pinpoint focus and controlled nerves when we hit 'Changes', I'd still missed the chorus change. I'd copped an evil glare from Flint on that one. *Fuck.* These guys played next level. I needed to pick up my game. Practice more. Be better . . . no . . . be perfect.

After LA, we traveled to Las Vegas, Houston, Atlanta, and Miami. From sunup to near midnight, we never had a break. If we weren't performing or greeting the fans, we were eating, sleeping, traveling, and on vocal rest. I loved singing backup with Slip. With our scheduled visit to San Francisco behind us, we landed in Seattle two and a half weeks after leaving LA.

We took to the stage at The Quarry Lounge, a huge live music venue in the center of the city. Dotted throughout the overzealous crowd, fans waved signs decorated with birthday wishes for Cole.

With a day off tomorrow, the guys and I looked forward to a few drinks after this show to celebrate Cole's twenty-fifth birthday. But until then, we had to give these partygoers one hell of a performance. As we hit the first track, I scanned the venue to find my focal point. Hot guys danced on the floor before me. Girls screamed in front of Flint. Through the flashing stage lights, I struggled to see Gena and Tristan at the control panels beyond the crowd. *But shit!* My heart skipped a beat. Was I seeing things? The lights blinked again. The girl standing behind Gena looked like Tia. But that wasn't possible. Tia was in LA.

Was I missing her? *Yeah.* We'd texted every day. We talked

when we could, often late at night. It was hard to have private conversations when I shared a room with Slip.

Focus. Play. By our second song, Flint had the audience in a frenzy, dancing and singing along to one of The Flintlocks' former hits. As we played "Changes," a spotlight pierced my eye. I glanced at Tristan and swiped my eyebrow, our signal to let him know I was being blinded. *What the fuck?* I'd have words with him after the show.

But just as I went to turn away, the spotlight died. My heart jumped an octave. I swore it was Tia. *Ergh.* I'd never been this messed up over someone before. *No, wait.* Yes, I had. And that had ended badly.

Fuck. Concentrate.

With steel-like determination, I strummed out "Changes." As I closed my eyes, images of Tia naked filled my head. *Think of notes ... not her sexy body.* Smirking, I pummeled energy into every raw progression.

I hit the chorus perfectly.

Nailed it. Yeah!

After thundering out two more songs, we hit our final track. Cole hammered out one last booming gallop across his drums and smashed down hard on his cymbals to end the show. The crowd erupted with cheers and applause. I yanked my bass strap over my head, placed my guitar on its stand, and joined the guys near Flint's mic. We bowed and waved to the audience, then rushed off the stage. Every time we played, I thanked God I'd landed this gig. I relished every performance. Loved playing with these three men. I was in my element again. I never wanted to lose sight of how lucky I'd been or take this opportunity for granted. I prayed being with Tia never jeopardized that.

As we passed the curtain, Flint let out an almighty roar and charged past our entourage and stage crew. He picked up Sutton and spun her around. "Argh! You're here." He rained down kisses on her lips.

"Tia?" Cole held his arms wide and shot forward to hug her standing beside Sutton. "What are you doing here?"

My heart filled my chest, pounding hard and fast. My night just got better and better. I hadn't been imagining things.

Tia *was* here. It had been her at the mixer, no doubt playing with the lights.

After picturing her naked body to help focus during shows, there was only one thing I wanted to do.

See it for real.

Chapter 22

LEWIS

"Happy birthday, Cole." Over Cole's embrace, Tia threw me a sexy wink. My hands twitched, wanting to reach out and hold her too. She hugged Cole, tight. "It's so good to see you. Sutton and Flint have been conspiring for weeks. She's planned a surprise party."

"Oh. My. God. This is brilliant." Cole swung her around in a circle then placed her on her feet.

Giggling, she wrinkled her nose and slapped his arm. "Now let go of me. You're all yucky and sweaty. Ew!"

Cole released her and grabbed Sutton, hooking his arm around her shoulders. "You're the best. Thank you."

Sutton laughed. "You're welcome. Maddy's here too."

Slip sucked in a sharp breath. Maddy weaved through the throng of crew and gave us hugs and said hello, but her gaze kept jumping to Slip.

Well, hot damn! They had a spark for each other.

Just like Tia and me.

How had I missed that at the launch? *Oh, that's right* . . . I'd been too messed up over Tia.

"Great show, guys," Blake hollered. "You've earned a night off. Let's celebrate. April, Falcon, and I will meet you at the bar. Don't dawdle."

"Happy birthday, bud." Flint hooked one arm around Cole's neck and patted his chest with his other hand. "Let's go freshen up so we can party. It's been killing me, keeping this a secret."

Hmmm. There were more secrets between the band than they let on. Me included.

As everyone headed toward the steps at the back of the stage area, I raked my gaze over Tia's long, silky black skirt and crop top. It was the first time I'd seen her in a skirt. And damn I wanted to get underneath it. Catching her around the waist, I whispered in her ear, "It's good to see you. But I hope you wore that skirt for a reason."

"You bet I did. Want a quickie?"

"God, yes." My dick strained in my jeans at the thought of touching and kissing her. I stopped in my tracks. "Boys," I yelled out to them at the bottom of the steps and thumbed toward the stage behind me. "I'll just help Joel and the crew pack up for a few minutes. I won't be far behind."

"Joel, hey?" A devilish grin slid across Cole's mouth. "Don't be long."

"Never." I grinned. I hadn't missed our stagehand's heated gazes or flirtatious comments. His interest provided a cover for me to steal a moment with Tia. I should have felt bad, but hey, I had to do what I had to do.

"Tia? You coming?" Cole waved as he walked backwards down the corridor that led to the dressing room.

"I'll meet you out front. I'm going to the ladies."

"All right. See you at the bar." He turned and took off at a run, catching up to Sutton, Maddy, and the guys.

I'd taken all of three steps, past some of our crew bumping out the gear, when Tia caught my hand. She dragged me behind the wall of stage curtains and into the small narrow tech room on the side of the venue, locking the door behind us.

I barely had time to draw a breath before she kissed me long and hard. Burying my hands into her silky hair and tasting her lips had me aching all over. I cupped her face and drove her back against the wall between the six-foot high racks of AV patch bays flashing with blue and green lights. As I pressed my body into hers, my whole system hummed. "Why didn't you tell me you were coming?"

"I wanted to surprise you."

"Oh. You have. I like that."

She dropped her purse on top of the stack of speakers, reached for my jeans, and unbuckled the belt. "Watching you on stage is such a turn-on." She yanked my boxer briefs down, grabbed my cock, and rubbed me up and down. *Oh, geez.*

"Everything about you drives me crazy." I slid my hand down her chest and squeezed her breast but headed straight for her skirt. This was a quickie, right? I grabbed the fabric and drew it upwards. Teasing my fingers across the front of her panties, I rubbed her up and down. Damn, her panties were wet. "Fuck, I want you. Have you got a condom? That's not something I carry on stage."

"Here." She dug into her purse, tore one off a strip, and handed it to me.

"Were you expecting a lot of action?" I raised an eyebrow as I ripped open the packet and rolled the rubber on.

"Hell yeah. I'm not just here for Cole's birthday." She grabbed the front of my shirt and pulled my lips to hers. "Get inside me, now."

I moaned against her lips. "You are dangerous, aren't you?" Falling to my knees, I tore her panties off over her ankles and tossed them on her purse. As I stood, I dragged her skirt with me and held it near her hip. I took hold of my cock in my other hand and buried myself inside her. *Oh . . . yes.* Heat coiled up my spine and rippled across my skin. "Fuck, you feel good."

She threaded her fingers into my hair and kissed the side of my neck. "Lew, we have to be quick."

The high from performing and having her here shot a fresh wave of heat through my veins. I thrust into her slowly for all of five seconds before manic lust took over. As I kissed her, I pounded and pummeled into her. Hard and deep. Fast and frenzied. Curling my hand around her raised thigh, I drove into her, pinning her against the wall. Her wet warmth and clenched muscles around my cock made me harder and harder.

Fire skipped through my veins.

My heart thundered against hers.

Our panting breaths were hot enough to set off the alarms.

"Lewis." She dug her claws into my shoulders. Her eyes fluttered shut. "Fuck. I'm gonna come. Seriously. Oh. Shit. You got me."

Smiling against her lips, I thrust into her again and again. There was nothing as exhilarating as fucking after a show. The rush of adrenaline and surge of endorphins were intoxicating. The madness of being with Tia enhanced the vibe. As she convulsed and shuddered in my arms, I pumped my own release into her. *Oh . . . yeah!* Grinding into her, I rode out the high, savoring each blissful jolt and shock coursing through my body, my bones, and my blood. I kissed her sweet lips, stroked her silky hair. "Hmm . . . that was a good quick fuck."

Cupping my cheek, she giggled. "It was. But we better go. We can't get caught." She grabbed a packet of tissues from her purse for me to dispose of the condom and for her to clean up.

I tucked my dick back into my boxer briefs and rezipped my jeans. I glanced at the door. *Shit!* I hoped we hadn't been too loud.

"I'm down for doing that anytime." She tugged on her

panties and straightened her skirt. With a mischievous smile, she stole another kiss. "So hot. But go. I'll meet you at the bar."

"Okay. See you soon." My head still spun as I slipped out of the room first. At a run, I took off down the hall and rushed into the dressing room. The guys had just finished showering and dressing in fresh clothes. "I'm back."

"He'd better have been worth it." Cole chuckled and jerked his chin toward the bathroom. "Hurry up. We'll wait for you."

Guilt and heaven crashed through me as I grabbed my bag and dashed into the shower. This sneaking around had better be worth it. *So far, so good.*

I freshened up, then headed out to the venue's bar with the guys to mingle with the fans. Being asked to autograph merchandise, sign T-shirts, and have selfies with people added a new high to being with The Flintlocks. Security was always nearby, keeping an eye on our safety. It took us more than an hour to join our group at the cordoned off area at the far end of the bar for drinks.

At a table, Blake poured shots of vodka for everyone, then handed them out. He raised his glass to Cole. "Happy birthday. May we rock on. Party hard. Keep making hits. Cheers."

I downed my shot. Tonight was the first time I'd seen Blake let his hair down. His Texan accent drawled even more with a few drinks under his belt. Just before midnight, April brought out a huge birthday cake and we sang "Happy Birthday" to Cole. Our entire entourage and crew of twenty people had filled two tables with empty beer bottles and stacks of used shot glasses. Everyone danced and chatted, swayed and staggered on their feet. *Including me.*

Not wanting to draw attention, I kept my distance from Tia. But the little smiles and winks we threw at each other made the evening entertaining.

Near one a.m., after too many shots, I sat at a bar table with

Slip, downing a couple of fresh, icy-cold beers. Just being in the same room as Tia made my balls ache for more action. Maybe it was the unleashed flurry of having sex again after so many dry months, or the notion that sex with a woman was new and intriguing, but I had to find a way to get her alone again. I took a sip of my beer. The bitter taste tingled my tongue, but it didn't quench my thirst. My new thirst for Tia. My eyes were on her as she talked to Gena and our tech crew, and the buzz of alcohol barreled through my body. Without diverting my gaze, I spoke to Slip. "Have you ever wanted to bury yourself inside someone so bad it hurts?"

"Are we talking on an hourly, daily, or weekly basis?"

I followed his tortured gaze toward Maddy. "How long have you two been getting it on?"

"What?" His brows pinched together.

"You and Maddy."

"I don't know what you're talking about." He shook his head slowly, swiveling his glass to and fro on the table.

"Dude, it's pretty fucking obvious."

"Just like you and Tia?" He arched an eyebrow at me.

"That's news to me." I grinned over the rim of my glass.

"You had a smear of pink lipstick on your lips when you came into the dressing room. It just happens to be the same shade she's wearing."

Warmth touched my cheeks. "It was nothing more than a friendly hello kiss."

"Yeah, right. Just like Maddy and I are *just friends*." He grimaced as worry flooded his eyes. "Fuck! Can you ignore I said that?"

"No. But I won't tell anyone." Seemed like we both needed someone to talk to. I missed my friends, especially Hayden and Reg. Thanks to time zones and schedule clashes, they were no longer just a quick phone call or subway ride away. Sharing a room during promo, I'd gotten to know Slip better over the past few weeks. We got along well. And clearly, we both had secrets. "So, how long have you been with her?"

He swiped his hand back and forth across his chin, then rubbed the back of his neck. "Since we met last year. I'm running out of excuses to spin to everyone when she's in town. I feel guilty if I chat to another woman. I hate sneaking around behind Sutton and Flint's back. Neither of them know. It's totally fucked up."

"Why don't you just openly date?"

"It's . . . complicated." He lowered his voice; heartache tore through his tone. "She's Sutton's best friend. I've been burned by a similar situation. I used to date Flint's ex's best friend. It didn't end well, for any of us." Sadness flooded his eyes. "Maddy and I were never supposed to go beyond a one-night stand. We agreed. I told her upfront I didn't want a girlfriend because I like my freedom. I didn't want to be casual because it causes problems. But when she's in town, she texts, she calls, and I end up on her doorstep."

"You've got it bad for her."

"Maybe. But I don't want to hurt her. I don't want to cause problems between friends. I don't want to get to that stage where we're awkward at parties or one of us doesn't go to places to avoid seeing each other."

"You're doing that right now. You're here talking to me, avoiding her."

A glint shimmered in his eyes. "Just like you and Tia?"

I grinned, downed a mouthful of beer, then placed my glass on the table. "Now that's complicated."

"I thought you were into dudes."

"So did I . . . I mean, I am. I'm not sure what is going on between us, but we'll figure that out. It's been really hard to *change*. We don't want everyone to know until we know what we are."

Slip shot air through his nose and shook his head in warning. "You like playing with fire, don't you?"

"Not at all, but somehow, I've landed in the center of one."

"You certainly have. Do the other guys know?"

"No. I'd like to keep it that way for now."

Slip leaned forward, resting his elbows on the table. "Fine by me. Flint won't care. But Cole? That could go either way. He's very protective of her thanks to his own messed up relationships and what's happened to her in the media." Concern mixed with too much vodka and beer flooded his dark eyes. "Tia's like a sister to me, too. I didn't know Rhett well, but I knew Phil. He broke her heart. I don't want to see her hurt again."

I straightened. "You knew about Phil?"

"Yeah," he said like it was no big deal. "I caught them together on more than one occasion."

I pinched my brows together. "And you never told the others?"

"Nope." He shrugged and swayed. "I'm not one to cause unnecessary drama. I'm not a gossiper. Tia and Phil had their reasons for wanting to stay on the down-low—they didn't want to cause more issues between Flint and Phil, and they loved their secretive games. But once we signed, things changed. Phil couldn't keep his dick in his pants." He pointed at me. "So if you're going to be an asshole and screw around on her, I will say something."

My former bandmates had never looked out for each other like that. My siblings would never have protected me like this. "I've never cheated on anyone. I've had my wild times, my fun, but every time I've met someone special, being with another person has never entered my mind."

"I've never cheated either." He sighed as he slumped back in his chair. "That's the thing—Mads is special. She's fucking awesome. I haven't been with anyone else since we hooked up. But after being burned in the past, I'm not sure I want to go down the relationship road. Got any pointers on how to get out of this fucked up situation?"

I chuckled and waved my beer at him. "Sounds like you're in a relationship but won't admit it."

"I'm in a mess, that's what I'm in." He wiped his hands back and forth on top of his jeans. "It's not just about being afraid of screwing up or being hurt; it's about priorities." He jutted his chin toward our group. "My world is this band. I love what I do. I've worked hard to get here. I love this lifestyle and everything that comes with it. The travel. The attention. The fans. Music will always come first. It always does."

My breath jarred my chest. Slip was right.

At the end of the day, music came first.

Love was too unreliable.

I'd learned from my mistakes and had to be cautious. That was why I wanted to take things slow with Tia. "I agree. Music is life. But there is always room for love and compromise. You're sitting here wishing you were with Maddy. You won't know what will happen unless you try. You might find a balance, like Flint and Sutton have."

He let out a low laugh. As he swished his head from side to side, his long hair brushed across his shoulders. "They're a rare exception to the rule. I'm not that lucky. Sometimes no matter how you feel about someone or how much you love them, there's too much other shit blocking the road to being together. On both sides."

"Baggage and barriers, right?" *Yep!* Tia and I had a ton of those to deal with.

"Truckloads."

I raised my beer glass. "Here's to being fucked up by love."

We chinked our glasses and downed a mouthful of beer.

He smiled a crooked smile. "To no light at the end of the tunnel."

I hated seeing him tortured over someone he liked. But I could relate to that. With a drunken sway, I clutched onto his shoulder and gave him a gentle shake. "There is always a light—it might be a freight train coming at you or a bright new opportunity on the other side. There's no way of telling what awaits you unless you take some risks." I quirked a grin and raised my eyebrows. He needed a nudge with Maddy. I needed to be with Tia. Hopefully my plan worked. "So, want to take one?"

"One what?"

I eased back on my chair. "Maddy is sharing a room with Tia. If you want . . . Tia could stay with me. You could get some time with Maddy."

He chuckled as he shook his head. "You like stirring the pot, don't you?" He stole a glance toward Maddy. A war of want and restraint swirled in his eyes. "But you'd do that?"

Hell yeah. I want to get laid. "Absolutely." The alcohol kept talking. "I'm no expert on relationships. But when something keeps pulling you back together, maybe you should stop fighting it. If you and Maddy are meant to be, you'll find a way to make it work. Letting go of the past is hard. Change is even harder. *Trust* me on that one. But give yourself a chance to find out if what you have is real. If it's right, you will survive anything. If it fucks up, I promise I'll be here for you to help you through the mess. You've been good to me, Slip. I'll always be here if you need me."

"You got this all planned?"

"Nope. I'm winging it." I grinned but then slid some seriousness into my tone. "I hope I can trust you like you can trust me. Tia and I need some time to work things out. Are you willing to do the same with Maddy?"

Slip's leg jiggled as he met Maddy's gaze. He rubbed the back of his neck, then ruffled his fingers through his hair.

"Fuck." He slid off his stool and pointed at me. "If this fucks up, it's on you." He downed the rest of his beer and slammed the glass down on the table.

"I've got your back."

"I've always had yours." He slapped me on the shoulder, then took a step backward toward Maddy. The biggest shit-eating grin lit his face. "Don't fuck up with Tia. I want you in the band."

"I'll do my best not too."

But just like in life, there were no guarantees.

My track record had proven that.

Chapter 23

TIA

At two a.m., I headed back to the hotel with Slip, Maddy, and Lewis. Traveling together provided the perfect cover for our secret, steamy rendezvouses. No one suspected a thing. On our floor, I fell into the room with Lewis. He had my top half off before the door clicked shut.

Another two mind-blowing rounds between the bedsheets with him were ten times hotter than our previous encounters combined.

I loved he was a fast learner.

He'd always asked questions, tried different things, and had taken his time exploring, tasting, and touching me. If we were going to keep seeing each other, I wanted to do away with condoms. We agreed on getting checkups before he got home from promo so we didn't have to use them.

The following afternoon, having to say goodbye to Lewis and act like nothing was going on between us in front of my brother and the rest of the band, had taken all my self-control. I'd wanted to kiss Lewis again, so freaking much. But as I gave him a quick hug goodbye, and breathed his earthy scent in, dizziness swam through my head like I was high up on a tightrope, with no safety net, afraid to take another step. He was right. We had to take our relationship slow. I didn't want either one of us to get hurt. Not again. But sneaking around had woken a desire in me that had been hibernating for way too long . . . the need to have some wicked fun. Just the thought of stealing hot moments and finding ways to have sexy rendezvouses with Lewis without being caught turned me on. For the first time in months, I had something to look forward to. Lewis would be home in two weeks. I couldn't wait to get him alone again.

I stepped over to Maddy. As I gave her a hug goodbye, I whispered a sweet thank you in her ear. She pursed her lips, blushed and nodded. Then she jumped in her car to drive north across the border to Vancouver, where she filmed her show. The small, sexy smile Lewis threw me as I left for the airport in an SUV with Sutton, quickened the flutter in my heartbeat. I was already counting down the days until the band's promo tour ended so Lewis and I could find out if this fire between us had any longevity.

The anticipation of seeing him again helped me through the next two weeks. So did his texts and pictures.

On the afternoon the guys were supposed to come home from their promotional tour, I couldn't sit still. As I lounged in a director's chair behind the cameras at work, I flicked through my script, unable to concentrate on the words. Today's scenes were taking too long. While Peyton and Mia ran through their takes, Sutton and I glanced at our watches every few minutes. The day couldn't end soon enough.

"Two weeks apart is too long." Sutton scanned her cell phone, checking out the latest social media post from the guys' performance in New York last night. I'd already done that.

"How are you going to survive being away from Flint when

he's on tour?" I rested my sore leg up onto a stool in front of me.

"They've planned the dates so Flint and I can catch up at least once a month."

"That's cool." *Hmm.* That would work for Lewis and me too. If we made it that far. "So after he gets home tonight and you *catch up*, do you have plans for the weekend?"

"Yeah. We're going to a spa resort in Palm Springs. I don't know what the other guys are doing. Do you?"

"Cole won't stop going out, bringing chicks home, drumming or running every morning. I'm not sure about Slip and Lewis."

"You sure about that?" She raised an inquisitive eyebrow. "You're always texting Lewis."

Shit. She's noticed. I gave her a causal shrug. "It's just friendly catch-up talk."

"But you light up at every message. Smile. Your cheeks flush."

I hugged my script to my chest. "He's fun to chat with. That's all."

Concern darkened Sutton's deep blue eyes. "Are you wanting more? Hoping he will change for you?"

He had. But that didn't eliminate my doubts that he'd wake up one day and realize I wasn't what he wanted, and he truly was gay. I'd come off second best before. "We're just friends." *With benefits. And more chemistry than a science lab.*

"I don't want you to get hurt."

"You have nothing to worry about." It was sweet that she cared, but I could look after myself. I knew what I'd gotten into.

"But I do. You're full of laughs and fun when we hang out with the guys and the crew, but here on set you're different. Your spark fades. It's there but just not as bright." She reached over and placed her hand on my forearm. "Is everything okay? Is there anything I can do to help?"

Sutton loved everything about our show. Her character. The

storyline. The fashion. But me? I couldn't find my groove. I must have been a decent actress because no one else seemed to have suspected anything.

"Sutt, I love you. Trust me, everything is fine." I hated lying, but she didn't need to know that I was exploring my options. Over the past couple of weeks, I'd been out several times. I'd had dinner with my agent and asked Jack to look for new roles—he'd been shocked out of his wits but had respected my wishes. He made too much money off me to question my decision. I'd caught up with Duke and Chloe at two of their gigs. Helping Chloe on sound had provided some fun and much-needed distraction from counting down the hours and days until Lewis got home. I'd even researched going back to school, exploring my options in TV and film, but nothing had caught my eye.

"I know you're not fine." She clutched my hand, all gentle and caring. "But I'm here if you need me. You can tell me anything."

"Thank you. You're cool. I can see why Flint loves you."

"Thanks. He's my one." She blushed, then groaned, slumping in her chair. "But boy, I wish this day would hurry up and end. I want to go home and be there when Flint arrives."

I couldn't argue with that. I wanted to see Lewis . . . be with him. How could I do that without Cole finding out? It would be a challenge—but a challenge I was up for.

Filming wrapped at six p.m. Sutton and I rushed to hug the other girls good bye, farewelled the crew, and took off. She sped out of the studio's parking lot in her Mercedes like a police car in pursuit of a criminal, but my driver wouldn't rush, going all *Driving Miss Daisy* on me. I couldn't wait until I could get behind the wheel again. But my leg showed no signs of getting better. Regular physical therapy every Thursday morning only ever provided temporary relief. The pain always returned within hours.

Would being permanently injured turn off Lewis? He loved

getting out with the guys. Snowboarding. Having adventures. I'd never want someone to stop doing something they loved because I couldn't. I never wanted to hold anyone back. *Ergh!* I didn't want to think about that now.

My driver pulled into the driveway at home. My stomach sank at the sight of another town car parked in front of the house. The chauffeur stood waiting, leaning against the hood and vaping.

Who was here?

Did we have visitors for dinner?

I hobbled through the front door, past Cole's bag laying at the bottom of the staircase, and into the living room. Cole and Lewis jumped up from the sofa and rushed to greet me. No one else was in the room.

"Hey, baby sis." Cole hugged me. "God, it's so good to be home."

I slipped from Cole's embrace into Lewis's arms. "Hi."

He nuzzled into my ear and whispered, "Missed you." But his hug was quick and fleeting. No need to raise Cole's suspicions.

"Tee, something's come up." Cole ruffled his hands through his hair and grinned. "I'm gonna head out to Vegas for the weekend and catch up with Irena and her friends. She's there doing a photoshoot for *Elle* magazine."

I had no idea who Irena was but my heart happy danced. *Cole was going away. YAY!* But I packed on the sulking and pouting. "Are your supermodels more important than me? I was looking forward to hanging out and hearing all the gossip from promo." Keeping my hopes on a leash, I kept my tone causal and carefree. "Is Slip going with you?"

"Nope." Trouble furrowed Cole's brow as he shook his head. "He bailed. Some cousin I've never heard of is visiting this weekend."

Cousin being Maddy. I zipped my lips, trying not to smile. My heart beat a touch faster as I turned to Lewis. "What about you? Are you going?" *Say no, please?* I prayed nothing had changed since we'd Snapchatted two days ago when we'd discussed our clear doctors' results and this weekend.

He gave me the sexy eye as he shook his head. "No. My brother, Lee, is coming to LA for a conference in Anaheim. We're catching up on Sunday afternoon."

Yes. We were on.

He threw me a quick wink. "With a few days off, I aim to *explore* some more of LA."

Warmth flooded my cheeks. *Oh yeah.* I loved that he meant me.

"Tia can show you around." Cole hooked his arm around my shoulders. "She needs to get out of the house."

"Maybe. We'll see." I rubbed Cole's arm. I should have felt guilty about abusing the trust Cole had in me and Lewis, but I didn't. Time together was what Lewis and I needed.

"Okay." Cole clapped his hands and headed for the door. "I'm out of here." He picked up his bag. "I'm gonna grab some sleep during the drive out to Vegas, then party the weekend away in a house full of hot chicks. I'll be back on Monday night."

"Alright then." I wanted to kick him out the door as fast as I could, but I casually leaned against the doorjamb and waved goodbye. "Have fun. Love you."

I held my breath as he hopped in the car and shut the door. The driver took off, and the security gate clicked shut. He was gone. Butterflies swirled in my gut as I stepped inside and locked the door.

Lewis stepped in beside me. His small smile didn't hide the anxiety swarming in his eyes. "We couldn't have planned that better even if we tried."

"No. My brother's addiction to sex and supermodels has paid off."

"Indeed." He tugged on my shirt. "So, what's on our agenda?"

"You nervous?"

"Not gonna lie. Yep."

"We don't have to rush. We have the house to ourselves for the whole weekend. We can take this slow."

"Are you fucking kidding me?" He snaked his hands around my waist and drew me in for a kiss. Long, slow touches and flicks of his tongue made my knees weaken. "I plan to have you naked as often as possible. I aim to explore every inch of your body, starting here." He ran his hand to the front of my jeans, cupped between my legs, and pressed my zipper into my crotch. *Oh wow.* "I'm not going to waste one second of this weekend with you. That okay?"

"I like the sound of that." My voice came out breathy and hot. "After a shower."

He scooped me up in his arms and carried me upstairs to my bedroom. As we shuffled into the bathroom, we undressed each other and fell into the cascading warm water. Sensual touches and kisses turned hungry. He buried himself inside me, pinning me against the cool tiled wall. Jolts of electricity charged through my core every time he thrust into me.

Sweeping his hair off his face, I whispered against his lips, "You're getting the hang of this 'fucking a girl' thing."

"I plan on being an expert by the end of the weekend. But I've much to learn. You up for that?"

"I am. I hope my leg will handle it."

"I'll make sure it does. We'll work with it. So, is this good for you?" He spun me 'round, bent me over and fucked my pussy from behind.

The breath shot from my lungs. "Oh yeah. That . . . is good."

This was going to be a fucking great weekend.

Chapter 24

TIA

I woke next to Lewis late the following morning in a tangle of bedsheets. Lying with my cheek against his shoulder, I glided my fingers over his collarbone, then traced the outer edge of the horned, bullock's head tattoo that covered most of his chest. I tilted my head back to look at him. "Why did you get this tattoo?"

He stared at the ceiling, took a deep breath, then met my gaze. Sadness darkened his eyes. "To remind me to be fearless. To face things head on. To fight for what I believe in and who I am."

His words struck the center of my chest. He bore some heartbreaking scars most would never see. But they'd given him an underlying strength that was admirable. "Is that about being gay? Or life in general?"

"Both. Pop taught me to be strong and to be true to myself. He never judged me, never cared about my sexuality, never hesitated in taking me in. He helped me through college, vetoed my boyfriends, and got my ass out of trouble on more than one occasion. He was awesome."

"You miss him?"

"Every day." Lewis entwined our fingers and held them against his chest. His eyes turned glassy. "He was always so full of life. The community adored him. He was always helping people, offering meals to the homeless, and surrounded by friends. Pop felt like home. He always just loved me for me."

And now, here Lewis was, with me in my bed. We were on a journey to see if this was something that could survive and not just a steamy fling. We had to be true to ourselves and see if we were worth fighting for. The path ahead was nowhere near clear.

He rubbed the back of my head. "What about your folks? Did they mess you up like mine did me?"

He made a joke of it but being disowned would screw anyone up. "They were never around much when Cole and I were kids. They're workaholics. Mom's now CEO of a big French pharmaceutical company. Dad was an engineer, designing infrastructure road networks, but now he just consults on various projects." I'd never miss their hounding and nagging. "They always pushed us to excel at school. Mom was a real tiger mom. We had tutors for everything, or babysitters—whichever way you look at it. We had to do music, sport, chess, debating. We had to be the best at everything. We got top grades. But no matter how much our parents tried to sway us toward the corporate world, Cole loved drumming and I wanted to be an action star."

Lewis drew tiny light circles across my back and played with the long strands of my hair. "But they never stopped you, right?"

"No, they didn't." I'd never deny that. "Doesn't mean they were happy. Even now, they keep telling us how disappointed they are in our career choices. We should be saving the world and building a better future, not playing around. For them, it's not about the money and fame—it's business prestige and academic accolades."

"Do you see them often?"

"No." My hand fell softly from his hold onto his chest. As I circled his nipples with my fingertip, little goose bumps dotted his skin. "I saw them at Phil's funeral. Before that . . . um . . . maybe when I came to LA for the Emmys the year before that. Our paths rarely cross—not even for the holidays. They aren't involved in my life or Cole's. It's less stressful this way. There's less arguments and bickering."

"Yeah. I don't miss the fights I had at home when I was a kid, or those I had with my old band, or my ex. Emilio used to dig at me all the time for not being a huge star. For me, music has never been about the money—always the passion."

"I was that way about stunt work too." I whispered against his skin. "It over-ruled wanting to be an actor. I was lucky I got to do both." With light strokes, I traced his collarbone, the line of his shoulder and down his arm, and stopped at the inked pair of playing cards on his bicep—a jack of hearts and diamonds. "What about this tattoo?"

He flexed his arm, bulging his toned biceps toward me. *Nice.* He smiled a small smile. "One night playing cards with Hayden and Reg, just after my twenty-first, I lost a shitload of money. I was a dick, being a cocky asshole, thinking I'd won. They wiped me out. That's the hand I lost with. That tattoo is my reality check to not be a stupid imbecile ever again."

"I can't imagine you being cocky about anything other than music."

"I'm not cocky." He playfully tapped the back of my head.

"You are, but not in an arrogant, asshole way." I lifted my chin to look up at him again. "You light up when you play with the guys, perform on stage, or when you find that touch of magic for a song. Your talent was wasted on The Saylors. Trust your gut, your skill, your creative ideas. The guys love that. There is nothing sexier than confidence."

"I'm a musician. There will always be self-doubt." He combed his fingers through my hair. "I'm still finding my feet and earning my place in the band. But yes, I'm getting better and more comfortable."

I stabbed my finger against his chest. "You've earned it. You've survived promo. You've met the next milestone to do the album launch."

"Yeah. I did, didn't I?" He caught my hand and kissed it. "God, I want to make tour."

The passion in his tone struck a chord in my heart. I missed doing what I loved. "I hope you do too." I lowered my voice. "I need to find something that makes me want to leap out of bed every morning again. I miss my daily hit of adrenaline and excitement at work." I planted a light kiss on his chest. "All I know is . . . I want to leave my show at the end of this season. It's not me. I talked to Jack, my agent, and I have him looking for new roles. If something doesn't come up, maybe I'll go back to school and change careers completely."

"You'd quit acting?" His eyes widened in an I'm-intrigued way, not with an are-you-mad kind of startlement. "But you're a huge star."

"For me, it's never been about fame and money, but action and thrills. If *Through the Smoke* had ended, and nothing as action-packed had come my way, I would've been happy just being a stunt person. It's been hard to accept I can't do what I love anymore. But I need to find something more exhilarating than what I'm doing now. So, I'm looking at my options and movie roles where the shoots aren't as long as TV shows."

"I can see you in movies. That would be cool." He swept my hair off my cheek and tucked it behind my ear. "But school? You'd go back to studying?"

"Yes. I've been looking at some TV and film courses, but nothing has caught my interest."

Rolling to face me, he drew the sheet over our waists. His silver eyes shimmered like ice in the morning sunlight as he stroked my arm. "What about stunt co-ordination or special effects?"

"I couldn't do stunt co-ordination; it's still very physical. And special effects involves sitting behind a computer for most of the day. That's not me."

He draped his hand over my hip. "Why don't you take some time off to figure it out? You could come with us on tour."

My heart rate quickened. Travel? "And do what? Be your groupie?"

"No, my lover." He chuckled and kissed my forehead. "You could work with the sound and lighting engineers. You loved helping in New York and at our launch."

I jerked my chin back a fraction and furrowed my brow. "On AV?" The cogs in my head turned. Warmth stirred in my belly. *Could I? No.* Operating mixers and lights was just a hobby.

Something I'd learned.

Something I *loved.*

As I dragged my thumb over the soft line of whiskers above his mouth, a small smile tugged at the corner of my lips. "I do like pressing your buttons. I've loved helping you guys out. The crowd at the launch was awesome, the tech was fun to play with, and the rush was wicked, but to do that on tour or as a career? I don't know. I love the band, but I'm not sure it's me." My pulse had quickened though.

He caught my hand and held it beneath his chin. "A fire just ignited in your eyes as you talked about it. You're smiling and your energy has totally changed. Life is too short and unpredictable. Do something you love. If running tech gives you a rush, follow it."

"The pay cut would kill me, but you're right." Something had flickered to life in the pit of my belly and had warmed my blood. "You might be onto something. Maybe I could find something similar in the film industry. That would be fun." I stole a quick kiss from his lips. "Let me look into it. I'll do some research into jobs and courses." Sound engineering, event management, show production . . . I had options to explore and was excited to investigate.

Confusion crinkled his brow. "Why wouldn't you work with us? Gena's going on maternity leave soon. You could be part of our team. And I wouldn't mind having you around every day . . . and in my bed at night." He pushed me down on the mattress and hovered over me.

"You'd put up with me flashing lights in your eyes, controlling your sound with a flick of my fingertips, and watching your every move?"

"Not the lights, but the rest kinda turns me on." He slid his leg over mine and nudged his growing erection against my thigh.

"Hmm. I like that." I linked my hands behind his neck. "But no. I don't want to be dragged back into that world of partying and gossip, and we need to be logical and sensible. Even if I moved into that field, I'd want to keep us and work separate. If we didn't work out, I'd hate it to cause problems for you and the guys." But the hole in my chest ached. In truth, hanging out socially with the band here at home was awesome, but being with them every day would remind me too much of Phil. Of my loss, my heartbreak, my old self. I wasn't that person anymore.

I was on the path to finding the new me. Lewis had just helped uncover a potential direction, something that had always been at my fingertips but had never been a consideration due to my love of stunts. But now the way was clear.

"We won't cause problems." Lewis dipped his head and

flicked his tongue over my nipple. I flinched and giggled. He grinned like he'd just tasted ice cream. "The guys and I will be fine. I don't plan on going anywhere."

I smoothed my hand over his soft hair. "And I want to ensure you don't." There were no guarantees, but I'd do everything to ensure he stayed with the band. Even if that meant maintaining separate lives.

He rolled on top of me and nestled between my legs. Mischief ignited in his eyes. "You will find something new, I'm sure of it. There's nothing wrong with starting over. I've done it more than once. So to celebrate new directions, we need to do something fun, and something that won't hurt your leg. *I* have something in mind."

"Like what?" I wriggled beneath him, edging him toward my opening.

"Do you trust me?" He brushed his soft lips across mine and smiled.

"Not totally."

"Fair enough." He chuckled. Sliding his hand around my waist, he rocked his hips against me. A gravelly groan rumbled deep in my throat. "*Mmm.* After I've made you come, we're going on a date."

I ran my hands over his shoulders. "But what if we're photographed together?"

He kissed the tip of my nose. "Cole gave us explicit instructions to get out of the house. So that's exactly what we're going to do. We just can't kiss and fool around in public."

"If that's the case, I better get my fix now so I can last the day." I hooked my legs around his waist and drew his body flush against mine.

"We won't be gone that long. A few hours, tops."

"Don't care. Just fuck me. Please?"

"I can do that." He eased into me, filling me, claiming me,

owning me. Shivers darted across my skin as he thrust and drove in deep. He teased his lips across my mouth, searing me with his hot breath. "I honestly never thought this would feel so good. So different."

I wrapped my arms around his shoulders and pulsed my hips in time with his movements. "Yeah, but you didn't tell me where we are going?"

"You'll have to wait and see."

Shit. What was I in for?

I didn't care. He drove into me, making me see stars.

Chapter 25

LEWIS

Ever since I'd met Tia, the guys had always raved about how outgoing she'd been. Dancing had caused her leg to ache too much. She couldn't drive yet; possibly, she never would again. She couldn't do stunts. But there was so much she could do. She just needed someone to show her. With Cole not home, I was more than happy to do so. It was a beautiful late April day, not one to be spent indoors.

This was our first date.

Me? Dating a girl?

My head still spun, struggling to be comfortable with a woman.

But Tia wanting to quit her job added new pressures and deadlines to firmly establishing how serious we were about each other. It was too early to tell. But if she pursued a career in AV, she should do it with The Flintlocks and her brother, not on some TV or film set. I had a couple of months to be more secure about my place in the band, pass more milestones, and be confident that they'd support our relationship. Slip had been cool, but I still had reservations about Flint and Cole's reactions. Flint got pissed every time I missed a beat during "Changes" thanks to my stupid nerves getting the better of me. Cole had warned me not to touch his sister from day one, and there I was, banging her senseless. It went against every grain in my body to not tell them Tia and I were seeing each other, but until I was more certain about how I felt for her, we had to stay under wraps.

But we had a free pass this weekend.

After a few hectic weeks of promo, I needed an afternoon of fun. With Tia.

While she ate a bowl of fruit salad at the kitchen counter, I made a few phone calls. With plans in place, we set off in her Mercedes.

I loved driving in LA. People complained about the traffic and chaos, but damn, it was so open and scenic. Instead of skyscrapers towering overhead and narrow streets, there were palm trees, wide roads, and sunshine. So much better than New York.

Forty minutes later, I pulled into a parking lot at Marina del Rey and headed toward the tourist office.

"We're going on a boat?" Tia asked as she hooked her backpack over her shoulder. Her yoga pants showed off her long, sexy legs. "Not a speed boat, right? The jarring will hurt my knee and ankle."

I didn't miss the anxiety in her voice. I caught her arm and drew her to a halt outside the office. "It's a pond out there today, and this is not an ordinary boat. I'm sure you won't hurt your leg. If you do, I promise to give you a full foot and leg massage all night long if I have to."

"Hmm." A wicked smile inched across her lips. "Ow! My leg is hurting."

Chuckling, I disappeared into the office and checked in at the counter. With directions in hand, I led Tia into the marina toward our berth.

"Holy shit." Tia gaped at the boat tied up beside a little blue hut. "Parasailing? I can't do that."

"Yes. You can. You've jumped out of planes, ziplined canyons, and abseiled off cliffs. This may not be as hardcore as those things, but it will be fun."

She stared at the speedboat decked out with parasailing rigging. Sheer terror darkened her eyes. "No." She shook her head and tugged on the back of my T-shirt to draw me away. "Lewis, I can't. I'll get hurt."

My chest shuddered. I hated that she was afraid of reinjuring herself. I wanted to show her that she could do so many things without getting hurt, like I'd done in New York. "Tia. Stop." I took her hands in mine. Her soft fingers trembled. Her skin was cold and clammy. I rubbed my thumb across her knuckles, wanting to erase her doubts and ignore my quickening pulse. "You won't. I promise. I'll help you. The guy assured me you don't have to use your legs and the landing is easy. We won't touch the water. You take off and land on the platform at the back of the boat. You've got this."

"Lewis?" She scanned the boat and gnawed on her lower lip. She took a few deep breaths then a flash of excitement shot through her eyes. *Oh, yeah.* She wanted to do this. "I don't know."

I squeezed her hands and gave them a gentle shake. "If the ocean is too rough, we'll come back."

She looked at the two operators, the big engines on the back of the boat, then at me. A nervous smile quivered across her lips. "Okay."

"Awesome."

We stepped onto the pontoon. It dipped with our weight, but not enough for Tia to struggle with balance. After meeting the parasailing operators, Aaron and Vance, and helping Tia onto the boat, we put on lifejackets and were ready to take off.

As I took a seat beside her, my fingers itched to touch her, but we couldn't do that in public. Tongues wagged. The paparazzi could be on the beach, tracking us with their telescopic lenses. But damn, she was beautiful. Cascading behind her baseball cap, her ponytail caught the breeze as we headed out of the marina. Her smile brightened as we sped up. *Yeah.* We both needed a day out.

Just off Venice Beach, the boat slowed to a halt and rocked gently from side to side. *Ergh!* Did it have to do that?

"Okay, folks," Aaron headed toward the back of the boat. "Time to get you harnessed up."

Tia clutched onto the edge of the seat. "Lewis, I've changed my mind."

"You can't back out now. We're here. Are you seasick?" As the boat swayed, nausea pooled in my gut. I wasn't at the point of having to hurl, but if it got any rougher, I'd be hanging over the side of the boat. Whose idea was this? *Fool.*

"No. It's just—"

"Just nothing." I tapped her thigh. "Your leg will be fine, so get your ass into that harness."

"Oh." She threw me a saucy smile. "Bossy Lewis. I like him."

Fuck! Why did every sexy comment from her spike my pulse? "Good. Then do as I say, and I won't have to punish you."

As she stepped into one of the tandem harnesses, she lowered her voice so only I could hear. "What if I want you to do just that?"

Blood rushed to my cock. Not good when I was been cinched into straps. I hovered my lips next to her ear. "I will do anything you want. Trust me."

She thumbed toward the marina. "Can we go home now? Please."

Chuckling, I nudged her arm. "After this, absolutely. And I'm prepared to get a speeding ticket to get you there as soon as possible."

"I'll pay the fine if we get pulled over."

"Deal." I handed Aaron my cell phone. He took a couple of photos of us, then I stowed it back in Tia's bag. As I stood beside Tia, Aaron clipped us onto the parasailing bar. I clutched onto the straps. My heart stampeded. I'd always wanted to do this. But as the boat took off, I questioned my decision. I didn't know who was more anxious. Me or Tia?

"How are you doing?" I hollered to her over the wind. "Leg check?"

"Yeah. All good." Her gorgeous green eyes glittered in the sunlight.

"You ready?" Aaron yelled louder than the roaring motors.

Tia gave me a nod. "I am. You?"

"Hell yeah," I shouted, gripping onto my harness for dear life.

"Let's fly." Aaron counted down on his fingers. "Three. Two. One. Go!"

The parachute shot out behind us. Seconds later, we lifted from the boat.

As the winch released and we rose higher and higher, Tia shrieked . . . but it wasn't from fear. It was excitement.

With the harness cutting into my thighs and way too close to my nut sack, we soared above the ocean. The coastline loomed to our right, the endless Pacific to the left. Sunshine sparkled on top of the ocean like shattered glass had been spilled across the surface.

As the wind whipped my hair against my face, I yelled to Tia, "This is incredible."

"Oh my God. I love this," she shouted.

My heart swelled. To see her smile was the best feeling ever. Mission accomplished.

For five minutes, we flew up the coast toward Santa Monica

Pier, then we looped around to head back toward the marina. We were winched slowly into the boat. I'd instructed Aaron to make sure the landing was controlled and gentle, so Tia wouldn't hurt her leg. Once my feet hit the deck, Aaron and I caught her, released her harness, and set her on a seat without her having to put a foot on the ground.

"How was that?" I swept the stray strands of hair off her face. "Your leg okay?"

She flung her arms around my neck and planted a huge kiss on my cheek. "Argh! That was brilliant. Thank you."

"You're welcome." I hugged her back, but my heart raced way too fast. "See? You can do things that don't hurt your leg."

"I needed this." She clutched onto me tighter. "So much."

She crushed her lips against mine. So much for remaining discreet. As I kissed her back, my heart hammered against my ribs. God, I wanted her. But not there.

"Tia." I broke our kiss and caressed her neck. "Too many eyes."

"Yeah. I know. What I want to do to you shouldn't be done in public. We'd get arrested."

"Hmm. You in handcuffs sounds hot."

"I have some at home in my room."

"Really?"

"Yes."

"Geez. We need to go. Now."

Chapter 26

TIA

Teasing Lewis, rubbing my hand up his leg, and hovering it dangerously close to his crotch had the desired effect during our drive home. We barely made it inside the house before he crushed me against the wall and showered me with kisses.

"You're so mean," he panted.

"No . . . it was foreplay."

"Then you'd better take as good as you can give."

"Try me."

He raked his hand down my chest, cupped and teased my breast. "God, I love touching you."

"I'd prefer you did that while naked."

He clutched the bottom of my T-shirt and yanked it over my head. My bra joined my other clothes. Dipping his head, he claimed my breast, licking and flicking his warm, wet tongue over my nipple. Goose bumps dotted my skin. But it wasn't enough. I wanted more of him. All of him.

I tugged on his shirt, pulling it over his head. My heartbeat quickened as I raked my gaze over his ripped, toned physique. *Hmm. Mine.*

He picked me up, I hooked my legs around his waist, and he carried me upstairs to my bedroom. As he lay me down on the bed, he hovered over me. "God, you're beautiful."

"And I can't keep my hands off you." I ripped open his board shorts and dipped my hand into his boxer briefs. Caressing his hardened cock, I rubbed him up and down. The heat of his flesh sizzled against my fingertips. "Lie down."

"Now who's bossy," he moaned against my mouth, then fell back onto the mattress beside me.

The second his head hit the pillow, I scrambled upright and tore off his shorts and boxer briefs. My yoga pants joined them. "I want to explore every inch of your body with my tongue." I circled my hand around his cock and swiped my thumb over the head. "Starting here." I took him into my mouth.

I wanted to satisfy him in every way possible, be the best lover he'd ever had. Do everything he wanted and needed. I'd been adventurous with Rhett and Phil; there weren't many things in the bedroom I hadn't tried. As I licked and flicked and circled my tongue over his cock, a moan fell from his lips. "Fuck, you're good at that."

"Want more?" Coating my fingertips in his beaded arousal, I slid my hand downward, massaging and teasing his flesh. With soft tickles and teases, I made my way toward his ass. I reached his puckered skin, circling and sleeking his entrance.

He flinched and wriggled. "Tia. You don't have to do that."

"I want to." I licked the head of his cock and pressed my finger against his hole. We'd gone down on each other, but this was next level. More intimate. Did he trust me? "Do you want me to?"

White-hot heat blazed in his silver eyes. His breath panted. Then, he nodded.

As I took him into my mouth, I eased the tip of my finger into his butt. His hips bucked, and the breath shot from his lungs.

Sucking and licking his hardness, I tasted and teased him. But as I drove my finger farther into his ass, the hottest moan I'd ever heard fell from his lips. Such a turn-on. His muscles squeezed around me. The pleasure fluttering across his face urged me on. I slowly worked my way in deeper, pulsing, taunting his depths.

"Oh geez, Tia. Yeah. That." He panted as he clutched onto the bedding. His hips jerked thrusting his cock deeper into my mouth. Every muscle on his glorious body flexed and rippled.

Swirling my tongue over his tip, I lapped at him. Sucked him. Tasted him. My head spun with a dizzy high. This was intoxicating, having him lost in pleasure caused by me. Bobbing my head, I quickened my pace. I added another finger, thrust into his butt, then wriggled and twisted them inside him.

"Oh, fuck." Lewis knotted his fingers into the long strands of my hair. "Babe. I'm gonna come. You don't have to—"

Yes, I did. I wanted all of him. Charging my fingers faster and harder into his ass, I took his cock deeper into my throat. The salty taste of him was totally addictive. I didn't slow down.

"Oh, sweet fuck," he hissed. His butt tightened around my fingers. As he fucked my mouth, his hot release spurted into me. His body jerked. Twitched. Throbbed. Pulsed. Laughing, and with the biggest smile on his face, he collapsed against the pillow. "Okay. Stop. Wow. But stop."

I eased my fingers out of him then crawled up beside him. My knee ached from the funny angle I'd been lying on. But I'd survived.

He swiped my hair off my face and kissed me. "Damn, you never cease to amaze me."

He kissed me like I was his oxygen. As he stroked my hair, there wasn't one inch of my face he didn't press his lips against. So tender. Sweet. Somewhat dreamy.

His hand glided down my side and eased between my legs. His finger slid through my slit. God, I was wet for him. "I want to make you come harder than you made me blow. And that was pretty fucking big."

"I've had more practice at giving blow jobs than you have had at going down on me." We'd had fun with him exploring between my legs with his fingers and oh, his tongue. He'd tried many different tactics, tuning into my reactions, with me telling him what I enjoyed. It was like he wanted to master my body and I was only too happy to provide him with the guidebook.

"I wasn't talking about going down on you." He worked his sleeked fingers toward my ass. "I meant do you take as well as you give? Here?"

"Yes. But would you like to make sure I don't run away?" I crossed my wrists above my head. "Cuff me."

"Fuck." He nuzzled into my neck, licked and nipped the soft, sensitive skin beneath my lobe.

"They're in my nightstand. Second drawer." I needed the rush, the thrill—another hit of pure, hot adrenaline.

"Bossy. But we do this my way." He reached into my nightstand and pulled out my silver cuffs with leopard-print padding. He dangled them from his fingertip and burned me with his smoldering gaze. "God, you turn me on."

"Likewise." I held out my wrists.

He undid the cuffs and clipped one band around my wrist. A wicked grin inched across his lips. "I'm glad you like to play. Anytime you want to stop, just say so."

"Trust me, I won't be asking you to stop."

Chuckling, he shook his head. "Roll over. Move to the edge of the bed. You can put your leg down if it hurts."

So thoughtful. I tossed the pillow aside. On my knees, I faced the headboard. He inched in behind me, nudging his returning erection against my butt cheek. Taking my hands, he placed them on the bed frame, linked the cuffs around the wooden top railing, then clipped the other band around my free wrist. "This okay?"

"Oh yeah." The space between my legs clenched in anticipation. My pulse quickened.

Scooping my hair back, he trailed his fingers down my spine. "You are so beautiful, Tee." He caressed and circled my butt cheek, then dipped his hand between my legs. With slow, languid strokes, he slid two fingers through my wet folds. Up. Down. Up . . . down.

My eyes fluttered closed. *Fuck.* I was going to come just from his touch.

Hovering his lips near my ear, he moaned. "Do you know how good you feel?"

My core clenched. "Lewis? Please?" I wriggled my butt against him.

Smiling, he kissed my neck and sleeked my arousal toward my ass. As he sank his teeth into the ridge of my shoulder, grazing and nipping at my flesh, his scorching breath sent goose bumps coiling across my skin. Nuzzling into my ear, he whispered, "I've wanted to fuck your hot ass since our first time. I want to bury myself inside you. Make you come. Hard. That okay?"

"Yes."

"How bad do you want me?"

As he dipped two fingers into my vagina, he pressed his thumb against my butthole, rubbing me, probing me, teasing me.

Oh, Lord. I rocked back toward his touch. "Mmm." I yanked on my cuffs; the padded steel dug into my wrists. The restraint, the submission, the need to trust him burned through my veins like a blazing inferno. "I'm gonna break the headboard if you don't get inside me now."

"Feisty. I like that." He eased his thumb into my butt and worked his way in deeper. I cinched around him. But as he slowly plunged and prodded me, and fingered my pussy, my body relaxed. My head fell back, dizzy from his hypnotic rhythm and pace. *So freaking good.* He bit and tugged on my earlobe. "My God, you're so fucking wet. I have to have you."

He withdrew his hand, then nudged his cock against me, sliding it between my butt cheeks. He teased his head against my hole, dipping and pressing into me gently. I rocked my hips backward, widened my knees. Gripping onto the headboard, I closed my eyes and exhaled. I wanted him more than anyone I'd ever wanted before.

Slowly, he entered my ass. Every one of my muscles gripped around him, sucking him inside me. Pleasure and pain coiled through my core, up my spine, and settled into the base of my neck. "Oh yes."

His heavy breath filled the air as he thrust gently, filling me with every inch of his length. "Tia." My name falling from his lips sent tingles rippling across my skin.

He took hold of my hips and drove into me with discipline and restraint. Time and time again. But then, hunger for more took over. He quickened his pace, adding more force and heat. As he penetrated me, my head lolled forward. I wanted to touch him, kiss him, but my cuffs held me in place. I was under his complete control. *So hot.*

Snaking one of his hands forward around my hip, he headed between my legs and embed his fingers inside my pussy. "You like that?"

"Fuck yes." My voice was a breathless hot mess.

He pumped his fingers into me, and buried his cock into my behind, deeper and deeper. A guttural moan rumbled deep in his throat. "Hold on, baby. I got you."

Rocking against him, I met every one of his thrusts. *So. Damn. Good.* But then, *oh my.* He hit that sweet spot deep inside me with a new vengeance. The combination of his fingers and cock hammering into me sent charged flames rushing to my core. Every one of my muscles gripped onto him. My toes curled. My breath panted. My knee ached but I didn't want to stop. "Lewis. There. Oh. Yes."

He slammed into me, filling me with his cock and fingers. Rubbing me. Pumping me. Riding me till I was on the edge.

"Lewis," I hollered. "Fuck." The most intense orgasm of my life shot through me. Sparks zapped every one of my nerve endings, even shocked every hair on my scalp. My body convulsed and shuddered as he pushed into me again and again.

"Argh," he groaned, spilling his own release into me. Thrusting. Quaking. Jerking. Wrapping his arms around me, he crushed my back into his chest. As we rode out the wave of bliss, our breaths panted. His heart pounded against my shoulder blades. Sweat licked our skin. He smiled against my ear and withdrew his cock. "Damn. That was so fucking hot."

He released my cuffs, then tossed them on the floor. He grabbed some tissues off my nightstand for us to clean up, then they joined my cuffs. Lying down, he drew me into his embrace. Facing each other, we kissed, touched, and smiled against each other's lips.

He swiped my hair off my face. "I've had a lot of anal, but that—touching you, feeling you clench around my fingers while I fucked you—just took it to another level."

"Gotta say, best anal I've ever had too."

"I've kinda had a lot of experience in that area." He chuckled, then softened his tone. "How are the wrists?"

I held up one hand. Red marks circled my skin. "Fine. Worth it."

"Definitely." He kissed me. Every flick of his tongue against mine made me crave more. Would I ever get my fill of him?

I didn't want this bubble to burst. Didn't want the way he turned me on to ever fade. As we touched, kissed, and came down off our high, my heart beat to a new rhythm. He'd brought me back to life. Made me feel like anything was possible.

Was I falling for him? *Yep.* How could I not?

But unease lurked in the pit of my gut. Every time something good happened to me, it all turned to shit. Was it possible to keep my relationship with Lewis a secret so nothing and no one could ever mess it up?

I wanted to stay out of the spotlight and didn't want our lives and careers to get in the way. But inevitably, they would.

As the late afternoon sunshine steamed through my windows, we dozed in each other's arms. We should shower. Get dressed. Go out to dinner. But being locked away in my room felt like heaven.

How long could we stay like this? Days? Weeks? Months?

Lewis's cell phone beeped with a message.

Seconds.

He reached onto the floor and grabbed his shorts to get it.

He stared at the screen.

His body turned cold and rigid.

"What?" Concern chilled my blood. "Who is it?"

His brow furrowed. "Um . . . Emilio. He wants to talk. Come see me."

My heart stilled. "Why?"

Lewis grimaced; heartache darkened his eyes. "He misses me."

Oh, shit.

With each passing second, the grooves in his brow deepened. A gazillion emotions swam through his clouded gaze. He let out a sharp breath then tossed his cell phone aside. "Tough. I'm not interested in anything he has to say."

But there was anguish in his voice. I understood heartbreak. And I knew sometimes, it didn't heal. I didn't want him to regret anything or always wonder if he'd made the right decision. Despite the doubts circling through my mind, I couldn't let him ignore the text. We had many bridges to cross if we were going to be together. Dealing with the past was part of the process.

I sucked in a deep breath, keeping a tight hold on my emotions and uncertainties. "I think you should call him. You haven't spoken to each other since he left. What if he has something important to return to you? Or he just wants to check in to make sure you're okay? You haven't had full closure on him walking out. Maybe this will give you that." *But what if Emilio wants him back?*

"You want me to call my ex?"

"I trust you." *Fuck. Do I?*

Hot sex was one thing but playing with my heart was an entirely different matter. I was falling for him, but did Lewis feel the same? What if he still loved Emilio and wanted a second chance?

My ribs ached and constricted. *Crap.* Was Lewis another Rhett? Destined to return to his ex?

Chapter 27

LEWIS

Emilio's text unhinged me. All through dinner at the local Italian restaurant and a movie at home with Tia, I couldn't get his message out of my head. Sleep evaded me. Just after midnight, I eased out from underneath the covers in Tia's room and ventured downstairs. I grabbed my acoustic bass from the music room and headed outside to sit by the pool. As I struck and strummed the strings, a million thoughts pounded my head. Why, after eight months of silence, had he finally contacted me? Memories bombarded me—the moment we met after one of my gigs in Brooklyn, lazing in the living room as we made music, the hot lovemaking after a wild night out . . . then the fights we'd had.

He'd vented. *"When are you going to record another album, Lewis? When are you going to tour again? We should be hanging out with your celebrity friends, like Everhide. We should be going to premiers and fancy restaurants, not eating slop at your pop's bowling alley. I'm tired of traveling to Boston. Leave The Saylors and help me DJ. Write more music for me."*

I'd fumed. *"But I love playing with my friends. It's not about the money. I love what I do."*

Despite my issues with my former band, I'd always loved playing. Emilio had never understood that. Our relationship hadn't been perfect, but God, I'd loved him. The good had far outweighed the bad. That moment, when I'd gotten down on one knee and proposed, flickered behind my eyelids. The words were still clear in my head.

"Em, the moment we met, my life changed for the better. Your smile captured me. Your love of music sealed you into my soul. I love that you put up with my crazy friends and band, and my dysfunctional family. You make me feel loved and cherished in a world that is often against us. But no one can deny how much I love you. I want to spend the rest of my days making more incredible music together, have a family, and spend my life with you. Will you marry me?"

"No!"

My heart shuddered and hurt my ribs. Now, after all this time, he wanted to see me. I plucked my fingers slowly across the strings and closed my eyes. The turmoil in my head tumbled from my lips.

> *I was lost, in a daze, going nowhere,*
> *The sun and the moon were my only friends.*
> *There was nothing left in my heart to care,*
> *The loss of your love hurt me beyond repair.*
> *Hearing your voice after so long is too hard to bear,*
> *Why, after all this time, are you messing with my head?*
> *I've tried to move on, thought I was doing just fine,*
> *One word from you and I'm falling off the line.*

"Hey?"

I jumped at Tia's voice behind me.

"Oh. Hey." I put down my guitar and drew her onto my lap. She swiped my hair back off my face, cupped my cheek.

"You okay?"

Am I? Nope. I wrapped my arms around her waist. "Just enjoying the evening. Music. The view."

"Thinking about Emilio?"

Is it that obvious? I lowered my chin, and nodded slowly. "I'm just thrown off-balance."

"Why don't you call him?" She placed her hand over my aching heart. "You won't rest until you do. Don't let this fester and become a problem. Whatever it is he wants or says, we'll deal with it."

My heart sank into my stomach. No doubt she questioned whether I wanted a second chance with him. I hated that for a split second, tiny cracks had appeared in my concrete resolve, but I'd been quick to reseal them. I wasn't like her ex, Rhett. There was no going back to Emilio. But so much had been left unsaid. "Em hurt me too much. I'm not sure if I could ever forgive him."

"You have a new life. You've moved on. You have me." She kissed my forehead. "But you need to do this to move forward."

I smiled and puffed air through my nose. "You are much wiser than your years."

"I don't want you to have any regrets." Concern loomed in her eyes.

I caressed the side of her neck then pressed my lips to hers. "I've had many, but you aren't one of them."

That was the truth.

After crawling back into bed with Tia, I still couldn't sleep. As she slept beside me, her eyes fluttered behind her lids. This beautiful, broken girl had wound her way into my heart. She'd changed me. Every day, I fell for her more and more. But how deep did my feelings run? Did I . . . no, could I love her? Maybe she was right. To answer that question, I had to put closure on my past. Then I could move forward.

Mid-morning, I slipped out of bed and pulled on my pajama shorts. I grabbed my cell phone, ambled downstairs, and headed outside. Nausea and nerves swayed in my stomach as I glanced at the time on the screen and did the quick calculation. It'd be near midday in Miami. *Fuck.* I had to get this over and done with.

My hands shook as I found Emilio's number and called him.

Ring.

Ring.

Ring.

Ring.

Crap.

Then, he answered. "Lewis?" Emilio's voice shook with controlled excitement.

"Hey." Wincing, I rubbed my eyebrows. "I got your text. What's up?"

"Babe. I miss you so freaking much. Are you good?" His sweet tone churned my gut and hurt my heart.

"I'm fine."

"Are you in LA?"

"Yep."

"Shit, Lew, so much has happened over the past several months. I hate to admit it, but Miami hasn't been all it's cracked up to be. It's tough out here. There are too many DJs competing for gigs. Many have established names and regular bookings. I'm up and down each week, working my ass off to get hired for events and shows." His tone softened. "But since I left, I've had a lot of time to think. I fucked up so bad. I love you, Lew. Turning down your proposal was the biggest mistake of my life."

My ribs constricted and cracked. "I haven't heard from you for eight months, Em."

"Absence makes the heart grow fonder, right? I needed time to make sure we were meant to be together. I'm sorry. I want to marry you."

A sharp pain sliced through the center of my head. If he'd said he'd made a mistake a day or two after he'd left, maybe things would've worked out differently. But he hadn't. He hadn't returned any of my calls or texts until now. "You can't say shit like that. I've moved to the other side of the country and have gotten my life on track."

"I've seen you on the news. You're with The Flintlocks. That's so freaking cool." The fervor in his voice set off a warning bell in my head. He'd be jealous of the celebrity circles I now walked in. The envy would be killing him. *Tough.*

I paced the length of the pool, staring at the glistening surface. "They're great guys. It's not all smooth sailing, but we're getting there."

"You've finally made it. You're a star. You've hit the big time. It's what we've always wanted."

There it is. I could picture the dollar signs swirling in his eyes. Fame and money were what he'd always craved. For me, joining The Flintlocks was never about making millions—it had always been about recording, and creating music, performing and doing what I loved. I'd never take being with them for granted.

His tone softened. "I'd love to see you, Lew. I'd love the chance to fix us."

"Fix us?" A spite-filled breath shot from my lungs. I stared out across the canyon. Hurt meshed with the red-hot anger churning in every cell of my body. "Are you shitting me? You only want to get back together because I'm doing well and finally making something of myself. You quit on me when times were hard. You don't do that to people you love. You never cared about what made me happy. All *you* wanted was money and a celebrity life. It's all you've ever cared about." *Damn.* It had taken me too long to realize that.

"Yes . . . no . . . I love you."

The words he'd often whispered to me suddenly held no substance. "I'm not sure you ever did." He'd tired of supporting me and now wanted to crawl back into my life just because I was in the spotlight, and he'd hit hard times. Well, fuck that. "Em, I loved you. So freaking much. But you broke my heart. You left. It's over."

As I sank onto one of the sun loungers, images of Tia flickered through my mind. Her smile. Her laugh. The ecstasy on her face when I was buried inside her. But there was so much more to her. She'd help rebuild my confidence in my music, in my ability to play and be the best I could be with the band. There was no ulterior motive to get something out of me in return. That was true respect and support. I glanced up at her bedroom window. I took a deep breath and filled my chest. She was my now and hopefully my future. "I've met someone."

"That didn't take long," he snapped. His true colors shone through.

"It's only new."

"Who?" Cynicism dripped off his tongue. "Some hot Californian surfer? A sexy Hollywood actor? A badass businessman?"

I chuckled. "Definitely hot, sexy, and badass. But not a guy."

"A chick?" His cold, callous laugh punched me right in the guts. "You? With a girl? Are you fucking with me?"

"It's crazy, I know." Every time I thought of Tia, warmth crept into my cheeks.

"Don't kid yourself, Lew. You? With a woman? Oh, please. You are gay as fuck. Always have been. You can't switch that off." He turned cynical and snarky. "You have your fun with her. Fuck her. But when you come to your senses, give me a call. You love me. Your future is with me. We belong together."

Daggers stabbed my chest. Tears prickled the backs of my

eyes. I refused to let him get to me. "No. You had your chance. There is no round two. It hurts just hearing your voice. Hurts even more that my success is all you're after. I want to be with someone who wants me for me. I thought that was you, but it's not. So, thank you. This was the closure I needed. You've made me realize that despite all the heartache and how much I hated losing you, it was the best thing that could've ever happened. I'm glad we never got married. I love you. Always will. But we're not meant to be together."

"And this chick is?"

I wished the answer was clear, but it was too soon to tell. "Maybe. She's never cared about where I came from. Never cared about my bank account. We've got a lot of territory to navigate and explore, and have reservations to overcome, but she has always accepted me for who I am. She's helped me adjust to this new life. Best of all, she makes me laugh and we have fun. We're good together."

"Is it that TV star from the club?"

"It's none of your business who I'm seeing." I couldn't spill her name; he'd go to the press.

"Stop being delusional, Lewis. Wake up. You can't change who you are."

Fire coiled through my veins. "Everybody changes, Em. Some do for the better—some for the worse. This person I've met is my better."

"Lew?"

"No. Enough. You gave up on us. Gave up on me when I lost my way when my band broke up and I didn't become the star you wanted. That's on you, not me. But I've always loved what I do. All you did was use me to build your career, then you walked away. Now life has changed, you want me back? No, that's not going to happen. I wish you the very best and every success. But we are over. Please, don't call again. I gotta go. Bye."

I ended the call and pressed my fingertips into my stinging eyes. *Fuck!* Five years of my life had been wasted on someone who had only held out for money and fame. Just because I'd joined The Flintlocks, I wasn't rolling in dough ... yet—although my first couple of paychecks had been a bucketload more than I'd earned in the past two years, and royalties were yet to roll in. But this could be a short ride if I didn't meet the next milestone. I didn't want to go backward. Not again.

Tia had known since the beginning I wasn't loaded with cash. It had never bothered her. We'd connected over our sexy banter, a ton of laughs, our shitty heartache, our outlook on life, and our passions. We'd become friends before lovers. Our attraction had put us through more emotional turmoil and challenges than a *Survivor* reality TV show. Everything about her made me question my sanity, but she'd made me grow. For that I'd be forever grateful.

Just as I was about to walk inside, she appeared in her window in her silky robe. I stopped in my tracks. She gave me one of her sexy smiles, undid her robe and dropped it on the floor. Naked, she leaned against the frame and wriggled a come-hither finger.

My dick sprang to life. *Hell yeah.* How could I refuse?

At a sprint I zoomed inside, took the stairs two at a time and yanked off my pajama shorts.

Snaking my hands around her waist, I pulled her down onto the bed. Drawing her on top of me, I kissed her. Touched her. Entered her.

Giggling, she kissed my lips. "Good morning."

"It is now." I threaded my fingers into her hair and crushed her lips to mine. It was nearly nine a.m. I had to go see my brother. But I had a damn good excuse to be late.

Tia placed her hands beside my head and rode me, hard and deep. Her breath teased my face. Her wet warmth around my dick quickened my pulse. God, I loved the feel of her.

But Emilio's words ricocheted through my head.

Was he right about not being able to change?

Did Tia and I have longevity?

Falling for her more scared me.

No matter how good this felt, how much I liked Tia, and how much I wanted this to work, there were elements of my upbringing that kept me guarded about giving my heart to a woman. I had to face the damaging wounds caused in my distant past. Catching up with my brother today couldn't have come at a better time.

There were binding chains around my soul I wasn't sure I could let go of.

Was Lee the one who would cut them free?

Chapter 28

LEWIS

After showering and dressing, I kissed Tia goodbye. "Are you sure you don't want to come meet my brother?"

On the bed, she stretched her arms above her head, and a sleepy smile curled across her lips. "No. I have lines to learn."

"Okay. I'll be home for dinner."

"I'll be here."

"Good." I wriggled my eyebrows. "We have to make the most of our last night together before Cole comes home."

"I plan on it."

"See you soon." I grabbed my wallet and cell phone, and took off in Cole's sports car. Two hours later, I pulled into the driveway at the resort in Anaheim and handed the valet the keys. "I'll only be a couple of hours. Keep it handy."

"Yes, sir."

Walking into the foyer of the hotel, I grinned. I'd never let fame get to my head, but there were some perks I enjoyed and could now afford. Valet parking was one of them.

Outside at the pool bar, I texted Lee to let him know I was there and ordered two bottles of beer. Taking a seat at a table underneath a poolside umbrella, I placed my cell phone on the table and adjusted my sunglasses. The sky was endlessly blue. Kids splashed in the pool and played underneath a fountain. Ladies sat nearby, drinking cocktails, keeping a close eye on their toddlers. Men hovered near the bar, chatting and laughing. I still had to pinch myself that I was in LA. Living my dream. But what a crazy few weeks. Finishing promo. Still having a hit on the charts. Being with Tia. And the call with Emilio.

I was determined to prove him wrong.

I could change. I wanted to erase the doubts lingering in the back of my brain and be confident in going forward with Tia. I hoped Lee could bat some hard sense into me.

Lee strolled out of the hotel. His polo shirt hung loose on his slim shoulders. His cargo shorts sat low on his hips. *Damn.* He'd lost weight. But with his pale silver eyes, sharp jaw, and blond hair, there was no mistaking he was my brother.

I rose as he approached. We hugged, slapping each other on the back. It had been too long since we'd seen each other, just over seven months since Pop's funeral. That felt like a lifetime ago.

"So good to see you, man. How are you?" I returned to my seat. "You've lost a few pounds."

"School accounting and continual budget cuts do that to you." He took the chair adjacent to me.

"Really? It sounds like you have one of the easiest jobs in the world." I handed him his beer.

"Can't complain." He took a sip, then placed the bottle on the table. "Before I forget, Lucy wanted me to give you this." He dug into the pocket on his shorts and pulled out a folded envelope. "It's an invite to her wedding for you and a plus-one."

"Thanks." As I glided my fingertips over the glossy cream envelope, my heart twanged. My twenty-year-old, youngest sister was getting hitched before me. She'd met a church-going military man two years ago. Word via my sibling grapevine was that our parents are ecstatic. This straight man of the faith and good provider ticked every box on their approval card. "When's the wedding?"

"Second weekend in July. You able to come?"

In just over two months. The thought of visiting my family in Ohio iced my blood. I had no fond memories from my childhood. Our parents had been strict with a stinging hand if you didn't obey. Their narrow-minded views, rejection and harsh opinions had done irreparable damage. At Pop's funeral they'd kept their distance, never acknowledging my existence. At three of my siblings' weddings, I hadn't been allowed to sit with my family. I'd been a mere guest, shoved on the table farthest from them. I hadn't even been invited to celebrate two of my other siblings' marriages. But Lucy was cool. Like my oldest brothers, Lee and Lyndon, Lucy hadn't succumbed to our parents' narrow views. Luke, Linda, and Lisa were a different matter. Lucy had been five when I'd run away. We'd reconnected via social media when she became a teenager. She was sweet and beautiful and had the kindest heart. I'd love to celebrate her special day. "If I can come, I will. I'll have to check our schedule. We have a lot of promo before the tour."

Could I handle another event being shunned by my family?

I smirked. Wouldn't it shock the fuck out of them if I turned up with Tia?

Thing was, I didn't want to give them the satisfaction of them seeing me with her. They'd turn it around and toss that straight-is-the-only-way bullshit in my face. Say that I should've gone to conversion school all those years ago.

Lee lowered his sunglasses onto the bridge of his nose. The glare off the pool was blinding. "She'd love you there."

I tucked the invite under my cell phone, resting on the table. "I'll do my best."

"So, tell me what's been happening?" He play-shoved my shoulder. "You big-time celebrity."

I chuckled as warmth crept up my neck and settled in my cheeks. "I'm far from big, but I'm loving the change. Sorry we didn't visit Cleveland during promo. But it's a scheduled stop on the tour. I'll make sure you and your family have tickets to the show."

"My kids would love that." He swiveled his beer bottle back and forth on the table. "But I'm not sure about Amanda."

"Why not? She loves concerts."

"Um . . ." He lowered his chin and picked at his beer label. "We're getting a divorce."

"What? Why?" *About fucking time.*

He stared across the pool. "I couldn't fight it any longer. I had to stop living a lie. You inspired me and gave me the confidence to take the leap. It's only taken fifteen years, but I'm finally coming out."

Me? Inspire? There was a first. But my chest swelled. I was so freaking happy for him. "That's awesome. How did Amanda and the kids take the news?" His wife was a gem. A true angel. But living states apart, I'd never had the opportunity to get to know his two now teenage kids very well. The three times Lee had brought them to New York for short vacations had been our only time together.

"Amanda has always known. The kids know. They've been the ones who've encouraged me and been my biggest supporters. We've talked about it a lot over the past several months. Amanda has been amazing and helped me to make the right decision. I'm thirty-seven years old and terrified about coming out. But I can't deny it anymore."

I knew all about wanting to make the right decision. Tia and I were doing just that. "So conversion school, all those years ago, didn't work." Other than successfully messing with his mind.

"No. It made me miserable. It clouded my judgment. Destroyed my soul." The anguish in his voice hurt every cell in my body. That could've been me. Thank God, I'd run away.

I pinched my brows together. "Why did you stay with Amanda for so long?"

"For the kids. When we were forced to marry, we tried to make it work. We honestly became best of friends. We respected each other. In many ways, we loved each other but weren't *in* love. We're divorcing on very amicable terms. There is no hate or anger. The kids are old enough to understand. I moved out two months ago. I'm finally being true to myself."

Tears prickled my eyes. Sometimes no matter how hard people tried to change you, they couldn't. *Shit* . . . was I in that category?

No. Changing had been my decision, no one else's. I'd taken the leap and was experimenting. I'd opened my mind and heart to new possibilities. Was it a solid flip? *No.* I still found men attractive. But Tia had captured me and intrigued me. Every day with her was new territory I wanted to explore. "Do you have a boyfriend?

A smile that made him look ten years' younger inched across his face. "Yes. His name's Mateo. We're lying low, telling everyone we're just roommates until the divorce is finalized. Amanda has met someone too. We're finally happy. Free from living a lie."

"That's awesome."

He knocked his knee against mine. "So thanks for all those times I visited you in Brooklyn when you took me to gay clubs. Every time, it was pure torture, pure temptation, pure heaven. But it was exactly what I'd needed to see the light."

I'd hated seeing him suffer in an unhappy marriage. But when he'd been in those bars, fire had ignited in his eyes. It wasn't about being turned on by the scantily clad men; it had been about finding the courage to be honest with himself. "Someone had to help you find the right path. I'm glad I played a small part."

He fidgeted with his wedding ring. "I haven't told our parents yet. They've never changed their views. I guess they'll disown me. But that's the risk I'm willing to take."

"People who can't accept you for who you are, aren't worth the energy. I was so scared and terrified when I ran away. But I had to be me. I knew who I was. Nothing would change that."

He clutched my hand on the table. "I've always admired how strong you were. It took guts to leave. I've loved watching you live your life the way you've wanted to. I've seen you in recent interviews, unashamed and proud of who you are. That's how I want to spend the rest of my days."

I wanted to laugh. I wasn't sure who I was now I was with Tia, but I was open to what I could become.

He sipped on his beer, then a curious smile quirked his lips. "So . . . have you started seeing anyone since Emilio?"

Half-grinning, I shook my head. "Yes. But you're not going to believe it. Please don't tell our folks. Don't tell anyone. We've got to keep it quiet for now."

"I kept being gay quiet for over half my life. Any secret of yours is safe with me. Promise."

"The guys in the band don't even know. But . . . I'm seeing a girl. Tia, Cole's sister."

"Holy shit." He fell back in his chair. "I was expecting you to drop some big, hot male celebrity name, not a female. Since when?"

"My head is still spinning, trying to comprehend what's happened. We met when I first flew out to audition for the band. This spark ignited between us the moment we spoke. We finally hooked up just over a month ago. It's crazy hot. We're trying to take things slowly but failing."

"My God. Look at you." He shook his head slowly from side to side, but the biggest grin lit his face. "I don't think I've ever seen you look so scared, and anxious, but so freaking happy. Not even Em made your cheeks flush, or turned you into a bashful fool. But I've got to be honest—I never thought I'd ever see you with a girl."

"Me either. I still have some reservations."

"Why?"

I picked up a spare coaster and fidgeted with it. "After Emilio, I'm so fucking afraid of being hurt, being deluded ... and dumped. Tia and I are into each other. On one hand, we have this wild, insatiable, almost uncontrollable attraction—but on the other hand, we're so fucked up by our past relationships. I'm in this constant battle. After being with men all my life, I don't know if I'm just experimenting or if we have a future." I tapped the coaster against the table as doubts swam through my head. "When I met Em, I saw forever. That didn't go to plan. With Tia, I fought my attraction toward her for months until I couldn't go one more day without being with her. I just don't know how to be certain that this is real. I'm still into men. I'm not attracted to other women—just Tia."

"Lew, that kind of powerful, unexplainable connection is so rare. You'd be mad not to see where it goes."

"She drives me fucking crazy, turns me on, blows my mind. I never thought sex with a woman would be so fucking good." I chuckled as warmth crept through my chest. "When I'm with her, I'm happy. So why do I doubt everything? Shouldn't being with someone be easy?"

"Not always. Lew, there are no certainties in life. All new relationships go through a process. At various stages, you have to decide whether you're going to keep seeing each other or not. Sometimes those decisions can be difficult when you're battling huge differences and changes. But don't deny yourself the chance to be happy. You've always loved love. It doesn't matter what package it comes in. Up until now, it's been men. Now, it's a girl. Being with a woman won't change you as a person or your beautiful soul."

"Some days, it's hard to process what's happened. Does that make sense?"

"Hello? This is me you're talking to. I denied being gay for fifteen years. Don't fuck up like I did. I took way too long to be true to myself. Your breakup with Emilio was awful. Yes, he broke your heart. It wasn't meant to be. But you've taken a step to moving on. Have faith. Be honest with yourself. Trust your instincts, and by God, listen to your heart."

My ribs ached. The truth tore at my soul. "I'm worried that long term, I won't be as happy with a woman as I would be with a man. What if we end up together with a family and locked in a life of misery like you and Amanda were?"

"Oh, Lew. No." He shot forward and clutched my hand. "Don't think like that. Amanda and I had some good times together. We have two amazing kids. Don't let what happened to me hold you back. Live *your* life. You've always done that. You just said Tia makes you happy. That's gold. Own that."

Yeah. Tia was special. My kindred spirit. My *person*.

But God, I never wanted to experience heartache like I'd had with Emilio again. I'd wanted to get married and have a family. Spend the rest of my life with him. But it had all been a farse.

I took a deep breath. A new wave of reality settled over me, easing some of the madness in my mind. *Anyone* could hurt you, leave you, or break your heart. I had to be prepared for anything.

As I took a sip of beer, my stomach swayed. There was one thing that I couldn't deny—not anymore. I was falling for Tia.

But was it a forever type of love?

Shit.

I needed more time. More certainty.

But how could I establish that when promo for the next single began at the end of next week? Plans for the world tour began next month. Music and everything I'd worked so hard for was about to dominate my life.

I wasn't going to mess up my chances with the band.

Crap.

I should've never gotten involved with Tia.

But I had.

Was I prepared to go all in with Tia and risk my heart and my place in the band?

If . . . no, when . . . the guys found out and it came down to a choice between her and music, which way would I turn?

My heart lurched.

I already knew the answer.

Chapter 29

LEWIS

Lying on my bed, propped up on my hands, I kissed Tia's lips, her cheeks, her eyelashes. My dick still throbbed with a delectable pulse after having hot morning sex. I wasn't completely awake— not at 5:45a.m. But sex had been worth it.

For the past four days since I'd met with my brother, being with Tia had consumed my every thought, and we'd stolen some crazy moments. I'd processed my feelings, put my past behind me, ignored Emilio's follow-up texts, and let her into my heart. I'd fallen fast, and I didn't want to hide anymore. I wanted to face any consequences with the band sooner rather than later. I was sure they wouldn't care that we were together. But if they did, they weren't the guys I'd thought I'd formed friendships with.

I nuzzled and licked the fine column of her throat. The taste of her sweet skin was pure heaven. "We need to tell everyone we're together."

"Lewis, no." She giggled and clutched onto my hair, drawing my head back. "Not yet."

"Why not?" I caught her hand and pinned it beside her head.

"I don't want to sneak around anymore."

"But sneaking around is fun." She pursed her lips and wriggled beneath me.

Hmm . . . she liked to cause trouble. *But no . . .* "Tee, be serious."

She sighed, but something deep in her eyes caught me off-guard.

"Tee?" I flopped down onto the pillow beside her and faced her.

Worry darkened her eyes. "I'm sorry. I'm not ready. I've been so focused on researching new careers and options for school; I haven't had enough time to process us."

Deciding to go back to college had only taken her a few days and had been a no-brainer for her. Pity she couldn't do the same about us. Being together was a big decision, a huge change for both of us, but I was in.

"Well, I have." I stole a kiss from her lips. "I want to be with you."

She smiled and cupped my face. "That's awesome. I'm getting there. I just need a little more time."

"What can I do to erase your doubts?" I softened my voice, entwined our fingers, and held her hand against my chest. "Is my call with Em still bothering you? You know that's over, right? I've gotten closure." He'd messed with my head and had lingered in my thoughts for a couple of days, but Tia had overruled everything.

A cold silence slammed into me. Her eyes glassed over, and she lowered her chin. *Shit.* That was it.

"Tee, it's over with Em. I swear."

Her voice came out as a pained whisper. "That's what Rhett used to say. You've been in a weird mood since you called him. Do you want to get back with Emilio?"

"No." There was no hesitation. "Em's call upset me, but

it reaffirmed that we are over. I've spent the past few days questioning my feelings for you, wanting to make sure this is right. And it is."

She fidgeted with my signet rings. "Yes. But it's not just Emilio. We've really only been together since Friday, just under a week."

Take out the night of the launch, our hot night in Seattle, and our texts and phone calls during my month of travel, she was right. "True. But this is good. We've fought our feelings for so long—let's see were this goes. Like my brother said, we just need to give ourselves the chance to be happy. We need to be honest with everyone."

She kissed my knuckles. "Yes. But now isn't the right time. I want to tell everyone I'm quitting my show. You leave at the end of next week to promote the release of your album. You need the spotlight on the second single and the tour announcement, not our relationship. The minute we step out the door together or go public, we'll be in the headlines again."

"We don't have to go public, but the guys need to know. I don't want to keep lying to them. It's not who I am."

"Please wait just a touch longer. You need to pass the next milestone to make sure you go on the tour. You need to get through this next promo."

I caressed the side of her head and stroked her hair. "No milestone is going to make a difference. They could kick me out at any time. Lying and being dishonest is just cause." That bore more weight than me dating Tia.

"I know I'm asking for a lot, but I just want to be more certain." She placed her hand on my chest. "Once I tell the others about school, I can focus on us. I want us to work. I honestly do. This is crazy and new and super-hot, but I need to see past that." She leaned forward and planted tiny kisses on my cheek, then my nose, then my lips. "I want to have some fun falling for you more, steal some crazy moments, go on a couple dates, spend hours talking, and make sure that this is right. Okay?"

"How long?" I kept my voice calm, but my insides were on the brink of snapping. "We can't keep doing this. I need a deadline. We're either on or off." My heart shuddered; this could go either way. I didn't want to pressure her, but we had to face reality.

She closed her eyes and nodded. "I know. How about the weekend after you get back from promo? That will give us a bit more time together, let the hype of the album launch calm down, and let the heat between us settle."

"I hope it never settles." I slipped my arms around her and drew her into my embrace. I kissed her forehead. I wasn't happy I had to keep lying to the guys, but I wanted her to be sure about us. There was no need to burst this bubble if she wasn't on the same page as me. "I'll just have to work on convincing you that we are a good thing."

She glanced up at me. A smile slid across her face, and her eyes shimmered with that fire that always simmered between us. "I look forward to it."

"Good. Me too." I glanced at the clock. *Shit. 6:10 a.m.* It was fucking early. *Too early.* Cole would be home from running soon. I patted Tia on the butt. "But right now, you'd better get out of here and go to work. You don't want to be late."

"Okay." She rolled to sit upright. Leaning over, she kissed me. "I'll see you tonight."

"Yeah."

She grabbed her robe off the floor, slipped it on, and disappeared out the door.

I sank into the pillow and draped my arm over my eyes. *Fuck!*

I could do this.

I could keep my mouth shut for a few more weeks. I'd be

gone for three of them.

She was right. We needed the fire between us to settle and not make any rash decisions.

She was worth the wait. Everything would be fine.

And just when I'd convinced myself of that . . . Emilio texted. *Again.*

> LEW, I LOVE YOU WITH ALL MY HEART AND SOUL.
> BE MY FUTURE.
> PLEASE CALL. FOREVER YOURS, EM.

Shit. I should've blocked his number. I wanted to put the heartache behind me, hoping that we could remain friends. But I wasn't sure that was possible. I had to cut the cord. So why couldn't I hit DELETE?

I had to.

I would.

Soon.

Just not today.

After a long day of rehearsals at Flint's for the album launch, the guys and I were wrapping up our last song when Sutton and Tia came into the studio and headed for the sofa. Tia raked her sexy gaze over my sweaty black T-shirt, and threw me a wicked smile and a wink—the kind that always made my day.

At the end of the track, Slip filled the room with an ear-splitting strike on his strings. The electric twang reverberated through my chest as I clapped and whistled. "Woohoo. That was awesome. Great rehearsal, guys." Today had been good. We'd nailed every track.

We grabbed our towels, wiped the sweat off our faces, and joined the girls. Flint sank onto the seat beside Sutton and planted a big, sloppy kiss on her lips.

She giggled and shoved him away. "Yum, but gross."

"You love it." He straightened, resting his arm along the back of the sofa behind her.

"Hi." I rubbed Tia's shoulder as I passed behind her. Tiny tingles shivered across my fingertips in the wake of touching her. Hooking my towel around my neck, I sat on the adjacent single sofa chair and threw her a little smile.

"You gals ready for dinner?" Cole sank onto the seat beside Tia and grabbed his cell phone out of his shorts pocket. "I'm starving. I need a fix of carbs. Everyone good for pizza?"

She patted him on the knee. "Yes, but can I tell everyone something first?"

"Sure. What's up?" Slip sat on the sofa arm next to Flint and guzzled down half his huge water bottle.

Tia's hands shook as she smoothed them over her linen pants. Excitement jumped in her voice. "I've made some big decisions. Life-changing ones, and I want you to be the first to know."

I smirked. I knew what they were—and they sure were life-changing. They just had nothing to do with the decision I was waiting on from her.

Concern darkened Cole's eyes; his shoulders slumped. "You're not leaving again, are you?"

Cole adored his sister, loved looking out for her and having her around. Good thing she wasn't moving away.

"No." Tia shook her head. "But I'm going to quit *Angels in LA*."

"What?" Sutton shrieked; her hand splayed across her chest. "No."

Tia threw her a sympathetic smile. "Sorry, Sutt. It's just not me."

Flint sank deeper into the sofa. His brows pinched together. "Did you get a better role?"

"Not yet. Jack, my agent, is looking." She took a deep breath and let it out slowly. "But if nothing comes up by fall, I'll go back to school. I'm going to study technical film and TV production.

I've found something I love doing, that I'm good at and want to pursue."

Cole gaped. Flint's eyebrows shot skyward. Slip bobbed his head in approval. Tears welled in Sutton's eyes. I just nodded and half-grinned, playing along since I'd known since this morning.

"I love my tech." Smiling, she rounded her shoulders and pressed her palms between her knees. "I love working the front of house and managing behind the scenes. So I want to become a production or floor manager, run events and award shows, or work on late-night talk programs where every day is different. As long as it's got a zany live audience, I'm there. I've taken the leap. Filming for season one of *Angels* finishes in mid-July. School starts in September."

"Whoa." Cole rubbed the back of his neck. "I didn't see that coming. Are you sure you want to give up acting? Are you prepared for the drastic lifestyle and income change?"

"Yes." Her face glowed with a stunning smile. "My choices in life have never been influenced by money, fame, or five-star luxury. But I'm lucky. I've worked hard and I'm set up for life."

Cole swiveled toward her. "I'm all for the change, but why wouldn't you come work for us? Gena's leaving soon. We have the tour. You can learn everything you want about production as part of our team."

"No. You're too big. I don't have the experience you need for a world tour. And I want to work in TV and film, not music. Every show or event would be different. Every function would present new challenges. Every day would be exhilarating. It's me."

It wouldn't be as much fun as it would be if she worked for our team, but we'd had that argument. I'd lost.

"Bullshit." Cole glanced at each of us guys like he was assessing us for reservations. There were none. "Tee, we perform every night in front of audiences that are bigger than the ones you'll find at any TV show or event. We have more tech than most studio productions. You love to travel. You're family. We belong together."

Her eyes glassed over. A knot at the base of my neck tweaked. Tia would thrive if she worked with these guys. She didn't need to protect my place in the band. I'd survive. "Tia, it would be fun. It would work out. *Trust* me." My tone came out more tense than I'd anticipated, challenging her to take the risk on us, on her dream, on living life. "Just don't flash lights in my eyes like you did in Seattle."

She threw me a saucy smile. "That was a once off tease. I'd wouldn't do that again. Not on purpose anyway."

"Good." All had been forgiven during our steamy encounters.

Cole jabbed his finger against her arm. "Tee, you can't fuck with us on stage. But if you promise to behave, we'd want you with us. No question."

She tucked her hair behind her ear, nodded, and lowered her chin. "Thank you, but no. I love all of you, but I need to do this my way. I want to take every step from the ground up. No help or favors required."

I leaned back in my seat. New theories hammered my head. Maybe her reluctance to work for the band wasn't about our relationship. Maybe she wanted to protect her relationship with her brother more than anything. I could understand that. Working with friends and family often soured.

Cole slung his sweaty arm around her shoulders and gave her a hug. "I know you're stubborn and like to do things your way. So whatever you decide, we'll back you. Just know you can come work for us at any time."

"Thank you."

Projecting her an I've-got-you smile, I rubbed the tip of my chin. "It's a big step and sounds exciting. Change is never easy but often worth it." I prayed changing for her would be. "You've gotta follow your heart, do what you love, and be honest and true to yourself."

We had to do that for our relationship too. We'd get there. The sooner, the better.

Slip shook his head. "You're crazy going back to school, Tee. I'd stick with the acting. More money. More fun."

"I'd love to do school and small movie roles. As long as I leave *Angels,* I'll be happy with either option or both."

"Oh, this sucks." Sutton pouted and folded her arms. "Tia, you're so good on our show. I'm happy you've found something you want to pursue but I'll miss you."

"I'm still here in LA. We'll see each other. I promise. This is a huge change, but it's the right decision. I don't want to tell the studio I'm not re-signing until next month when our contracts are up for renewal. So please keep this quiet for now." She rubbed her hands together. "But enough exciting news for one day. Let's order dinner. I'm starving. What's on the menu?"

I'd like that to be Tia.

But that would have to wait.

And just when everything seemed to take a step forward and life was sorting itself out, the following morning, Emilio texted again:

> BABY, PLS CALL ME. YOU'RE ALL I THINK ABOUT.
> WE CAN BE HAPPY TOGETHER.
> I WANT TO COME SEE YOU.
> LOVE YOU, EM

Fuck. Fuck. FUCK!

I ignored it.

Over the next few days, Tia and I fell into a routine at home. Every morning when Cole went out running, Tia snuck into my bed. We fooled around, went to work, occasionally saw each other for dinner, crashed in our separate rooms each night, and set repeat.

But I wasn't a morning person.

By nine a.m. each day, I headed out with the guys. As we were driven to meetings and photoshoots and rehearsals for the album launch, I tried to catch some naps, but the growing hype and excitement around our schedule made it near impossible.

Despite the long days, I stayed true to my word and snuck in two dates with Tia when Cole headed out to catch up with some girls. We went to the Break Room in North Hollywood. Tia smashed the shit out of everything—plates, cups, bottles, even an old desk. The second outing was an evening picnic on the beach. Both were awesome nights.

But I was exhausted before the promo had even started.

The day before we headed to New York, Cole and I headed to Flint's for one last practice session. In the studio, I picked up my acoustic bass and hooked the strap over my head. I rubbed the stinging sleep from my eyes. I'd caught a couple more hours of dozing after Tia had left this morning, but it hadn't been enough. Every bone and muscle in my body ached.

I'd brought up the idea of telling everyone with her again this morning. I wanted to leap. She'd been adamant about taking it slow. *Tia? Slow?* I'd never thought I'd see the day.

We were more than lust-crazed lovers. I knew we were. I was just impatient.

Our deadline couldn't come soon enough.

Flint pulled up a stool beside his mic. "Let's nail the stripped-down version of the new single."

Slip grabbed his acoustic guitar and sat cross-legged on the floor. Cole fetched a single snare drum and his sticks.

Just as we were about to play, my cell phone pinged. I yanked it out of my pocket, hoping for some sexy text from Tia, but no . . . It was from Emilio. *Shit!* I clenched my hand around my cell phone and closed my eyes. A tornado of turmoil tumbled through my head. My heart hurt.

This had to stop.

I typed out a reply:

```
STOP TEXTING.  WE ARE OVER.
```

Letting out a slow breath, I tucked my cell phone away, cleared my head, and set my fingers over my strings to play. I glanced at the guys who were waiting for me. "Sorry. I'm good."

"Let's roll." Flint tapped his fingers against his guitar. "One. Two. Three."

Slip led with the intro. I was quick to join in, but I lacked concentration. Tia's reluctance to tell the guys still ate at my insides and knotted my gut. The texts trickling in from Emilio tainted my veins. I was over secrets, my ex, and delays.

I needed a fucking decent sleep.

As the stripped back tune filled the room, Flint's deep voice haunted the air.

> *It's been one of those weeks, yeah,*
> *One of those days, oh yeah*
> *Where nothing's gone right, oh no,*
> *Nothing's gone to plan, nah-ah.*
> *Now I'm beyond frustrated,*
> *Fired up and irritated.*
> *So before I go out of my mind,*
> *There is only one thing I have to do . . .*
>
> *I need to jump in my car,*
> *Pick up my friends, hit a cool bar.*
> *So we can dance all night,*
> *Have fun until sunlight.*
> *So I can forget,*
> *Yeah, forget about you.*
> *Oh yeah.*

I puffed air through my nose. I wished I could forget my ex. He hadn't taken no for an answer. I'd refused to respond until a few minutes ago. He knew I was seeing someone. Why did moving on have to be so hard?

> *I hate that you're on my mind,*
> *Can't sleep or put the hurt behind.*
> *I'm over all your games,*
> *I've changed, I'm not the same.*
> *I won't ever fall for you again,*
> *No, not ever, not again.*
> *I don't want to ever feel down,*
> *It's time to hit the town.*
> *So before I go out of my mind,*
> *There is only one thing I have to do . . .*
>
> *I need to jump in my car,*
> *Pick up my friends, hit a cool bar.*
> *So we can dance all night,*
> *Have fun until sunlight.*
> *So I can forget,*
> *Yeah, forget about you.*
> *Oh yeah.*

My fingers twisted and tensed. *Guilt.* That was what had irked me about Emilio's' texts. He'd made me feel guilty for moving on. I shouldn't feel that way. No . . . I refused to feel that way. Tia and these guys had been the fresh start I'd needed. I had a new confidence. I'd grown. I was in a much better place and surrounded by better people.

Fuck Emilio.

Flint threw me a questioning look, but he hit the chorus. I joined in for our harmony, but my voice came out tight and scratchy.

> *I need to jump in my c—,*

Pick up my friends, hit a cool bar.
So we can d—nce all night,
Have fun until s—nlight.

"Cut." Flint sliced his hand across his neck. "Lewis? You're off. What's eating you?"

So much I couldn't fathom where to begin. Frustration drilled into my head. "Sorry. I'm just tired. What do you think about playing this song slower?"

He scratched his stubble. "But it's a party song?"

"On the electrics, yes. But when broken down raw, it needs to be sultrier and have a fuck-you-I'm-going-out-with-my-buddies attitude." My exact thoughts about Emilio.

Cole groaned and tilted his head back. "Why can't you just play the fucking song how we wrote it?"

Ouch! That stung. "It doesn't sound right."

"It's freaking awesome as is." He drove his fingertips into his brow, massaging at the grooves. "For once, can you leave a great song untouched?"

"Sure can." I shrugged my shoulder. My tone, too clipped. We'd all clashed heads while we were breaking down some of the songs that were harder to play live. I'd contributed my thoughts. They'd often loved my suggestions—Flint and Slip more so than Cole. He loved his music and was protective of his creativity, and of his friends and family. I hoped I was now included in that group. Time would tell when Tia and I told him we were together . . . if she wanted to be with me. *Ergh!*

Brushing off the tension with a pluck of my bottom string, I let my suggestions go. "It was just an idea. Leave it. We'll play it as is." I didn't want to piss them off. I loved the song.

"Lew?" Flint leaned forward, resting his arm across the top of his guitar. He looked at me from underneath his long hair that fell across his eyes. "Are you okay?"

I nodded, my neck stiff as a board. "Yep. Just got a few things on my mind."

"Is it Joel?" Cole chuckled and raised a curious eyebrow. "Have you two been hooking up? Is that why you're so tired?"

"No." Agitation sliced through my tone. At every full rehearsal, soundcheck, or performance with our road crew present, Cole made suggestive comments toward Joel and me when he saw us talking together or having a laugh. I felt bad for Joel. He was a nice guy. I'd made it clear to Joel I wasn't interested. And I'd told Cole to back the fuck off. "He's not my type."

"So who is your type?" he asked.

I smirked and let out a short, sharp breath. "Wouldn't you like to know."

Slip laughed low and shook his head. I loved that he'd respected the fact that Tia and I needed time to work things out. "Lew, ignore Cole. One day he might grow up. But something is bugging you. So spill."

"Oh, it's a guy." Emilio's texts had pissed me off more than anything. "My ex has texted a couple of times. I stupidly called him two weekends ago after he contacted me. He wants to get back together."

Flint struck his strings with a loud twang. "Please tell me you said no."

"Of course I did."

"But are you having second thoughts?" Concern flooded Slip's eyes; he was no doubt looking out for Tia.

My heart thudded hard against my ribs. *Am I? Is that why I'm bothered?* I sucked in a deep breath and stared out the window. Did I miss Em? . . . *Yes.* Did I want to get back together? . . . *Fuck no.* Did I miss being with men? . . . *No.* I missed being loved. Tia had turned my world upside down, but there was no doubt about how I felt for her. *None.* She was it. I just wanted her to feel the same way about me. We'd gotten together in such a hot blaze; I wasn't handling that we were now traveling at different speeds. I wanted her to catch up. "I've run through those scenarios and questioned my feelings, but no. He hurt me too much. Em was selfish, self-centered, and used me."

I clenched and unclenched my fist. I wanted to say, *'No, I'm not having second thoughts, because I've met someone new'.* But I didn't. Tia needed more time.

I hated being in limbo. We were crazy about each other.

What was holding her back? What had I missed?

Oh, shit!

A wave of nausea flooded through me and rolled through my gut. An electric shock jolted through the center of my chest. I winced and clutched my bass against my belly.

Was she just using me?

She'd loved sneaking around with Phil, and now she loved doing it with me. And she loved her games. Was that all I was to her? A game? Was that why she didn't want to tell the guys about us?

No! Don't go there. She was into me. I knew it. I felt it. *Do I?* Or was I being delusional?

A chill shot over my skin. Was this Emilio all over again? Had she let me believe she was crazy about me but was afraid of commitment?

Fuck. Stop!

Being tired had messed with my head. I trusted Tia. I trusted us.

I had to kill those thoughts. We had enough challenges ahead without adding more worries onto the pile.

Cole twirled his sticks. "Dude, go out. Get drunk. Get laid. You've had countless opportunities during promo and at functions."

"You guys have been my priority, not hooking up with someone. I've been too focused on music, on finding my feet in LA and passing the milestones. I've had some personal curveballs to deal with—some were unexpected and left wing. But I'm sorting them out."

"Are you sure?" Worry flooded Flint's eyes. "Do you need help? We're here for you. There is *nothing* you could say that would change the way we feel about you." His gaze burned into me, pinning me to my stool. *Shit!* I hoped he meant that about Tia and me. He leaned forward. His voice deepened with true sincerity. "We'd do anything for you. You can trust us. You're a Flintlock."

I wished I could be one hundred percent certain about that. "Thanks. I'm good. It's nothing a good sleep won't fix. But we need to practice first." I strummed my strings. "Let's play."

"Oh yeah." Slip struck his guitar.

But I didn't miss the shake of his head.

Secrets caused problems. I'd learned that. I didn't want mine to blow up in my face. I just had to make it through promo.

Tia was worth the wait. Worth the risk.

But as I left LA with the guys and our promotional schedule kicked in, my palms sweated during every interview when the reporters asked about my love life. My head ached every time Cole encouraged me to hook up with some hot dude who'd batted his eyelashes at me when we were at a party or a function. My gut knotted every time we performed and practiced. It was getting harder and harder to lie. More importantly, I didn't want to. I wasn't being true to myself, which I'd always prided myself on. Every phone call I'd had with Tia, tension hovered between us.

Fuck.

I wanted to be with her.

What issues hadn't we resolved?

Why did I feel like I was standing on the San Andreas Fault, and everything was about to rip apart?

Chapter 30

TIA

So much had happened in the past three weeks while the guys had been away, I'd struggled to keep up.

I'd been accepted into school. I was set to start in the fall.

I'd hung out with Chloe and Duke. They'd asked me to join them for a few weeks at the end of August on the festival circuit doing sound, just to have some fun before school started. I'd taken up their offer.

I'd upped my physical therapy to two sessions a week in my efforts to improve the strength in my ankle. It still ached like a bitch every day.

I'd had dinner with my agent again. Jack hadn't found me any roles yet; a few things were coming up next month that looked promising. If someone in Hollywood wanted a crippled, limping, scarred woman for a part, I was so there. I doubted those roles came up often. Jack had spent more than an hour trying to convince me to stay on *Angels in LA*, but he hadn't altered my decision. I'd officially tell the studio I wasn't re-signing this Friday.

There was no looking back.

I was on a new path.

Everything was falling into place.

Telling everyone about Lewis was my final frontier.

But every time Lewis and I had talked about it while he'd been away, I'd broken out in a cold sweat. Something inside my head and heart prevented me from standing at the top of Griffith Park and shouting out to the world we were together. Something I couldn't get a grasp on. It went beyond being worried about his place in the band. I was sure it was just nerves about the weeks of ridicule we would face when we went public. I'd done this before. I could do it again. If the nausea in my gut would subside, I'd be fine.

Lewis had come home from promo two days ago and had been utterly exhausted. He'd slept for most of the time. So had Cole. The travel and non-stop hype had knocked them flat. My hectic filming schedule threatened to do the same to me. We were behind on production and our hours of shooting went from sunup to sundown.

After a long day at the studio, I caught up with the guys on Tuesday night.

Just after eight o'clock, I sat at the table with Cole and Lewis, eating the steak and fries I'd cooked. Cole's eyes were bloodshot, tired, and Lewis struggled to stay awake, but the high from their promotional tour still rippled through the air.

"Tee, you should've been there," Cole said over a mouthful of meat. "The fans were amazing. The parties were wicked. The shows were unreal."

The evidence had filled my social media feeds every day they'd been away—the TV interviews and performances, the footage of them greeting fans, the photos with overzealous partygoers. Endless images of Flint hugging girls, Slip copping kisses on his cheek, Lewis downing shots with handsome guys, and Cole licking Jell-O off some girl's tummy had filled my cell phone. The headlines had flashed: *'The Party Boys Are Back,'* *'Hot Album, Hot Shots,' 'Lewis King – New Flintlock Doesn't Disappoint.'*

Lewis munched on some fries. "And this was only promo. Tour will be ten times better and bigger."

"I'm glad you had fun." I sipped on my water. "I've been so busy, I hardly noticed you were gone."

But I had.

Each story and photo online had hurt my heart.

Flint, Cole, and Slip had moved on from losing Phil.

Some days I still struggled.

I didn't miss wild parties or being the focal point of gossip. The guys could have that. But what had gotten to me the most— even more than missing Phil— were the pictures of the four guys climbing the Harbour Bridge in Sydney, zooming down the River Thames in a speed boat in London, and taking on the City Climb skyscraping adventure in New York.

They'd done activities I could never do again. I missed the fun we used to have together.

Accepting the limitations of my injured leg had been hard. Thanks to Lewis, every day I'd gotten better and more comfortable with venturing out. That didn't change the fucked-up fact I still wanted to jump off buildings for fun.

After a long day at the studio, I needed an early night. "Guys, I'm going to hit bed." I stood and rubbed the back of Cole's shoulders. "I have to leave here at six for shooting on location tomorrow." I had a full day of filming at a café in West Hollywood.

"Have fun. We'll clean up." Cole waved his finger at the dirty dishes and empty beer bottles.

I stepped over to Lewis and gave him a half-hug. Nothing that would draw attention from Cole. "Night."

"See you tomorrow." Lewis wrapped his arm around my

legs and gave them a rub. "We should be home early tomorrow night. We'll *talk* then."

By talk, he meant about us. Sex would be good too. I could see the need for both in his eyes. "Okay." I wanted to get lost in him, love him, feel our fire, and throw away my worries about opening my heart to him once and for all.

I twinkled my fingers at the guys and headed to bed.

The following morning, my driver pulled into the lane way just off Melrose and drew to a halt. I stepped out into LA sunshine and breathed in the warm air. Four huge white studio trucks, along with cameras, trellises, panel lighting, and cast member trailers blocked the access to the small street. *You can do this. Don't limp.*

Pinning my best, fake, good morning smile into place, I headed toward my trailer. I dug my nails into my palm and focused on the cutting pain in my hand rather than the dull ache in my ankle.

I couldn't wait to finish this show.

I wouldn't have to hide my injury.

No more having to be perfect in front of the cameras.

As I lifted my chin, I drew my shoulders back and strode around the crew setting up for the day. I clenched my teeth, quickened my pace and clambered up the steps into my trailer. Wincing in pain, I slammed the door behind me. I clutched my foot, massaged my ankle, and fought back the tears. The agony eased as I took a couple of slow, steady, breaths. I was okay. I was good. *That's better.*

After swallowing a painkiller, I met with wardrobe, was dressed in a Prada suit and patent-leather flats, and had my hair and makeup done. Time for action.

I grabbed my script and my cell phone and headed for the door. But as I reached for the door handle, my phone beeped. *Lewis.*

A big grin curled across my lips as I read his message.

MISSED YOU THIS MORNING.

I replied:

XOXOXO.

Was I one hundred percent sure about being with him? *No.* But I was ready to give us a shot.

As I headed outside, I flicked through the pages of my script. I couldn't have written a better storyline to end the season on. My character landed a promotion. It'd make penning an exit easy for the writers of the show. They could just add in I'd had to move cities. *Done!* Today's first scene was me telling the girls about my new job at the firm.

Underneath a portable gazebo, Sutton hugged me hello. Looking stunning, in a silky floral wrap dress, she beamed a radiant smile. I loved seeing people in their element. This was hers.

"You ready for a big day?" She squeezed me tight.

"Always." *Not.*

"Okay, girls." Frank, our director, clapped his hands. "Let's knock over this scene as quickly as possible. We have a lot to get through today."

"Let's go, ladies." Sutton dragged Mia and Peyton out of their director's chairs and headed over to the café's alfresco tables. The three of them loved this show. They'd easily survive without me.

"Tia?" Frank talked with his hands, pointing at no particular spot down the street, then to the girls. "I want you to run up to the ladies. In your excitement, knock into waitress Fiona's shoulder, spin around, then plonk onto your chair beside Peyton. Okay?"

Run? My blood pressure spiked. My ankle throbbed at the

thought of pounding the pavement. "Wouldn't it be more in character if I slink up to them, sat down, bursting with energy, then delivered my lines?"

He dipped and bobbed his head from side to side. "That may work. Let's try it both ways." He slapped his folder against my arm and headed over to the camera.

"Yeah. Great." *Crap!* I smoothed my hands over my dress pants. Knots twisted in my stomach as I walked down the street into position.

Twenty extras came out of their holding area underneath another couple of portable gazebos and took their positions at the outdoor tables.

The camera crew did last minute lighting and audio checks.

"Okay." Rodney, the second assistant director, stepped in front of café, held up his hand, and hollered, "Quiet on set," then dashed to stand beside Frank.

Frank pointed at me. "Action. Rolling."

I let out a slow breath and hooked my purse over my shoulder. Digging deep into my soul, I found my inner lawyer goddess and morphed into character. I took off, scuttling along at a fast walk toward the café tables. I bumped into Fiona, who was serving some guests, spun around, and sat on my chair next to the girls. My ankle throbbed in protest. Ignoring it, I delivered my lines. Perfect execution. *Thank goodness.*

"Cut," Frank yelled and grimaced. "Nope. I'm not feelin' it. Let's amp it up. Tia, run this time. Really knock into Fiona. You've just been promoted. I want to *feel* your energy. *More* excitement. Do it again, please?"

"Um ... yeah. Sure." I could do this. Focus. Just like I'd taught Lewis to do. Like I'd done for years on my previous show. *Visualize the execution. Pick your path. Don't deviate.* But run? I wriggled my toes, stretched out my ankle. I'd be fine. It was only a short distance.

My heart tapped against my ribs as I headed down the sidewalk for the retake. Unease swirled through my stomach as I scanned every inch of the footpath. I searched for every crack or divot, rock or area of unevenness. *All clear.*

Rodney silenced the extras and crew.

Frank pointed his finger at me again. "Action. Rolling."

Shit. I refused to risk being hurt. But I could do this. It wasn't far.

Setting grit into my veins, I took off. In a walk-a-step, run-a-step awkward stride, I headed toward the girls. Pain shot up my leg, stabbed deep inside my ankle, and speared my knee. I slammed into Fiona, knocking her forward onto the table. *Shit, that was hard.* I went to say sorry, but as I turned, my ankle rolled. *Snap.* I screamed. "Argh! Fuck!"

Tripping, I stumbled and fell. My elbow hit the edge of a table, then connected with the concrete sidewalk. Rolling onto my side, I clutched at my foot and cried, "Fuck. Oh fuck."

People leaped from chairs and scurried to my side. Strangers' faces loomed overhead.

"Oh my God. Tia?" Sutton shoved through the sea of people. "Are you okay?"

Tears trickled from my eyes. My chin trembled. I winced and shook my head.

"Get the medic," Sutton shouted. "Tia's hurt."

"Fuck. This is not what I needed today." Frank cursed and ordered a crew member to fetch the onset medic. "It's just a fall, Tia. You'll be fine."

"No." The pain in my knee throbbed as much as my ankle. "I need to go to the hospital. I think it's broken." *Shit. Shit. SHIT!*

Everyone cleared the sidewalk of tables and chairs. Two young gentlemen scooped me up and carried me to my trailer. Frank and the girls followed. Seconds later, Jen, the medic, arrived. As I stretched out on the sofa, she eased off my shoe and grimaced at my scars. "You've been hurt before?"

"Uh-huh." I clenched my teeth as she brushed and pressed her fingers over my skin and bones.

"It's hard to tell if it's broken without an x-ray. How long ago was your original injury?"

"Injury? What the fuck?" Frank hissed as he paced in front of the trailer's kitchenette.

"It's nothing." I shuddered. My ankle was already swollen and turning black. "Just an old break from last year."

Jen glanced at my scars then raised a you-can't-fool-me eyebrow. "That's no normal fracture. I think it best to call an ambulance and get you to the hospital. Until then, we'll keep your ankle iced, and I can provide you with some pain relief."

"Oh yeah, bring on that shit." I nodded. "Give me the hardest stuff you've got."

Twenty minutes later, the ambulance arrived. I changed into my own clothes, grabbed my purse, was put on a gurney, and rolled toward the vehicle. It was overkill for a busted ankle, but at least it wasn't as horrific as the last time I'd been carted off a film set.

Hovering beside me, Sutton squeezed my hand. "You want me to come with you?"

"No." I patted her arm. "I could be hours. I'll give you and the guys an update after I've had an x-ray." No need for them to be bored out of their brains while waiting at the hospital.

"Okay." She stroked my hair, sweeping the strands off my face. "Love you."

"Love you too. Sorry I've messed up a day of filming."

"Don't be silly. We'll be fine."

At least they would be. *Me?* I wasn't so sure.

As I was driven to the hospital, new tears fell. The ice pack wrapped around my ankle was heavy and uncomfortable. The chill made every bone in my lower leg ache and throb. *You idiot.*

I shouldn't have run. I shouldn't have pushed myself beyond my limits. *Stupid. Stupid. Stupid.*

I'd grown to believe I'd be okay—Lewis had spent the past few months convincing me I was okay. That I could do new, but limited, activities. Yet here I was, back at square one. Injured. Broken. Fucked up. I shouldn't have listened to him . . . or Frank. The drugs eased the pain in my leg but not my head.

After a lot of sitting around and having x-rays done, I lay in the emergency bay bed, waiting for the results. The one person I wanted by my side wasn't anywhere in sight. I was over this shit. Over acting. Lying. Being a mess. *Fuck.* I flicked the tears off my cheek, grabbed my cell phone out of my purse, and texted Lewis . . . and Cole:

> HURT ANKLE ON SET.
> AT HOSPITAL FOR X-RAY.
> WILL TEXT YOU ONCE I GET RESULTS.

But my brother never listened. He rushed into my bay in the emergency department thirty minutes later . . . by himself. My heart twanged. I'd thought Lewis would've insisted on coming.

"Hey, Tee." He ran to my bedside, clutched my hand, and kissed my forehead. "What have you done to yourself?"

"I had to run on set. My ankle snapped." It throbbed, just to remind me of that fact. I glanced at the curtain's edge, hoping Lewis would appear. "Did any of the others come?"

"No. They're tied up in tour meetings. They wouldn't get into emergency anyway. They're not family or next-of-kin or any of that crap."

Valid point. My heart sank into the pit of my stomach. I should add the rest of the band members' contact details to my medical insurance. The guys were my family.

"Have you got the results yet?" Cole pulled up a chair close to my bed, the legs scraping across the floor.

"No." Over waiting, I slumped deeper into the pillow. The

painkillers fuzzed my head. "I'm still waiting for the doctor. I told you not to come."

"That wasn't an option."

God, I loved my brother. Loved that he cared.

Fifteen minutes later, the doctor arrived. I raised an eyebrow. In my druggy haze, I could have sworn he was Tom Hanks' twin.

"Morning Tia. I'm Dr. Carlton." *Shit!* He even sounded like Tom. "How are you feeling?"

"Keep the drugs coming and I'll keep feeling awesome."

Chuckling, he pulled my x-rays out of the packet and held up the one of my ankle. The black and grey film shimmered in the fluorescent light. "You've had a bad bust up, haven't you?"

That was an understatement. "Don't sugarcoat the news, doc. Is anything broken?"

He continued to examine my x-ray as if totally intrigued by all the plates and pins holding my bones together. "The bones? No. Your knee is fine. Your ankle is just sprained."

The air shot from my lungs. I clutched Cole's hand and squeezed it. My ankle wasn't broken. *Oh, thank fucking Christ.*

Cole rubbed my arm. "That's great news."

But the doctor still eyed my x-ray. A groove formed between his brows, growing deeper and deeper by the second. I clutched at the blanket and twisted it into a knot on my lap. "Is there a but?"

"Yes. A big but." Holding the x-ray higher, he pointed to two pins in my ankle. "These pins in your talus and calcaneus concern me. Do you get a lot of pain when you walk? Continual swelling?"

"All the time. Every day."

He lowered the x-ray and turned to me. "They could've been positioned better. If redone, it could alleviate some, if not all, the pain you're experiencing."

More surgery? No. No. NO! But no pain? Whoa. "Would that involve months of non-weight-bearing bed rest again?"

"Yes." He stuffed the film back into the envelope. "Eight to twelve weeks."

"Shit." The blood drained from Cole's face. "That long?"

I twisted my head on the pillow. "I was out of action for four months when I broke half my leg, then had three months of leg braces, and crutches, and I still have physical therapy every week. Eight weeks is nothing." But it was. It was a lifetime. It had taken me twelve months to heal this much—the idea of going back and starting again was too hard to comprehend.

Cole rubbed my shoulder. "So sorry, sis. I hate seeing you hurt. If you want to get it redone, you won't have to recover alone. I'm here for you."

"Thanks. But that won't be necessary. I'm tough." But I wasn't. Not right then.

"More surgery is only a recommendation, but I honestly believe it would help," Dr. Carlton said. "I'm an orthopedic surgeon. Legs and ankles are my specialty. You don't have to decide today, but in the future, if you want to discuss options, come see me at my practice." He handed me a card. "For now, I'll get one of the nurses to strap your ankle. Take it easy for a few days, keep your foot elevated, iced and rested. The swelling and bruising should disappear in a week or so."

"Thank you." Relief flooded through my veins. But my head ached. More surgery? More recovery? Did I want to go through that again? I struggled every day. I'd never be one hundred percent. But was the possibility of less pain and improvement worth going under the knife for? *Crap.* It was something I'd have to seriously consider. Just not then. Not in my drug-induced state. I wanted to go home.

After being dismissed from the hospital, Cole dropped me off at the house near one o'clock. Not wanting to burden him,

I sent him back to his meetings. I'd survived for months on my own with a broken leg; I could do the same with a sprained ankle. I had crutches. I could run a fucking marathon with those things.

But as the drugs wore off, the crippling pain in my ankle returned. I grabbed an ice pack for my ankle, clambered up the stairs, popped some of my strong painkillers, and crawled into bed. I tugged the pillow underneath my head then drew the quilt over me, hugging it beneath my chin. After the emotional and tiring day, my eyelids grew heavy. With the drugs fogging my mind, I drifted off to sleep.

A soft knock on my bedroom door woke me. I glanced at the clock. *Fuck.* It was eleven in the evening. Where had the day gone? Sitting upright, I rubbed my bleary eyes. Lewis tiptoed to my side in his pajamas and placed his cell phone on my nightstand. He sank onto the bed and wrapped his arms around me. "You okay? You didn't return my texts this afternoon."

"Sorry." I wiped my hand down my face. "I took some strong painkillers. They zonked me out."

"Sure did. You haven't moved an inch since we got home. Cole and I have been checking on you to make sure you're still alive. He's gone to bed. I came to check on you one last time before I crashed." He stroked my hair. "I'm glad your ankle isn't broken."

"Me too. But it's not good. I might need more surgery." I flicked the quilt off my legs and unwrapped the heavy towel and no-longer-cold ice pack from around my ankle. After tossing them on the ground, I crawled out of bed, used the bathroom, and returned to the covers.

Lewis slid his hand up and down my bare thigh. "Cole told me what the doctor said. Are you going to have the surgery? It'll be a long recovery."

"Does that bother you?" I grabbed another painkiller off my

nightstand, knocked it down with a mouthful of water from the glass, and wiped my mouth on the back of my hand.

"No. Why would it?"

I sucked in a deep breath as I closed my eyes. My heart cried. "Because I'd be out of action for months. It might not make any difference to my ankle. Even then, it's never going to be perfect. I'm always going to be injured. Limp. Hobble. Be an invalid."

"Tee, your injury has never bothered me." He shuffled closer and looped his arms around me again, drawing me to his chest. "I'm here for you. Whatever you decide to do."

I sniffled against his white T-shirt. "I may end up with more scars. I'll never wear short skirts and tiny dresses like most girls do." Not that I ever had.

He chuckled, then kissed the top of my head. "Have you not learned anything about me? Pants are kinda my thing."

My heart twisted and tensed. I didn't want his jokes, or quick wit or sympathy and pity. I pushed off his chest to sit upright. "I was a fool to believe I was getting better. I shouldn't have gone dancing or parasailing or had crazy sex or run onset today. My ankle wasn't healed enough. It wasn't strong enough. Now I'm hurt again."

He clutched and squeezed my hand. "Today was a freak accident. You'll be okay."

"I won't ever be able to do the things you and the guys love doing. I can't run, or snowboard, or ride a fucking bike. I can't even drive. I don't ever want to hold you back."

"You're not." He caressed the side of my head. "Stop this crazy talk. I'm not going anywhere."

My shoulders slumped. "Why do you care so much?"

"Because I'm yours. I hated not being by your side today. I'm tired of hiding. I want to tell the others we're together. Tomorrow."

"We can't. I have night shoots for the rest of the week." I

rubbed at the tension throbbing in my temple. "We have to wait till the weekend. Please?"

He drew my hand away from my face. "Aren't you sure about us? A few days won't make a difference, will it?" Anguish swallowed the silver shards in his eyes.

Today had made a difference.

I wasn't the same as I had been that morning.

The concept of undergoing more surgery, repeating the past twelve months of recovery, and having to start again had messed with my head. *Crap.* I cupped his cheek. His soft, barely-there stubble tickled my fingertips. "It's just been a crappy day. Please. Just wait."

The light faded in his eyes. Shaking his head, he lowered his chin. "Shit. It has. I'm sorry. I was just worried about you and hated not being with you. Of course we'll wait. But that's it, Tee. Not another day longer." He squeezed and rubbed my hand. "For now, you get some sleep. I'll see you in the morning." As I lay down, he pulled the quilt over my waist and gave me a quick kiss on the forehead.

He stood and went to step away, but I caught his arm. "Lew?" My head wasn't in a good space. My foot throbbed. I cared for him so much. I didn't want to think about the future, the past, or risking my heart on a new relationship. I just wanted the here and now. "Can you hold me? For five minutes."

He hesitated, then nodded. "Yeah. I can do that."

He crawled under the covers and drew me into his embrace. With his heart beating a steady rhythm beneath my ear, the warmth of his body surrounded me. The scent of his skin intoxicated me. This was good. Being in his arms calmed me. When we were together . . . alone . . . nothing could hurt us, and no one harassed us.

This was what I wanted. *Just him.*

Why couldn't we stay like this forever?

Locked away.

Sliding my hand over his chest, I kissed his bare skin. The drugs had eased my pain, not my want for him. We hadn't had sex in three weeks.

He was here, in my bed. That was dangerous. Risky. Hot.

Was it wrong that I wanted to savor these secret moments for a few more days? *Probably. Yes. No.*

My pulse quickened, and my body took on a mind of its own. I kissed my way up his throat, licked his neck, nibbled his ear.

"Tia?" he moaned, then chuckled softly. "I thought you wanted a cuddle."

"I changed my mind. I've missed you."

"We can't." He raised his shoulder, blocking my lips' access to his neck. "Your brother's across the hallway."

"We'll just have to be super quiet." I dipped my hand into his boxers and rubbed his rock-hard cock. I loved that my kisses and touch turned him on.

A low growl rumbled deep in his throat. "You'll be the death of me." He rolled me onto my back, eased my boyleg panties off, yanked off his pajamas, and made hot, dreamy love to me.

The day certainly ended on a better note than how it'd started.

Sleepy and relaxed after a blissful orgasm, I curled against his chest. I kissed his pec, my head too heavy to lift any higher. "Lew, you better go."

"Yeah." His voice sounded faint. Distant. The soft trails of his fingers down my back had stopped.

Shit. I had to shake him awake. He had to go back to his room. But my arms had turned to lead. His heartbeat was like a soft lullaby against my ear.

I was unable to stay awake. My eyes fluttered shut.

Chapter 31

LEWIS

"Lewis. Wake up?"

"Ow!" Why was I being poked in the arm?

Blinking, I struggled to open my eyes. Two electric greens greeted me, but they weren't full of morning sunshine or sexy happiness. Sheer terror and hurt shimmered in their depths. A chill shot through my veins. *Oh, shit!* I was still in Tia's room. The digital clock on the nightstand blinked 5:12 a.m. *Fuck.* Cole would be heading out for his run soon. He'd check on Tia after her fall yesterday. I had to get out of there. But before I could untangle my naked body from the sheets and roll out of bed, Tia shoved my cell phone into my face. "What the fuck is this?"

"What's what?" I rubbed the sleep from my eyes, then focused on the fine print. My heart stilled. Every ounce of blood in my body drained into my toes. Another message from Emilio lit the lock screen.

> LEW, WE CAN DO THIS.
> WE BELONG TOGETHER. CALL ME.
> LOVE YOU, EM.

What the fuck? My head throbbed. He had to stop texting.

"What's going on?" Sitting facing me, Tia clutched the quilt across her bare chest. "Have you been lying to me?"

I glanced toward the door. *Shit.* We had to be quiet. This wasn't good.

"No." I sat upright and wiped my hand over my face to make sure I wasn't in the middle of a nightmare.

"Why is he texting?" The razor-sharp edge in her harsh whisper could cut diamonds. "You said it was over."

"It is."

"Do you want to get back together?"

"No." I softened my voice. "Absolutely not."

"Are you still in love with him?"

The sadness in her tone tore at the scars on my heart. God, I wasn't Rhett. "I'm not. I swear I'm not."

"This is how it started with Rhett and Michaela. First, the texts. Then, the calls. Followed by the we're-just-friends bullshit." She closed her eyes and shuddered. "I can't go through that again."

Um . . . she was the one who'd wanted me to call him. And I was glad I had. It was over.

I slid my hand up her bare thigh then snaked my hand around her naked waist. It was too early for this kind of conversation. I did my best to focus. "You have nothing to worry about. We're not getting back together. Not ever." I brushed my lips against hers, but she didn't return the gesture. *Shit.* "But babe, right now, I have to go. I'll come back once Cole leaves. Promise." I yanked off the sheet. *Where the hell are my clothes?* Searching the covers, I found Tia's T-shirt and panties and tossed them to her.

"Thanks," she grumbled, kicking back the sheets and straightening her sore leg. Her strapped ankle had swollen to the size of a baseball. A bluish-black tinge radiated outward from the bandaging. It needed more ice.

"How's the foot?" I asked.

"Painful." She ripped on her clothes and flicked her long hair out of the collar. The setback of possible surgery and a long recovery had played on her mind last night. But like always, she'd shoved it aside with some crazy talk and sexy seduction rather than discussing the pros and cons. But I'd given in. *Damn.* I had it bad for her.

As I searched the covers again for my boxer shorts, my blood pressure spiked. I swore I'd left my pajamas by my feet. I looked under the pillows, over the edge of the bed, and through the sheets once more. *Fuck.* I'd grab her towel and head back to my room.

But just as I was about to jump out of bed, Tia caught my arm. Trouble etched her brow. My chest ached. I didn't want her to worry about my ex. Or surgery. What could I do to put her mind at ease?

Nothing right then.

I had to get my ass out of there.

"Lewis? Do you miss being with men?" Her pained voice was barely audible.

My head ached. This was not the conversation we should've been having at five o'clock in the morning. But the text from my ex had obviously rattled her.

I rolled toward her. Hooking my finger beneath her chin, I turned her face toward me. *Damn, she was beautiful.* "No. I haven't missed *being* with men. Needing time to process us was about accepting change and committing to someone new. Was I ready to let someone in? Are you my last first kiss, my last first time, my future? I want to find out." I brushed my thumb across her smooth jawline. "I get blown away every time we're in the same room together. You make me laugh. The sex we have is phenomenal. I'm into you. Falling for you. I want to see where this goes. I've been waiting for and wanting you to feel the same way."

She half-turned away from me and stared out of the window.

My heart cinched, and my skin prickled all over. "Tee? What's going on? We're good, aren't we?" What had I missed? I scooped her hair back over her shoulder, letting it cascade in waves down her back. "Talk to me."

"I should've seen this coming. I'm stuck on repeat. I may be out of action for months if I have surgery. The band is taking off, taking all your time. Your ex is texting. My future career path has changed."

I kissed the tip of her shoulder. "Hey? I'm not going anywhere."

Tears welled on the rims of her eyes. "You can't be certain about that. What if Cole and the guys hate us being together and kick you out?"

My stomach clenched. The scars on my heart ached. "It wouldn't be the first time someone has rejected me for who I am or who I want to be with. I'd get another job. I'd find another band to play with. I've done that before—I can do it again." But God, I didn't want to. My love of music had been restored. I've found a great band. I'd found *her*.

She shook her head. "I don't want you to do that. You love playing with the guys. You're so good. The perfect fit. I don't want to jeopardize that."

"You're not. I came to LA for them. You're an unexpected bonus."

"Falling for each other wasn't part of the plan. We fought our feelings for so long, gave in to them, took a chance and explored them."

We certainly have. A saucy smile slid across my lips as I ran my hooked finger down her sexy arm. "Hmmm, think of all the exploring we could do if we stopped sneaking around, and you ditched school and worked with us instead."

She winced, hugging the sheet to her chest. "I don't want to work for you guys."

"I want to change your mind." I edged closer, kissing my way toward the small of her neck. But I got no playful flinch or smile, only a cold shoulder.

"You won't." She swiveled toward me. "I've found what I want to do with my life and something that makes me happy. I have you to thank for that. But I can't work with the band. Not ever."

Confusion hammered the center of my brain. "So what are you saying?"

She lowered her chin and fidgeted with her hands on her lap. "We're at a turning point. We're in different places now compared to when we first met. I'm going back to school. You're about to tour with the guys. I don't want to stand in the way of you having fun. You don't need me to be a burden."

Panic crept through my veins. I didn't like the direction this conversation was heading in. "You're not."

"We have other things to focus on. Life is pulling us in opposite directions."

I clutched her hand and gave it a tight squeeze. "No. It's not. It's brought us together. You saw a text from Emilio and freaked out. I get that. But I'm not Rhett, running back to my ex. You're concerned about me being surrounded by temptation on the tour—I understand that. But I'm not Phil. I'm not a fucking teenager. I've had my fair share of hookups. I can control myself. Am I nervous about telling everyone about us? Too fucking right. But I have faith that my friendship with the guys is strong enough to survive. I'm in love with you. That is worth the risk."

She closed her eyes and shook her head. "No. It's not."

Not the reaction I'd expected when I told her I loved her. Nor the ideal circumstance. "Yes. It is."

"Don't you get it?" Her shoulders collapsed. "I care about

you. I want you to enjoy the ride you're on. The extra media attention on us will add more pressure you don't need. Gossip and scandal have killed every relationship I've ever had. I've lost Phil and Rhett. I don't want to add you to that list."

My heart rate doubled, not in a good way, making my head spin. "You won't lose me."

She swept my hair off my forehead, then cupped my cheek. Too much sadness darkened her eyes. "I don't want you to change who you are for me."

I caught her hand in mine, entwined our fingers, and lowered them to my thigh. "Tia, I changed the moment we kissed. There was no turning back once we slept together. You opened my mind and heart to new possibilities, to things I didn't think would ever happen in my lifetime. I don't care what people say. Neither should you. I will start again if I have to. But no one, not the band, nor gossip, nor some stupid dibs rule, is going to dictate who I can and cannot love. I want to love who I want, when I want. And that, right now, and hopefully for the rest of my days, is you."

She was scared, I understood that. But we'd had this conversation. I couldn't go 'round and 'round in circles.

I gave her hand a gentle shake. "Tee, we can't hide anymore. I hate that you never spend the night in my bed. You keep wanting to sneak around, not wanting Cole to find out. You're going back to school to keep some separation and your independence from the band—that's fine. But I want to be with you. So what's the real issue? Now that it's come down to the eleventh hour to tell everyone we're together, you want to back out?" I couldn't believe her insecurities still lingered even after months of spending time together.

She closed her eyes and withdrew her hand from mine. "It's about doing the right thing. I don't ever want you to have to choose between music and me, so I'm choosing for you. You're a Flintlock. In a year, after the tour, things might be different. But until then, let's not worry about us."

My heart splintered like kindle. There didn't have to be a choice. I wanted her and music. We'd make it work. Why couldn't she see that? "No, we have breaks in our tour dates so we can see each other."

"We will . . . as friends."

The back of my eyes stung. "Are you fucking with me?"

"No," she whispered. "This way, no one loses. No one gets hurt."

"Too late for that," I snapped. "You just can't let go of the past, can you? This hasn't been easy on either of us, but up there on that ridge"—I pointed out the window—"the night we got together, you said you were in. What's changed?" But something else struck me hard, low in the guts. "Are you ashamed or embarrassed to be with me? Because I was gay? You want to fuck me but not be seen with me? Is that it?" My chest ached. I didn't want to hear the answer.

"No, this is for the best."

I wasn't convinced. "You don't know that when you haven't even given us a chance. My God . . . you were so patient and understanding as I processed being with you. I fell in love with you. You wanted this too, but now you're just giving up?"

She winced. "I'm setting you free."

Pain shot through the center of my chest. "Being free is living life to the fullest, taking chances, and being with the one you love with no limitations or boundaries. So stop being afraid." I dug my fingers into the bed to steady myself, to stop myself from spiraling. "We've all been burned before. Hell, I had my heart ripped apart by Emilio. But you brought me back to life. Tee, Phil's gone. So has Rhett. I'm here, wanting to love you. Why won't you let me?"

She lowered her chin, as if she were avoiding my gaze. *What the fuck?*

But as I took a shaky breath, ice stabbed my heart. The blood drained from my face. "I've been a fool, haven't I? I tried to talk myself out of having feelings for you but couldn't. I couldn't believe you felt the same way about me, but this was all an illusion, wasn't it? Just like the stunts you used to do. You wanted me to believe this was real, but it was all trickery and bullshit." *Fuck.* This was Emilio all over again. "You loved the thrill of the chase, the game, the secrets." I should've listened to the guys; they'd warned me. "In all this madness, I fell in love with you." *Shit.* I hadn't just fallen for anybody, but a woman. She'd changed me where my parents had failed. *Ergh!* "Now, instead of taking the next step, you want to walk away. No . . . run as fast as you can. Fuck that."

"Lew." She reached for me, but I blocked her hand. "I'm sorry."

"Save it." I scrambled out of bed, searching for my pajama shorts underneath the quilt laying on the floor. *Not there.* I walked around to her side of the bed, searching through the sheets. *Found 'em.* I yanked my boxers on. "I fell for a girl who was willing to take chances, have new adventures, and was willing to try new things, but in reality, all you want to do is play it safe and stay locked away from the world to avoid getting hurt. That's not me." With anguish twisting every one of my muscles, I placed my hands on the mattress. I leaned forward and loomed before her. "Tee, we're good together. You know we are. We have an insane connection and can't keep our hands off each other. But you just want to throw away what we have?"

She stared at me; water pooled in her eyes. I wanted her to grab me, kiss me, say she'd made a mistake. But instead, her chin trembled, and she nodded.

Fuck! I slapped the mattress hard. "I can't believe I fell for you." All my hurt and heartache poisoned my tone. "You're just like your fucking brother. You're afraid of developing real feelings for someone, afraid of relationships and love. So be it. You want out? I got the message, Tia. You happy? We're done."

There was a knock on the door. "Hey Tee. You awake? I heard noises." Cole's face appeared in the opening.

Oh fuck!

So. Not. Good.

His eyes widened. The door flung open, slamming against the wall. His face blazed red as he glared at me in my boxers. His fists clenched beside his running shorts. "What the actual fuck? Are you fucking my sister?"

"Was." I stormed past him and grabbed my cell phone off the nightstand. The icy, daggered glare Cole threw at me annihilated what was left of my shattered heart. As I headed for the doorway, I brushed against his shoulder. "Past tense. It's over."

I left, slamming the door behind me.

Chapter 32

TIA

"Lewis!" Cole yelled. Turning, he reached for the door handle. "Get your fucking ass back here. NOW!"

"Cole. Don't," I cried, clutching a pillow against my chest. Tears streamed down my cheeks. "Please. Let him go."

Cole's breath rasped in and out of his lungs. "Fuck." He slapped the back of my bedroom door, then spun toward me. He rushed over to me and sat beside me on the bed. The confusion and hurt clouding his eyes ripped my rib cage in two. "What the hell is going on?"

My head ached. The stressful combination of my injury, work, and the texts Lewis had received had compounded, causing too many alarms to go off in my head. I refused to be blindsided again. Emilio had been texting Lewis, just like Michaela used to do with Rhett. She'd eventually weaved her way back into his life. Old feelings had never died. The temptation and their love had been too strong. Before Lewis did the same thing and shattered my heart, this had to end. "I don't know where to begin. It was good but it all fell apart."

"Clearly." Sarcasm shot through his tone. "I'll fucking kill him."

"No." I shook my head. "It's not like that."

"Then tell me what this is because my mind is spinning out of control. Did he hurt you?"

My chin quivered. Nausea flooded my gut. "No . . . I hurt him." I'd hurt him before he hurt me. This pain now would save us from destroying each other in the future.

"Tia." He wrapped his arms around me, letting me sob against his T-shirt.

"We didn't want you to find out like this. We were going to tell everyone we were together, but it all turned into a hot mess . . . No, I'm, the mess."

He rested his head against mine. He rubbed my arm, hard. The tension in each stroke, rough. "This is a problem, Tia. We don't do problems, us or the band."

"This isn't a problem for the band. Lewis is devoted to you. He gave up his life to be here and loves playing with you guys. But his ex has been texting. He says it's over. I want to believe him. I do. In my heart, I do. But school's happening. My leg's fucked again. Life is pulling us in different directions. It just got too complicated."

"That's why we have the dibs rule. Getting involved with someone close fucks things up."

I sat upright. Fire shot through my veins. "Fuck the dibs rule, Cole. We're adults. You can't stop people from falling for each other. I left LA because of your stupid dibs rule." *Shit.*

"What . . . what are you taking about?" Turmoil shot through his tone.

My heart shuddered, but it was so broken, there was nothing left of it that mattered. "I left because I loved Phil."

"What?" he gaped.

"We were crazy about each other. But after he and Flint fought over Shelby and the dibs rule was set, he didn't want to upset Flint or you or Slip. So when we got together in junior high, we kept it a secret. Then when you guys got signed, he changed. He became an addict, always in search of the next high. He wanted no ties. He chose music over me. Every post online of him causing havoc, making out with and fucking other girls tore my heart. I couldn't stick around and watch that. I had to leave. Landing the role on *Through The Smoke* was perfect timing."

Cole's chest collapsed as his mouth struggled to form words. "You loved Phil?"

I wrapped my arms around myself, hoping it would contain the pain. "So fucking much. But in Chicago, I moved on. I loved my job. I made new friends. I stupidly fell for Rhett. But, like Phil, he loved something more than me. That just happened to be his ex-wife."

A muscle in his jaw ticked. "And Lewis?"

"He's . . . amazing." Everything about Lewis made me want to unravel my soul and wrap myself around him. Everything from his good looks to his sense of humor to how he made me feel like anything was possible. It defied logic. "I came back here to be with you. I needed to sort out my life. Rebuild. I never expected Lewis to be part of that."

"But he's gay. Did he lie to us?"

"He never lied. We both struggled to comprehend our attraction and tried to resist each other. But something kept pulling us together. It was a huge change for him. For both of us. We just needed time to work things out. Time to see if the feelings were real. To see if we could be more. But we can't. You're going on tour soon. I'm going to school. The timing isn't right." I wasn't sure it ever would be.

"Timing?" Anguish flooded his eyes. "You should've never been together."

"Cole, stop. This is hard enough as it is. I just broke up with him so he can focus on the band. Not me." And so my cracked heart would heal quicker.

He sucked in a sharp breath, held it, then let it out as he shook his head. "Shit, Tia. That's so fucked up. You like causing havoc, don't you?"

I swiped a tear from my cheek. "I didn't mean to." But like always, I had. *Fuck.* "I didn't want either of us to get hurt. I failed epically on that front."

"I'm so mad you didn't tell me," he seethed through his teeth. "I hate that you're upset. I'm pissed at both of you for lying and fucked off you didn't trust me. You could've told me you liked each other."

"We needed time to figure things out. Can't you understand that?"

He closed his eyes, clenched his jaw, then let out a strained breath. "So, what went wrong?"

"Me." Sadness swallowed my soul as I sobbed. "I don't know how to let go, Cole. Of what Rhett did to me. Of missing Phil. Of being afraid. I'm just not ready to be in a relationship. I fucking hate not being able to move on."

"Oh, baby sis." He hooked his arms around me again and kissed the top of my head. "It's okay. You will when the time is right. I'm here for you. Always. But do you think it would help to talk to someone? See a therapist?"

I hadn't been to one since I'd returned to LA. I was doing okay, ready to move on with my life, but clearly, I'd spiraled downward. "Maybe."

"Good." He rubbed the center of my back in soothing circles. But then he stilled, tensing around me. "So right now, what are you going to do?" Controlled anger rippled through his low tone. "What do you want me to do?"

I sat straight. "Me? I'll call Duke and Chloe and stay there for a few days until things settle down. But you?" I sniffled and wiped the end of my nose. "Please let this slide. This was the right thing to do for you, for him, for everyone."

He grimaced. "But was this the right thing for you?"

Was it right to fall for a man I shouldn't have been with? *No.* Was it right to let him go and put everyone's happiness before my own? *Yes. Always.*

I smiled a sad smile. "I'll be okay. It just hurts at present." I'd be fine. I had to be. I cared about the band too much. They were my family. Family made sacrifices for one another, and that was what I was doing. I didn't want to cause more problems. It was best to stay away. Like I'd always done. That way, nobody would get hurt.

He clutched my hand on my thigh, tight. "I hate seeing you like this."

I'd done this to myself; I'd deserved it. But Lewis didn't. "Just don't kick Lewis out of the band. He's done nothing wrong other than fall for a screwup like me. He's a Flintlock. Be the friend he needs. He's never had a close family. His last band didn't end on a good note. He's lost people he's loved and trusted. Don't let him down or hurt him like I did." I stuffed the broken pieces of my heart into the depths of my chest. I'd deal with them later. "Please. Just give us some time. We'll get over this mess."

Cole shook his head. "I'm not sure what I'm going to do about Lewis. You're hurting because of him, and I don't like that." But the breath shot from his lungs and his shoulders slumped. "Was I that naïve? That I didn't see you two were more than friends?"

I puffed air through my nose. "Yep."

He wiped his hand over his face, then rubbed the back of his neck. "I suck at seeing the truth. Too little, too late ... again."

"I'm okay." *Nope, I'm not even close to that.*

He pinched his brows together "No, you're not." Raw anguish tightened his tone. "Don't lie to me anymore. Love sends people off the rails. I don't want that to happen to you. Don't end up like Aidan . . . or Phil."

"I won't," I whispered. "I don't want to die." Even though my insides felt like they had. I clutched and rubbed his hand. "This had nothing to do with you. You're fucked up by your past as much as I am. Stop blaming yourself for what happened to Phil and Aidan. You aren't responsible for their deaths. Phil was an addict. Aidan had mental health issues. You were an incredible friend to those guys. But after Aidan died and Priah broke your heart, you changed."

"I should've done more to save and protect them. I should've been there for you. I just want everyone to be happy, and get the most out of life . . ." He lowered his chin and his voice. "Because you never know when it's going to end. I miss Phil and Aidan. And Priah. I worry non-stop about Flint and Slip and you . . . and Lewis."

"You love the guys more than life. I love that. But maybe you missed the signs because you've put up an emotional wall and refuse to let anyone else get close." *Damn. We are so alike.* I loved my brother, but like me, he just had to own his shit and be more honest. "You're blind to what's going on around you because of it. You forget I know you, Cole. You may hide it from everyone else, but I see right through you. You run for miles most days, screw one supermodel then the next, and live the rock star life, hoping it will keep your secrets hidden. It won't. It won't erase what happened three years ago at Christmas. I saw you with her. You've never mentioned it. Am I on the money?" I raised one catty eyebrow. "Guilt's a bitch, right? Have you told Flint?"

The color drained from his face. Fear darkened his eyes. "I won't hurt the people I love. I'll take it to my grave."

"So much for the dibs rule, huh?"

"Fuck you. I won't lose my best friend. So kill it," he snapped.

My heart hurt for him. "Secrets have a funny way of coming out. Lewis was mine. Look how that's turned out."

"No. Mine is buried." He stabbed a finger at me, hovering way too close to my face. "Don't ever bring it up again."

"I promise." I crossed my heart. "I won't." It wasn't my secret to tell. It would never pass my lips.

"Good." He shot to his feet, raked his fingers through his short hair. "Fuck. I'm going for a run. I need to pound out a few miles—maybe ten. Then, I will deal with Lewis. This shit show isn't over yet." He stormed out of the door and took off down the staircase. "Fuck," he shouted, rattling the entire house.

Secrets destroyed lives, broke hearts, and made you miserable. Now mine was out in the open, I could put the pain behind me. I could move on . . . again.

Lewis and I were over.

Done.

So why did my heart hurt so much?

I fell back against the pillow, drew the quilt over me, and let the tears fall.

I'd been right about one thing.

Ending things with Lewis had hurt but it was for the best.

There was no way I wanted to risk falling in love.

If it ended, I wasn't sure I'd survive.

Love wasn't worth the risk.

Chapter 33

LEWIS

After storming out of Tia's room and dressing, I jumped in Cole's Corvette. I took off toward the beach with no destination in mind. I wasn't running away or afraid to face the consequences of sleeping with Tia. I wasn't like that. But going by Cole's livid reaction, I knew what was coming. He'd kick my ass to the curb. I'd betrayed his trust and ruined our friendship. My chest constricted, sending a shudder through my soul. *Damn it!* What had I done? I'd fucked the most important thing to me . . . music.

I just needed a few hours to clear my head. Process everything. Harden my fucking stupid heart.

Prepare to start again . . . again.

Fuuuuck!

Two hours later, I found myself in Santa Barbara. I drove along the palm-tree-lined road, past old white Mediterranean buildings with red-tiled rooftops, and pulled into a parking lot by a quiet section of the beach, away from the tourist-popular areas and Stearns Wharf.

Leaving my shoes in the car, I jammed a baseball cap low onto my head and headed along the shoreline. The beach was quiet for the early morning hour. As I dug my toes into the soft sand, I absorbed the warm sunshine and breathed in the fresh ocean air. Thoughts of Tia exploded in my mind. How had we gone from making love last night to being broken today? Nothing made sense. No matter how much I'd tried to convince her Emilio was my past, she hadn't accepted the truth. No relationship could survive a lack of trust.

But I knew *my* truth.

I sat in the sand and grabbed my cell phone out of my shorts pocket. As I scanned the years of messages from Emilio, memories flooded my mind and hurt my heart. I was over being used, manipulated, and taken advantage of. Over not taking a stand. I'd loved him . . . but we were done. *So done.*

With a shaky finger, I deleted his number.

That wouldn't erase the thousands of photos or memories of our time together, but it was a start. There was no going back.

As I went to turn off my cell phone, I accidentally hit the photo gallery icon. An image of Tia and me harnessed, ready to parasail, filled the screen. My breath shuddered against my ribs. Her eyes sparkled. Her smile shone. The wind tossed our hair around our faces. But my gaze was on her. It had always been on her.

I rubbed the ache in my chest. I loved her. More than I cared to admit. But we were over, and I'd fucked my future with the band.

Now I understood the reason for the dibs rule.

Being involved with someone close to or related to the band caused problems. She was family. I wasn't. The guys would choose her over me.

Fuck.

I was such a fool.

An idiot.

A complete FUCKING moron.

Just past nine o'clock, a group of college-aged guys ran onto the beach, ripped off their shirts, and played football near the water's edge. Hot bodies. Nice tans. Toned arms to die for. *Mmm.* Not a bad view.

But they weren't Tia.

Five minutes later, a bunch of girls rushed across the sand to join them. In their skimpy bikinis, sun hats, and sunglasses, I didn't give them a second glance.

They weren't Tia.

Fuck.

We'd had our fun. I'd fallen in love. But now it was time to move on.

I had no idea where I'd go. I had nowhere to live. My best option was to head back to New York. I'd crash with Hayden or Reg for a few weeks, then head to Europe like I'd planned as a backup all those months ago. Or maybe Hayden could give me some session work at Everhide's record label until I found a new band to play with. I had options. They just weren't what I wanted.

After walking the beach for hours, and having a coffee and lunch, I couldn't delay the inevitable any longer.

I headed back to LA. To Flint's. The guys should be there practicing.

I pulled into the driveway, but Slip's and Cole's cars weren't there. I used my key and code and let myself inside. "Flint? Sutton?"

No answer. No one was there at four o'clock on a Sunday afternoon.

Shit! Were they at Cole's, consoling Tia? Talking to Blake, working out a plan to let me go?

Fuck.

I headed into the music studio to pack my basses and my belongings. But as I sat on the floor, rolling up a cable, I glanced around the room. Jamming with the guys, working on songs for the album, and the ton of laughs and ups and downs we'd had rattled my brain. I'd tried to fill Phil's shoes but had failed. Before I left, I wanted to hear this room hum with music one last time.

Taking to the digital piano, I tinkered with the keys. With each note I played, my chest grew heavier and heavier. I'd loved being part of this band. The guys had considered me as one of them from the moment we'd met. I'd learned so much. For that, I'd be forever grateful.

I'd leaped. I'd fallen. I was broken. Again.

Shit.

Why had I let someone mess with my head and heart? *Easily.* Because I fucking loved her.

I couldn't remember meeting anyone else who made me laugh so much. She put everyone around her first. Even me. Seeing her face light up when she did something she loved, and being by her side when that rush of adrenaline and zest for life hit her soul, had become my daily addiction. I wanted those things to become everyday occurrences. I wanted to see her smile, live, follow her newfound passion.

Falling for her had been unexpected. Mind blowing. She made me feel like no one had before. Not even Emilio had ignited my soul like Tia did. Together, we were complete. Bound by some unexplainable force. But we hadn't been strong enough to survive. Our fire had burned us to the ground.

As my hands flew over the keys, the tune morphed into a song. Words I'd wanted to say to Tia . . . should've said to her . . . pummeled my head.

> *You stole my breath the moment we met,*
> *You owned my heart the moment we kissed.*
> *Loving you was what I was meant to do,*
> *I never wanted my past to hurt you.*

Don't walk away from me,
What we have is too rare.
Don't walk away from me,
My heart cannot bear . . .

To lose you.
I can't breathe without you.
Can't sleep without you.
I want you for the rest of my life,
Can't you let go and just be mine?
We'll travel every road together,
Fight every battle and face the weather.
Spend every day right here.
Baby, can't you see
Can't you see.
We were meant to be.

"Hey?" Cole's voice made me jump.

Fuck.

I sucked in a deep breath and spun around on the stool. My pulse throbbed inside my temples. As he stood in the doorway, I searched his face, trying to read his mood, but every feature was set in stone—except his fiery eyes. *Shit.*

"What the fuck?" He strode into the room. "You went to Santa Barbara."

Damn cell phone tracking. "Yes. I needed some time out."

Six feet away, he paced in front of the desk. "Tia told me everything," he hissed.

I grimaced. "What exactly is *everything*?" That we fucked up? That I was a total mess? That we shouldn't have lied? None of that was new to me.

He stabbed his finger toward my face. "I trusted you with her. You abused that. I'm so fucking pissed at you right now."

"Ya think?" I snapped, thick with sarcasm. "I didn't plan this."

"Were you just fucking her for fun? Sneaking around behind my back for some cheap thrill?"

I clenched my fists, my jaw, my muscles. *How dare he?* "No. Don't be a dick about this. I wasn't just fucking her. She's gotten inside my head from the moment we met. I questioned my sanity on more than one occasion. We fought our attraction for months, but we couldn't deny being into each other." My heart shuddered against my ribs. "Being with her changed everything about who I am. Do you think taking that step was easy for me? To be with a woman?"

"Lewis." Cole slapped his chest. "I, of all people, understand what it's like to be curious and question sexuality."

"I never had until I met her." I lowered my chin. "I know you get this. Tia told me about Aidan."

His shoulders slumped; anguish took hold of his tone. "She told me she called it off. Is that right? Or was she *your* experiment?"

I stared out the window; my vision blurred. Tia had been a whirlwind of unexplainable forces. She'd lifted me up, swept me away, knocked me down, but I'd never regret being with her. "Isn't the start of any relationship an experiment? To explore and question your feelings for each other? Ours were real. But it got complicated and hard, and shit got in the way."

"She won't admit it, but she fucking loves you."

"I was deluded to think she did. But she's just fucked up and can't let go of the past. We were good together, man. But she got scared. Scared of you, of hurting the band, and of change, and most of all loving someone again. That destroyed us." I met his hard gaze with steely grit. "I'm not sorry for falling for your sister, but I understand the consequences. You don't have to sweet-talk around the issue."

"Oh, I won't." His face reddened as he shook his tensed hand near his throat. "You're neck deep in shit, Lewis. The thing is . . ."

He closed his eyes, drew in a deep breath, then let it out slowly. Muscles in his tensed jawline ticked. "I'm too fucking mad to think straight. I hate seeing Tia hurt, and you're the reason."

Clutching my knees, I dug my fingernails into my bones. She was the one who'd ended it, not me. I had nothing left to lose, so I let loose. Drawing my shoulders back, I glared at Cole. "I wanted us to work, to stop sneaking around once we knew how we felt. But she didn't. She's so protective of you and has always put you and the band first." I flicked my hand at him. "She has always tried to honor your stupid code and not get involved with anyone close to you guys. But your fucking dibs rule has done nothing but hurt her, made her miserable and too afraid to take chances."

Cole staggered back a step and sank his ass onto the desk. *Yeah. Truth hurts, asshole.* As he rubbed his brow, sadness fogged his eyes. He stared toward the floor. "She told me about Phil. I never knew. After all these years, it's like I don't know my sister at all."

"That's right—you don't. She's not a kid anymore. If you spent time with her, you'd see that."

His voice softened but flames still licked through his tone. "We used to be close and told each other everything. We used to hang out. Tia and Phil were always a package deal growing up. They were the life of the party. Always up to crazy antics. Then we got signed, our music took off, and she left for Chicago. We lost a piece of our soul. Phil changed. Now I know why."

I shook my head and shot air through my nose. "There are so many secrets in this band, it's insane. If we were upfront and more honest with each other, maybe no one would get hurt."

"I'm not so sure about that." A flash of pain rippled through his eyes before they burned red.

I'd hit a nerve. He had secrets too. *Don't we all?* No, I didn't. Not anymore.

Cole's voice sliced through his teeth. "I'll do anything and everything to protect those I love. I will never falter on that."

"I got it." My heart shuddered. I just didn't fit under that umbrella.

The door flung open and in strolled Flint and Slip. Flint held his arms wide. "What the hell is going on?"

"Lewis has been fucking Tia." Cole flicked his hand at me.

"Oh." Slip straightened, clearly trying to sound surprised but failing.

"Damn." Flint wasn't much better than Slip.

Cole glared at them. "You two knew?"

"Yeah." Slip shrugged. "I've known since your birthday."

"I've had my suspicions for a few weeks." Flint scratched his stubble.

"Why did no one fucking tell me?" Cole's voice shot through the roof.

Shit. Flint had speculated too. God, I should have trusted our friendship more. I'd been such a fool.

"Nope." Flint shrugged. "They needed time to work their shit out without us breathing down their necks. They would've told us when they were ready." He leaned his elbow against the end of the piano and crossed his ankles. Turning toward me, he shook his head, wrinkled his nose, and chuckled. "But fuck . . . with Tia?"

"Yes." I closed my eyes and nodded. The pain still burned inside my chest. "But it's all turned to shit. Emilio texted again. She saw his messages. We had a huge fight. She won't believe me when I say it's over. But trust me, it's so over. I've deleted his number." Too little, too late.

"You and Tee were so good together." Taking a seat on one of the Marshall amps, Slip leaned forward and rested his elbows on his knees. "She's had a lot to deal with since losing Phil. Being dumped by Rhett and injured hasn't helped. But you're the one who put a smile back on her face, got her out of the house, and helped her live life again. Tia hates being a burden on anyone and would've been petrified you'd get bored with her."

A sly smirk curled the corner of my mouth. Her in cuffs flickered through my mind. "Oh . . . she's never been boring. We were good, but it's over. Don't fall in love. It fucking sucks."

"Nah." Flint grinned. Shuffling forward, he slapped me on the shoulder. "It just takes a few goes until you find the right one."

One day, I'd find what Flint had found with Sutton. But not today.

"Is there any chance you two will sort things out?" Slip asked.

"No." I lowered my chin. "I tried to reassure her that Em was out of my life, but it wasn't enough. She won't take a chance on us or let go of our pasts. I'm sorry we got involved. But I knew there'd be consequences. I understand it if you want me to leave." With a heavy heart, I scanned the room. Was there anything I had left to pack?

"What?" Slip gaped. "No."

"It's okay, man. Family comes first." Eyeing a notebook I'd left on the coffee table, I headed over to grab it. I picked it up and tossed it in with my Fender bass and clipped the case shut. As I stood staring at my gear, my stomach sank to the floor. "Tia belongs with you guys. She should be on our . . . I mean, your . . . production crew. She goes on about school and tv production careers and new movie roles, but in all honesty, this is where she wants to be. She comes alive behind a mixer, and when she's monitoring every stage light and tuned into our performances. Tia loves this band as much as each one of you. But she's afraid of making mistakes and letting you down. The continual reminders of all the crazy shit she used to do don't help. She's worried you'll never take her seriously and was worried our relationship would cause issues. But you don't have to be concerned about the last one if I'm not here. You'll find another bassist."

"Lewis, stop." Taking a step toward me, Flint held out his hand. "We don't want another bassist. We want you. You're one of us. You're like me . . . adopted. We can't let you go."

Wait. What?

"Hold on a sec," Cole interjected. "This is about Tia."

"Yes . . . but no, Cole." Flint threw him a fiery glare. "This is about everyone. We've suffered enough after losing Phil. Family sticks together. We'll work through this. We're not going to stop people from being together anymore. We're not going to make any more stupid mistakes. We've all made too many and have all been hurt. Lewis stays."

My breath shuddered in my chest. Tears prickled the back of my eyes. I'd never had anyone fight for me before. Not ever. I'd been so used to people shunning me, kicking me out . . . disowning me. I'd expected the same from these guys. I'd never had someone care for me so much.

I'd given my heart and soul to this band. Loved them. Flint was right. I had to stop making mistakes too, and trust them more. I deserved to stay. "You mean that?"

"Yes." Flint nodded. "We're musicians. Causing emotional havoc and heartache is what we do." He stepped over to me and place his hands on my shoulder. "On that first plane ride from New York, I said I'd have your back. Before the album launch, when I suspected you were seeing Tia, I said that there was nothing you could say or do that would change the way I feel about you. I meant every word." He flicked his head toward Cole and Slip. "So do these guys. Cole's a little overheated right now, but he'll calm down. He's a softy at heart. He's just pissed he was the last to know." Flint gave me a little shake. "I'm not going to lose anyone else I care about. You were one of us from the moment you played in that audition. You're a Flintlock. Trust me. Trust the guys. So unpack your shit. You're not going anywhere."

Overwhelmed, I flung my arms around Flint and gave him a heartfelt hug. He'd become a true friend. The best lead singer anyone could ask for. "Thank you." As I stepped back from him, I shook my head. "Women . . . who needs 'em, right?"

Cole gave me an icy glare. Steam still came out of his ears.

I hated seeing him upset. "Cole, I'm so sorry I messed up with Tia. If you want, to make things easier, I'll move out. I'll give you and Tia your space."

He winced, then nodded. "Stop fucking apologizing. But so Tia doesn't leave. . . that might be best."

What? Tia is leaving because of me? Fuck. "Where's she going?"

"Just to Duke's"

Oh . . . Thank God!

"Come stay with me," Slip added. "My house renos are nearly finished. All that's left is the kitchen and that's supposed to be installed next week. Everything else is done."

My head wobbled in some form of nod. "Thanks, man. That would be great."

Slip had stripped most of his huge old house back to the bare frame and rebuilt the entire thing into a sleek modern home with a touch of Balinese finesse. I'd never owned a house; I'd only rented in Boston or lived with Pop. The possibility of putting permanent roots down here in LA after the tour was a new dream that had sprouted. Every day it had grown stronger and stronger. I'd wanted that to come to fruition. *Another reason not to fuck up again.* "After tour, I'll find somewhere to live. Promise."

"Deal." Slip rose to his feet. A fresh, wicked glint shimmered in his dark brown eyes as he wrung his hands together. "So, boys? When someone fucks us up, are we going to keep the tradition alive?"

"What tradition?" I asked.

Slip grinned, big and wide. "No girl . . . or guy . . . will ever tear us apart. So let's get drunk. Drown our sorrows. Write some wicked songs. Move the fuck on."

Now that sounded like a good plan. "I'm down with that."

"Always." Flint patted and clutched my shoulder. "I'll grab the bourbon and vodka."

As Flint headed for the door, Cole lurched off the desk and blocked his path. "Um, Flint? When you get back . . ." Cole's gaze burned into me like a branding rod. Yeah, it was going to take a while for him to forgive me. I'd do everything in my power to make things right. He was a good guy—a bit messed up like the rest of us, but I'd never blindside him again.

Deep grooves furrowed his brow as he rubbed the back of his head. "You need to hear the song Lewis played before. It was awesome. Tops that 'broken heart' shit you write."

What? But I winced. "You heard that?"

Cole dipped his chin. "Every word."

"Fuck." I stepped over to the sofas and sank onto one of the seats. Some things blew me away. These three guys were often on that list.

"Can't wait." Flint slapped Cole on the arm, then headed for the door. "I'll be back."

Cole headed over to join me. He clipped me on the back of the head, hard. I'd deserved that. I was surprised the guy hadn't decked me. But the night was still young. "That song was awesome. Own that. Let's play around with it and record what you sang."

Not all was forgiven, but at least we'd taken a step in the right direction. "Get a few drinks into me and I'd be happy to."

I did have a family.

A home.

These guys were it.

But it felt incomplete without Tia. Some time, space, and distance were all I needed to reset. I had to refocus on music. It had never let me down and was the only constant in my life I could rely on. *Hmph.* Now I could count on these guys too.

That night, we drank an absurd amount of liquor.

We jammed.

We wrote lyrics.

It was amazing, but on the inside, I was fucking miserable.

A week later, I was no better. The days had disappeared in a blur of meetings for the tour and rehearsals for some up-and-coming awards shows. I'd texted Tia just to see if she was okay. To let her know I wasn't. *No reply. Fuck.*

On Wednesday, almost three weeks after Tia and I broke up, the guys and I had flown to Las Vegas to attend the USA Rock Music Awards. We'd won best single. *We'd fucking won!* What should've been one of the best nights of my life had been overruled by the lingering emptiness in my chest. I'd smiled for the cameras. I'd waved to the fans. We'd partied hard until dawn. But it had all been an act.

So much for moving on.

No person was worth feeling this crappy over for this long. But my heart was stuck. My head hurt. Why was getting over Tia so much harder than getting over any partner I'd had before? We'd only been together for a couple of months, not years.

On Friday, back in LA, as a summer day blazed across the city, I sat beside Slip's lap pool, downing a beer. Just after lunchtime, Cole walked through the doorway, dripping in sweat in his tank top and exercise shorts. Had he run there? *Why?*

"Hey man, how are you doing?" He dipped his hand into the pool and splashed his face and arms with water. *Damn.* I could appreciate his hot, glistening body . . . but he wasn't Tia.

"Just great," I mumbled.

"Liar." He sat on the edge of the sun lounger next to me. "Where's Slip?"

"Asleep."

"Fair enough." He glanced across the pool and combed his fingers through his damp hair, leaving tousled tracks in their wake. Then he tapped his fingers together and fidgeted with his watch. Something was off.

"What's up?" I asked.

He stilled. Concern darkened his eyes. "I'm worried about Tia. She cries nearly every day, and it has nothing to do with her show finishing filming this afternoon. That's not normal."

My chest cinched. I hated that. "No, it's not."

"She's still messed up over you. I've tried talking to her, but she won't listen. She comes home from work, barely eats, then goes to bed. You two were always laughing and goofing around. I miss that."

So do I. "Shit happens."

"Yes, it does." He leaned forward, resting his elbows on his knees. "What I've struggled to comprehend is that you risked being in the band and were willing to give up everything to be with my sister. So, man, be honest with me. Do you still love her?"

I downed a mouthful of beer, then wiped the corners of my mouth with my fingertips. Did I love her? *Yep.* Did that matter anymore? *Nope.* "One thing I've learned is sometimes love isn't enough. I'm sorry it's taken longer than I expected to put this behind me. But I'm getting there."

"No, you're not. She isn't either. You're stuck, unable to move on because you're still ridiculously into each other."

"And how would you know that?" *What suddenly makes him Mr. Observation?*

"Because you're mopey sacks of shit. I hate that I didn't

know you were into each other." He lowered his voice. "Lewis, I can barely begin to fathom the emotional hurdles you would've gone through to be with my sister. Changing sexuality is a huge fucking deal. Anyone who'd do that must truly love her." He closed his eyes. "I just wish you'd been honest with me. I would've been an asshole and lost my shit for a few days. I would've been concerned and worried about how Tia would've handled the gossip, but I would've come 'round. I would've been there for you. Been your friend. Like I have been and always will be. I get ruffled and heated and lose my shit every now and then, but so does everyone. So if you still care for her, please fix this."

Ice set around my heart. "I'm not the one who broke us." I stared at the rippling pool surface. "I've tried to fix things, but she won't talk to me. I've texted. Called to check on her. But I've been ghosted." Just like I'd been when Emilio and I had broken up. I wasn't going to waste any more time.

"Shit. I didn't know that." He straightened and edged forward on the sun lounger. "Come over. Talk to her face to face. She needs you."

"No. She had me." I waved my beer bottle at Cole. "She wasn't prepared to fight for what we had like I was. I *was* willing to give up everything for her. I fought for her. We talked and talked and talked. But I can't do that anymore. There is nothing left to say. I'm sorry." I let my head fall back against the chair and stared at the cloudless sky. "I'll be fine. This weekend will help me reset. Trust me."

I should pack soon. I had to leave in an hour to catch my late afternoon flight. Friday traffic was always cactus.

He jerked his chin back. "By going to your sister's wedding? How's that supposed to make you feel better?"

"Oh, it won't be a love fest when it comes to my family. Being around them will kill any lingering flames I have for Tia.

Guaranteed. Then, I'll come home and focus on nothing but the tour. Deal?"

"Lingering flames, huh? So you do love her?"

Hmph. He'd picked up on that. "I won't after this weekend."

"Not sure it works that way."

"It has to."

"You're as stubborn as she is."

"I learned from the best."

My conversation with Slip a couple of months ago slammed into my mind. *Sometimes no matter how you feel about someone or how much you love them, there's too much other shit blocking the road to being together.* Tia's inability to let go of the past had been our block. There was no way around it.

But was the flame I held for Tia eternal? Unable to be extinguished?

I still felt her in my soul, in every cell, and in my heart.

No. Stop. We are done.

I had to kill those flames.

Visiting my family for Lucy's wedding would help see to that.

Chapter 34

TIA

On the last day of filming *Angels in LA*, the summer heat and brutal sunshine reminded me I was in hell. I sat at a shaded table with Sutton, just outside the studio on our afternoon break, sipping on iced water. When I'd come home last December, I'd prayed this city wouldn't burn me again. But it had. The City of Angels was the breaker of hearts, destroyer of souls, and the crusher of dreams. I was a mess . . . again. No matter how often I'd told myself that letting Lewis go had been the right thing to do, it didn't make it hurt any less.

The days were supposed to have gotten easier, but they hadn't. I missed him. So much so, I ached all over, inside and out. I'd cried myself to sleep too often. The house felt empty without him. Something had to change.

That change would happen today.

Once work finished in a couple of hours, there'd be no more acting in front of these cameras or behind them. The producers had been devastated when I'd quit a month ago. They'd promised to write my character out of the show, leaving the door open for me to return if I changed my mind.

I wouldn't.

I had my whole future ahead of me. School started in two months. I'd tried to psych myself up every day since enrolling but had always fallen flat. Jack had found me two small, local movie roles, but neither of them thrilled me. I had a few weeks to mull over them before deciding. And surgery on my foot had to wait. In a few days, I'd join Duke and Chloe on the festival circuit, one month earlier than planned. I needed to get out of there. *Leave LA*. But every time the high of joining them hit, so did a deep ache inside my chest.

Duke and Chloe were fun to hang out with. But they were nowhere near as full-on as my brother and the guys. That was the problem.

They weren't The Flintlocks.

They weren't my family.

Once our break was over, Sutton and I ambled inside. I sat beside her in our chairs, waiting to film our final scenes. She curled her arm around my elbow and rested her head against my shoulder. "I can't believe this is your last day. I'm going to miss you."

"Yeah. I'll miss you too." I rubbed her arm. "But we'll see each other all the time." *Hopefully.*

"But why aren't you excited about finishing?" She sat upright and smacked me with her rolled up script. "Every time I've asked you lately if you're okay, you've brushed me off. I've never seen you so focused on your lines before. I know you've been lying when you've said you're too tired to come over for dinner and hang out with the band. I know you miss Lewis. So stop avoiding him. He's just as messed up as you are."

I winced. Hearing his name made the hole in my chest ache. I hadn't meant to break his heart. That was what I'd wanted to avoid. *Epic fail.* "For now, it's best to cut all ties so we can move on quicker. Down the track, we'll be friends. I'm sure of it. Stop worrying."

She shook her head and lowered her voice. "I can't do that because I care about you. I went through the same thing with Flint. I walked away from him, thinking it was the right thing to do. But I was miserable without him. I thought my career was more important. I was a complete and total stubborn cow. But how I felt for him ended up overruling all logic. It was hard, but love is worth fighting for. Don't make a mistake and throw something amazing away."

"I'm happy you worked things out. Flint is a good guy."

"So is Lewis."

"Yeah. But no matter how crazy we were for each other, we couldn't make it work."

She swiveled toward me, clutching my hand on her lap. "Being crazy for each other should be a reason to stay together. Love is so hard to find. He fell in love with you. Not anyone else. Make it work."

She made it sound so easy, but it wasn't. "Sizzling-hot chemistry isn't enough to survive. That burns out."

"Not if you don't let it." She smoothed her hand over the back of my hair. "Every time you were with Lewis, you got that sexy banter on, you went on crazy adventures, you hung out with the band, you had fun. Don't you miss that? Isn't that worth building on?"

I lowered my chin and fumbled with my fingers in my lap. I'd never connected with anyone else on so many levels. He'd made me laugh. Seen through my bullshit. Pushed me to try things within my limitations. He was perfectly flawed, perfectly fabulous, and perfectly fucked up—as much as I was. But he deserved to be with someone who wasn't as broken as me. "It's not enough."

"Yes, it is." She jabbed her sharp fingernail into my bicep. "You've got to stop being so stubborn. You could do what you love and be with him every day. Be with the guys. How amazing would that be? I'd be so jealous." She sank back into her chair. "Stop letting your past rule you. Focus on the future and what makes you work."

"That's just it. What could I possibly offer him long-term?"

She lowered her voice. "What can you give him that no one else can?"

I searched my brain but came up blank. *Crap.*

There was a shuffle and disturbance behind us. We spun around, and in walked Flint, carrying a tray of takeout coffees.

"Argh!" Sutton jumped from her chair and rushed over to him. Flinging her arms around his neck, she kissed him on the lips. "Hi. What are you doing here?"

He snaked his free hand around her waist, clutched her ass, and tugged her forward, flush against his body. "I came to see you before I have to head to a meeting and thought I'd drop off better tasting coffees than what the canteen provides for you and Tee."

She swiped her thumb across his lips, then cupped his cheek. "Have I told you I love you?"

"Yes. Love you too."

My heart stumbled against my ribs. I loved that they were so happy. Flint always went out of his way to be with Sutton. He surprised her and made her feel special and never hesitated in letting everyone know they were together.

Shit. Lewis had wanted to do that. He'd never wanted to hide behind closed doors like Phil had, and he'd never lied about his ex like Rhett had. He'd wanted to be mine.

My stomach fluttered for all of two seconds before it fell flat.

I'd fucked us up. I was too afraid of being hurt.

I'd ignored his texts. His calls. His efforts. There was no fixing us.

It was time to build a bridge and get over Lewis.

Move on.

Filming wrapped just after five o'clock. Gathered around the studio set, I shared a few tears and hugs over too many glasses of champagne with the cast and crew. They were an amazing bunch of people, but the show wasn't for me.

I stumbled through the door at home just after ten o'clock, drunk. I curled into a ball on the sofa and hugged a cushion to my chest. My head and heart wouldn't stop spinning, hurting. I didn't want to feel like shit anymore. I wanted the chains around my soul to break. I had a new life ahead of me. I should be happy. I should be excited.

But a tear slid down my cheek.

Cole came out of the music room and fell onto the seat beside my head. He stroked my hair. "Hey, Tee. You look and stink like shit. Congrats on finishing the show."

"Thanks." I sniffled.

"Why aren't you dancing around and jumping for joy?"

"I'm just processing the day."

"Have you come to any conclusions?"

"Yeah. Love sucks."

He chuckled but then took a deep breath. As he swiped hair off my brow, he softened his tone. "I hate seeing you like this."

"I'll be fine."

He clipped my head. *Ow!* "I've let you wallow, cry, and mope around for long enough. I hoped this would've passed by now, but it hasn't. Lewis is the same. Clearly being apart isn't working. So here's a mad idea. Try being together. Call him. Sort your shit out." *Fuck.* Cole was Sutton on repeat.

"There's nothing to work out."

"Tee, you've always gone after what you've wanted. You chased your acting and stunt career. You pursued endless excitement and thrills. You put others first. But . . . you've never fought for love. Why not?"

"It hurts too much."

"I know it does. I've been there. I was gutted when Priah left. I fought with every breath to get her to stay, but too many other factors pulled us apart. There is nothing standing in the way of you and Lewis being together." He rubbed my arm and gave me a little squeeze. "I never meant for our stupid dibs rule to hurt you or for you to be afraid of being with someone you loved. Stop worrying about the band. The guys and I will continually have our ups and downs, but we'll always work through them. Stop worrying about your leg, and your job, and what the headlines will say. No matter what happens, I'll be here for you. So if you love Lewis, fight for him. Life is too short. Don't waste another fucking second."

My breath shuddered in my chest. "What if it doesn't last?"

"What if it does?"

"What about the backlash we'd cause in the media?"

"Tee, you're a Flintlock. It comes with the territory. You've survived worse than anything they'll publish about you being with Lewis. Gay man gone bisexual—isn't that scandalous. Rather than covering up your relationship with some bullshit, just be honest and admit you're dating. The majority of the population won't care. They'll be happy for you. For those who aren't, fuck 'em. We know the truth, and we'll stick together."

"I have so many doubts."

"We all do. No relationship is perfect. Learn from your past breakups and put your energy into making the next one better. You have to decide if the way you feel for him is strong enough to push those concerns aside so you can give each other a real shot. Only you can answer that. Does he treat you well and make you happy? Does he make you feel invincible? Does he make you forget all the bullshit going on around you and love you for being you?"

Sniffling and nodding, I sat upright and nudged him on the knee. "For someone who's messed up too, you're pretty amazing."

"I try to be."

"You are. You look out for everyone. I love that about you." I rubbed and patted his thigh. He cared about his friends and family and took the weight of the world onto his shoulders when things didn't go right. Like most of us, he wanted to avoid being hurt again. "I'm sorry I hurt you too. I never meant to lie about being with Lewis."

"I know." He placed his hand on my shoulder and gave it a gentle squeeze. "You're my baby sister. I love you no matter what. But it's time to stop hiding and stop being afraid. I want you to be happy. Lewis did that. So fix it. Oh . . . and one more thing . . ." He leaned back on the sofa and hooked his arm behind me. "When you get back from the festival circuit with Duke, please come and work with us. You're family. You belong with the band. Go back to school, study online, do what's right for you. But you have more experience under your belt than some of our current stagehands. You have stepped up and helped us with audio whenever we've asked without question. Lewis was right—you shine pressing our buttons. Our crew wouldn't be complete without you. If you hate working for us, you can leave. I won't stop you. But think of the wicked fun we'd have if you came on the tour?"

Tears prickled my eyes as I gave him a half-hearted nod and another sniffle. "Let me think about that, okay?"

"No." He shook his head. "You've done enough of that. It's time for action. I'm officially kicking your butt. You love Lewis. Don't let him go. I'm here for you if it doesn't work out. But I'll be your biggest supporter if it does. I promise."

"I do love him." My shoulders slumped. "But I hurt him so much. He'll never forgive me."

"There's only one way to find out." A mischievous glint flashed in his eyes. "I hear there's a wedding on and the invite was for 'Lewis plus one.'"

My heartbeat quickened. "I can't go to Ohio."

"Why not? The wedding is tomorrow afternoon. You'd easily make it in time."

"What if he turns me down?"

"Give him a reason not to."

Fuck.

What was the one thing that made our love better than anything we'd ever experienced before? What would help us put all our hurt behind us and look forward to the future?

I had no idea. But I had time to figure it out.

I'd always loved taking risks. This one was the biggest of all.

My pulse quickened. Nerves flitted through my gut.

At pace, I had to scurry through airports, fly over half the country, and race across many miles.

That was me!

It was time to fight for what was mine.

Fight for love.

Fight for Lewis.

Chapter 35

LEWIS

My hometown of Fremont, halfway between Toledo and Cleveland, Ohio, had turned on the sunshine, skies of blue, and gardens full of green for Lucy's wedding. More than two hundred people had packed into the old church, filling every pew. The majority of my family and their friends present hadn't been a part of my life for more than sixteen years. I didn't miss them. Not one little bit. I sat in the second back row with my brother, Lee, and his kids, waiting for Lucy to arrive. We hadn't been invited to sit toward the front with the rest of the family. No shock there.

The ceiling fans overhead whirred, failing to provide any relief from the unrelenting summertime heat. I ripped off my tie, tucked it into my pocket, and popped open the three top buttons of my white dress shirt. I ripped the hairband off my wrist I pulled my hair back into a man bun. But that didn't provide any reprieve from the sweltering temperature either. Why the hell had I worn a suit? Mine was at least linen. I felt sorry for the groomsmen, standing near the altar in their gray tails. Blaine, my sister's husband-to-be, mopped his brow every few seconds, no doubt suffering from the heat and wedding jitters. But my sister had good taste. With his buzz cut, broad shoulders, and Chris Pine blue eyes, he was definitely handsome. His three friends weren't bad either.

Lee and I quietly cracked jokes, questioning people's choices in attire, and caught up on the family drama. Three weeks ago, he'd come out to our parents over dinner. It hadn't gone well.

"So are you doing okay? You know . . . since you told everyone at home?" I glared at the back of my mother's head. She sat, regal as a queen in a cream mother-of-the-bride dress, in the front row next to my sisters and brothers. But there was nothing majestic about her heart. We'd been at the church for fifteen minutes. She hadn't looked once in our direction.

"Yeah, I am." A new strength mixed with an edge of heartache rippled through his tone as he fanned himself with his booklet. "They told me to never step inside their house again. I was prepared for that." Yep. I'd heard those words before.

"You're strong. I admire that."

"Thanks to you." He patted and squeezed my knee. "Best thing I ever did was come out. I've discovered who my true friends are, and I've gotten rid of those who can't accept change. It's so freeing. Empowering. I wish I'd done it years ago."

"I'm happy for you." I wished I could draw on some of that strength he'd talked about. The chaos in my head since breaking up with Tia still bombarded me every day. Why did breakups hurt so fucking much? Leave you in a mess? Take so damn long to get over? *Ergh.* I shouldn't have come to the wedding. I couldn't pretend to be happy when I wasn't.

The organist played a droning chord, announcing the bride's arrival. The congregation rose to their feet. As Wagner's "Bridal Chorus" whined through the air, and my sister, Lucy, glided down the aisle in a stunning yet simple white dress with pearls around the neckline, a stabbing pain speared my ribs. I'd wanted to marry Emilio and spend the rest of my life with him. But in that moment, all I could think about was how beautiful Tia would look, floating down the aisle in a gorgeous gown . . . toward me. *Fuck.*

Without her around, not even music had been the same.

I needed to snap out of this hellish cycle this weekend. I'd promised Cole. We started tour rehearsals next week. If my sappy ass continued like this, I'd kick myself out of the fucking band. No one needed to put up with this shit. Me included.

Lee leaned toward me and spoke low into my ear. "You've been distant ever since you arrived late last night. Is it band or girl dramas?"

Hmph. I kept my eyes forward. "Girl. Next question?"

"What's happened?"

"Tia got scared and was afraid to commit. She didn't love me as much as I loved her. Do you want me to go on?" Rejection still hurt like a bitch.

"There's nothing wrong with being scared. Hell, it took me fifteen years not to be."

"I was right about one thing. A woman couldn't make me happy."

"Tia did. Even if it was only for a little while."

Yeah, she had. But it was over.

"You really loved her, didn't you?"

"Yes." I shrugged my shoulder like it was no big deal. But it was. My heart was still in tatters. "I'd thought that about Emilio too. Look how that turned out."

"He wasn't your forever. I'm not saying Tia is either. But when I last saw you, you lit up when you talked about her. Your soul ignited. To have that spark for someone is rare. Are you sure it's over?"

I lowered my chin and nodded. "Yeah, we're done. It was good while it lasted. But now I'm just gonna focus on the tour.

I'll be fine." *Eventually.*

"I'm here for you if you need me."

"Thanks, man." I spoke low so we didn't disturb the congregation. "You and Mateo should move to Cali. You need to get out of this town and be around people who don't care who you're fucking."

Wait. Who was I kidding? LA thrived on gossip and scandal. I'd been prepared to deal with that. Growing up gay, I'd learned not to care what spiteful people said. I'd wanted the world to know I was with Tia. We would've been in the headlines for a day or two, then some other celebrity would have claimed the spotlight. But she'd been trolled and bullied and shamed online one too many times, and hadn't wanted to face the firing squad again. I would've been by her side. She'd never have to go through that alone.

"Funny you mention Cali." Lee straightened his wilting buttonhole carnation, but it re-flopped in the heat. He fiddled and fumbled with it before he gave up and just let it hang. "We've seriously considered that option. Mateo and I want to start our new life together. It will be hard to leave the kids, but they'd be excited about summer vacations at the beach."

"Yeah. It's nice out there." But it wasn't the same without Tia.

Fuck! No more dwelling. I was done. I was over men . . . and women.

At the reception dinner held at the local golf country club, Lee and I were stuck on the table in the farthest corner from our parents and the bridal table. The venue was nothing like the luxurious wedding places you found in LA; this was much more laid-back and basic. We had the best time drinking, laughing, and meeting some of Blaine's out-of-town friends. We were loud and turned heads. *Fuck 'em.* After dinner and speeches, half the guests hit the dance floor.

As music filled the room, my sixteen-year-old cousin, Maggie, rushed up to me and nervously asked for a photo. I couldn't deny I was humbled and flattered. The second after she took the snap, she beamed an oh-wow smile and typed madly, posting it online. "My friends so don't believe I'm related to a famous rock star. Now I have proof. Thanks, Lewis. Love you."

"You're welcome." I gave her a quick hug. *Some* of my family members were cool.

Once Maggie disappeared, six other cousins and friends of Lucy and Blaine's rushed forward, surrounding me, begging me for photos. This had never happened before at any previous family function. I freaking loved it. Lucy giggled and made her way toward me. She sashayed through my little gathering of groupies and drew me into a small clearing on the dance floor. "Looked like you needed saving."

"No. I love meeting the fans." I took her hand and twirled her 'round to dance. We waltzed and swayed from side to side. "But I don't want to draw attention. This is your day. Sorry about that."

"Don't be." She shook her head. "I had to steal one dance with my famous brother. I always knew you'd be a big rock star one day."

I chuckled. "It just took a while, didn't it?"

"Yes. But you deserve it. You've worked hard, and never gave up on what you love. That's cool. Thank you for being here today. I know it's difficult for you to come home. But having you here means the world to me."

"I'm glad I made it. You look beautiful and happy." Her gorgeous dress shimmered in the soft lights. Her smile was full and bright. "I hope you and Blaine have an amazing life together."

Lucy gazed at Blaine as he talked to some of his friends. "He makes me feel like a princess and that anything is possible.

God, I love him. He's perfect."

"You don't deserve anything less."

"Neither should you."

"Thanks, Luce."

Blaine waved at her to join him. Lucy nodded. "I better go. We'll catch up soon."

"Absolutely."

As Lucy swayed her hips and made her way over to Blaine, my head throbbed. Emilio had never made me smile like that. We'd been great friends. We'd had a great relationship and loved each other. But there had been none of that all-consuming passion, love, and fire. The world had never stopped when he walked into the room. But *shit.* It had with Tia. She'd tipped the earth upside down, set it in a spin, and knocked it off its axis. *Fuck.*

Sweat broke out on my brow. My heart drummed against my ribs. I glanced out of the huge windows across the fairways, blanketed in evening's darkness.

The truth slammed into me.

I wasn't over Tia. Not even close. I wanted to be with her.

Did I have one more fight in me?

Out of nowhere, my ten-year-old niece, Daphne, slammed into me, knocking the breath from my lungs. She grabbed my hands and jumped up and down. "Uncle Lewis, dance with me."

Blinking, I regained my composure. "Sure."

She latched onto my fingers with a vise-like death grip and swung my arms from side to side as "Levitate" by Dua Lipa boomed through the speakers.

Yep. I was spinning too.

Halfway through the song, Daphne twirled away from me and ran off to join some other kids dancing nearby. Chuckling, Lee joined me on the edge of the crowded dance floor and slapped me on the shoulder. "You okay?"

"Um . . . yeah . . . sure." I swiped my hand over my hair. "Not my first rejection."

He smiled and shook his head. "Not Daph. I saw that stunned, what-the-fuck-am-I-doing look on your face before Daph attacked you. That look when you finally admit that it's not over, that there is no one else, and you're finally being honest and true to yourself. I'm sure I had the same expression when I couldn't deny who I was anymore and when I had to be with Mateo." He placed his hand on my shoulder and gave it a gentle nudge. "Luce won't mind. Go get your girl."

My girl?

Was Tia mine? . . . Fuck yes!

Dizziness swam through my head. My pulse hit overdrive. My breath shuddered in my chest as the brakes I'd put on my feelings for Tia gave way. *No more lying or denying.* I had to go home. To Tia . . . *But shit!* I glanced at my watch. *8.54 p.m.*

I blinked the bewilderment from my eyes and struggled to form words. "I want to, but I can't. I won't make the last flight out of Cleveland or Toledo." But I'd give it a damn good shot. I was happy to break the land-speed record to get there.

"Why fly?" He jutted his chin toward the door.

A shiver ran up my spine.

I turned toward the entrance.

My heart stopped.

Tia walked into the room.

Chapter 36

LEWIS

Dressed in a stunning navy strapless gown that reached the floor, Tia outshone everything and everyone in the room. She'd stolen my breath and blown my mind. Operating of their own accord, my feet carried me toward her. *Oh my God. She's here.*

But I stopped an arm's length away.

All my shock, hurt, and heartache tangled and twisted with my uncanny and unrelenting want and need for her. I wanted to draw her into my arms and kiss her until she saw stars. Hold her close. Forgive her in one breathtaking moment.

But I couldn't.

She wouldn't have flown halfway across the country if she didn't want to fix us, right? I was down for that. But after she'd shattered my heart, caution ruled. I needed to make sure we were aligned. I wanted her to fight . . . for us. For me. Like I was ready to do for her.

Clenching my hands to prevent myself from reaching for her, I let out a raspy breath. "What are you doing here?"

A nervous smile curled across her lips as she fidgeted with the chain-link shoulder-strap on her clutch. "I'm your plus one.

Remember?"

She was my only one. But I didn't want to make this easy for her. *Did I? No.* "That invite was revoked the moment we broke up."

She winced. "Lew, I'm sorry. I'm here. For you." She glanced around the gathering. All eyes were on us. It wasn't every day that this town saw an A-list TV celebrity. But I couldn't blame them. It was hard to take your eyes off her. *Damn, she's breathtaking.* "Can we please go somewhere to talk?" Her eyes pleaded with me.

"Why?" My heartbeat quickened as I raked my gaze over her bare, sexy arms. Arms that had wrapped around me, held me, loved me. *God.* I wanted them touching me again. I was failing at playing hardball. "What is there left to say? Do you have more reasons to add to the list for us not being together?"

She took a tiny step forward. Anguish surged through her tone. "I made so many mistakes, I don't know where to begin. I got scared. I took the easy way out. I thought I was doing the right thing, but it just hurt us and made us miserable. I'll do anything to make this right."

I swayed on my feet, dizzy from wanting the same thing she did. Holding onto a fine thread of composure, I tilted my head to the side and arched one eyebrow. "Anything?"

"Yes . . . Lewis, I love you. So freaking much."

My heart swelled, doubling in size. Warmth flooded through my body and pooled in the center of my chest. *She loves me.* Yep, I was a lost cause. "Fuck, Tia. I can't do this anymore."

"Do what?" Sheer panic flickered through her eyes.

"Keep up this act." I'd never be an actor. I sucked at pretending.

Grabbing her hand, I dragged her out of the room into the deserted foyer. By the golf tournament notice board, I spun her 'round to face me. Before she could draw in air or utter a word, I pinned her against the brick wall and kissed her. Kissed her hard and deep. Fiery, hot hunger coiled through my veins. The taste of her lips was pure heaven. Each lick, nip, and suck, each hungry bite and crush of her mouth against mine blazed through my soul. Her arms around my shoulders were the touches I needed. Her body pressed against mine was what I craved every day.

"Oh wow." She curled her fingers around the back of my neck, sending shockwaves down my spine. "I nearly died in there. I thought I was too late. I'd thought I'd lost you."

Catching my breath, I murmured against her lips, "I was seconds away from catching a plane home to you."

"Yeah?" Tears glistened in her eyes. "I'm glad I caught you in time and got here first. I don't want to waste another second being apart."

I caressed the sides of her head, tipping her chin a fraction upward. "Is everything a race to you?"

She threw me a saucy smile. "I like coming first."

I chuckled. God, I'd missed her sass. "I know you do. I like making you come first." Standing in the middle of the foyer wasn't the best place to contemplate sex, but my hardening dick disagreed. Tia's touch didn't help. Grinding my hips forward, I crushed my groin against hers to let her know how happy I was to see her. *Hmm. So good.* Closing my eyes, I inhaled her sweet perfume into every cell in my system. "What made you change your mind about us?"

Her body melted into me. *Yeah.* That was where she belonged.

"The truth did." Serenity softened her voice. "I fucked up. Big time. I was trying to make everybody happy and put everyone's needs before my own. It just ended up hurting everyone. Injuring my ankle again sent me spiraling backward. Needing more painful surgery and time to recover messed with my head. Even with the sprain, I didn't want to burden anyone or be waited on. I'm stubborn like that."

I smoothed my thumb across her cheek. "You are stubborn, but you're not a burden. I'll always be here for you. Even if you didn't want me as a lover, I'd be here as your friend." It'd kill me, but I wanted her in my life.

She brushed her thumb across my lips. "I wanted you so much, but the texts from Emilio frightened me. So did my past. So did the way I felt about you. I went into flight mode. But no more running. I'm here. For you." She slid her hand onto my chest and played with one of the open buttons on my dress shirt. *Hmm.* I'd be happy if she undid the rest, took my clothes off, and had her way with me right there in the foyer. The desire darkening her eyes suggested she wanted to do just that. But she drew in a deep breath, then let it out slowly. Clearly, she had more control than I did, and more was on her mind. Within a heartbeat, tears welled in her eyes. "I'm so sorry I hurt you. I was afraid to love you more, even more afraid to lose you. I've lost too many people I've cared about. I don't want to lose anyone else."

"Me either." I pressed my forehead. "I want us to work. But I don't want to fall for you more and more to have you leave and break me again."

"I won't. I'm in this for the long haul." Smiling, she stared at my chest. She traced her fingertips across the top of my bullock's head tattoo. It was as if she was drawing on its powerful meaning for strength. She lifted her chin. Her gaze connected with mine. "I was so messed up when I came home to LA, but you helped me find my way. You taught me it's okay to take time to question things and to not be afraid. It's okay to start again." She flattened her hand against my skin. "But I don't want *you* to start again. Not this time. No more running away or moving to another city or finding a new band to play with. You have a home and are surrounded by people who love and care about you. Especially me."

My heart pounded against her touch. I hadn't had a place to call my own or family to care about for so long. LA had given me so much more than I'd ever dreamed of.

I clutched her hand against my tattoo. That ink was there for a reason. I was strong. I had new confidence. I'd gotten a little off-course over the past few weeks, but I was back on track. With Tia. What we had was worth fighting for. "I'd like to stick around if that's okay?"

"Yeah. I'd love that." She kissed my knuckles. "I was worried the fire between us would burn out. That one day, you'd come to your senses and go back to men. I thought it was a sex thing . . . but clearly *that* hasn't presented any boundaries." She flashed me a wicked smile but was quick to turn serious again. "I questioned what I could offer you no one else could. Why would you love me more than anyone else? What made me special? I had to dig deep—"

"Tia, you are special," I cut in, pressing her hand closer to my heart. "You're amazing and stronger than you think. At first, it was impossible to fathom being with you. But this blaze that ignites in my soul whenever you're near drives me crazy. You're impossible to ignore. At the end of the day, I just wanted to find someone, a person, to love me. With all my flaws, and history, and messed up life . . . just love me, no matter what. It took time to process and let someone new in, but that person is you."

Her eyes glistened and she nodded. "That's why the answer to what I can give you became so clear. I can give you *everything.* We're more than friends; we're soul mates. Kindred spirits. We have incredible fun together. You're embedded in the band that is a huge part of my life. Our careers align. We like the same things in the bedroom . . . That's so freaking hot and horny." She cupped my cheek. "Lewis, I love you. I want our future to be together. I want children. One day, we can have a family. We can grow old together. So, what makes me special? I'm a little damaged and dented, but I'm the complete fucking package."

I swayed on my feet. She saw us having a family? *God.* I wanted that. She *was* my everything. I clutched the back of her head and drew her mouth to mine. Kissing her had never tasted so sweet. So warm. So fine. Every touch of her lips sent an inferno rushing through my body. I rubbed the back of her head, smoothing my hands over her silky-soft hair. "Tia, you're *my* package—no one else's. I've missed you so freaking much."

"I'm yours. I've never felt this way about anyone. Not Phil. Nor Rhett. Only you. I can't let that go." She gripped the lapels of my jacket and gave them a gentle pull. "If you ran away, I'd find you. I'd fight for you, hunt you down, follow you to the ends of the earth. That's how much I want to be with you. I want to travel and take on the world with you and be by your side every day. I've never been more madly in love with anyone than I am with you."

I teased my mouth against hers and smiled against her lips. "You're sounding a touch obsessive." Thing was, I liked it. It made my blood rush to my dick.

"Mmm. Maybe a little." She slid her hand down my chest, then snaked her arms around my waist. Clutching my ass, she pulled me forward, hard up against her body. "I might tie you up, but you'd like that."

"That would be a yes." My balls ached in anticipation. It wasn't too early to leave the wedding, right? But wait . . . I needed some final clarity. "So no more secrecy, right?"

She shook her head. "No more sneaking around. No more lies. No more games. You never wanted to hide from the world once we got together, nor lie about it. I want to be your girlfriend and for everyone to know I'm yours. You're right. Fuck what people say. There is nothing . . . absolutely nothing . . . the media could write about me that hasn't already been printed. Let them brand me as your scandalous lover, your sexual-converting vixen, your tempting tigress. We'll probably get backlash from the queer community too, saying you can't change who you are or you were always bisexual. Whatever the haters post, print, or preach, I don't care. We know the truth. We found each other, fell in love, went through emotional hell, but now we're here. I love you and just want to be yours."

"I want that too."

She snaked her hands around my neck and kissed me. "Let's ride or die."

"Oh, I'm definitely in for the ride." And I prayed it would be a long one, hopefully forever. I pulled back, but it was only so I could kiss her again. And again.

And press her hard up against the wall.

Feel her breasts crush against my chest.

Have her heart beat against mine.

Have her hands on my body.

So freaking hot.

The door to the reception room opened and an elderly couple I didn't know headed toward the exit. They stopped in their tracks when they caught sight of Tia and me making out by the wall. Disgust and shock flitted across their faces. I smirked at them. I'd much rather be doing so much more than kissing Tia.

And that was exactly what I intended to do.

Chapter 37

LEWIS

I grabbed Tia's hand and led her down a small hallway and into the bridal preparation room. I'd seen Lucy, Blaine, and the bridal party use it to freshen up after having formal photos. Luckily, the door was unlocked, otherwise I would have smashed the damn thing open. I drew Tia inside and locked the latch behind us. Four padded chairs, a small round table holding a pitcher of water, and a mirror graced the room. A single door with a restroom label on it was in the far corner. Spinning Tia toward me, I drew her into my embrace and pinned her against my chest. "I still can't believe you're here."

She touched her lips to mine. "I'm sorry it took so long for me to come to my senses." Her voice turned sultry as she dropped her clutch onto the floor. "Is there any way I can make it up to you?"

Grinning, I nipped and kissed my way up the fine column of her neck. "I'm sure we can think of something."

She peeled off my jacket and tossed it on the ground. "Sexy suit, by the way, but it would look better off."

"This is only the second time I've seen you wear a dress. I

remember what happened during the first." *Seattle. Tech room. One mind-blowing quick fuck.*

"That was hot." Raising a saucy eyebrow, she took hold of my hips and guided me backward. My knees connected with a velvet-cushioned chair by the frosted window. Blood rushed to my groin as she fumbled with my belt, yanked my suit pants open and freed my hardened cock. "But I'm all for variety. Sit."

"Yes, ma'am." I lowered onto the seat. My eager hands slid beneath her dress, glided up her legs, and yanked off her boyleg panties.

The second they were free of her ankles, Tia hooked up her skirt and straddled me. Rocking her hips forward, she teased her bare pussy against the tip of my dick. Her lips found mine, and she whispered, "Don't be gentle."

Oh, geez! I circled my hands over her back, lowered her zipper—I was much better with zips than bra hooks—and let the dress fall open. My whole body ached to have her. "Good, because I'm hard as fuck and want to be inside you."

Taking hold of my hard-on, I slid it through her warm wetness, rubbed it against her clit, and stroked her up and down. Her hot arousal sleeking me was too much.

She nuzzled into my ear. Her hot breath sent goose bumps darting across my skin. Taking her weight on her legs, she eased forward, and lowered onto my cock. With a quick thrust, I buried myself inside her.

A sexy moan fell from her lips. "Fuck, I need you."

I closed my eyes to stop them from rolling toward the back of my head. She had no idea how amazing she felt. So warm, wet, and wicked. I swirled her ponytail around my hand and drew her lips to mine. "God, I've missed you."

Planting fiery kisses against her skin, I kissed her mouth, her throat, her shoulder. Tugging the front of her dress down, my fingertips brushed her soft flesh. I cupped her breast and raked my thumb across her hardened nipple. Dipping my head, I took it into my mouth. Licking. Tasting. Teasing.

She arched toward me. "Lew, your mouth is magic, but I just wanna fuck you. That okay?"

"Yeah." Returning my lips to hers, I kissed her, hard. The fire between us set the room ablaze. My heart raced faster and faster.

Grabbing onto the back of the chair, she slid up and down my cock. With each move, the chair squeaked and thumped against the wall, but nothing deterred us.

Rocking her hips, she rode me. Driving me deeper and deeper.

I couldn't get enough.

I took hold of her hips. As I thrust forward, I pulled her toward me.

I did it again.

And again. And again.

Fuck!

"That's it, baby." Her breathy whisper teased my lips. "Like that."

Clawing and clinging onto handfuls of her dress at her waist, I tugged her body against mine. I wanted to savor her heat. Drown in the smell of her sweet skin. Hold her closer so I could hammer into her harder. I dug my fingers into her hips, gripping them tighter and tighter.

Flexing my butt, I drove into her pussy . . . and set the motion on repeat. *Thrust. Thrust. Thrust.*

Our breaths smoldered. Our fevered kisses grew hotter.

Each drive made my cock harder.

Each touch quickened my heart rate.

Each rush made my head spin.

Her core clenched around me. *Fuck.* I loved that. It was like her body never wanted to let me go. That she wanted more of me and my touch. I'd gladly give her what she wanted.

But geez . . . I was close. I couldn't hold on much longer. I cradled the side of her neck. Panting against her lips, I struggled to speak. "Tee?"

She nipped and licked her way toward my ear. Shivers ran down my neck and along my arms. *Crap.* I was losing control. She took hold of one of my hands and guided it between her legs. Her faint voice tumbled against my lobe. "Touch me and I'm there with you. I want to come together."

I growled, something bordering on demonic.

I embedded my thumb onto her clit, then circled and pressed it into her hot arousal. She wrapped her arms around my shoulders and crushed me to her chest. Driving into her hard, I surrendered to pleasure.

"Fuck." The air shot from my lungs. My release exploded, spilling into her with each pump and pulse. Hot waves of heaven coiled up my spine, shuddered across my skin, and wrapped around my heart.

Tia rocked against me, quaking against my chest. "Oh God, that's good."

Her head fell back, and she giggled, pure sweetness. Watching her come was hot. Magical. Blissful. As I circled my hands over her back, I held her close, riding out my orgasm. I savored our connection, our touch, our hearts beating as one . . . as well as each throb coursing through my cock, my bones, my body.

This was where I belonged.

With Tia.

We had a long journey ahead to work out our relationship, but at least this time, we had a solid start. A chance to find out if this was something special.

How could it not be when I loved her so fucking much.

I kissed her heated flesh, grazed my teeth over her earlobe, then whispered in her ear, "I love you."

"Same." She swept my hair off my face, then brushed her fingertips down my cheek. "If all our quickies are this hot and fast, we are going to have so much fun."

"Mmm, I agree." I ran my hand down her chest and cupped her boob, then realigned her dress. "I also like taking my sweet time exploring every inch of your body. I'll do that after the wedding. But for now, we should head back inside."

"Yeah. I'll just clean up." She winked as she eased off me and dashed into the restroom. I lurched to my feet, my knees weak in the aftermath. *So worth it.*

Once Tia returned, and I used the bathroom to freshen up, we redressed and realigned our clothes. The most adorable smile skipped across her lips. I liked seeing that back in place. She stepped in close and straightened my shirt collar. "So now we've made up, can I meet your family?"

I curled my arm around her waist and kissed her gorgeous lips. "You might change your mind about us after you meet them." I had my suspicions about how introducing her to them would go down. None of the scenarios were good.

"I won't change my mind. I promise." She entwined our fingers, and we headed for the door. "No more hiding. I want everyone to know we're together. Whatever happens, I'll be right by your side."

Nerves flitted through my gut. This wouldn't be easy. But any time I got anxious or overwhelmed, all I had to do was find a spot to focus on. Now, that spot would always be Tia.

I opened the door, and we made our way into the wedding reception. I took a deep breath and scanned the large crowd. "Hope you're ready for a shit show?"

I was certain there would be one.

"Now that . . ." she squeezed my hand, ". . . is my area of expertise. Let's go."

Chapter 38

LEWIS

I led Tia straight to the bar and we downed two bourbon shots. I didn't need the drink for liquid courage; it was more to enhance my ability to tolerate some of my less-than-favorable relatives. Just holding Tia's hand on the way into the room had raised many eyebrows. Most of my extended family shared my parents' views on sexuality—that anything aside from being hetero was the devil's doing, an illness, and downright wrong. During the wedding ceremony and dinner, they'd kept their distance, ignored me, or been civil but fear had flickered in their eyes. I was used to it. I'd grown immune to their behavior. But my heart hurt for Lee. The people he'd cared about had turned their backs on him.

I had no time for narrow-mindedness.

I was here for Lucy and to see the handful of family and friends who didn't give a shit about a person's sexuality . . . and now, so I could introduce them to my girlfriend.

I snaked my hand around Tia's waist and pulled her close. "Are you ready for this?"

She rubbed her hands up and down my forearms. "Yes. I

want to meet all your family. They can't be as bad as you say they are."

I puffed air through my nose. "Do you want to place a bet on that?"

"Okay." Mischief ignited in her eyes. "If I lose, I'll take you back to the hotel, use that tie you have stuffed in your pocket, bind you to the bed, and have my way with you again."

Hugging her close, I chuckled against her ear. God, I loved her. "How is that a bad thing?"

"It's not. I'm hoping I don't win."

"So do I." I held out my hand for her to take. "Let's get this over with. We'll start with the nice members of my family. Come meet the bride and groom."

I led her over to them, sitting at a table, talking to friends. "Excuse me, Lucy. Blaine. I'd like you to meet Tia."

Blaine's eyes widened, and he jumped to his feet. The chair went sliding backward into the person sitting at the table behind him. He stuttered a quick apology then spun around to face Tia. "Holy shit. Hi. I love your show."

Tia shook his hand, taking his fluster in her stride. "Thank you. But congratulations. Sorry for the very late arrival. It's nice to meet you. I hope you've had a fabulous day."

Lucy stood and drew Tia into a huge hug. "Oh, wow." Her voice came out a touch shaky. "I didn't know Lewis hung out with huge TV stars as well as famous rock stars."

Tia giggled. But before she could say anything, I cut in. "Actually, Tia's my girlfriend."

Lucy's jaw hit the floor with a thud. "Did . . . did you say girlfriend?"

"Yes." Tia hooked her arm around my back and tucked into my side.

Lucy blinked and shook her head. "How? What? Since when?"

"We've been together for a couple months," I said. There was no need to go into all the sordid, finer details. "There was a lot of craziness involved, trust me."

"There certainly was." Tia placed her hand on my stomach and drew closer. Her beaming smile and touch were all the comfort I needed. "But we made it."

"Well, holy shit." Lucy's voice ricocheted off the roof. I laughed; I'd never heard my sister swear. I guess marrying a military man had changed her. She flicked the back of her fingers against my arm. "You're going to tell me all about this when I get back from the honeymoon. We're going to Niagara Falls."

"Okay, I promise." I nodded, slipping my free hand into my suit pants pocket. "You'll have fun there. It's awesome. Make sure you go ziplining and check out the bar at the top entrance to the boats."

Lucy threw a raunchy smile at Blaine. "We don't plan on seeing anything outside the bedroom. Right, pumpkin?"

He blushed, turning red and bashful. "We'll at least get to the Falls."

After a quick chat and a couple of photos with their starstruck friends, Tia and I continued around the room. I headed toward Lee and Lyndon next. With each step I took holding Tia's hand, my parents' glares drilled into the back of my head. They weren't friendly, come-over-here-and-introduce-us stares—more like they wanted to banish me to hell. My brothers sat at the farthest table from the bridal table, downing a ton of beer. The surface was littered with a dozen empty glasses. *Go, boys!*

"Argh." Lee jumped to his feet and bear-hugged Tia. "I finally meet the infamous Tia. The woman who stole my brother's heart. I've heard all about you."

"So it's not all good then." Her eyes twinkled as she wrinkled her nose.

"No." He slumped back in his chair, grabbed his beer, and raised it at us. "But it's good to see you're working things out."

"Yes." She nodded. "We are."

"Never thought I'd see the day you'd be with a chick, Lew. But I'm glad you're happy." Lyndon shook my hand, then Tia's. "Lovely to meet you, Tia."

"Thank you."

Skirting around the busy dance floor, we wandered through the cluster of tables, chatting to a few family friends. But anytime we neared my parents, they were quick to move away. *Typical.* I'd need another drink before I faced them.

At the bar, I ordered a round of bourbons as Tia slipped onto a stool. She hooked her fingers into the top of my belt and drew me closer. "Damn, you have a big family."

Wedged between her legs, I rested my hip against the counter. "This isn't even all of them. There are more aunts and uncles and cousins who aren't here."

"Wow." Her eyes widened as she rubbed her brow. "My pool of relatives is nowhere near this huge. You have way too many siblings. I want a family one day, but not seven kids. That's way too many."

"Two or three would be nice." I leaned forward, snaked my hand around her waist, and nuzzled into her ear. "You want to start trying?"

"God no. Let's stick to dating for now." Giggling, she jerked her chin back. "We go on tour soon, and we're not married."

My breath hitched. "Did you say, '*we* go on tour?' Are you gonna come with us?"

She looked up at me from beneath her long lashes. "Yeah. That okay?"

"*That* is perfect. But the marriage thing?" A dull ache flared in the center of my chest. As the waiter placed our drinks on the counter, my past rejection swam through my mind. I wanted forever with Tia, but did that have to include a ring? "Do you really want to do that one day?"

"Yes."

My pulse spiked as I downed my shot. I slammed my glass onto the counter. I turned on a playful tone, but lingering fear rattled my heart. "I'm not sure I ever want to risk proposing again."

"Then don't." She shrugged and swallowed her drink. "I understand why you wouldn't want to. So when the time is right, I'll ask *you*."

Weight evaporated from my shoulders. I breathed easier. "I like the sound of that. But for future reference, don't do anything outlandish, and I wouldn't want a big wedding like this. The alcohol is good though." I waved down the bartender and pointed at our glasses for a refill.

After our bourbons were refreshed, Tia raised her glass at me. "I'm down for no fanfare. I'd do anything to avoid the paparazzi, the stress over dresses, food, venues, and guests, so let's elope. After tour. If we survive that, we'll be together for a very long time. Deal?"

Warmth filled my belly and spread throughout my entire body. I'd found the perfect person. I chinked my glass against hers. "I am loving you more and more by the second."

But as I stole a kiss from her sweet lips, a shard of ice shot down my spine. I straightened and sucked in a deep breath. My mother and father threw us evil stares from across the dance floor. They stood with two friends, talking in hushed tones. No doubt talking about me . . . and Tia. I downed my bourbon and wiped my mouth on the back of my hand. I couldn't delay this any longer. "Tee? Are you ready to meet my folks?"

"Absolutely." She slipped her hand into mine.

Together, we made our way over to them. The couple my parents had been talking to made a quick escape. My mother turned to follow them, but I blocked her path.

Her lips drew into an icy, thin smile. She wrapped her cream shawl around herself like it was a shield. My mother's figure may have been slightly more curvaceous than it was when I saw her at Pop's funeral, her styled hair a touch grayer, and a few more lines crinkled the skin near her eyes, but clearly nothing else had changed.

My father sniffed, and his spine went rigid. His small blue eyes narrowed as he looked down the bridge of his nose like he'd smelled something rotten. But that was just the way he'd looked at me for years. His leathery skin from working long hard days at the ketchup plant and thinning gray hair aged him well beyond his sixty years. But otherwise, in his simple black dinner suit, he looked fit and healthy.

I held out my hand for him to shake. He glared down at it, sucked in a deep breath, then shook it, once. After he'd let go, he was quick to wipe his palm on the back of his suit pants. He'd always been adamant being gay was contagious and dirty.

It boiled my fucking blood.

But I held my tongue.

I was here for Lucy, not them. I was and would always be the better man.

"What are you doing?" My mother's harsh whisper cut through the air. "You're making a spectacle of yourself with this young lady. No one wants you here."

My mother's frosty tone didn't faze me; it didn't even ruffle a hair. I'd grown immune to their lack of respect and locked all care for them away a long time ago. After many years, and despite the changes that had happened in the world, they still didn't accept me. I no longer gave a crap. I was better off without them. "Yes, Lucy and Blaine do. They invited me." Undeterred by their reaction, I pasted on a warm smile and slid my hand onto the small of Tia's back. I drew her forward and directed my hardened tone at my folks. "I've admired your efforts in avoiding me throughout the day. But so you can get your facts straight for your little whisper conventions and town gossip, I'd like you to meet Tia. My girlfriend. Tia, my parents, Esme and Warren."

"I . . . I beg your pardon?" My mother blinked a gazillion times. She turned her ear toward me as if she hadn't heard me correctly. "Your what?"

I kept my smile in place, but my insides twisted. I wanted to clip that ear of hers. She'd heard me perfectly fucking well. "Girlfriend."

In a wave of hot air, her frozen aura melted. It was as if the sun had invaded the room.

"Oh . . . oh, my." My mother's thin smile grew wide and big. Her gaze brightened. Delight lit her face. She stood three inches taller and shook Tia's hand, nearly shaking Tia's arm from its socket. "It's so lovely to meet you. My goodness. A girlfriend."

I scrunched my hand into the back of Tia's dress, wanting to tear her away from my mother's clutches. I couldn't believe my mother's reaction. *No wait . . . yes, I can.* This was exactly what I'd expected.

"It's about time you came to your senses, Lewis." Dad's tone was full of smack. "Hello, Tia."

"Hi," Tia said, but she grimaced, tilting her head to the side. "What do you mean, Lewis had to come to his senses?"

"Oh." The blood drained from my father's face. He swallowed, backpedaling at full speed. "I'm sorry. I don't want to cause any problems, but have you had conversations about his previous relationships?"

Tia slipped her arm around my waist and clutched onto my hip, hard. Her voice jumped three notches, attracting the attention of the relatives standing close by. "Do you mean do I know Lewis was gay? Yes. Do I care? No. Lewis is amazing. It's a shame you've missed out on having him in your life because you've never accepted his sexuality."

My mother lifted her chin and strained every muscle on her face to form a smile. God, it looked so unnatural, out of place, and almost disturbing. I wasn't falling for this bullshit.

"But that changes now he has a girlfriend." Her soft voice, full of love, grated against my skin. With each word that spilled from her mouth, a foul taste rose in mine. Then she took a step toward me and held out her hands. "You can come home, my son."

What. The Actual. Fuck?

I blocked her wrists and took a step back. Like a warrior, my heart stood its ground. The tattoo on my chest burned. "Are you fucking kidding? This doesn't change anything. If you couldn't love me when I was with men, why would you accept me now just because I'm with a woman?"

"Because you've found the right path." Light shimmered in my father's eyes. "You've changed and seen the error of your ways. You're now with this beautiful young lady."

Ergh! He was just as bad as my mother.

I clenched my teeth and closed my eyes. I took a few breaths to find my calm. *Breathe. In. Out. In. Out.* Tia's touch and the scent of her perfume helped. "Yes, I'm with Tia. But I'm still me. Being gay was never an error, nor is being bisexual." *Never.* Fire snaked through my veins. My calm slipped. "You should've loved me regardless of who I was with. You'll never accept my past. I know that because you've cut Lee out of your life. You should've never sent him to conversion school. He's *gay*. Always has been. *You* can't force people to change."

"But you did." My father's voice hardened.

Tia shook her head. An inferno blazed in her eyes. "Yes, he did." She hooked her finger through the belt loop on my pants and drew my side against hers. "We both did. But it wasn't *forced* upon us or drilled into us via some twisted therapy. *We* made the decision to be together. The more we got to know each other, the more our attraction became undeniable. I'm not some sweet girly-girl. Trust me. I'm a tomboy. I wear long pants and suits way more than skirts. I love my sports. I hang out with men more than women. The band Lewis plays with now is my life. I may be female in body, but don't be fooled. Lewis and I get along so well because I'm more manly than half the men on this planet."

"Hmm." Grinning, I clutched her ass and kissed the side of her head. "When you put it like that, you are, aren't you? I knew I loved you for a reason."

"Shh." My mother patted the air. Mortification flitted across her face. "Both of you. Lower your voices. Please." She glanced around the room, throwing onlookers an innocent smile. *What a freaking joke.*

But Tia didn't falter.

I loved her fire and passion, and was overwhelmed by her standing up for me. Just like Flint had done. I'd always fought my own battles, could fight them, but being surrounded by people who loved me made it easier.

She straightened and shook her head. "Lewis is one of the most incredible people I've ever known. He's brilliantly talented. He loves me, his band, his friends, and adores his family members who accept him. But you've failed to see that. Who he takes to bed shouldn't matter."

"Well, it does." The chill returned to my mother's tone.

"Why?" Tia's shoulders slumped. "How can loving someone, man or woman, be wrong?"

"So he's corrupted your mind too," my father snapped.

"No, love did." Threading my hand beneath Tia's long hair, I cradled the back of her neck. I gazed into her beautiful eyes. "When you meet someone who takes hold of your soul, consumes your every thought, blows your mind, fills your heart, makes you happy, and turns you into a better person than before, it doesn't matter who that person is. I've found love in a completely unexpected, fabulous new package."

Tia's eyes glistened as she smiled. Leaning into me, she kissed my cheek. "I'm yours. Don't forget it."

"Never." I turned to my parents. That thick, protective steel shield I'd set around my heart all those years ago remained firmly intact. "If you can't accept Lee is gay, or who I was, am, or may be in the future, then I won't ever be setting foot in your house again. I don't need you in my life and haven't for a long time. I have a family. A new one. One who doesn't judge. Who loves me wholeheartedly. Unconditionally. And accepts who I am."

"Lewis?" My mother gaped.

"Save it."

I stepped back to leave, but Tia halted me. She squeezed my hand. Hers trembled within my hold. Closing her eyes, she took a deep breath, as if she were reining in all the anger, frustration, disbelief, and shock my parents had caused. Then, she glared at them. "My parents weren't around much when I was growing up. When they were, they often voiced their disappointment in my brother's and my career choices, but they never stopped us from pursuing what we loved. They never faltered in loving Cole when he was with a man, never told me to stop wearing boys' clothes at school, and never interfered with our relationships. We dated losers, jocks, stars, skanks, and people who broke our hearts. No matter who we were with, they always supported and loved us." Tia clutched onto my arm, tight. I wasn't going anywhere. "You should've been there for Lewis when he discovered his sexuality. He ran away because you gave him no other option. Instead of wanting to change him, *you* could've gotten help to understand homosexuality and learned how to be more accepting. But you didn't. You failed him big time."

My father's face reddened. "Enough."

"You're right. It is." For once, I agreed with him. They weren't worth wasting air on. "I'm not asking *you* to be queer. Just stop being hell-bent against those who are."

"No," my mother snapped. "It's not right."

"Then once again, we're done." I hooked my arm around Tia's shoulders and kissed the side of her head. "Thank you, but it's okay. Let's go."

But she didn't budge. She swiveled to face me and cupped my cheeks. Tears welled in her eyes as she injected love and seriousness into her tone. "Our children will know nothing but unconditional love. We'll always be open-minded and accepting. They'll be surrounded by people who care for and support them. We'll love them, no matter what. You hear me?"

My breath shuddered through my lungs. She stole my heart all over again. Tia was exactly who I needed. I kissed her palm and nodded. "Yeah, I do."

She shook her head at my parents. Acid filled her tone. "That won't include you. You'll never be a part of their life."

"Lewis?" My mother scolded me, fumbling with her shawl. "Control your rude girlfriend."

Chuckling, I slid my arms around Tia's waist. "No chance."

She raised a saucy eyebrow at me. "Are you sure about that?"

Okay . . . maybe in the bedroom.

I had to keep my mind off getting her between the sheets.

Dragging my gaze away from Tia's sexy lips, I looked at my parents. They may have been my blood relatives, but the ties were truly severed, and I didn't need to mend them. "I agree with every word Tia has said. If you can't see that being gay has made my life, not destroyed it, that's your problem, not mine. I've loved some incredible men, have great friends in the queer community, and every relationship I've had, the good and the bad, has made me who I am. They put me on a path that led me to a new incredible life and to Tia. I'm happy . . . and in love. That's all that matters."

My father folded his arms, drew his shoulders back, and hissed, "I'm already questioning your choice in women."

I held up a finger. "Don't. She's the one. Like always, at every family gathering I've been fortunate enough to be invited to, you've reassured me that running away all those years ago was the right decision. Tia loves me for me. That's more than you've ever done. So before you say another word, we're leaving." I took Tia's hand. "You want to get out of here?"

"Yes, please."

Without a backward glance, we walked toward the exit, past the gaping mouths and shocked glances on half the guests' faces. I got a nod and salute from Lee and a quick hug and kiss from Lucy, then Tia and I rushed out the doors.

On the sidewalk, I pulled Tia toward me and cradled her face between my hands. "I'm so sorry about that. But I fucking love you for standing up to my folks."

She clutched onto my forearms. "They don't have to like everyone on the planet. But to be so hateful, and unaccepting, and to disown your own children over sexuality are things that are impossible for me to comprehend. To change that view and welcome you home at the flick of a switch was a hard 'hell no' for me."

I brushed my thumbs across her cheeks. "Same. Thank you for being you."

"Always." But she swayed and closed her eyes. "Did . . . did you want them back in your life because you're with me?"

My heart didn't shudder or falter. "No." I tilted her head back so I could touch my lips to hers. "My family is now in LA. You're the one I want. I'd follow you to every corner of the universe just to be with you."

"How about just to the hotel?" Her smile turned sheepish as she toyed with a button on my shirt. "I lost the bet. Your parents were horrid."

I arched my eyebrow. "You gonna deliver?"

"You know I will." She slipped her hand into my suit pants pocket and pulled out my tie. She hooked it around my neck and whispered against my lips. "And I'm going to make good use of this."

Unable to contain my grin, I kissed her. Breathed her in. Drank in her scent. "What were you going to do if we didn't get back together?"

"Failing wasn't an option."

"No. It wasn't." I wrapped my arms around her and kissed her delicious lips. But before things got too heated between us and I was caught for incident exposure and having sex in public again, I reached into my jacket and ripped out my cell phone.

I called an Uber.

Five minutes to wait.

They'd better not be late.

Chapter 39

TIA

I'd never fully comprehended how strong Lewis was until I'd met his parents last night. I had a new profound respect for him. To have such a grounded belief in yourself from such a young age, and to not let anyone tell you otherwise, was admirable. Inspirational. I'd met some awful people—haters, preachers, downright bullies, and shady characters—during school and college, and at work, but Esme and Warren took the prize.

The wall Lewis had built to protect himself against his parents' attitude was justified. I'd never question it. The loss of their love ran deep in his heart. I'd seen it. Felt it. Heard it in his voice sometimes. But I was glad that bridge to his family was broken, and I would be happy if it was never repaired. They'd have to change—not Lewis. I couldn't see that ever happening.

His family made mine look like a fucking dream.

I'd often resented my parents for not being around, but now I had a different perspective, thanks to Lewis. They were living *their* life to the fullest. Being honest with *themselves*. Doing what *they* loved. Just like he'd done. My parents had given Cole and me everything and anything we'd needed so we could become strong, independent people. *Sometimes too independent.* But that had given us the courage to follow our hearts, our passions, and our careers. We'd fallen off the track several times and had our hearts trampled on more than once, but we'd learned from our mistakes. Regardless of what had happened in our lives, our parents would never disown us. They'd always love and support us, even if it was from afar.

Now, I had someone else who loved me. I'd found a man who had taught me not to be afraid anymore. No more dwelling in my past heartache and pain. I was determined to live my life to the fullest, do what I loved, and be surrounded by my family. And I wouldn't worry about what people printed in the press.

I had Lewis.

I couldn't be happier.

After a wicked, spine-tingling, toe-curling night in bed at the hotel, and a late morning brunch with Lee and his boyfriend, Mateo, Lewis and I arrived back in LA on Sunday evening.

With a few in-flight drinks under our belt, we struggled to keep our hands off each other during the limousine ride home. I wanted him naked . . . again. But as we fell through the front door and dropped our luggage onto the floor, we were met by a welcoming party. I hadn't expected that.

Music drifted from the sound system. The guys sat in a row on the sofa with beers in hand. Sutton lazed sideways with her legs hooked over Flint's thighs. Their conversation stopped the moment we stumbled inside.

My stomach somersaulted backward. Despite everyone knowing about Lewis and me, and after keeping secrets for so long, it was nerve-racking to finally admit we were together.

I took Lewis by the hand, and we sheepishly made our way over to the group. My ankle ached after too much walking around the wedding venue, down long hotel hallways, and through airports, but to have Lewis by my side, the pain was worth it.

"Hi." I twinkled my fingers at them. Why were my cheeks burning? "Um . . . so Lewis and I have some news."

"Looks like the trip worked out." Concern, happiness, and relief flooded Cole's eyes.

"Yeah, it did." Lewis draped his arm around my shoulders. "We're good."

"Yay!" Sutton clapped.

"You sure about this?" Flint waggled his finger at us.

"Yes." I snaked my arm around Lewis's waist and rested my head against his shoulder. "We're sorry for all the sneaking around. Sorry for the drama we caused. No more secrets. Promise."

"Lew, we love you, man." Cole splayed his hand over his heart but then stabbed his finger at Lewis. "But you fucking hurt my sister, I'll kill you."

"Noted." Lewis chuckled. "But I hope I never do."

"Glad you sorted your shit out." Slip nodded, raising his beer toward us.

"Yeah." I glanced at Lewis and smiled. "It wasn't easy, but we got there."

"We need to celebrate." Sutton swung her legs off Flint's lap and jumped to her feet. "More drinks, anyone?"

"Um." I scratched my cheek, then thumbed toward the staircase. "We were planning on celebrating in a different manner."

"You can fuck later." Cole grinned as he stood. He stepped over to us and gave me a big hug. "I love you. I just want to see you happy."

"I am."

He turned to Lewis and threw him a cocky smile. "While I don't want to think about you banging my sister . . . or hear it, for that matter . . . if you ever need tips on how to please a woman, us three guys can help you out."

Lewis's eyes glinted as he rubbed the tip of his chin. "I seem to be managing in that department. Tia has been a good teacher."

Slip laughed and joined us, slapping Lewis on the shoulder. "Has she pulled out the handcuffs yet?"

"Wait. What?" Cole's eyes widened. "How do you know she has cuffs?" He spun back to me. His eyebrows raised. "Do you?"

I shrugged, unashamed of my toys. "Yes. Slip was with me when I bought them a couple years ago for Christmas."

"It doesn't surprise me you two went to an adult shop." Flint scooted over to the bar to help Sutton pour the drinks. He jutted his chin at Lewis. "Are you sure you want to be with Tia? Do you want to back out now before you can't escape?"

"Nope." Sexy, hot love sparkled in Lewis's eyes as he took my hand and led me over to the bar. "I've had my fair share of wild sex. I was gay, not naive."

Was.

Not anymore.

I loved that he was mine.

"Good thing you're not clueless or you'd get a fucking shock, hanging out with us." Flint grabbed the bottle of bourbon and cracked the lid. He waggled a finger at Cole and Slip. "These two make Mötley Crüe look tame."

I'd witnessed some of the shit Flint had done in the past. He wasn't innocent either. Laughing, I slipped onto one of the stools. Lewis, Cole and Slip stood beside me as Flint handed us shots across the bar; bourbon for Lewis and me, vodka for everyone else.

As we readied ourselves to swallow our drinks, Lewis slipped his hand down my back and tugged on the hemline of my shirt. When our gazes met, my hunger for him spiked.

Oh yeah. One or two drinks, then we were out of there.

Cole raised his glass. "To more music, fun, and wicked times ahead."

Flint hooked one arm around Sutton and held up his vodka in his other hand. "To love, happiness, and family."

"Love you." Sutton kissed his cheek. "But don't go too wild on tour without me."

"Sutt." I grabbed my bourbon. "I'll be on crew. I'll keep an eye on him."

"You're joining us?" Slip's face lit up. "Fucking awesome."

"I have a lot to learn but I can't wait." I'd spend a couple weeks with Duke and Chloe on the festival circuit, defer school for a year, and see what happened when we got home from the tour. I loved my study; I wasn't going to rule it out. But being with the band, my family, was where I belonged.

"To new beginnings." Flint raised his glass higher. "We've survived a crazy year. We've recorded and released an album. We've had two top-ten hits. The third single drops next month. Rehearsals for our first *global* tour start next week. How incredible is that?" His tone had sailed higher and higher, but then he dialed it down. "We may have lost Phil, and I miss him every fucking day, but we have gained a new brother. Lewis, we can't wait to tour with you. Write new music with you. And have a fuck-load of fun. You are, without a doubt, a Flintlock." His softened gaze drifted to me. "Tia, you are home. You belong with us. Always have. Always will."

God, I loved these guys. I splayed my hand over my chest. "Thank you, Flint. I won't let you down. Cheers."

Around these people, I didn't have to hide my injury, cover up my scars, or pretend to be someone I'm not. They loved me for being me.

I'd found my true place in life.

Everyone chinked glasses, and we downed our shots.

Lewis clutched onto the back of my shirt and nuzzled my

hair, near my ear. He whispered, "We need to get out of here."

I swallowed hard. The air between us began to sizzle.

And spark.

And grow hotter.

Oh, yes we do.

But I had to clear the air about one more thing with Cole first. After placing my glass down, I turned to him. "Are we cool?"

"Yeah. Always." He grabbed the bottle of vodka and refilled the glasses. "No more sneaking around, okay?"

"No. We won't." I smoothed my hands over my jeans and rounded my shoulders. "But can I stretch a favor?"

"Depends on what it is." He leaned against the bar.

The slow, sensual circles of Lewis's thumb on my bare skin beneath my T-shirt were getting harder and harder to ignore. But I could do this. Cole first. "My original plan was to move out once I got settled in LA. With work and career changes and Lewis, life got a bit off track. Now we're together, we want to find a place of our own." We'd talked about it on the flight home. "But with the tour coming up, are you okay if we wait until we get back?"

"God, yes." Cole downed his shot. "I love having you here. Stay as long as you like. My home is your home."

I wouldn't overstay my welcome that much, but I'd take it for now. "Thank you."

He play-punched Lewis on the arm. "Make this work. I want you two to be happy."

"We will." Lewis nodded. "Thank you."

"Good. Now let's go sink some balls." Cole pointed toward the games room on the other side of the kitchen.

"Um . . ." Lewis pursed his lips, then winced. He turned to me, then back to Cole, as if he were torn between hanging out with the guys and wanting to take me to bed. But then he shook his head at Cole. "Rain check." A mischievous smile inched across his mouth as he took my hand and drew me off the stool. "We have some unfinished business."

"I'm amazed you've lasted this long." Slip waved his shot at us, then tipped it down his throat.

I placed my free hand on Cole's arm and kissed him on the cheek. "Better turn that music up even more if you don't want to hear us. Love you."

Grinning, he grabbed his cell phone, and upped the volume on the sound system. "You're right—I don't. Not ever."

Lewis waved to everyone. "Night."

Flint chuckled. "You won't be sleeping if Tia's involved."

Lewis pointed at him. "Good thing I'm okay with that."

"See you tomorrow." I blew everyone a kiss. "Love you."

Hand in hand, Lewis and I ambled toward the stairs, but at the bottom, he picked me up, threw me over his shoulder, and carried me to my bedroom. Laughing, he placed me on my feet and kissed my lips. "I'd waited long enough to get you alone."

I locked the latch behind us. No more Cole walking in on us. I'd learned from that mistake. "Me too."

He smoothed his hand over the back of my hair. "It's still surreal we're here, not sneaking around."

"True, but I'm glad we're not. I love you too much to hide anymore."

He slid his hands up and down my arms in slow, gentle sweeps, tickling every hair on my skin. A moan rumbled deep in his throat, like he got off on just touching me. "Want me to show you how much I love you?"

"Uh-huh." I yanked off his T-shirt. His tousled hair fell in soft layers across the tips of his shoulders. *So hot.* His silver eyes glistened in the dim light as he reached for my belt and undid my jeans.

A hot wave of anticipation pooled between my legs. "Do

you want to play?"

As he pressed his crotch against me, his erection grew harder and harder. He skimmed his hand over my chest, then tweaked my nipple through my T-shirt. A jolt of electricity zapped my core. *Oh yeah.* He licked his lips and my knees weakened. God, I had it bad for him.

Hot desire ignited in his eyes. "I like to play—you know I do. But tonight, we don't need any toys. The only restraints we need are my hands to pin you against the bed. The only things I want to play with are your boobs. The only games we'll be playing will involve me teasing you with my tongue, and fingers, and driving you over the edge. I just want you. In my arms. Making love."

My heart melted. "You're definitely a keeper."

"Good." He grabbed the bottom of my T-shirt, eased it off my head, then dropped it on the floor. Snaking his hands around my back, he unhooked my bra. He'd mastered that. It joined my top on the ground.

The rest of our clothes were quick to follow.

After flicking off the bedcovers, we eased onto the mattress. His bourbon-flavored kisses made my head spin. My tongue wanted more of him to taste, and my hands wanted more of his flesh to explore. Every time we were together, I wanted the experience to be fun, safe, and fucking hot. My body was his to love and adore. So was my heart.

Lying on our sides facing each other, I skimmed my palm over his bare chest and ripped abs. Each groove, each muscle, was pure perfection. Making my way lower, I wrapped my hand around his velvety hard cock. As I stroked him up and down, I kissed his hot lips. Everything about him made my body hum and heat all over.

A soft moan fell from his lips. "God, I love you touching me."

In a rush of fiery kisses, he stole my breath. He threaded

and knotted his fingers into my hair. But as a wicked grin curled across his lips, he eased my hand off his cock. "Not the way I want to come tonight."

I bit my lip. *No. Not me either.*

He rolled toward me and hooked his leg over mine. He trailed soft nips and licks down the side of my neck, sending goose bumps shivering across my skin. I flinched and giggled and dug my fingers into his shoulders. His gentle hands roamed over my arms, my waist, and my belly, warming my flesh. I loved how every one of his touches made me feel like I was something precious, shiny, and new. But I wasn't fragile.

"Lewis." Threading my fingers into his hair, I kissed his lips. "I want you."

"Begging, are we?"

"Yes." Between my legs tensed, craving some action.

He dragged his thumb along my jawline, traced my lips, then dipped it into my mouth. I sucked on it, licked it, and swiveled and circled my tongue around it. Each stroke made me wetter and wetter.

"Hmm," he groaned. "I love what that tongue of yours can do." He glided his wet fingertip down my throat, between my breasts, over my stomach and headed between my legs. "But I want to touch you. Tease you. Taste you."

Oh, please. Arching toward him, needing him, my whole body lit on fire.

With fiery kisses, he worked his way downward. My eyes fluttered closed as he worshiped my boobs with hot licks and gentle nips. The flick of his tongue over my sensitive nipples sent another shudder coursing through my core. God, I was gonna come just from him taunting my tits. But then he headed lower, and made his way between my thighs.

His mouth claimed me. His warm tongue lapped, licked, and fucked me. Circled and stroked me. *Oh, yes.*

"Lewis." His name tumbled from my lips in a breathy pant. I clawed at the sheets. I was too pent up with want. Need. Fire. Tension. I pulsed my pussy against his mouth and tongue. *Yes. There. Yes. Yes. Fuck.* Arching off the bed, I exploded like a detonated bomb. Every nerve ending quaked and quivered. Jolted and jerked. Electric sparks coiled up my spine and shivered across my scalp. Sinking into the mattress, I giggled and crushed my thighs around his head to stop his delectable onslaught. "God, you're good at that."

Grinning, he crawled his way upward. "I'm a quick learner, and you taste good; I want to do that to you every fucking day." He planted a kiss on my lips. "See how delicious you are?"

I licked my lips, undeterred by the taste of me on his tongue. The lingering flavor of bourbon sweetened the saltiness. "You taste nicer."

"Hmm. You can blow me anytime. But right now, I want this." He nudged and teased his cock against my opening, then buried himself inside me. The breath rushed from my lungs. My head sank into the pillow. My body melded to his. As I drew my legs higher and widened my knees, he clutched onto my thigh and drove into me, deep and slow. "God, you feel incredible."

Wrapping my arms around his shoulders, I held him close. As I was still sensitive from orgasming, every hair on my body tingled. My core clenched around him, grasping for more. More of him filling me. More connection. More heat.

But as the fire blazed between us and we moved as one, our kisses stayed sensual and sexy. Our touches, soft and graceful. Our whispers, low and raspy. Even better than those things were his rhythmic movements. The gentle thrusts, hot penetrations, and gradual rocks of his hips sent waves of heat rushing through my blood and wrapped around my heart. Slow lovemaking made my body purr and my soul soar.

In the past, sex for me had consisted of mad quickies, hot

fucks, and crazy antics. To strip it back, take our time, and use nothing but our bodies to explore and savor one another was magical. To find someone I truly connected with on all aspects in the bedroom was uncanny. Lewis and I were made for each other.

As our body temperatures rose, he caught my hands, entwined our fingers, and pinned them beside my head. Moaning, he swiped his lips across mine. "I don't think I will ever get enough of you."

I wound my legs around his waist. Our steamy, panting breaths united. With our gazes locked, he pushed and rocked and drove into me harder. Deeper. *Oh, God.* I needed more. More of him. "Good, because I'm totally addicted to you."

The biggest grin lit his face. I'd put that there. I hoped it always stayed in place.

He drove into me, heating my core. Each thrust sent fire through my veins, seared heaven into my soul, and pushed me closer and closer to the edge. With a guttural groan he ground his hips against me, plunging into my depths.

He hit that spot. That spot that drove me wild. I dug my nails into his back.

"Oh yes." My orgasm shot through me. My whole body shuddered. Zaps skipped across my skin. Giggling, I whispered in his ear, "Hmm. So hot."

"Mmm!" A husky growl rasped deep inside his throat as he closed his eyes. Sharp jerks shocked his body. Tiny tremors quivered through his muscles. As he pumped his release into me, a glorious smile inched across his mouth and smoldering bliss shimmered in his gaze. He planted dreamy kisses against my lips. "Fuck, you do it for me."

I caressed his cheek, then tucked his loose hair behind his ear. His cock throbbing deep inside me still made my core hum.

I could stay like this forever. Be locked in his gaze, connected to his body.

Perfect.

But he collapsed beside me. Close was just good. He stole a deep kiss from my lips then smoothed his hand over my hair. "Every time gets better and better. I didn't think that would be possible."

"There are still so many things we haven't tried."

"I look forward to every new experience with you. You blow my mind every time." He caught my hand and kissed my fingertips. "I love you. We've had a few long weeks, a crazy weekend, and a big day. Now all that matters is you're here. With me. We have a lot of making up to do. So after a shower, we're gonna do that again, only with you on top. You up for that?"

"You know I am." I slid my hand around his neck and drew his lips to mine. Kissing him filled me with love, hope . . . and happiness. I'd come back to LA to start over. I'd never expected to find a new career I was excited about or a love that changed my life. I'd never expected to find Lewis.

I'd learned from my past, treasured my family, and now . . . I was home.

I was in love.

I was ready to take on the world.

Lewis had mended my heart, my soul, and all my broken bridges.

Chapter 40

LEWIS

Seven weeks later, at the end of August, I sat in a stretch limousine with Tia, Sutton, and the guys, heading toward the Prudential Center in Newark, New Jersey, to attend the MTV Video Music Awards. I fixed the cufflink on my dress shirt and realigned the sleeve of my Valentino jacket. Nerves flitted through my gut, and my palms sweated as we approached the center. Twelve months ago, the idea of attending events like this during my lifetime seemed far-fetched. Now, here I was with my new band. Tonight, wasn't just about our nomination for Group of the Year—it was my first public appearance with Tia . . . my girlfriend.

As I raked my gaze over her dressed in a stunning silver satin power suit with nothing on underneath her jacket, my heart swelled . . . and so did my dick. The diamond-encrusted pendant dangling in her cleavage and the matching earrings made her sparkle like an angel. Just add wings, and she would be.

But the closer we got to the venue, the more Tia paled, like she was about to throw up. Walking the carpet wasn't the issue.

Tomorrow's headlines were. But she'd promised to not let the gossip upset her.

Only time would tell.

I placed my hand on her thigh and gave it a squeeze. "We've got this."

She clutched my hand and nodded. "Yeah. I know."

April had prepared us for any difficult or out-of-line questions from reporters about our relationship. We were there to promote our music and the tour—not our love life. But I knew things didn't always go to plan.

"You ready?" Cole's eyes lit up as he leaned forward on his seat, opposite Tia. He rubbed his hands together, ready to hit the spotlight. But knowing him, he'd also be looking forward to the drinks, the after-party, and the hot single women. Luckily we weren't performing.

Sutton linked her arm around Flint's elbow and gave Tia and me an encouraging smile. "Just follow Flint. He knows how to work the cameras and deflect reporters. He helped me though our first appearance when I was nervous." Her eyes shimmered as she looked at him. "Our fake-dating stint didn't stay fake for very long."

Flint chuckled as he threw Sutton a sexy glance from beneath the curtain of long hair covering his cheek. Damn man was too hot for his own good. "We didn't even make it through one night. You couldn't keep your hands off me."

"Nope." She kissed his cheek, then wiped her lipstick mark off his skin. "Worth it."

"We'll be fine." Tia fidgeted with my signet rings. "This isn't my first event. I've probably walked more red carpets than you have."

"I'm sure you have, Tee." Beside me, Slip didn't look up from texting someone on his cell phone. I'd lay bets on it being Maddy. She was meeting us at the after-party. "The difference is, we love it. You don't."

"True." Tia linked my fingers with hers and leaned against my arm. "But I'm here for you guys. Tonight isn't about me. I like that."

"Oh, this will no doubt include you." Cole splayed his palms wide. "But we're all prepared. Put that gorgeous smile on, wave to the cameras and fans, and have fun."

"Will do." Tia nodded, but her hand shook in mine.

"We're here." Cole slid toward the door, waiting for a security guard to open it.

"About time." Slip tucked his phone away, then ripped and ruffled his fingers through his long hair that our hairstylist had spent thirty minutes straightening. His messy, I've-just-got-out-of-bed look returned. *So Slip.* He grinned a mischievous grin. "That's better. Let's nail this fucking party."

The limousine halted and we climbed out, one after the other. The cool evening breeze offered no relief from the late summer heat.

Flint took Sutton's hand, and they led us down the red carpet. Sutton's stunning blue dress with a rhinestone neckline sparkled underneath the bright lights.

With each step I took, butterflies skipped in my stomach. I'd done promos, and shows, and appearances before, but nothing on this televised scale. The crowds, the noise, and the flashing lights were overwhelming. Taking Tia's trembling fingers in mine, I drew her toward me. "You've done this more than me. Show me the way."

She hooked my hand behind her back and stepped in close, her chest pressed flush against mine. She lowered her voice. "I'll show you the way to heaven later, but for now, let's walk this damn carpet."

Hmm. I'd be counting down the hours for this party to be over. "Deal."

Following the guys and Sutton, Tia and I waved to the crowd behind the barricades, and weaved our way around TV cameras and the production crew. Once we reached the main media section, Flint and I had to leave Sutton and Tia to join Cole and Slip to be snapped by photographers. I couldn't deny I loved being in front of a lens. It did wonders for my confidence.

Just as I took Tia's hand after the fifth pose with the guys, a female reporter called out to me. "Lewis? Lewis King?"

My heart skipped a beat. She'd called *my* name. Not Tia's or one of the other guys'. *ME!* A reporter knew *my* name. There was another first. I wasn't an egotistical person, but fuck, that felt good.

Tia and I drifted over to her as a cool smile crept across my lips.

"How are you this evening?" Catherine from *E-Times* held her mic toward me.

Chatter from other artists and reporters nearby filled my ears. The panel lights above blazed in my eyes. Where were sunglasses when you needed them? But I had this. *Be honest. Truthful. And keep a clear head.* I took a deep breath and replied, "Great, thank you. It's so good to be here, to be nominated, and to celebrate the success of other fellow artists." I was nailing this PR shit.

Catherine glanced from me to Tia and back again. "And you're here with the lovely Tia Tanner this evening."

"I certainly am." Warmth touched my cheeks and spread across my chest. It was hard to think about the band and music when Tia stood this close.

Catherine waved her finger back and forth between us. Her tone took on a curious yet cautious edge. "As in, you're dating?"

"Yes." I placed my palm on the small of Tia's back. Her eyes flooded with love and anxiousness as she faced me. I gave her a reassuring nod. I had her. She had nothing to worry about. "We have been for a couple months."

"Well, this is an unexpected development." Catherine's eyebrows shot skyward. "Lewis, you just broke the hearts of millions of men tonight."

"Oh, a few have broken mine over the years. But I'm lucky— I've found someone very special. Tia is amazing. Meeting her and The Flintlocks, has been the best thing that has happened to me in a long time. I hope everyone is happy for us."

"I'm sure they are. You two look great together." Catherine gave us a heartfelt smile. But then she pointed her mic at Tia. "You've managed to steal the heart of another man who seemed to be off-limits. How did you do it? What's your secret?"

Tia drew her shoulders back, and sucked in a deep breath. During media training with April, Tia had responded with snappy, snarky comments ranging from '*I'm fucking good in bed*' to '*None of your goddamn business*' to '*I'm just too irresistible.*'

All were true, but April had suggested toning it down. *"Act. Be disgustingly nice to the reporters so they won't be able to say anything bad about you. How do you think I've managed to smooth over all the crap the guys have caused off-stage? I've taught them, hounded it into them, beaten it into their thick heads to be angels in front of the cameras."*

Whether Tia listened to her advice or not was totally up in the air. I braced myself for whatever would come out of her mouth.

But within a heartbeat, Tia curled into my side, all loving and warm. She softened her voice and packed on the charm. "There's no secret. We became friends, then that evolved into something more. We were meant to find each other. Thank you." She gave the cameraman a dazzling smile, then tugged me on the arm.

I chuckled, stunned at her short and sweet comment. There were no quick-witted or heated comebacks. April must have gotten to her. I loved Tia no matter what, but yeah, she'd impressed me yet again.

Before we were asked more probing questions, we moved on. "Have a good night." I waved farewell and we continued along the carpet.

As we joined the guys who were waiting patiently for the Twenty One Pilots to finish being interviewed in front of us, I caught Tia around the waist. "Are you feeling okay? You were nice to a reporter."

"I'm trying a new tactic." She swiped lint off the shoulder of my jacket, then straightened my tie. "But you were a total ass-kisser."

"That reporter loved us. And I meant every word." I drew her closer to me. "You are special. Amazing. And the person I love. You were right. We were meant to find each other."

Her eyes sparkled in the flashing lights. "There was no need for stories or lies or scripted comments. There was no need to act. I was just honest. And that . . . felt amazing." She stole a quick kiss that made my stomach flutter. "I love you."

"Hoy!" Cole laughed. "Keep that smooching up and you will be the headline on every gossip site tomorrow."

"Bring it." Tia smiled against my lips.

As my heart pounded loud and proud, cameras flashed and clicked around us. Ignoring the hollers and hoots from the reporters, I took Tia's hand, and we continued toward the venue. I joined the guys for more photos and interviews, but I couldn't take my eyes off Tia nor the smile off my face.

Fuck, I was in love.

And I freaking loved it.

I hoped the press loved seeing the two of us together. For Tia's sake, not mine.

Guess we'd find out tomorrow.

***

I woke to Tia straddled across my hips in her red boyleg panties and tank top. Her long hair tickled me as she licked and sucked my nipple. Each swirl of her tongue sent a jolt straight to my hardened dick. That wasn't my normal morning glory. I clutched the back of her head and rolled her down onto the hotel mattress. "Are you still drunk?"

We'd had a wild night at the after-party and hadn't been fazed by not winning our category. Everhide had taken the statue. Some of the night had gotten blurry.

"Yes . . . and horny." She clutched my butt and wriggled against my crotch.

"You're insatiable." I kissed her lips, caressed her hip, then slid my hand around to clutch her tidy ass. I drove my hard-on against her panties. Too much fabric lay between us.

"Hmm. I want that, but . . ." She shoved me on the shoulder, then waved her cell phone in my face. "Look at this?"

I blinked at the screen, struggling to focus. A bright picture of us last night on the red carpet blazed before my eyes. "Hmm. We look good."

"It's more than that." She wriggled out from underneath me and sat upright against the headboard. "We're out there. We're on every news site."

I flopped back down onto my pillow. My boner was not happy about the situation. "How long have you been awake searching the Internet?"

She glanced at the alarm clock on the nightstand. *10.12a.m.* "Half an hour. You were too cute sleeping beside me. I didn't want to wake you. But I got hot just looking at you. Sorry, I got carried away."

Yeah, my balls were suffering because of it. "You can jump on me anytime." I loved sleeping beside her and waking next to her every day, but burying myself inside her and making her come was even better. I wanted to finish what she'd started, but she was fixated on her cell phone. *Damn it.* I rubbed my eyes and blinked the sleepiness away. "So hit me. What do the headlines say? The good and the bad."

This was important to her. I'd listen to every crappy gossip report if needed.

I rolled toward her. Draping my arm across her waist, I hugged her hip.

She sucked in a deep breath, then let it out slowly. "Okay." Her fingernail tapped against the screen. "*E-Times* says, '*Hollywood Star Steps Out With Hot New Beau,*' JustJared wrote, '*Didn't know Lewis King was bisexual. How hot is this couple?*' *Glamor* voted us as one of the best-dressed couples of the night." Her voice rippled with excitement, then it dive-bombed. "There are some bad ones. *Fabulous Freaks* posted, '*Tia Tanner Stole One of Our Men—Bitch,*' *GossipOnline* wrote, '*Tia Tanner Can't Be Dating Lewis King. He's Gay. Fake-dating Alert,*' and *AngelTownNews* wrote, '*Tia Tanner's at it again. New Lover. New scandal.*'"

I kissed her gorgeous, toned bicep. Slipping my hand beneath the hem of her tank top, I rubbed and tickled her tummy. "Hmm. I like being your scandalous lover."

She giggled and playfully clipped me on the head.

"Ow!" I tickled her ribs. She flinched, giggled again, and sank a few inches. Leaning over, I kissed the top of her boob. "Those headlines were okay. There's always good and bad."

"Yeah. There was nothing written about me being hot-headed, so that was a huge win. Being nice and not lying helped. Lesson learned. I'm not going to let the bad articles get to me. I'll focus on the positive ones . . . or even better than that, no headlines at all . . . after today." She curled towards me; her legs rested against my chest. "The posts about us being a hot couple and making the best-dressed list were cool."

"Those headlines are a first for me." I slid my gaze and my

wandering hand over her scarred leg. I loved that she no longer hid the marks from me. They were part of her, and I loved every inch of her body.

"I like being your first." Her eyes glinted as she clutched her cell phone against her chest.

"And my last." I kissed the tip of her knee, resting against my chest. "You are the one and only woman for me. And I am *your* man. See here?" I traced the scars on her lower leg. "If you look at these marks from this angle, they form an L and a K. My initials. I'm permanently etched onto your skin, like ink."

"Really?" She swiveled her leg to see the lines. "Oh my God. I will never unsee that. That's so cool."

"We're destined to be together forever." I kissed her sweet lips.

"Yeah." She pressed her forehead against mine.

I curled my hand over her injured ankle. It was swollen after too much walking and dancing the night before. "Have you made a decision about the surgery?" She'd been to appointments and had gotten two more professional opinions. They'd agreed more surgery would help.

"Yes." She swiped her fingertips down my scruffy cheek, tickling the fine hairs and whiskers above my lip. "I have to do it. It won't make it any worse, but the chance to be better is too enticing. I'll be zooming to rehearsals in a wheelchair for a while. And you'll have to wait on me hand and foot. That okay?"

"Always." I slid my hand up the back of her leg. Each touch of her skin ignited my blood, sent it rushing toward my dick. "There is one more thing I need to take care of."

"What's that?" Her eyes glittered in the soft morning light.

"You were horny before."

"Still am."

My dick jumped from half-mast to full hoist. "So am I." I crawled to the end of her feet, tugged off her panties, then pulled her flat onto the bed. Nestling between her legs, I buried myself inside her.

Fuck!

Life couldn't get much better than this.

But . . . I was wrong.

Chapter 41

LEWIS

By the end of September, our set list had been finalized, stage construction for full rehearsals had been built, merchandise had been approved, and marketing schedules were set for the kickoff of our global tour in November. But before we entered full tour mode, we had to deliver a gig Flint had promised Molly, the manager at Hayley's Bar in Pasadena.

I didn't miss the days of playing at small venues, but Molly was cool. The guys would do anything for her.

"Holy shit!" I gaped out the window of the SUV as we approached the bar. The traffic was bumper-to-bumper, and the massive line of people snaked from the entrance, through the parking lot, and out onto the street. "You said this was a small gig. Three hundred, max." I planted a play-punch into the side of Flint's thigh.

"It was supposed to be." Flint's energy jumped as he surveyed the crowd. "Guess word got out we were performing."

Yeah, that happened when we posted the details on social media.

Butterflies swirled in my stomach as security waved our

driver through the sea of people and we pulled up outside the back door. The fans waved and screamed and took photos of us. "This is unbelievable."

For a small bar, this was insane. They'd be turning away people at the door.

"This is a warmup for the tour. Get used to it." The buzz coming off Cole was electrifying. He loved this life. I couldn't blame him. I did too.

"Let's rock this joint." Slip opened the door and jumped out.

Another security guard ushered us inside and into the green room.

I hadn't seen Tia since we'd done soundcheck earlier that afternoon. She'd be out in the bar area at the mixer. She'd had ankle surgery three weeks ago but zoomed around in her funky wheelchair like she played center for the paralympic basketball team. *Crazy woman.* But I loved her. She should be at home resting, but no one could tell Tia what to do. She'd insisted on coming to the show. With Gena on maternity leave, Falcon had hired Kieran, an experienced sound and lighting engineer, to head our technical team for the tour. Poor guy had to teach Tia everything he knew. Good thing they got on like a house on fire.

The loud chatter from the crowd and music playing in the bar reverberated in the tiny green room. Blake, Falcon, and April huddled near the sofa, talking away as they typed on their cell phones. They thrived on the pre-show hype as much as we did.

Five minutes before showtime, the guys and I helped each other put on our transmitters and thread our in-ear monitor cords through our shirts.

As I clipped my transmitter onto my belt, Flint squeezed my shoulder. "Ready to rock this joint?"

"Yes." I clapped and rubbed my hands together. "Let's go." Nerves no longer crippled me before taking to the stage. I nailed every track when we played, even "Changes". I couldn't wait to perform with these guys.

As Blake led us out of the room and toward the stage, Flint stepped in beside me. "Oh. Forgot to tell you. We made a change to the set list for song five. Just go with the flow. It's for someone special here tonight." He rushed forward to catch up to Blake.

My pulse spiked. "Who?" I called out to Flint. "What change? What song are we playing instead?" *Fuck!*

"You got this, Lew." Cole glided past me. "It's all good."

I held my hands wide. "What song are we now performing?"

Cole kept walking like he hadn't heard me.

"This is news to me?" Slip shrugged as he scooted past me, but then he winked. "Just follow Flint's lead."

"What the hell?"

I knew all the songs backward, but still . . . what the fuck? Who changed the set list five minutes before a show? *Crap.*

As we stood off to the side of the stage, my nerves threatened to return. But I looked out across the packed room and could just make out the mixer. Tia would be there. *My focal point.* Calm instantly washed over me.

With a mic in hand, Molly walked up the steps and onto the center of the stage. "Good evening, everyone. Welcome to Hayley's." The crowd whistled and hollered, but then was quick to fall silent. Molly introduced us. "I have known these handsome young men since they were in high school. I'm convinced I played a huge part in them being discovered. If a certain record label exec hadn't had a flat tire outside this very bar and come in here for a drink while he waited for roadside assistance, these boys may have never been signed." Molly placed her hand over her heart. "These are my boys. And I'm claiming their newest member as mine too. He's a total hottie, very talented, and a true treasure. I've been begging these boys to come and play for me again for months. I'm glad they're finally here. So, would you please welcome to the stage Flint, Cole, Slip, and Lewis . . . The Flintlocks."

The audience screamed, cheered, and clapped. The noise, almost deafening. Every holler hit the center of my chest. God, I loved my job.

"She gets me every time." Cole tapped his fist against his heart, then stuffed his ear monitors in. "I love Molly so much."

"Let's raise her roof." Flint's eyes glinted, hungry to entertain the crowd.

"I'm right beside you." I nodded.

"Fuck yeah." Slip pointed to the stage. "Let's go."

We ran up the steps and took position. I grabbed my bass and hooked the strap over my head. Joel, our stagehand, passed Flint his electric, raced over to adjust my mic, then moved a cord out of Slip's way. He gave the thumbs up to Cole, who was sitting behind the drums.

Flint stepped up to his mic, struck his strings once, and nodded in Kieran's direction.

The lights dimmed.

My pulse quickened. Curling my fingers around the neck of my bass, I took a deep breath and glanced over the darkened crowd. I couldn't see much farther than the first few rows. But Tia was at the back. I could feel her eyes on me.

I smiled. I liked her watching me. It gave me this slow, burning ache for her throughout our performances and rehearsals and led to some hot encounters once I got off stage.

Oh yeah. The tour would be fun.

Cole tapped his drumsticks together and counted down. "Three. Two. One."

With a smash of his sticks on the cymbals, we launched into our first song. The stage lights flashed bright. Our music boomed through the speakers. The sardine-packed audience jumped, danced, and clapped.

As I sang backup vocals, strummed my bass, and moved about the stage, adrenaline zipped through my veins. I couldn't wait to do this every night of the tour. I loved feeding off the crowd's energy. I loved playing and performing.

At the end of the fourth song, I stood by my mic and turned my attention to Flint. Panting and sweating, I took a deep breath to clear my mind. I had no idea what we were about to play. I ran through the list of our hits in my head, ready to jump into whatever Flint threw our way.

I wiped the perspiration off my face onto my shirtsleeve, then positioned my fingers over my strings.

I was set.

Flint took to his mic. "Good evening, everyone. We hope you're having a good time tonight. And we hope every one of you fuckers has bought tickets to come see us on our tour."

The crowd erupted. Their loud whistles and shrieks rattled the walls and roof. *So. Freaking. Cool.*

"Awesome." Flint flicked his sweaty hair off his face. "Now we love Molly to death. But she's got one thing wrong. Sorry, Moll, but Lewis is ours. While many of you may just think he's ridiculously handsome, hot as fuck, and a great bassist, and you wish your ass looked as good as his does in jeans . . ."

Fuck! Heat blazed in my cheeks. What was Flint doing?

He held up a finger. "But . . . we want you to know, he's also a very talented songwriter. If y'all have listened to the deluxe edition of our new album, track thirteen, 'Coming Home,' was written and composed by Lewis." He waved at me, then turned back to his mic. "We'd barely met him when I'd said we had to have that song on our album. Luckily, he agreed. I just got news an hour ago from Blake, our manger, that Lewis's song has outperformed our latest released single in sales and streams across all platforms, making it the third-most-popular track on the album."

What? Holy shit. I clutched onto my mic to steady myself.

Flint continued, "As a result, we'll be releasing it as our official fourth single next week. Y'all okay with that?"

The crowd hollered, whistled, and waved their hands above their heads.

Tears prickled my eyes. My head spun. *My song is a hit? It will be released as a single? Oh wow!* My thundering heart was about to escape my chest. Playing with these guys was a dream come true. Having my song included on the album had been mind-blowing. But for it to become one of our bestselling tracks was beyond anything I could've ever imagined. Life just hit a new high.

"Lewis?" Flint swiveled toward me as he hovered his lips against his mic. "In honor of your amazing song, I'd like you to step over here, take the lead, and sing it for us."

I gaped. I actually gaped. "No. Dude, you sing it."

"Nuh-uh." Flint waved me forward. "The stage is yours."

Slip started to chant and clap. "Lewis. Lewis. Lewis."

The crowd joined in. "Lewis. Lewis. Lewis."

Shit! I trembled all over. My stomach knotted. *Me? Sing lead?* I glanced at Slip, then at Cole, then back to Flint. They waved me forward. *Damn.* They'd all been in on this.

Humbled, honored and shocked, I placed my hand over my heart, grinned and shook my head. There was no way out of this. So, I'd own it. Taking a deep breath, I stepped over the cords and cables snaking across the stage floor and made my way over to Flint. I gave him a hug. "Thank you."

"No. Thank you for a fucking awesome song."

Slip dashed over to me and gave me a fist-pump. "Well done, man. Let's rock."

"LEWIS!" Cole cheered from behind his drum kit and clapped his sticks together. "Woohoo!"

I stole a glance in Tia's direction. I couldn't see her, but I threw her a huge smile, and tapped my chest. This wouldn't have happened if she hadn't encouraged me to play my music to the guys all those months ago. Now . . . here I was.

"You ready to back me up?" I asked Flint as I stepped behind his mic.

"Just this once." Grinning, he winked, tapped my shoulder, then headed over to my mic.

My chest swelled as I scanned the jostling audience. This was freaking awesome. I'd never sung lead. I wasn't going to waste the opportunity.

I sucked in a deep breath and let it out slowly.

I spoke into the mic. "Evening all. Anyone out there ever been hopelessly in love? I'm talking about the kind of love that keeps you awake at night, go a little stir crazy when you're apart and has you counting down the minutes of every day until you can see that person again. Anyone had that kind of love?" A wave of whistles and yeses drifted across the audience. "Yeah, you know what I'm talking about." I plucked my bottom string. "When you find the one that turns your world upside down, it's fucking awesome. I hope y'all find a love like that. I have." I pointed toward the mixer. "Tia, I love *coming home* to you. Every fucking day."

I strummed my strings. Cole thudded the intro beat on his bass drum, then galloped his sticks across the tom toms and hit the snare. Flint and Slip ripped into the vibrant track on their electrics. I added the groove with my heavy bassline.

Each note reverberated through my chest. I took a quick breath and sang:

> *Another day breaks over the horizon,*
> *Another bed I wake up alone in.*
> *Another city I am seeing,*
> *Different air to you I'm breathin'.*
> *But now there'll be no more dreamin'.*

I've been away for so damn long,
I've lost track of the hours and days.
But the difference about this morning,
I'm gonna pack my bags, be on my way.
Oh yeah, I'm coming home to you.

I can kiss the lonely nights goodbye,
Stop staring at the endless sky,
As the miles disappear,
And the city grows near.
I'll turn up the radio,
Sing to songs I don't know.
I can't stop my heart from racing,
Knowing it's you I'll be embracing.
Before this day is through,
Oh yeah,
I'll be home with you.
I'll be home with you.

I've stayed awake too many nights,
Thinking about you, oh yeah.
I've stared at too many ceilings,
Wondering what you're doing.
I toss and turn, dreamin',
I touch myself, wishing,
Wishing, it was you.

But now . . .
I can kiss the lonely nights goodbye,
Stop staring at the endless sky,
As the miles disappear,
And the city grows near.
I'll turn up the radio,
Sing to songs I don't know.
I can't stop my heart from racing,
Knowing it's you I'll be embracing.
Before this day is through,

411

Oh yeah,
I'll be home with you.
I'll be home with you.

As I struck my bass and flicked my sweaty hair off my neck, my heart hammered against my ribs. I spun around, ripping out the beat. I glanced at Flint, Cole, and Slip. I may have written this song, but it had become one of *our* songs, a Flintlocks hit. Being part of a team made the success so much better and more rewarding. I couldn't wait to write new music with these men, go on the tour, and be part of their future.

At the end of the track, Flint retook his mic. We churned out several more hits before we finished our show. The fans roared and clapped as the four of us bowed, then rushed off the stage. We jumped around in a group hug, riding out the high from performing. But I was quick to excuse myself. With the aid of security, I charged through the crowd, promising a few zealous fans I'd talk to them soon. I reached Tia at the back of the venue. She was sitting in her wheelchair behind the mixer. The moment she saw me, she held her arms wide. I dropped to my knees in front of her and gave her a huge, hot, sweaty hug. Then, I kissed her. "I love you."

"You were amazing." She cupped my heated cheek.

"I just wanted you to know I love coming home to you."

She smiled a big smile and brushed her thumb across the top of my lips. "You already said that."

I caught her hand and kissed her fingers. "I wanted to make sure you haven't forgotten."

"No. Never."

"It's so good to see you smile. Are you ready to party?

"You bet. Me and my wheelchair have a date with the bar."

"I'll go shower and be back soon."

But before I left, I kissed her again.

I'd originally come to LA for two days—now I never planned

to leave. I prayed I'd never have to start again.

I'd found a new family. *The Flintlocks.*

I had a home. *LA is it.*

I'd found a new love. *Tia.*

My heart couldn't lead me astray anymore.

I'd found where I belonged.

***

At three a.m., a few hours after our show at Hayley's had finished, the doors to the venue closed behind the last group of dawdling drunk fans. But the buzz from the night still kicked through our veins. The band, our entourage, security, crew, and some of Molly's staff sat around tables, having a few drinks and winding down from the epic night.

"Man, the tour is going to be wicked." Beside me, Slip took a swig of his beer.

"Fuck yeah," I agreed, then waved my beer toward Blake and Falcon, sitting across from me and Tia in our jagged circle. "I can't believe you want to release my song. Thank you. I'm honored."

"It's a great track." Blake dipped his chin. "Just write thirty more with these guys so we have a ton of new material to choose from for the next album."

I chuckled. "I'll do my best."

"Let's get through this tour first." Flint cracked the lid on his fresh beer. "I want to enjoy this ride."

"Oh shit." Blake clicked his fingers and dug inside his suit jacket. "Cole, I almost forgot. This was delivered to the office today."

He stood, took a step toward Cole, who sat adjacent to Tia, and handed him an envelope.

"What is it?" Cole asked.

"I don't know." Blake shrugged. "It's marked confidential from some lawyers in San Francisco."

"San Fran?" Puzzlement flitted across his brow. He opened the letter and unfolded the pages.

But as he read it, the blood drained from his face. Tears welled in his eyes. He covered his mouth with his hand.

"Cole?" Flint, sitting diagonally opposite him, shot forward. "What is it?"

"Um . . ." He sniffled and shook all over. "Shelby was killed in a helicopter accident."

"What?" Flint gasped. "As in, my high school ex, Shelby? Oh, Jeezus." As he rubbed the back of his hair, water welled in his eyes. Sutton hooked her arm around him and hugged him.

My brain scrambled to put the pieces together. "Is that the dibs rule Shelby?" I asked no one in particular.

"Yeah." Cole stared at the letter, then dropped it and his hands into his lap. "Fuck."

Beside me, Slip swiveled toward him. Confusion furrowed his brow. "But why are the lawyers sending you a letter?"

Cole's hands trembled. Tears pooled on the rims of his eyes. "I have to meet with them next week."

"Why?" Tia asked.

"She had a child." Cole closed his eyes. "Three years ago."

The anguish in his voice stabbed my chest. No kid should lose a parent, by death or other means. I knew that for a fact.

But a chill shot through the air.

Flint's face turned white. "So, what's that got to do with you?"

"I didn't know. I swear. I haven't seen, or talked to, or heard from her for years." The letter quivered in Cole's hands as he struggled to form words. "This says . . . it's my kid."

"Our friend is dead . . . and you fucked my ex and never told me?" Flint shot to his feet, sending his chair tumbling backward and crashing to the floor. "Asshole." He stepped across the circle, swiped a right hook into Cole's jaw, and stormed out of the bar. Sutton rushed after him.

Everyone froze, clearly stunned by the news and the loss of an old friend. But I'd never seen Flint lash out. He'd never hurt a fly.

Tia grabbed my hand and squeezed it. Sadness and shock rippled through her eyes. Then she swiveled toward Cole and clutched his thigh. Her voice came out soft and full of anguish. "I told you, didn't I? Secrets have a funny, twisted way of coming out. Guess you didn't expect it to happen like this."

His eyes glassed over as he rubbed his reddened jaw. "It can't be my kid. It just can't be."

Slip wiped his hand down his face, then leaned forward. "But what are you going to do if it is yours?"

Cole stared at the letter. He shook his head. Closing his eyes, he said. "I don't know. I have the tour coming up. I have a life. I can't take care of a kid."

A kid? Holy shit. What could I say? All I could do was be the friend he needed. "We're here for you. We'll help. Always."

"Thanks. I know." The rims of his eyes blazed red. Then every muscle in his jaw twitched and tensed. He roared. "Fuuucck! This can't be happening. Not a kid. Please, God. Not a kid."

As I caught Tia's hand in mine again, my heart bled for Cole. I'd been through many drastic life changes over the past year ...

Guess Cole was about to do the same.

... Bring on more of The Flintlocks.

THANK YOU

Thank you for reading BROKEN BRIDGES, Book 2 in The Flintlocks Rockstar Romance Series. I hope you loved Lewis and Tia as much as I do.

Be prepared for another emotional story full of sizzle. TORTURED TONES, Book#3 will be available in early 2024.

BONUS BOOK

Find out how my world of rockstars started with the Everhide Rockstar Romance Series for FREE.

ROCKED – The Price of Dreams is the origin story of how the band met in high school. It is not imperative to read this before the series. It is a pre-romance of the adult relationships that develop throughout the six books (3 x standalones, 3 x follow-ons – all happily ever afters, no cliffhangers).

From friends-to-lovers, enemies-to-lovers, roommates to lovers and more, the Everhide Rockstar Series will have you falling in love, shedding tears and laughing out loud.

Read the prequel, **ROCKED – The Price of DREAMS,** for **FREE** if you subscribe to my newsletter.
Join at: https://taniajoyce.com/subscribe

PS. If you loved BROKEN BRIDGES, would you kindly take a moment and leave a quick review on Amazon or Goodreads. They are music for an author's soul. Thank you.

BOOKS BY TANIA JOYCE

The Flintlocks Series

The Everhide Series

Billionaires and College Romance

NEWSLETTER

To stay in touch and to be notified about my new releases, sales, giveaways and more, please subscribe to my monthly newsletter. Join at: https://taniajoyce.com/subscribe

***

FOLLOW TANIA JOYCE

You can follow and find me on the following social media platforms.

Amazon: https://amazon.com/author/taniajoyce
BookBub: https://www.bookbub.com/authors/tania-joyce
Facebook: https://www.facebook.com/taniajoycebooks
Goodreads: https://www.goodreads.com/taniajoyce
Instagram: https://www.instagram.com/taniajoycebooks/
Pinterest: https://www.pinterest.com/taniajoycebooks
TikTok: https://www.tiktok.com/@taniajoyce
Web: http://taniajoyce.com